DOUBLE DEAD

Also by Gary Hardwick

Cold Medina

DOUBLE DEAD

GARY HARDWICK

A DUTTON BOOK

DUTTON
Published by the Penguin Group
Penguin Books USA Inc., 375 Hudson Street,
New York, New York 10014, U.S.A.
Penguin Books Ltd, 27 Wrights Lane,
London W8 5TZ, England
Penguin Books Australia Ltd, Ringwood,
Victoria, Australia
Penguin Books Canada Ltd, 10 Alcorn Avenue,
Toronto, Ontario, Canada M4V 3B2
Penguin Books (N.Z.) Ltd, 182–190 Wairau Road,
Auckland 10, New Zealand

Penguin Books Ltd, Registered Offices:
Harmondsworth, Middlesex, England

First published by Dutton, an imprint of Dutton Signet, a division of Penguin Books USA Inc.
Distributed in Canada by McClelland & Stewart Inc.

First Printing, August, 1997
10 9 8 7 6 5 4 3 2 1

 REGISTERED TRADEMARK—MARCA REGISTRADA

ISBN 0-525-93920-2
CIP is available.

Printed in the United States of America
Set in Plantin Light
Designed by Leonard Telesca

PUBLISHER'S NOTE
This is a work of fiction. Names, characters, places, and incidents either are the products of the author's imagination or are used fictitiously, and any resemblance to actual persons, living or dead, events, or locales is entirely coincidental.

For Mary Louise Hardwick,
who loved her children too much

The lawyer's truth, is not Truth.

—HENRY DAVID THOREAU,
"Civil Disobedience" (1849)

In cities, men are more callous to
the happiness and misery of others . . .
because they are constantly in the habit of
seeing both extremes.

—CHARLES CALEB COLTON, *Lacon* (1825)

Families are created in flesh, bound by blood, and
destroyed in humanity.

—JOE BLACK

PART ONE

GLASS HOUSE

i

The Colonial

Harris Yancy, mayor of Detroit, watched the young woman with joy. The girl's body shimmered with sweat as she writhed on top of him. She had a curious habit of singing when she made love. Strange, but he liked it. She moved with urgency, and he struggled to keep up with her.

The young woman moved Yancy's hands to her breasts. He squeezed them hard; then she moved her hands away, leaving him to the task alone.

She arched her back, and her body stiffened. She let out a moan that escalated into a little yell. She breathed heavily, mumbled something, then let out a large breath, patting him on the chest.

"Lord," she whispered. "I was quick today. Been missin' you." Then she laughed. "Your turn."

She rolled over, and Yancy pushed himself up on his arms. He had to make it quick. This was a young man's position, and he'd just turned sixty-two.

He moved inside her, savoring her beauty. She whispered to him, giving added passion. Soon his desire built into a surge of pleasure, and he climaxed. Yancy let out a deep breath, then lowered himself on the woman.

He lay on top of her, feeling younger for a moment, like he was twenty again, like in a few minutes he'd be hard and ready for more. Then the feeling slipped away, and he was sixty-two, tired and already thinking about the business he had to conduct.

"I can feel your heart," she whispered.

"The whole state can hear that bum ticker going," said Yancy.

"I don't wanna hear none of that talk tonight. You're gonna live forever, and you know it."

Yancy rolled over on his back. The young woman got up and walked to the bathroom. She was exquisite. Beautiful brown skin, long black hair that was done in braids, and a lean, trim body that was full in all the right places. Men dreamed of women like her, he thought. He was lucky to have enough money and power to possess one.

Yancy checked the clock. Almost time. Mr. Nicks was always punctual. "You taking a shower, Ramona?" he called.

"Yes. Wanna join me?"

"No, just lock the door for a while. I'll let you know when you can come back out."

"Okay, Yanny."

He hated that name, but it was better than Daddy or Poppy or the other names young mistresses called him.

Ramona was very obedient. Some of her predecessors had been too nosy. That was not good for him. Not only was he cheating on his wife, but he was the mayor of a city. And even though everyone knew that all men like him had a piece on the side, the political rule of the day was "Just don't let us catch you."

He heard the shower turn on. He went to the bed, reached behind the headboard, and fidgeted with something. After a moment he was done and started looking for his shorts.

Just then he heard a muffled, distant sound like something falling to the floor. Yancy looked around. Where had that come from? The colonial was old, built in 1925. It had been his home before he moved into the mayor's mansion. Now he and his wife, Louise, used it to host parties and hold private meetings and for a little recreation, he thought gleefully.

Yancy checked the clock again. He grew excited. This was a moment that would change many lives. He'd made many decisions in the past that affected the masses, but this one was different. This was a political and social volcano that would consume everything in its path. He recalled a verse he'd learned as a boy: "Great men move life with their passion." He was certainly about to do that.

Yancy heard the doorbell downstairs. He went to the bathroom door and listened. The shower was still going. He buttoned his shirt and walked out of the room.

★ ★ ★

"Time," whispered one of the killers. "Remember, no shooting. And they both have to go down. Double dead. That's our contract."

The other man said nothing. He just nodded.

Quietly they began to move, slow, deliberate actions, like two bears awakening from hibernation. They were near the door to their hideaway. One of the killers reached over and pulled on it, opening the way to the colonial.

"Everything's cool tonight," said Walter Nicks. His voice was deep and scratchy.

"It had better be," said Yancy. "The last thing I need is my wife coming around here."

The two men stood in the foyer of the house. Walter Nicks, Yancy's personal bodyguard, was well over six feet and towered over his boss. Nicks took off his black fedora, exposing his balding head. He quickly put the hat back on, as if embarrassed.

"What's this all about?" Nicks asked. He handed a black metallic briefcase to Yancy.

Yancy took the case without a word and walked back upstairs. "I'll contact you in a few days. Be ready when I do."

Nicks watched Yancy move up the long staircase. Then he turned, adjusted his hat, and let himself out.

Yancy reached the top of the stairs and went to the master bedroom. He opened the door, and his eyes widened as he saw a large man wearing a red mask about to force open the bathroom door.

Yancy gripped the black briefcase tighter and ran toward the nightstand, where he kept a loaded .45. He'd taken only one step when he was hit hard on the back of the head. He stumbled, then fell to the floor. He slid face first, and the carpet burned his cheek.

A man wearing a green mask came toward Yancy. He had a knife with thick plastic wrapped around the handle.

Yancy saw the man coming at him and got to his feet. He heard the other intruder ramming into the bathroom door.

"Ramonnaaa!" Yancy yelled.

The man by the bathroom door broke it open. The room was empty. The window was partially open. He looked around and saw that the shower curtain was pulled shut. He took out a knife and walked over to the shower. He was pumped up and ready to deal with the woman.

He pulled the curtain back and immediately heard something move behind him. He spun around and saw a woman swinging her hand at his face.

"Aaaahhh!" he yelled as a razor blade slashed him in the right cheek. The little blade cut easily through the red mask, and blood poured from the wound. The injured man dropped his knife and fell to his knees, grabbing at the wound on his face.

Ramona, dressed in her underwear, stepped out of the big bathroom closet. Her heart raced, and she could hear herself breathing. She quickly dropped the bloody razor, picked up the killer's knife, and moved to the door.

Through the door she saw a man in a green mask coming at Yancy. Yancy fended off the killer with a black metal case. The man in the green mask moved defensively, as if he didn't want to hurt Yancy. He measured the mayor, looking for an opportunity. Yancy swung the case, and the intruder grabbed Yancy's arm and pushed him to the floor, face first.

Ramona ran into the other room, yelling and drawing back her arm to throw the big knife at the killer. She was suddenly grabbed from behind. The knife flew from her hand and fell on the floor.

The red-masked man grabbed Ramona, grunting and cursing in pain. Ramona struggled with the man behind her, trying to shake him off.

In the bedroom the green-masked killer forced the metal case from Yancy's hand and turned the mayor over on his back. Then he raised the big knife and brought it down into Yancy's chest.

Ramona screamed as the killer struck Yancy again and again. She kicked her foot backward and struck her assailant in the knee. He loosened his grip, and she wrestled herself free.

Ramona looked up and saw the green-masked face of Yancy's killer coming at her. She tried to dodge him, but he landed on her. Ramona fell backward, knocking down the killer behind her and landing on top of him. She screamed, sandwiched between the assassins.

The man on top of Ramona pulled a small knife and flicked it open. Then he brought it down toward Ramona. She caught his arm, holding the weapon at bay, but slowly the knife came down at her face.

Without warning the man below grabbed Ramona around the

waist. She grunted as air was forced from her by the grip of the killer below.

"Good-bye . . . bitch," said the killer on top of her.

This was it, Ramona thought. She would die here between these two men like an animal.

The man in the green mask shifted and brought the knife down with all his weight. Ramona's arm weakened and began to bend. She twisted her body to one side, pushing off the man above her. She turned like a bottle spinning on its side. The knife came down into the shoulder of the assassin below her.

The man in the red mask screamed, a long, screeching sound that hurt Ramona's ears. The man on top was now off-balance, and Ramona shoved with all her might, pushing him free. He fell awkwardly to one side.

Ramona scrambled to her feet and ran out of the bathroom, looking at the bedroom door, which now seemed miles away. From behind her she heard a man getting to his feet. She saw the metallic briefcase sitting on the floor. Without thinking, she grabbed it with both hands. She lifted it, spinning and swinging the case upward. The corner caught the advancing killer in the temple, making a dull thud. He fell to one knee. Ramona stepped toward him and swung again with all her might. She hit him in the head with the side of the case, dropping him on his back. The big man in the green mask grunted hard and tried to get up but fell again. Ramona hit him in the head once more for good measure.

She stood motionless for a moment. She was spotted with blood, sweating and scared. She saw Yancy on the floor in a pool of blood. His eyes were open, and one hand was sticking up as if reaching for something.

"Oh, no. No, nooo . . ." she said. She took a half step to Yancy's corpse.

Someone groaned, and Ramona jumped. The men were not dead, she thought suddenly. "Gotta get outta here," she muttered to herself.

She grabbed her clothes and her purse. In a flash she remembered that she had no money and grabbed Yancy's wallet from the nightstand. She ran out of the room, taking her weapon, the black briefcase, with her.

Ramona fumbled as she put on her dress and tried to walk down the stairs at the same time. Yancy always had guards parked outside watching the place. She had to get to them, tell them what had happened. She ran down the stairs and out the front door. She looked around in horror.

There was no one there. The guards were gone.

Ramona searched for her car keys. She found them. They played a strange song as her hand shook uncontrollably. She ran to her car and drove away as fast as she could.

2

Jackin' the Box

The Frank Murphy Hall of Justice sits on a block of St. Antoine Street in downtown Detroit. It is just minutes away from its big brother, police headquarters at 1300 Beaubien. Frank Murphy houses Recorder's Court, a special segment of the Wayne County Circuit Court that handles only criminal cases.

Recorder's Court is one of the busiest courts of its kind in the country. Its judges and court staff are part of a complex machinery, handling thousands of cases a year. It is also a court in which seventy-five percent of the judges are black, and its jury pools draw heavily from a city that is ninety percent black.

On the seventh floor of Frank Murphy, Assistant Prosecutor Jesse King was about to put another one away. He stood in front of the witness stand in the crowded courtroom.

A defendant was on the stand, and that made him happy. It was always a mistake for a defendant to testify. But this guy was arrogant. He thought he could face the conscience of the community and fake it. The prisons were filled with men who'd made the same mistake.

The witness, Michael White, had date-raped a woman named Gilda Reese. He said the sex had been consensual. The bruises on her body and trauma to her vaginal area said differently.

White had a history of sexual assault, but all that had been excluded from evidence thanks to the prohibition of evidence on a defendant's prior bad acts. Jesse had tried to get around the rule, but the judge did not buy it.

Michael White was a huge black man, six feet six, two-fifty or so. He was a construction worker who drank too much and was a big man with his friends. But White was not smart enough to plead the Fifth and had taken the stand over his attorney's fervent objections.

". . . so, Mr. White," said Jesse. "It's your testimony that after Ms. Reese took off her clothes, she danced for you?"

"Yeah, that's right," said White.

"Did Ms. Reese put on music?" asked Jesse.

"Uh, naw, she just danced, you know, moving sexy like she wanted it."

"*It?*" asked Jesse. "What 'it' did she want?"

The defense counsel, a skinny, balding little man named Dennis Kendricks, stood up. "Objection, Your Honor. We all know what this case is about."

"Your Honor," said Jesse, "the witness made a vague reference to an 'it.' I'm just trying to clarify what he meant."

"Overruled," said the judge. She was a fiftyish black woman named Barbara Radford. A thorough and no-nonsense judge.

"So, Mr. White," said Jesse, "what 'it' did my client, Ms. Reese, want?"

"You know, the dick," said White.

The gallery in the courtroom laughed. There were about thirty people or so. Jesse waited patiently until they quieted down, then: "The dick?" he asked. "You mean, your penis?"

"That's right," said White. "She wanted it."

"And so you gave it to her?"

"Yes, I did. All of it," said White arrogantly.

"Really?" said Jesse. Then he homed in on his real point. "Isn't it true that you're sensitive about that part of your anatomy?"

White looked unsure for a moment. He glanced at Kendricks, who shook his head ever so slightly. "Naw, man," White said with gusto. "I don't like to brag, but I'm packin'."

More laughter; this time even the judge smiled.

Jesse took the moment to walk back to his table and take a drink of water. He took his time. White had crossed the line that he wanted him to.

"I can call one of your ex-girlfriends and have her testify about whether you're packing, as you say," said Jesse.

White looked at Kendricks again. White's defense attorney nodded.

"Go on," said White. "They'd be lying. They'll say anything because I dropped their asses."

"Watch your mouth, Mr. White," said the judge.

Nonchalantly Jesse asked: "So any woman you've had sex with would be biased, that's what you're saying?"

"Yeah, that's right," said White.

"Okay, so let's get into this 'packin' ' business," said Jesse.

As he stopped to take another drink of water, a black woman in a red blouse walked into the courtroom. Michael White registered shock at seeing the woman. Jesse saw this and smiled. He walked back to the witness stand.

"So, Mr. White, you're packin'?" asked Jesse.

"Your Honor," said Kendricks, "can we get on with something relevant?"

"This is relevant," said Jesse. "This man claims a large physical endowment; said endowment allegedly was used to rape the victim. Our medical report shows trauma, but nothing consistent with a giant penis."

The gallery laughed again.

"Overruled," said the judge. "But get on with it, Mr. King."

"Thank you, Your Honor," said Jesse. He turned back to White. "Mr. White, isn't it true you have a very small penis?"

"Objection!" yelled Kendricks.

"Overruled, Mr. Kendricks," said the judge. "Your client made this an issue."

Michael White was silent. He couldn't take his eyes off the woman with the red blouse.

"Well, Mr. White?" asked Jesse.

"Naw, it ain't little," said White.

"You're a big man, Mike. Six foot six, two fifty something. Big muscles, but you have a small dick, true?"

"Hell, no!" yelled White.

"Isn't that why you got mad at the victim?" asked Jesse. "It was your first date, she'd been drinking. She saw it and made a joke."

"No, I didn't do it," said White.

"Your Honor," said Kendricks, "who's to say what small is? This is all too vague to be relevant."

"He has a point, Mr. King," said the judge.

Jesse went to his desk and grabbed a book. "Your Honor, this is *Gray's Anatomy*, the bible on the subject of the human body." Jesse opened the book to a page. "Your Honor can take judicial notice of *Gray's* relevance and credibility in the medical community. The book says the average male penis is about six inches when erect. So let's say three or four inches would be considered small."

"Three or four?" said the judge, a little shocked at the number. "Is that okay with you, Mr. Kendricks?"

"Your Honor—" said Kendricks.

"I think it's a good number myself." The judge tried not to smile. "Well, I'm convinced that in this instance size does matter. Judicial notice taken, objection overruled."

"Okay, Your Honor," said Kendricks. "But I take exception."

"Noted for the record, Mr. Kendricks," said the judge.

Jesse returned to White, who was still transfixed by the lady in red seated in the gallery.

"You whipped it out," said Jesse; "she saw how small it was and said something that made you mad, didn't she?"

"No. You don't know what you talkin' 'bout, all right!" said White.

Jesse moved right in front of the defendant, looking him in the eyes. "She said, 'Where's the rest of it?,' didn't she?"

"No!" White said. He looked around Jesse at the woman in red.

"Perjury is a serious crime," said Jesse. "If we find out you lied, you could get even more time than you're going to."

"What's she doin' here?" Michael White pointed at the woman in the red blouse. "She gonna testify or somethin'?"

"Sidebar, Your Honor," said Kendricks.

"Yes, I think so," said Judge Radford.

Jesse and Kendricks walked up to the judge's bench. She turned off her microphone.

"Your Honor," said Kendricks, "my client has obviously been upset by the woman in the red blouse back there. I'd like to ask counsel who she is and if she intends to testify."

"Mr. King?"

"Never seen her before, Your Honor."

"Bullsh— Excuse me, Your Honor," said Kendricks.

"Mr. King, do you intend to call that woman as a witness?" asked the judge.

"Your Honor," said Jesse, "I've never met that woman, and I swear that I am not going to call her as a witness in this case. The state's case is ending right after this cross-examination."

"Happy, Mr. Kendricks?" asked the judge.

"No," said Kendricks. "I want an adjournment until I can find out who she is."

Jesse expected this and knew he had to stop any adjournment. For the first time he grew upset. "This is silly, Your Honor! Whoever this woman is, I'm not calling her to testify, so it's irrelevant. Why not run a check on everyone in the gallery while we're at it? I object."

"So do I," said Judge Radford.

"But, Your Honor, my client—" said Kendricks.

"Your client is in the busiest criminal court in America. And in case you didn't know, Recorder's Court is also the most efficient. And there's a reason for that. We don't adjourn trials on the day scheduled for conclusion because some woman walked into the room."

"Exception," said Kendricks.

"I'll add it to the rest of them," said the judge. "Now get back."

Jesse and Kendricks both thanked the judge, a requirement even if she reamed you. Jesse returned to White, who was starting to look irritated. He moved closer to the big man. "Mr. White, when the victim made fun of your penis, you got mad, didn't you?"

"I told you. No," said White.

"She made a joke and laughed and couldn't stop laughing. She kept asking, 'Where's the rest of it?,' so you hit her and kept hitting her."

"No."

"And you decided to teach her a lesson, so you raped her. That would teach her never to say it was small, right?"

"*No!*" White started to rise from his seat, then sat back down.

"Then you bragged to your friends, didn't you? You said, quote, I jacked her pussy. Like carjacking. Jackin' the box. That's what the fellas call it on the street, right?"

"I'm not answerin' any more damn questions," said White.

"Oh, yes, you are, Mr. White," said Judge Radford. "Or you will be put in jail. And if you swear in my court again, I'll throw you in myself."

Jesse glanced at opposing counsel. Kendricks looked angry and frustrated. Jesse then turned to the jury. They were staring at Michael White. One woman was very slowly shaking her head. It was almost over.

Jesse resumed: "Mr. White, don't waste our time here. You're already in a lot of trouble. Don't make me prove you a liar in front of all these good people. Now, for the last time. Do you have a small penis, three or four inches when erect?"

Michael White was silent. He looked at the woman in red, then back at Jesse. Hatred and violence were in his eyes. "I don't know how big it is," he said.

"You just said you were packing, but now you aren't sure?" Jesse asked, looking at the jury. "Are you sure you didn't date-rape Ms. Reese?"

White hesitated, then: "She wanted it."

"Yeah," said Jesse. "All three inches."

"I'll kick your ass, you muthafucka," said White. Kendricks jumped up, but it was too late.

"Mr. White, you're in contempt!" said Judge Radford.

"Your Honor," said Kendricks, "counsel's question was improper. So, under the circumstances—"

"Too late, Mr. Kendricks," said Judge Radford. "He was warned about his language. However, the jury will disregard Mr. King's last statement. Mr. King, you're on the line here too."

"Sorry, Your Honor," said Jesse. "I have no further questions for Mr. White. The state rests."

Jesse went back to his table. Kendricks tried to redirect examination, going through White's story, but the damage was done. White was nervous and appeared to be lying about everything he said. White got down from the witness stand and returned to his seat next to Kendricks. He stared at the woman in red all the way to his chair.

"Closings," said Judge Radford. "Mr. Kendricks?"

Kendricks got up and tried to save his case. He reminded the jury that Gilda Reese was the only witness and she admitted being drunk on the night of the incident. He told the jury that the victim was promiscuous. And lastly Kendricks alluded, ever so carefully, to the fact that White had not hidden behind the Fifth Amendment.

Jesse waited patiently as Kendricks finished. Defense lawyers always hit the same points, trying to convince someone on the jury to go against the evidence. All they needed was one person to hang a jury. Kendricks finished, and Jesse got up. He started speaking, as he always did in closing, from behind his table.

"Ladies and gentlemen, you might not believe this, but my job is not to convict the defendant in this case. I represent the people of this state. And the defendant is one of those people. He is innocent until proven guilty. My job is to find the truth, whatever it is and no matter how terrible it might be."

Jesse moved slowly toward the jury. He kept his eyes on the elderly black woman who had shaken her head at White's outburst.

"We've had some laughs here about the size of men's sex organs. But it was nervous laughter, wasn't it? And we are all nervous because we know in this day and age that violence is closer to us than it has ever been. It's one door, one car, one angry word away from us. Close. Too close. The victim, Gilda Reese, got too close to Michael White. She got drunk, said one word too many, and violence claimed her. You've seen the defendant and heard what he has had to say. Is he telling the truth that I am trying to find? No. None of us here believe that. He's a liar, a rapist, and he wants us to ignore all that because he had the arrogance to face you. His attorney's truth is only an echo of Mr. White's lies. We've all seen my truth here today. It was in Gilda Reese's tragic story and in the callous and evil attitude of the defendant. Michael White beat and raped a woman whose only transgression was having a few too many drinks. So, now that we've found my truth, help me do justice with it. Send Michael White to prison."

Jesse sat down. The judge charged the jury and sent them to deliberate. They were back in a half hour with a guilty verdict.

"Sentencing in two weeks," said Judge Radford. "Bailiff, take Mr. White to our lovely accommodations. Court's adjourned."

Michael White was taken away in handcuffs. He stared at the woman in the red blouse as they dragged him out of the courtroom. The woman in red smiled at Jesse and walked out without a word.

Jesse was congratulated by the victim and her family. The women kissed him, and the men clapped him on the back. Jesse smiled broadly. This was his favorite part. The long hours, low pay, and an unappreciative public disappeared in these moments. The victim and her family lingered for a while, then left. Jesse packed his things.

"Okay, Jesse," said Kendricks. "My client says that woman was a paramedic."

"Who?" asked Jesse.

"Don't fuck with me," said Kendricks.

"Oh, that woman," said Jesse. "Yes, she is. She treated Mr.

White when he got hurt in a basketball game not long ago. She did a *thorough* examination, if you know what I mean."

"You bastard," said Kendricks. "You said you'd never seen her before."

"I hadn't. We only talked on the phone. She said she might come but wasn't sure. She also said she couldn't remember your client at all. So I never intended to call her."

"God's gonna get you, Jesse." Kendricks laughed a little.

"Hey, he can take a number."

Kendricks shook Jesse's hand and left. It was a tough loss, but defense attorneys never took these things personally. Behind all the confrontation they were all in the brotherhood of lawyers. Jesse finished packing his briefcase and left the courtroom.

In the hallway attorneys, court watchers, and courthouse staff workers were leaving. The people all filled the elevator cars going down. Jesse walked over to a bank of elevators and pushed the up button. The hallway became mostly empty as Jesse waited for a car to come up.

"You ain't shit, you know that?"

Jesse turned and saw Michael White's brother, standing behind him. Ricky White was about twenty years old and big. He was six-two and at least two hundred pounds. He had a bald head with a nasty-looking scar running across his scalp. The whole family was scary, Jesse thought.

Ricky stared at Jesse as he moved closer. Ricky had sat through the whole trial and even testified as a character witness for his brother.

"I'm perfectly glad not to be shit, Mr. White," said Jesse.

"You know what I mean," said Ricky. His voice was tinged with anger. "You make money putting brothers in jail."

Jesse quickly checked the hallway. There was only a thin black woman in a yellow dress talking to another older woman in the hall. No bailiffs.

"I don't have time for this," said Jesse. He impatiently pushed the button again.

"My brother ain't no rapist," said Ricky. "He ain't perfect, but he didn't do it."

"Your brother beat and raped a woman because he's sensitive about his little dick," said Jesse. "He's a long way from perfect."

"You niggas all the same," said Ricky. "The white man wave

some money and you sit up and beg. What they pay you a week? Or do you get paid for each brother you take down?"

Now Jesse was angry. He took a step closer to the bigger man. "I'm black, your brother's lawyer was black, the judge was black, and nine members of the jury were black. Where did the white man come in today?"

"Fuck you. You muthafuckas always twistin' everything," said Ricky. "You know what I'm talking about. You just another Uncle Tom like that nigga out in L.A. who tried to put O.J. in jail."

"O.J. was guilty," Jesse said flatly.

"Just like I thought," said Ricky. "Fuckin' sellout."

That was enough. Jesse put his heavy briefcase down. Ricky White was angry, big, and looked dangerous. Thank God the court screened for weapons, Jesse thought. After years of dealing with lowlifes, he was unafraid of men like this.

"You know," said Jesse, "before there were blacks in the prosecutor's office, almost every brother who walked into a courtroom in Detroit was convicted. Guilty or not. You should be happy we're here, because we can make sure none of that injustice happens again. Black people run this court and this city. There is no racism here. Your brother was guilty, and I did my job putting his ass in jail. And you know what? If you ever screw up, I'll put yours away too."

"I don't care what you say," said Ricky. "The white man is still holding your nuts. That's the truth about this world."

"No. That's your world," said Jesse. "My world is not black and white. It's guilty and innocent."

"You full of shit," said Ricky. "You ain't nothing but—"

The elevator door opened. Jesse grabbed his briefcase and turned to walk away. Ricky White's arm shot out and grabbed Jesse by the shoulder.

"Don't be turnin' yo' back on me—" said Ricky.

In one fluid move Jesse grabbed Ricky's thick arm and twisted it. Ricky doubled over, bending forward. He tried to jerk away, but Jesse kept the pressure on him.

A woman screamed.

Jesse stuck out a foot, pushed Ricky forward, and tripped him. The big man fell flat on his face.

"I'm gonna kill you!" Ricky screamed on the floor.

"You'll be doing it with a broken arm," Jesse said. He twisted Ricky's arm again.

From behind him Jesse heard, "I got him, Mr. King."

Jesse looked over his shoulder and saw a court bailiff and the woman in the yellow dress. Jesse let Ricky go. The bailiff grabbed the fallen man, pulled him to his feet, and started to take him away.

"Let him go," said Jesse.

"Excuse me," said the bailiff, "didn't he attack you?"

"Just a misunderstanding, right?" Jesse posed the question to Ricky. Jesse looked at the angry man. If Ricky was as dumb as his brother, he would say no and be put in the lockup.

"Yeah," said Ricky weakly.

The bailiff let Ricky go. "I'll escort you outside, sir," he said sternly.

Another elevator came, and Jesse got on. He watched the doors close on Ricky's angry face. As Jesse put his briefcase down, he felt the fabric of his jacket move. He took it off and checked it. The sleeve was ripped a little at the shoulder from the scuffle.

"Damn," he said. "I should have had his ass locked up."

The car stopped. Jesse put his jacket back on and walked out of the elevator and into the Wayne County prosecutor's office on the eleventh floor.

The office was quiet. It was not the frenzy it usually was. There were no people running around, carrying the mountains of paper that were the blood of the office. The phones rang, but no one rushed to pick up. People just stood around, talking.

A secretary ran up to Jesse. He thought for a moment that she had business on her mind, but as she came closer, he saw she was teary-eyed.

"Jesse, someone killed the mayor," she said.

3

The Nasty Girls

The roller quickly transferred the drugs to the man, who shoved some cash at him. The roller counted it and waved the young man off. The man quickly sped off in his car on the dark street, burning rubber as he did.

"Scared-ass white boys," said the roller.

He walked down the deserted street and turned at the bright lights of Chene on the east side. Old cars rambled past. Derelicts stumbled along, talking to themselves. Night people.

The roller watched the street carefully, looking for customers. Normally the heads would come around eleven or so, after their supply ran out. They'd have to get money first, then come to see him. He didn't care how they got the money as long as they had it.

The roller was careful not to have his back in any direction for too long. Since the drug gang called the Union had self-destructed, the streets were in chaos. Dealers were engaged in petty wars, trying to recruit workers or put rivals out of business.

The roller, Keith James, was independent and would never work for any of the new drug gangs. He had a loose crew of three rollers he dealt with. No bosses and all that shit. They just sold the product and got paid. Keith hoped that all this silly-ass ambition would blow over and he could stop watching his back.

A young girl came his way. She walked slowly, looking from side to side. She was dressed in a tight little skirt and high heels. Her hair was done in short braids, and she wore a tube top that bounced along with her breasts. As she got closer, Keith saw that she couldn't be more than sixteen.

"Whassup, baby?" the girl said.

"Past yo' bedtime, ain't it, little girl?" said Keith. He saw that she was cute and maybe older than he had first thought.

"I go to bed all time of the day," said the girl. She turned for him, smiling. She was nice-looking, fine legs and a nice little behind. Too bad he was about business tonight.

"Sorry. I ain't interested," said Keith.

"You sure? This stuff is the best you can get out here."

"Sorry."

"Maybe I need to change your mind."

She was lifting up her dress a little when a car of teenagers rolled up to the corner. They stopped, looked, and drove on.

"Damn!" said Keith. "You gotta go. I ain't buyin' none of yo' stank ass. So get on while you still can—"

Without warning Keith felt a cord wrap tightly around his neck. Just as quickly the young girl stepped forward and brought a knee into his groin. He buckled over at the hot flash of pain. Behind him he heard a husky laugh.

"Never turn down the booty, dumb ass!" the young girl said.

Keith desperately grabbed the cord around his neck, but it was no use. He choked as the cord was stretched. The young girl patted him down and took his gun. Then she pushed Keith around the corner onto the dark street that he'd just left.

Under a broken streetlight a short black woman with a ponytail stood. As she stepped forward, the shadows made her face seem broken and dark. She was dressed in baggy pants, a flannel shirt, and sneakers.

"You rollin' up in my 'hood," said the short woman. She removed a gun from her pants. "He strapped?"

"Not no more," said the young girl. "I got it."

"Let him go," said the short woman.

Keith felt the cord loosen. He was still hurting from the hit on his balls and dropped to one knee. He looked up to see a tall woman walk over to the short one. The tall one was big, real big.

"This is my place, Keith," said the short woman. She moved closer, keeping the gun on him.

Keith's eyes showed recognition. "What the fuck is this, LoLo?" he asked.

"You know what it is," said the woman. "It's join-up time."

"Like Uncle Sam," said the young girl. The big woman was silent. She just looked on.

"I'm my own man," said Keith. "And if I did join a gang, it sure wouldn't be a pack of hos."

The big woman stepped out, slapped Keith hard in the face. He fell on his ass. He tried to get up, but the big woman was already on him. A quick punch to the chest sent him back down. The big woman drew back her fist, ready for the next try.

"Hold up, Yolanda," said LoLo. "Don't bust him yet."

LoLo walked over and knelt next to the fallen man. "Look, Yolanda and Sheri here want to do your ass, but I said no. I said, Keith is a smart nigga, he won't give us no trouble. Now, I know you a man and all that shit, but it's a new day in Detroit. You brothas been capping each other left and right, dying, going to jail, and what not. Us women have had to take up the slack. Now you can go on being all hardheaded and shit, or you can join up and get rich with the Nasty Girls."

Keith spat blood. He was getting his ass kicked but good. Yolanda was watching him, waiting. And LoLo still had the gun.

"Okay, okay," he said. "You want me, you got me."

"Cool," said LoLo. "All you gotta do is give me all your money, tell me where your stash is, and bring your crew to me."

Keith looked shocked and angry at the request but said, "Yeah, yeah. All right—"

Suddenly Keith kicked out a leg at Yolanda. It caught her in the knee, and the big woman stumbled back. Keith grabbed for the gun in LoLo's hand and managed to knock it loose. He had just gotten to his feet when he was tackled by Sheri. Turning, Keith got off a punch that caught Sheri in the side of the head. Sheri fell, recoiling from the blow. Keith got to his feet and ran.

The first shot caught him in the back of his calf, the second in the hip. Keith fell to the ground, yelling in pain. He heard them cursing, coming closer.

Keith rolled over on his back and saw LoLo above him, gun in hand. Her long ponytail was draped over one shoulder. She dropped down on him, bringing her knee in his chest. Keith coughed dryly as the wind flew from his lungs.

Lights were going on in nearby houses. Curtains parted, but it was too dark to see and too late for the cops to come in time.

"Good night, punk ass," said LoLo flatly. Then she put the gun over Keith's heart and fired.

4

Jesse

The city was in turmoil. Harris Yancy had been butchered in his own home. There were rumors of a woman being involved, but the cops were being unusually tight-lipped.

You couldn't find a copy of a newspaper, and the TV stations were doing around-the-clock coverage. The president had even made a statement at a press conference expressing his condolences.

Jesse sat in his office trying to do some work. New prosecutors had tiny offices that were always filled with messy, stacked files. You couldn't get rich working for the state, and they never let you forget it. And in the biggest irony of all, the offices were about the same size as a state prison cell.

Yancy's death meant there would be a shift in power unlike any seen in Detroit. Several would-be kings had already hinted at filing for a special election.

Jesse was deeply saddened by Yancy's murder. The mayor had always stood for equality and action. He had been trying to save the city from itself and doing a pretty good job. More than that, Yancy had represented the future for young blacks like Jesse. It was like losing a relative.

Harris Yancy had given the commencement speech at Jesse's graduation from law school. It was a moment that no law student ever forgets. Yancy had no love for lawyers, but he'd agreed to give the speech because Jesse's graduating class contained the highest number of blacks in the history of the school.

"The law is a thing that men make to govern themselves," Yancy had said. "So society is bound by its better intentions. Young lawyers are the guardians of that sacred trust."

Jesse had never forgotten those words. And now Yancy, father of an entire generation of black professionals, was dead.

There had been a funeral to end all funerals last week. Hundreds of friends, relatives, dignitaries, politicians, and celebrities jammed Detroit's Church of God. Loudspeakers had to be set up because hundreds of people had gathered outside the church to listen to the speeches and eulogies. Frank D'Estenne, county prosecutor, was one of the many speakers at the funeral. He had been a friend and ally of the late mayor's. His eulogy had brought people to tears.

There were parades, candlelight vigils, and prayer meetings all over town. And the overwhelming statement heard was "We want the murderer."

He'd sent condolences to the mayor's wife, Louise Yancy. Jesse was sure that it was lost in the thousands of other such messages at Manoogian Mansion, but it made him feel better.

Jesse King was in his fifth year at the Wayne County prosecutor's office. He was good at his job, some would say brilliant. He attacked his cases as if his own life were on the line, and he possessed a keen awareness and understanding of human nature, especially black human nature. He used these talents to fuel his relentless and crafty courtroom style. Juries loved him, judges respected him, and defense attorneys hated to see him coming. As a result of his talents, he'd won the vast majority of his cases and had never lost a murder case.

Jesse stood and stretched. He was six feet tall, dark, clean-shaven. He kept his hair cut low because it was curly at the roots and he thought it made him look better. He was handsome, but he didn't know it. Jesse figured that women were attracted to him because of his job. He was a professional black man and a premium in the community.

He was born into poverty in Detroit's Herman Gardens housing project. But this garden only grew anger, fear, and hopelessness. His parents had separated when Jesse was young. Jesse's father, a quiet man named Walter, was a dreamer, but dreams were for men with money. Jesse's mother, Estelle, wanted no part of Walter's life speculation. So Walter King had packed up one day and left. They never saw him again. Years later Jesse heard that his father had died of a heart attack. He did not go to the funeral.

His mother was a good but weak woman who tried to help her family by taking up with one worthless man after another, failing each time to connect with anyone who could better their lives.

When they got older, Jesse, his sister Bernice, and their brother, Tyrus, all acquired their mother's welfare mentality. For years Jesse believed the world owed him something, that he was a victim of America and could not help himself without the efforts of those better than he was.

He grew up knowing what it was like to want. There were times when they didn't have enough food and had to scrounge for what they could get around the neighborhood. They wore old clothes and had to suffer the humiliation of taking handouts. Poverty was heartless, he thought, but at least it forced the realities of life upon you.

After they moved from Herman Gardens, Jesse fell in with a group of neighborhood boys from the east side. A life of crime followed. His two best friends were Kelvin Ingram, a big, athletic boy who loved to play basketball, and Oscar Wellman, a handsome dark-skinned boy everyone called Cocoa.

Jesse and his crew shied away from serious crime. They were young but not completely stupid. Dealers died for dope, and none of them wanted that. The most they ever did was sell weed and steal. They drank, cut school almost every day, stole when they needed money, and had sex with willing young girls. It was one big good life, and like all kids, Jesse thought it would never end.

At sixteen Cocoa was picked up by police for burglarizing a house. Jesse and Kelvin thought Cocoa would get juvenile detention and be out in a few months. But days later Jesse found that Cocoa had been convicted of the rape of a young girl in Hamtramck.

They went to see Cocoa in jail and found out that he'd signed a confession. Cocoa couldn't read very well, and the cops had railroaded him. Jesse had known the boy all his life and just took it for granted that he could read.

Cocoa's family cried foul and got a lawyer, but it didn't do any good. The confession stuck, and Cocoa was sent to prison, real prison. Cocoa turned seventeen waiting for trial and was tried as an adult.

When he was in prison a month, Cocoa sent Jesse and Kelvin a chilling letter describing the day he was raped by two other cons.

The letter was childish, filled with misspellings and non sequiturs. Cocoa's last words were: "Don't ever come here."

Later that same year Kelvin joined a real drug crew. He invited Jesse to join with him. Jesse thought about it, but in the end he was too afraid of the life, as they called it. Kelvin went on with his crew and was shot to death by a rival gang within the year. Jesse was alone, left with the startling truth: that he was next.

He went back to school at Pershing High, looking for another crew to hang with, but instead he found a man named Daniel Perry. Mr. Perry was a history teacher. A black man who threw out their history book on the first day of class and gave them a real lesson in American history, one that included blacks at every important juncture.

Mr. Perry took a liking to Jesse, and soon Jesse saw the world differently. Perry was a believer in self-help, no welfare, and black power. Jesse adopted this philosophy and soon was among the better students in his school. This led to community college, a four-year university, and eventually law school.

At Wayne State Law School in Detroit, Jesse became a so-called black conservative. He believed that blacks were wretched only because they chose to be. And unlike most conservatives, Jesse knew this was true, because he'd grown up poor and become a professional through hard work and sacrifice. He'd lived on both sides of the tracks and knew what it took to make it from one life to the other.

There were not many people like him in the professional ranks. Most of the people he met, black or white, had always been solidly middle-class or better. So Jesse felt separated from his current peers as well as his old neighborhood. The 'hood, as they say, was vile and somehow foreign to him now. He did not belong to either world, yet he was tied to both. His journey from poverty to middle class had divided his consciousness and his soul as well.

Jesse got up and walked out of the little office and down the narrow hallway. He had the midafternoon hungries and was going to cop a quick snack.

"Hey, Marcia, what's up?" Jesse asked a middle-aged black woman in the office next to his.

"Ramsey Felder," said Marcia Daniels, a ten-year prosecutor. She was tough and smart with a quick wit.

"Ramsey Felder," said Jesse with disdain. "Jesus, Esquire."

"Right. Anyway, you know Ramsey, he's always preaching to the jury, waving that gold-plated Bible. I got him cold on the law, but our jury pool is looking like a choir of old church mamas."

"You got a problem," Jesse said. "Ramsey is good at that stuff. When I went against him, I beat him at his own game. I looked at his old case transcripts and took notes on the Bible passages he always quotes. Then I used them before he could. The notes are in my office, and you're welcome."

Marcia smiled in appreciation as Jesse moved across the hall to another small office. Jesse said hello to the two young men in the office. They were Peter Saunders and Peter Janowski, a black and white team everyone called Pete & Pete. They did mainly murder cases and often cochaired them.

Pete & Pete didn't say hello; they just waved and kept working, their faces down in papers on the desk. They were married to the job.

"Hey, Jess," said a pretty blond woman down the hall. She looked upset. "Listen, I need your help on something."

"Sure."

Denise Wilkerson was a two-year prosecutor whose mother was a federal judge and father a senior vice-president at General Motors. Denise was polite to everyone, but it was obvious that she was on her way to a big law firm one day. She walked out of her office to Jesse.

"I'm trying to find a witness in that Villard murder case."

"The lead pipe murder?" asked Jesse.

"Right," said Denise. "The cops turned me on to this snitch, a probation officer, but he—"

"Hardaway?" he asked.

"Yes," said Denise. "He's driving me crazy. He says he knows where the witness is, but he won't tell. I thought paying him was bad enough, but he's jerking me around for some reason."

"He wants a hook," said Jesse.

"A what?" Denise looked confused.

"Where is he?" asked Jesse.

Denise led him to her little office in the middle of the hallway. Jesse liked the fact that so many of his peers relied on him. He had a reputation for being smart, thorough, and capable of dealing with the scumbags of the system.

Jesse was the only lawyer ever to get an offer from the prose-cutor's office in his junior year at law school. He was doing a mock trial in school, and the county prosecutor was acting as judge. Jesse so impressed him that he was given an internship that summer. At the end of the internship they made him an offer. He was a rising star, and everyone in the office knew it.

Jesse went into the prosecutor's office right out of law school. The county prosecutor even used his power to help expunge Jesse's juvenile record and get him past the state bar ethics panel.

Jesse and Denise entered the office to find Thomas Hardaway, a short, heavyset man sitting in a chair. Hardaway was about fifty, overweight, and mean-looking. He had slick, wavy hair, what used to be called a process, and was chewing on a long toothpick.

He was a state probation officer, regarded as one of the best, but he had a side operation. Hardaway would get information from his clients and sell it to the cops. He was good, fast, and reliable. Unfor-tunately he was also a sleazy, double-dealing bastard. He got cash from the cops, but from the prosecutors he needed something even more important.

"Jesse, my man," said Hardaway. He got up and shook Jesse's hand.

Denise sat at her desk. Jesse stood with Hardaway in the middle of the little room. They stared at each other like gunfighters.

"What's up, Hardaway?" asked Jesse. "You got your money, so give it up."

"Hey, I told her what I knew," said Hardaway. "The man you want is about five-eight, black, bald-headed and goes by the name of G."

"That's about five thousand people in Detroit," said Jesse.

"That's all I know right now," said Hardaway breezily. The toothpick bounced with each word. He smiled and sat down.

"Okay," said Jesse. "I got a big drug case where the defendant is going to get probation. The kid's name is Clark."

"How connected is he?" asked Hardaway.

"He worked for the Union before they disbanded," said Jesse. "Claims he actually met T-Bone himself."

"How big was his crew?" asked Hardaway. He was almost salivating.

"Ten, eleven guys. You want him or not?" asked Jesse.

"Cool," said Hardaway. He reached over to Denise's desk and wrote out a note. "You'll make sure I get him, right?"

"Sure," said Jesse. "But I want you to give Denise here a freebie on her next capital case."

"No problem." Hardaway passed the note to Denise. "Peace." Then he got up and walked to the door.

"Look at this, Jesse," said Denise. "He wrote the eyewitness's name and address on this paper. He knew it all along."

"Hardaway's only useful if he keeps getting clients who are connected," said Jesse. "Sometimes after he gets money from the cops, he comes here to hook another street informant. I hate his guts, but that's just the way it is."

"He's almost a criminal himself," said Denise disgustedly. "Damn, I gotta get to the cops and have them pick up this guy. I'm sure with an eyewitness the defendant will plead." Denise got up and shook Jesse's hand. "I owe you," she said.

"You're welcome," said Jesse. Jesse left the office and moved on. He approached the next office, the big one that belonged to Richard Steel. He was a group leader and Jesse's boss. Richard was white, late thirties, and a vicious lawyer. He and Jesse were the only ones in the office who had never lost a murder case, and Steel had ten years on Jesse.

It was no secret that Richard Steel wanted to be county prosecutor. He often associated himself with high-profile cases just to take the credit for a victory. Behind his back they called him Dick Steals.

Jesse and Dick Steals did not get along. They were too much alike, hard-driven, bright, and competitive. Jesse was every bit as good as his boss, maybe better. This caused a serious rivalry in an office where whites ruled, but they worked in a city where blacks had power.

As Jesse passed by Steel's office, he tried not to look in, but he couldn't resist. The office was empty. A rarity this time of day. Steel didn't do many cases these days and was usually in his office wheeling and dealing with his many political connections.

Jesse walked into the refreshment area, a sad little place with three vending machines and several tables. Clerks, paralegals, and other office workers sat, talked and got food, and left. No one lingered. It was not the nature of the office. There was just too much work.

Jesse got a bag of chips and a Pepsi and started back to his office. He had a pile of work, and he didn't want to take any of it home. He was almost back to his little cubby when Marcia came up to him.

"Boss man wants you, Jesse," said Marcia.

"Dick Steals got his underwear in a bunch again?" asked Jesse.

"Not him, the *real* boss."

Jesse stop munching on his snack. "Why?"

"Don't know. But I guess you'll find out soon enough."

Marcia walked away. Jesse hurried back to his office, put on his jacket, and went to see the head of the prosecutor's office.

5

D'Estenne

François ("Frank") D'Estenne was an elegant man. He was tall, silver-haired, and slim for his fifty-eight years. He was always immaculately dressed and had a stride that looked as if he were gliding across the floor. It was said that he could charm a nun out of her panties, then sell them back to her. He was a calming influence in a nerve-racking business, Valium in a six-hundred-dollar suit.

D'Estenne was also a hard-ass, no-nonsense veteran of smoke-filled rooms and cutthroat politics. He dined with governors while ruining livelihoods, and laughed with senators while destroying would-be opponents. He was as mean as he was classy, and that was why he'd been county prosecutor for a decade.

D'Estenne was weak in the black community, however. And in the coming election he was being challenged by Xavier Peterson, a black community activist, ordained minister, and successful defense attorney. Peterson was not the first black man to challenge D'Estenne. Several had tried their hand, but none of them had even come close to succeeding. But Peterson was different. He was well liked across the board, and that made D'Estenne nervous. This election was going to be a war.

Jesse worked for D'Estenne but was a friend of Peterson, a fellow black lawyer. This put him squarely in the middle of the coming fray.

D'Estenne's legacy of power and the equally powerful challenge he faced were on Jesse's mind as he entered the big office one floor up from his own.

Jesse walked into the room with its tasteful French decor. D'Estenne took his heritage seriously. He peppered his speech with French and visited Paris every year. A bust of Napoleon sat on a column by his large mahogany desk. Behind the desk was D'Estenne, dressed in a flawless steel gray suit and cranberry tie. And standing next to the head of the little general was Richard Steel.

"Jesse, come in," said D'Estenne. He shook Jesse's hand heartily.

"Frank, Richard, what's up?" Jesse asked. He was nervous enough being summoned. Richard's being here only made it worse.

"Have a seat," said D'Estenne. All three men sat down. "Excuse me if I'm a little upset," said D'Estenne. "You know Mayor Yancy and I were close. He's in a better place now. *Grâce à Dieu.*"

Jesse didn't think D'Estenne looked upset. Just the opposite in fact. He looked great. All the same, Yancy and D'Estenne had been good friends. Yancy had backed D'Estenne in every election since he became county prosecutor.

"I have a special assignment for you and Richard," D'Estenne said.

"What is it? Or should I say, *who?*" asked Jesse. The prospect of working with Dick Steals did not thrill him.

"It's the Yancy case."

"We have a suspect?" Jesse said. He almost rose from his seat.

"Yes, we do, but it's . . . complicated. You see . . . well, that is—" D'Estenne hesitated. This was something that never happened, Jesse thought. D'Estenne was a master at controlling situations. Jesse became even more anxious. What could be so complicated as to make D'Estenne at a loss for words?

"What we want to do," Richard said, "is deal with—"

D'Estenne gave Richard a look that stopped him dead. D'Estenne's eyes narrowed into slits of severity, and his smile fell into a flat line. Here was the other D'Estenne, the bureaucratic killer who took no prisoners.

"Sorry," said Richard.

D'Estenne shifted in his big leather chair. His face went back to that of the congenial boss. "Jesse, you're one of my best soldiers, a star actually. I plucked you right out of law school because I could see it."

"Thank you, sir," said Jesse. A compliment. Now he knew whatever it was, it was very bad.

"And I don't want to bullshit you because I can't," said D'Estenne. "The suspect in the mayor's case is African American, a woman. In this town, with my reelection looming, we can't have whitey wielding the sword of justice alone."

"I know what you mean, sir," Jesse said, realizing how big this case was. "The defense will make a racial issue out of it if there is no black prosecutor on the team."

"Yes," said D'Estenne. "And I will not give them an advantage like that, not with the large numbers of African American judges and jurors in our system. This isn't Los Angeles, where they add the black lawyer as an afterthought. *Pas ici.*" D'Estenne picked up a crystal paperweight with the Arc de Triomphe etched on it. "But I don't like anyone telling me how to run my office. I don't see color, Jesse. I'm making you cochair on this case because you're good, but you happen to be African American too, so it suits the cause of justice."

"Thank you. I accept," said Jesse. He was elated at the news. Working with Dick Steals would be a drag, but a chance to put Yancy's killer away was something he was not going to pass up.

"Great," D'Estenne said. "Okay, now that we're all on board, we can work with the police to bring our suspect in with as little fanfare as possible."

"Agreed," said Richard, feeling as though he needed to say something.

"She's not in custody yet?" asked Jesse. "Why don't we just have two uniforms pick her up? I mean, I know she's black, but she's still a murder suspect."

D'Estenne leaned across his desk. He looked troubled, yet his eyes were full of intensity. "It's not that simple when the woman you're arresting is the mayor's wife."

6

Cane

Gregory Cane stood at the edge of the roof. It was almost morning and the sky was a deep, eternal black. The roof's coarse tiles felt rough and strangely good on his bare feet. A thin breeze cooled his nude body, causing his flesh to tingle.

Cane waited. Every day He came, ushering in new possibilities of life. But He also brought chances of death. And that's why Cane was here, naked, with nothing but what God had given him when he arrived to this misery.

Gregory Cane had been born to a heroin-addicted mother in the county hospital. He struggled in the intensive care unit for months, before his tiny body purged the drug from his system. He lived, but his left eye was rendered useless, a lifelong reminder of the battle.

After he recovered, Cane's mother reclaimed him. It would have been better if she had left him an orphan. Cane's life as a child and young man was filled with beatings, hunger, neglect, and hopelessness. He watched his mother turn from addict to prostitute to helpless invalid.

Cane's hard life turned him immediately to crime. He started stealing cars for a man called Tango when he was ten. After that he was in and out of juvenile detention on a regular basis.

Juvenile prison was just as bad as its older brother the penitentiary. Cane was hardened even further, learning to fight off rivals, perverted rapists, and cruel "guardians." He killed his first time at twelve. The bigger boy had attacked Cane on kitchen detail. Cane cut the boy's throat with the top of a tuna can and watched him bleed to death.

When he was sixteen, Cane ran afoul of two guards in a facility called Clearwater. The guards were running contraband, and Cane had gotten in their way with his own deals. The guards took Cane to an unused basement they called the Pit. They beat him savagely and left him there for four days in total darkness.

Cane thought more than once that he'd died during the ordeal. But in that unending darkness, hungry, bleeding, and smelling his own waste, he'd found himself. He saw that patterns of life were built on violence, and the strongest men were the ones who had no fear of that. And the average man feared his worst nightmare: sudden, painful death.

Cane walked out of the Pit after four days, looking like death. The juvenile facility's doctor couldn't believe he was still alive.

The corrupt guards were transferred, and Cane became a legend. But he was changed. He realized now that God had cursed him. God brought him into the world, realized the mistake, but could not take Cane out. Cane had defied God at birth and again in the dark basement. He and God were enemies now, and that would be his life's work, to beat Him at the game of life.

So Cane did not fear what the new day brought because he was already dead. Dead in his heart and in the eyes of society. He was a black drug dealer, a thief, and a killer. But at least he was the master of his own fate, and not even the power of the morning could change that.

The night faded, and the day spilled over the horizon, shining with crimson rays. The light turned golden and rushed over the earth into Cane's face. His eye blinked, and his mouth curled downward. He looked into the glow, into the face of God. He spoke, his voice a rumbling whisper.

"Fuck you," he said.

Cane stepped off the roof of the old house and went back inside, where he got dressed and put a big knife in his pocket. He never carried guns. He didn't believe in them. Guns made weak people think they were strong.

Gregory Cane was six feet three inches of thick, wiry muscle. His body was hard like an old piece of iron. His arms were longer than they should have been, and his hands were oversize. His face had a perpetual scowl that only changed to different levels of menace. His eyes were brown. At least one of them was; the other was gray in a milky white pool, a reminder of the day when God had almost won.

Cane finished dressing and got into his car, a Lincoln, and drove to a house a few miles away. The old house was a meeting place on Grand Boulevard where he and his crew got together to do business.

Cane got out of his car and went inside the huge house. It was three stories high, old and abandoned. It stank of garbage and urine. Broken furniture was on the floor, and debris was piled in corners. Two black men were waiting inside. Cane walked up to them.

"He's in the back," said Tico, one of Cane's men. Tico had known Cane since they were both sent to Clearwater. Tico was a brown-skinned man with a bald head and big gold teeth. He was a tough roller, but not as ruthless as Cane. Tico liked the money and women, but he could never get used to the bad part, the violence that supported these things.

The other man was Walker Lakeston. Walker was thin, dark-skinned, with a head of long dreadlocks. He always wore a pair of dark shades and lots of jewelry.

Walker had been born in Jamaica and come to America illegally. He'd joined Cane's crew a year ago, but Cane had known him a long time before that. Walker was a fierce competitor in the drug business. He had a reputation for having a lot of women and kicking ass. The only reason Walker had joined Cane was his own crew was busted by the cops and Walker had almost gone down with them.

"Muthafucka won't talk," said Tico.

"That's why I want him to meet my friend," said Cane.

"I ain't goin' down there," said Tico, a tinge of fear in his voice.

"Don't have to," said Cane. "I'll do it. This is the last time anyway. Smell's gettin' too bad."

"Why don't we just cut off one of his fingers, snip, snip?" asked Walker. His Jamaican accent ran smoothly under his words. "Always works for me."

"I want him to see what death looks like," said Cane. "And I want to see her again."

Walker was about to protest, but Tico cut him off with a look. Cane walked into the back of the house and grabbed a man who was tied hand and foot and lying on the floor.

"Time to talk," Cane said. He got the man to his feet and headed toward the basement.

Cane was the leader of a big crew on the west side. After the Union had collapsed, everyone had been confused for a while. The streets were filled with independents, nickel-and-diming and shooting one another over nothing. Cane got a crew together and slowly incorporated as many of the others as he could.

Cane's crew was rolling strong, and times were good. He and Tico dealt with the white suppliers, and Walker was his man for everything else. Detroit still had many crews, but his was now by far the largest. At least on the west side.

On the east side of town a group of women had assumed power. They called themselves the Nasty Girls or just the Girls. They had grabbed prime pieces of territory and consolidated power just as Cane had. And now they were expanding, adding to their numbers and pushing out each day—closer to him.

LoLo Wells and her women were tough, smart, and very careful. But LoLo was a hothead. She had a bug up her ass about the men in the business, and she was easily set off. That would be her downfall, Cane thought. Those who made it in the life needed to have level heads.

Cane walked down the creaky wooden stairs to the house's basement. The man he pushed along was probably one of LoLo's. The man had found one of Cane's supply houses and tried to rob it. The thief obviously had been watching the home for a long time. The man was caught, but he wouldn't tell who he worked for.

"Last chance, Earl," said Cane to the man. "I want to know who sent you to steal from me." Cane ripped the duct tape from the man's mouth.

"Fuck you," said the man named Earl Young. "Go on and shoot me, but I ain't droppin' on nobody."

Cane took Earl the rest of the way down the stairs. It was a long staircase. The house had been built pre–World War II and had what used to be called a root cellar, a deep, cavernous room below the house.

The basement was cold and dark. They were almost at the end of the stairs when the smell hit them. The house already smelled bad, but this was worse. It was like an open sewer, a hard and thick stench. Earl choked as the smell filled his lungs.

"Death don't mean nothing to you," Cane said, "because you haven't seen it. I'm gonna show it to you, and then you'll tell me what I need to know."

Cane took Earl into the basement and turned on the lights. For a second both men were blinded. Cane closed his good eye to the light. When it strained, it watered, and he hated that.

When the room came into focus, Cane saw the big cat chained in the corner. Earl saw her too and began to back away.

"What the—"

Cane hit Earl hard in the stomach. Earl fell but didn't take his eyes off the corner.

The tiger roared. It was a weak, sickly sound but still scary. Her eyes were evil yellow lights in the shadows.

"She's hungry," said Cane. "The other people I brought here yesterday talked, so she didn't eat."

The tiger was about twenty feet away. There was a large brown spot directly in front of her.

"See that spot?" asked Cane. "Those are the muthafuckas who was like you. Now, for the last time, who sent you?"

"Man, you can't do this," said Earl.

Cane picked the man up and pushed him closer to the cat. Earl struggled like mad as the cat advanced and stopped when her chain reached its limit. Man and tiger were now only ten feet apart.

Cane had purchased the half-grown tiger from a white man two months ago. He paid five thousand dollars for her. They chained the cat up while she was still sedated. When the tiger came to, she was hungry and mad as hell.

Cane admired the cat's beauty and strength. But he really wanted her to establish a reputation on the street. Rollers were ready to kill and to die, but not like this.

"Please don't," said Earl.

The tiger took a swipe with a big paw. She was weak and sick, but still fast. The cat growled and walked back to the wall, waiting.

"Okay, okay," said Earl.

Cane took the man by the seat of his pants and pulled him away from the tiger.

"Tell it."

"I was watching the house before I hit it."

"I know that. Who sent you to do it?"

"Take me upstairs first."

Cane shoved the man at the tiger. Earl hopped on his bound-up feet, digging in his heels and pushing himself back. The big cat leaped with a loud roar, instinctively pouncing at the man.

The chain went to its limit, and the tiger missed, making a choking sound as she was pulled back. Earl screamed, a high-pitched scream that sounded almost like a child.

"Who the fuck was it?" yelled Cane. He slapped Earl hard in the face.

"Okay . . . okay." Earl caught his breath. "It was the Girls . . . the Nasty Girls. . . . One of them told me the place was ripe for a hit. I took it from there."

"You work for them?" asked Cane.

"Naw, man, I'm just fucking her, that's all. I swear."

"Which one?"

"Sheri, Sheri Foland."

"Okay," said Cane. "Now it's time for you to see why they call them predators." He tightened his grip on Earl and moved him toward the tiger.

"Wait, man," Earl said. "I got something else."

"Not interested," said Cane. He pushed him closer.

"Someone is stealing from you."

Cane loosened his grip. "Who?"

"Get me out of here first."

"No. Tell me now or I'll give you to the cat."

"I know this guy, he works for you, he's been taking money. Braggin' about it too."

"Who?" said Cane. "What's his name?"

"Take me away from this animal first," said Earl.

Cane waited a moment. He hated people who stole from the crew more than anything. Maybe this guy was lying, but he had to know. A thief breeds rebels, and he didn't need that right now. Cane pulled Earl away from the big cat. "Okay," he said. "Now tell it."

"Jaleel over by Grand River and Fenkell, skinny dude, always carries this little dog."

"Jaleel Jackson," Cane said. He knew the man. He was a good roller and reliable—so far.

"Me and Jaleel was gettin' high with these two white girls one night, and he was braggin' about how he was stealin' from the house. Couldn't shut up about it."

Cane took this in. It would be easy to check out. "Okay," said Cane. "Let's go."

Cane released Earl, who wobbled a little. Cane had turned to go back up the stairs when he wheeled around and pushed Earl and sent him flying at the big cat. The tiger struck, this time hitting her mark.

The sound of the man screaming sent chills through Tico. He hated that damned tiger. The neighbors had called the cops about the smell and the roaring, but so far the police hadn't believed it. There were a lot of strange things in the city, but nothing like this.

Tico had tried to stop Cane from buying the cat, but Cane had been tripping that day. Cane wanted to make everyone scared of him in Detroit. He talked about dying, cheating death, God, and all that weird shit. Tico had known Cane long enough to know there was no reasoning with him when he got like that.

"Nigga's crazy," said Walker, shaking his head. "He'd do well on the island. Crazy men prosper in Jamaica."

"He's crazy, but it works," Tico said. "Four years ago I had nothing. Now I'm running out of places to put the money."

"Soon I'll be like that too," said Walker. "I can go back to Jamaica a rich man. I can't wait."

"Why'd you leave if it's so good in Jamaica?" asked Tico.

"More opportunity here. I love Jamaica, but there's no place like here for making money."

"I heard Jamaica is a shit hole," said Tico.

Walker grew angry. "You should not talk about what you don't know. We were building hospitals and colleges in Jamaica when your people were picking cotton."

"Fuck Jamaica," said Tico. "You in America now, boy. That backward island shit don't play here."

Walker turned sullen. He scowled at Tico, then covered it with a smile. "So, I hear Cane don't like the ladies," said Walker. "That true?"

"He ain't no fag if that's what you mean," said Tico. "Cane is just . . . he's above all that kinda shit."

"Above pussy? Bullshit," Walker said. He laughed.

"You don't wanna go bringing that up around him," said Tico. "Believe me."

Tico and Walker stood in silence for a moment. They listened, but no more sounds came from the basement.

"You think he did it this time?" asked Walker.

"Sounded like it," said Tico. "We gotta get the hell out of here."

They heard footsteps, and soon Cane walked into the room carrying Earl. Earl's legs were bloody where the cat had mauled him and he had passed out.

"Cat's weak," said Cane. "She almost didn't get him." Cane dropped Earl to the floor. "Walker, take him out and dump his ass somewhere."

"Damn," said Walker. "I just got my car washed. Come on, fool." He picked up Earl and dragged him out.

"It was the Girls, then, huh?" said Tico.

"Yeah," said Cane. "Plus this thief says Jaleel is skimming on me."

"He's full of shit," Tico protested. "Jaleel is cool people."

"Maybe," said Cane. "I want you to check it out."

"All right," said Tico. "Look, Cane, this shit with the cat has got to stop."

Cane walked to the door. "Yeah. Have someone call the cops."

"The police won't believe it. They've ignored every call that went in."

"Then call them animal rights people," said Cane. "They believe everything. And make it this morning. I don't want her to die down there."

7

Ramona

Ramona awoke with a scream in her throat. She rose up and looked around the room, making sure there were no killers at her bed. She calmed herself, then lay back down but could not get back to sleep.

Yancy was dead, she was almost murdered, and now the cops were looking for her. She'd been wearing a wig to cover her braids and lots of makeup to mask her face, but she still felt vulnerable.

She'd thought of turning herself in, telling the cops what happened, but that would be stupid. The cops would never believe her, and *if* she survived a night in county jail, she'd surely go to the penitentiary anyway.

Ramona was in a high-rise condo in Southfield. It was the home of a friend named Venita Washington, whom everyone called Vinny. The condo was Vinny's secret place. Even her husband didn't know about it. Ramona had her own key and watched it for Vinny from time to time.

She got into the shower. The hot water felt good, soothing. She tried to let go of her anxiety, but she couldn't. The ordeal with the masked killers had unnerved her.

She had no idea who the killers were, how they got in, or why Yancy's guards were gone from outside. She had tried to get inside the black metallic briefcase but failed. It was solid, no seams, just a big, heavy metal block and a handle. When she shook it, she heard nothing move inside. The case had not been there before Yancy was killed, so someone must have brought it. And if Yancy had the case, then whatever was inside it was important.

Ramona got out of the shower and dried herself. She glanced in the mirror. She had never been modest about her looks. She was beautiful. The face and body in the mirror were her prime assets. They had gotten her money, cars, a nice apartment, and trips to exotic islands. They had also saved her from Detroit's neighborhoods.

Ramona Blake was raised in a blue-collar household on the east side. Her mother was what they called a picture model back in the sixties. Bethel Blake's face graced the pages of the few magazine ads that catered to Negro women. Bethel was a striking woman who was high on the list of many neighborhood suitors. But when she made her choice, she picked a laborer, Henry Blake, a strikingly handsome man. He had swept Bethel away with his dark good looks and easy manner. Bethel became pregnant, and after a hasty marriage Ramona was born.

Shortly after Ramona came into the family, the marriage began to crumble. Henry was a good man but was never able to deal with Bethel's constant pressure to make more money and lift the family into the middle class. Henry was long on good looks and short on talent. He lifted boxes, not lives.

After a few years the marriage broke Henry's already fragile resolve. So, by the time Ramona's third sister, Sarah, was born, Henry was ready to go. And after a few years of being a weekend dad, Henry never showed his face again.

Bethel was shattered. Henry's leaving was the last proof she needed that her life was over. She became stricter on her girls, especially Ramona. She pushed them, punishing them for what Henry had done to her.

Ramona and her younger sisters, Sarah and Cheryl, were given the discipline of the church by their mother at an early age. Bethel Blake was a God-fearing woman who wanted her daughters to learn virtue. They went to church services at least four times a week. Bible class, Sunday school, early service, late service, choir practice. It was forced upon them and reinforced with beatings. Bethel Blake had been raised by the code of "spare the rod," and she saw no reason to change, especially with no man around. A whipping was the cure for any infraction, no matter how small.

Ramona grew tired of her mother's tyranny and stopped going to church over Bethel's objections. She became what the old church ladies called a fast girl. Ramona began to stay out late and hang with her friends. They taught her to be free, independent, and strong. The other fast girls had none of her inhibitions, ignorance, and Baptist guilt.

Ramona and her friends began their education hanging out in the streets, getting into trouble, fighting, and stealing. Ramona became a hard, rough-edged girl who would never back down from a fight. She was teased by her friends because the one thing she hated was getting any kind of scar on her face.

As they grew into womanhood, Ramona and her friends started hanging with young men. They partied, stayed out late, and smoked dope. Ramona lost her virginity to a man named Carlos on a cold night in a Cadillac and never looked back.

Many of the men they hung out with were drug dealers. They were dangerous, but they always had money. When they began to die or went to prison, things started to change. Ramona's friends started to sell drugs themselves. To them it was a natural extension of their already perilous lifestyle. For Ramona it was more of a problem. She tried it for a while, but she was not good at it. You had to deal with nasty people and sell to innocent kids. The money was good, but it was much too dangerous.

One day, while she and her crew were making a deal, some rival dealers came after them in a car and began shooting. Ramona and her friends all scattered, running in different directions. Ramona ran through the neighborhood, cutting through yards and alleys. Finally, when she was sure she had lost them, she went home.

Ramona arrived at her house but found the rollers were on her street, looking for her. She was never one for using guns, but she had one that day. When she saw the dealers getting out of the car, she fired at them. They ran for cover, and she slipped into her house.

The rival dealers sprayed the place with bullets. Ramona could still see the holes in the cheap walls and the cracked pictures of Jesus as the house was riddled.

Ramona's mother and her middle sister, Cheryl, were not hurt, but her little sister, Sarah, was hit. Bethel had consigned Sarah to kitchen work, and the young girl caught a bullet while washing dishes.

Sarah was taken to a hospital. She lingered for one awful week but didn't make it. Her sister, little Sarah, who sang in the bathtub, kissed her Tevin Campbell poster, and put sugar on her spaghetti, was dead.

Ramona took all the blame. Their family was not rich, but it was proud, and she had brought shame and death upon them. To her mother the tragedy was a result of Ramona's spreading lack of faith and rejection of God. To Ramona it was a bitter reminder of the cruelty of poverty and the sad choices for those living in it.

Ramona moved out of the house after her sister died and broke ranks with her drug-dealing buddies. It was a sad parting, but they could not talk her out of it. Hanging with them had cost Ramona her family.

She left home, got a job as a waitress in a bar, and began to hang out with women like Vinny Washington, pretty women, who taught her that she was wasting herself on silly neighborhood boys.

Ramona began to date men, some married, some not, who gave her anything she wanted. Suddenly she had money, clothes, cars, and a nice apartment.

But she didn't think of herself as a whore. That was a streetwalker, and she didn't walk the streets. Nor was she a call girl. They were just whores with gold cards. Ramona was a professional girlfriend, a woman who dated wealthy men and asked nothing in return, but if they gave her something, she was not about to turn it down.

Ramona rose through the ranks of the unofficial "girlfriends club." They were always at political fund-raisers, private clubs, working vacations, wherever the fiancées or wives weren't. Eventually she caught the eye of Harris Yancy himself.

Ramona got dressed in a pair of tight jeans and a little blue blouse. She chose a red wig, put on heavy makeup, and started out. She was working on getting out of town. But she was still too hot. She was planning to visit a friend who could get her a fake ID so that she could slip out of the city undercover. She was thinking of D.C. or Atlanta, where she could get lost in the large black population.

Ramona picked up the metallic briefcase before she went to the door. She checked it again and could see no seams or ways to get into it. She shook it again—nothing.

She always kept the case close to her. She had a feeling that Yancy's killers were after it, so her life would be worth nothing if she lost it.

When Ramona went to the elevator, she found one of the two elevator cars out of service. The servicemen had the doors open, and were working on it. She had to step over their tools, which were scattered on the floor. One of the two men looked at her and smiled. Ramona smiled back. He was a grunt, but she'd learned long ago never to be uppity to any man. It was not good for business.

"Lookin' good, honey," he said.

"Thank you," she said. She rubbed the side of her butt. The man's eyes immediately went there. She hadn't meant to do that, but it was a habit.

The other elevator's doors opened. The man inside was big and had a bandage on the side of his head. Ramona hardly looked at him. She got inside the elevator. The big man got out. The doors started to close.

"Hey, baby, can I get your number?" asked Don, stopping the elevator door.

"Move this shit off the floor," said the big man.

Ramona went rigid. She recognized that voice. The big man's back was to her, but she was sure it was the man in the green mask, one of Yancy's killers.

"Sorry, I gotta go," said Ramona.

Hearing Ramona's voice, the big man turned abruptly. Ramona pushed Don backward and slammed her fist on the close door button. The big man ran to the elevator but crashed into the falling serviceman.

The elevator doors closed. The car descended, and she heard a struggle above her. The killer was fighting the serviceman.

Ramona frantically pushed the button marked B1. "Come on," she said.

The elevator car jerked to a halt. The door opened slowly. Ramona positioned the briefcase to strike, expecting death on the other side of the door. The door opened, but there was no one there.

She ran out of the elevator into the underground garage. She looked at the valet booth. No one was inside. She moved back to the elevator, but it was already gone. She walked in the garage drive lane headed toward space 33B. Ramona had ditched her car, but Vinny kept an extra one here.

Suddenly she heard a loud pop. A figure rose next to Vinny's little Miata. It was a man. Ramona could not see his face, but she knew in an instant it was the other killer. She ran quickly toward the garage opening. She hadn't gotten far when she heard footsteps behind her, blunt crashes on the cement. Panicked, she ran faster, toward the light of the big garage door.

Something whizzed past her ear and hit a red Seville with a metallic clang. Ramona heard it clatter on the pavement. The killer had thrown his knife at her.

She raced outside. She saw a bus loading across the street. She ran for it, crossing the street against the light. Cars swerved and blew their horns. She looked over her shoulder at the condo's garage but did not see the killer come out.

Ramona reached the bus as it was pulling off. She ran alongside, beating on its door until the driver stopped, let her on, then drove into traffic. Ramona climbed the stairs. This was better, she thought, lots of people.

"Fare," snapped the driver.

She looked at the man's stern face. She was tired, scared, and still shaking. Ramona coughed a little laugh, fumbled in her purse, and put the fare inside. She went to the back of the bus and sat down, keeping her eyes on the condo. The killers did not emerge.

Ramona could hear her heart beating in her ears. She took several deep breaths, collected herself. The metallic briefcase felt cool on her lap.

She got off at the next stop, ran for a few blocks, then hailed a cab. Terrified that the killers would round a corner and shoot her dead, she stood in dread as it approached. She gave the cabbie directions, and the car pulled off, headed for Detroit's east side.

Ramona had enough street smarts left to know that the killers would find her again if she didn't wise up. She needed help, and it had to come from people she could trust.

She set the briefcase on the floor of the cab and at that moment broke her promise never to see her fast friends again: LoLo Wells and her crew.

8

Into the Wind

Jesse and Richard Steel had checked the crime scene early in the morning. They'd gone early to beat the news crews, who were doing remotes from the street.

The crime scene was in great shape, meaning that it contained plenty of usable forensic evidence.

Jesse couldn't help but feel happy as he sat in his little office going over his notes. He was on his way to something big in his career. Despite the tragedy involved, this case was a godsend for him. The publicity from this would put his name on the lips of every major legal player in the country. He was stepping into a storm, but he was determined to ride the wind.

"Not a lot of room in here for all that stuff."

Jesse turned and looked into the face of his friend Ellis Holmes. Ellis was a colleague from law school days, an upper-class kid who not surprisingly had made good.

"Hey, man, what brings you down here to the ghetto?" asked Jesse, shaking Ellis's hand.

"Just wanted to say hello," said Ellis. He was about Jesse's size, not bad-looking, and light in complexion.

"Well, thanks," said Jesse. "Come on in and grab a seat."

"Where?" asked Ellis. "Man, this is the smallest office I've ever seen."

"Yeah," said Jesse. He moved a heavy stack of papers from a chair. "At least I don't have to share it," said Jesse. "I have so many important cases I get the run of the cracker box."

Jesse liked Ellis even though they were an unlikely pair. They'd become friends in a study group at Wayne State Law School. And though Jesse's grades were always better, Ellis had landed the better job. He should have hated a guy like Ellis, but what was the point? Men with better families had better lives.

Ellis worked in a so-called silk-stocking law firm called Chapel, Swiss, & Silverstone. Big clients, big money, and a big fat deal for any black lawyer to get in. And Ellis was in solid. His father was the general counsel and part owner of an insurance company, and his mother was a state representative. Parents like that can steer a lot of business to a law firm.

"So, you hear anything about the Yancy case?" asked Ellis.

"No," Jesse lied. "They don't tell me anything here. I'm just a hired gun."

"I can't believe Yancy's gone," said Ellis. "Man, I was at the mayor's mansion the same day he died. How creepy is that?"

"I didn't think people at your firm cared much for Yancy," said Jesse.

"Are you kidding? We get a lot of business from the city. We're the municipal bond experts. The city keeps us happy with billable hours. You know they really like you over there."

"Not again with that," said Jesse. "You know I'm not for that place." He was uncomfortable whenever Ellis brought up the subject of joining the firm. It made him feel even more inadequate.

"They always need good litigators," said Ellis. "You're black, but you're also conservative. They like that. And just look at me. I got in."

"You know my response to that," said Jesse. "You were born in."

"It's gotta get a little darker over there," said Ellis. "Times change. There might be a place for you there—and soon. And hey, what's another nigger, more or less?" Ellis smiled broadly.

Jesse laughed to himself. Rich, affluent black men like Ellis always felt the need to refer to themselves as a nigger, in the way that only black people can, as a term of endearment. Still, Jesse disliked the wretched word. He never used it, especially to refer to himself.

"Thanks, but no thanks," said Jesse. "You still the only brother over there?"

"No. There's me, the senior associate, two new junior associates, and the partner."

"A black partner?" Jesse said.

"*The* black partner," said Ellis. "Louis Franklin. But he's old. Pretty soon he'll be gone. Then it's my turn. I can bring you in."

"Yeah, but I'll be cleaning the toilet." Jesse laughed, and Ellis joined him. "So, why are you really here, Ellis? This place must make your suit hairs stand up."

"I just came by to invite you and Connie over for dinner. Penny and I would love to have you. It's been awhile."

"Connie would love that, Ellis. I'll tell her."

"And here, come to the firm's breakfast for The New City Project at the River Front Ballroom." Ellis held out an envelope.

"Aw, I hate those things," said Jesse. "They're so . . . early."

"Come on," said Ellis. "This thing is very important. The New City Project is going to rebuild Detroit."

"Okay, okay," said Jesse. He took the tickets. "But I know you just need to get some black faces in that crowd for the press."

"Damn, you're cynical," said Ellis. "And also very right. Thanks, man. I appreciate it."

Ellis got up and left. He was slick but still a pretty good friend. Jesse wondered if Ellis could really get him into Chapel, Swiss one day.

"Who the hell am I kidding?" said Jesse out loud.

He spent the rest of the day becoming more familiar with the case against Louise Yancy. The police report said Yancy had been murdered by a single, frenzied killer. Yancy was stabbed ten times in the chest and abdomen.

Jesse went to Dick Steals's office to compare notes. They examined the massive crime report. Yancy had been killed between nine and midnight. And the guards who were supposed to come had never checked in.

"I talked to the guards"—Jesse checked the files—"Detectives Broadhurst and Reed. They said they weren't assigned to guard the mayor that night. And they both have alibis."

"Look," said Dick Steals, "Louise Yancy knew he was cheating on her, and she got tired of it. She snapped, and bang, she killed him."

"That doesn't make sense," said Jesse. "I'm sure she knew the mayor had women on the side. Hell, everyone knew it."

"The report also says there was probably only one killer," Richard said.

"But look at this," Jesse said. "It says here that there was a possible blood residue in the bathroom. Type undetermined."

"I saw that," said Richard. "People cut themselves in bathrooms. I know I do."

"And another thing," said Jesse. "When we were at the crime scene, I'm sure you noticed how clean the place was?"

"Clean?" asked Richard.

"Yes, it was . . . it's hard to describe, almost like no one had ever been there. It was too neat. I mean, the man had just spent the night there, supposedly with a woman, and the place was immaculate."

Richard leaned back in his chair and folded his arms. "Are you trying to say there's a cover-up?" He stared at Jesse as if defying him to say it.

"No," said Jesse. "But we should keep this in mind as we go along."

"You sound like a defense counsel," Dick Steals said.

"Every good prosecutor is a defense counsel. You know that."

"Look, Jesse, Louise Yancy is our suspect. She has no alibi, and we found traces of a narcotic in Yancy's system. So she may have tried to poison him."

"I didn't see that." Jesse shuffled through papers.

"It's in the toxicology report," said Dick Steals. "Got it this morning. Mayor Yancy had a heart condition. The autopsy found a drug called Procan SR in his system."

"SR? What's that stand for?" asked Jesse.

Dick Steals checked the report. "Slow release," he said. "Yancy had a prescription, but there was a lot more in his blood than should have been there. Procan SR treats heart arrhythmia, but if too much is taken—"

"Heart attack," said Jesse. "If she had given him enough, Yancy would have seemed to have died from a natural cause. How much did he have in his system?"

"More than he should have, a lot more. So we should ignore the details in the report and focus on the big stuff because I think we got her cold."

"Defense counsel won't ignore those things. We'd at least better explain them away. You know how these juries don't trust the cops."

"Well, I'm counting on you to handle those people," Richard said.

"Those people?" asked Jesse. His back straightened.

"The jury, I mean," said Dick Steals. "Look, you know it's going to be a mostly black jury—"

"I'm *cochair* on this case, Richard," said Jesse. He put his papers down and gave Richard a cold look. "I'm not going to play the happy black lawyer, smiling at the black jury while you do all the litigation."

"I never said that," said Richard.

"Don't play that denial shit with me," Jesse said. "I know what goes on in this office. You and I are *equals* in this case. As hard as that may be to accept, it's a fact. So don't even think about relegating me to some second-class status."

"Don't be so sensitive, Jesse. I'm just not good with juries, and I'll need your help, that's all."

Jesse knew that was a lie. Richard was fantastic with juries. Jesse had witnessed it firsthand. What Richard wasn't good at was dealing with race in the courtroom and in the office. Richard was known to have had terrible arguments with several black judges. He was also known to make offensive racial jokes, and he resented women lawyers in the office. It was a shame that he was so good at his job. He'd be easier to hate.

"As long as we understand each other," Jesse said. He returned to the file. "Now, I see there was evidence of a woman with Yancy."

"Yes, we found some fingerprints and ran them through the system," said Richard. "She has a record, but the cops haven't found her yet. Her name is Ramona Blake. Yancy was balling her regularly. We're looking for her, but I'd bet she's long gone by now."

"Did we get Yancy's phone records?" asked Jesse.

"Yeah," said Richard. "I checked them. The mayor called a few people that night, but they all look like business."

Jesse grabbed the phone records. Harris Yancy had made a lot of calls in the days leading up to his murder.

"The mayor's guards botched the assignment that night," said Jesse. "We need to find this guy Walter Nicks. He's the captain or something. He set the schedules."

"We tried, but he's gone," said Dick Steals. "Disappeared. Not at his house or anywhere else we know of."

"Quite a coincidence," Jesse said. "A major fuckup, and now he's gone. The security was run out of the mayor's mansion. I think I'll go over there and talk with some people."

"Don't hurt yourself, Jesse," said Dick Steals. "We've got our killer."

"But it's gonna be a hard case to sell in this town," said Jesse. "Louise Yancy is the first lady of Detroit. People love her."

"Well," said Richard, "we have one more piece of evidence. I'm sorry I didn't tell you about it before, but the boss told me not to breathe a word until tomorrow. But what the fuck, you should know. If he gets mad, just back me up."

"Okay," said Jesse. "What is it and where is it?"

"I don't have it with me. D'Estenne is keeping it under lock and key."

"Okay, then, what is it?"

Richard leaned in closer to Jesse. His eyes had a familiar gleam. It was the look a prosecutor gets when he knows he has a bombshell to drop on the court.

"The murder weapon," Richard said. "We found it yesterday night, wedged in the back of a cupboard in the basement. And it has Louise Yancy's fingerprints all over it."

9

Visitor

Jesse headed home, reeling from Dick Steals's information. Tomorrow there would be a press conference following the arrest of Louise Yancy. D'Estenne was going to contact her attorney and set up a time and place for her to surrender. He wanted as little fanfare as possible.

Jesse walked back to his office. A tall woman in a police uniform passed by, talking urgently to a new young prosecutor named Sharon Reed. The young prosecutor looked over at Jesse with a worried expression. Then she smiled like an angel at him, her face taking on new life. Jesse waved as they passed. Sharon said hello; then her face fell back into its worrisome cave. She's adjusted already, Jesse thought. The job divided your emotions. And you learned to switch them on and off at will.

"Jesse," said the tall woman, "how are you?"

"Fine," said Jesse. He didn't recognize the woman's face.

"It's me, Nell Parker," said the woman. "You never could remember my name."

Jesse took a closer look. Then he remembered. "Oh, Nell, I was your first," he said.

"First?" asked Sharon with more than casual curiosity. "First what?"

"Jesse was the prosecutor the very first time I testified," said Nell. "You never forget your first time, right, Jesse?"

"It was an armed robbery, and the defense counsel tried to say you manufactured evidence," said Jesse.

"I was terrified," said Nell. "But Jesse settled me down. Then we convicted those bastards."

"Nell is closing out a case with me before she starts undercover," said Sharon quickly, trying to get a word in between the two old friends.

"Congratulations," said Jesse. "Big move up."

"Thanks," said Nell. "I'm gonna love it."

"We'd better get going," said Sharon. She took a few steps to prove she meant it.

Nell and Jesse shook hands and said good-bye. Jesse went to his office. He had been planning to do some more work but decided against it. He left the building, got in his car, and drove east on Jefferson. The early October night was crisp. This was the best time of year, Jesse thought. Past the muggy summer and just before the cruel Michigan winter.

Jesse turned into The Harbor, a tower of apartments on the near east side. The building was close enough to the river that one side of it had spectacular views of the waterway. Jesse lived in a one-bedroom unit facing the city, away from the water. It was cheaper if you didn't get the view. But he had no complaints. He was lucky he could make the rent on his salary.

Jesse parked, then took the elevator up to the tenth floor. He walked toward his apartment, only to find a young black security officer at his door.

"I'm sorry, Mr. King, but this lady said she was a relative, and she looked sick, so I let her in."

"What lady, Renaldo?"

"She's inside your unit. Please don't report me. I really need this job." Renaldo looked terrified.

"It's okay, man, just go."

"Thanks, Mr. King." Renaldo left.

Jesse opened the door to his apartment and entered. He didn't see anyone inside. Jesse had a fondness for African art and had bought a lot of it. The apartment had put him in debt, but he had to have a nice place. He'd lived in some of the worst places in Detroit and had vowed never to go back.

A thin black woman walked out of the kitchen. She was in her late thirties; her clothes were shabby; her hair was unkempt. She looked a mess. She might have been pretty once, but her face had grown haggard and hard. She smiled beneath the dark glasses she wore.

"Jesse," said the woman.

"What do you want, Bernice?" Jesse said flatly.

Bernice walked over and hugged Jesse. He did not return the embrace.

"What do you want?" asked Jesse again, pushing her away gently. Instinctively he checked her hands. They looked bloated and shiny.

"I just dropped by to see my brother, the big-time lawyer," Bernice said. She fumbled with her purse as she sat on the sofa. Her movements were slow, sluggish.

"Don't waste my time, Bernice. What do you want?"

"Damn, you suspicious." Bernice laughed a little. Her words were slurred, and she hung on them, picking them carefully.

Bernice King was Jesse's older sister. She was a drug addict, a crackhead mostly, although she'd use anything if she had the money. And when she wasn't using, she could have been Jesse's twin. But Bernice was always using. Jesse couldn't bear to see her this way. She reminded him of the life he'd left behind and the way it always reached out to find him.

Bernice was his only sister. Their brother, Tyrus, had run away from home at sixteen and never returned. Unlike Bernice, Tyrus was strong. He was just not very smart. Tyrus at least had the decency to stay out of Jesse's life. Bernice was not the same.

"I told you never to come here when you're high," said Jesse.

"I ain't on nothing," Bernice said. She took out a pack of cigarettes.

"Don't smoke in my house," Jesse said.

"Damn, somebody gone die if I have a smoke?"

"Put the fuck— Put them away."

Bernice put the cigarettes in her purse. She scratched her arms. "I itch, some allergies or something."

"Look, Bernice, I don't have a lot of time to waste on you," Jesse said. "I can tell you're using again."

"Why you always think somebody on drugs? That's all you think about."

"Your hands are swelled, you can barely make a sentence, and—" Jesse grabbed her glasses from her face.

Bernice shielded her eyes. "Damn!" she yelled.

"Drugs always aggravate your eyes." Jesse handed her back the glasses.

"Look, I just got outta that county detox thang last week," said Bernice. "I'm trying to get it together. I just need some money for my kids." She put the glasses back on.

"No," said Jesse angrily.

"Jesse, your niece and nephew need clothes." She scratched her neck vigorously.

"Last time I gave you money, you went right to the dope man with it," said Jesse harshly.

"I ain't gonna do that, I swear," said Bernice. "I get my check next week. Just let me hold a couple dollars until then. My kids is starvin'."

"I thought they needed clothes."

"Food, clothes, they need everythang," she said without missing a beat.

"No, Bernice."

"Okay, Jesse, you go with me . . . buy the food. Will that make you happy?"

"Last time I did that, you sold the food, *then* you went to the dope man. I know you, Bernice. You don't get a dime from me, you hear? Now get out."

"Fuck you!" Bernice yelled.

She jumped up and glared at him. Up close Jesse could see his mother's face in Bernice's haggard, angry visage. "Mr. Big Fuckin' Lawyer!" Bernice said. "You think I gotta get money from you?"

Jesse didn't react. Anger was always stage two in the act. "Bernice, I can get you back into rehab."

"Rehab on my ass! I told you I did detox. I'm tired of you and your shit." Her hands were waving excitedly. "I'm your big sister. I used to change your nasty shitty-ass diapers. Just gimme the goddamned money!"

"I'm not gonna do that," Jesse said calmly.

Bernice sat down in the chair. She was shaking. But to Jesse it was a familiar show. Bernice put her face into her hands and began to cry.

Jesse was silent. Crying always came next.

"I'm really trying, Jesse. I know I let you down in the past, but this time—"

"It's always *this* time, Bernice. No."

"I was thinking about Mama yesterday, how she wanted us to be close."

"Mama is dead!" Jesse yelled. He hated when she brought up his mother's deathbed statement. "I tried to help you, but you dogged me out every time. I paid my debt to Mama, so don't even try it!"

She looked at him with her tear-stained face. "You here, living in this nice place. My house is worse than where we grew up. I got bugs all in my house, Jesse, roaches. You remember how we hated them growing up?" She pulled a handkerchief from her purse and wiped her eyes. "We ain't got no hot water. We gotta boil water to take baths."

"No, Bernice," said Jesse. "No money. You have to learn to be responsible."

"Okay . . . okay," she said, resigned. "I just gotta do what I gotta do. I ain't a bad-lookin' woman. I'll just get me a short skirt—"

"Do it," said Jesse. "It's better than begging me every day. At least it's a job, not welfare." He couldn't believe the words came from his mouth, but he meant them.

"You ain't shit, you know that." Bernice sniffled. "You think you better than me, don't you?"

Jesse stood over Bernice, looking down upon her. "I am better than you, Bernice. We both lost our way, but I found my way back. You had every chance I had growing up, and you chose the easy way out of everything. And every time I tried to help, you pulled me down with you."

"Why—why do you try to hurt me like this, Jesse?"

"Get out, Bernice. I've gone as far as I'm going with you. I got behind on my rent trying to help you. I took out loans to help you, and all you did was let me down. No more. It hurts me, but I have to have a life. And I can't save yours."

"But this time—"

"Don't come back. I'm gonna tell security not to let you in anymore."

In a burst of fury Bernice got up and turned over Jesse's coffee table. African statues and a wooden candy dish fell to the floor as the table turned over on them.

Jesse grabbed her. Bernice started hitting him, but he pulled her toward the door.

"Go to hell!" Bernice hit him in the side of the face.

"Don't make me hurt you, Bernice. Just . . . get out!"

Jesse dragged her out the door into the hallway. Bernice lost her footing and fell on the thick carpet, crying.

Jesse watched her lying in the hallway, and for a moment he didn't see Bernice the crackhead. He saw his ten-year-old sister, a skinny little girl who wore ugly print dresses and wanted to be Diana Ross when she grew up. He could not even remember when this all started. All he knew was that she was more trouble than she was worth.

Bernice turned and stared at him, her eyes hurt and angry, a combination that frightened Jesse for some reason. She started to get up, and Jesse closed the door, shutting her out.

Later that night Jesse sat alone in his car parked on the east side. He was on McKay Street near Victoria, a working-class neighborhood that had seen better days. There were still houses on the street, but vacant lots now dotted the once-uninterrupted row of homes, like missing teeth in a smile.

Jesse parked about four houses from his sister's home. He could see it from where he sat. It was in sad shape. The paint job was faded into a sad blue. Two of the wooden stairs leading to the porch were gone. It looked bad, unwholesome.

He didn't like being here. It was his history, but he'd left it all behind. He'd watched almost every childhood friend he had die, go to jail, become addicted to drugs, or locked into poverty and hopelessness. He sometimes remembered their faces, guys like Kelvin and Cocoa, young, bright, and full of life. Then they would change into visages of violence, drugged-out torpor, utter despair, and death.

A boy emerged from the side of the faded blue house. The kid walked slowly toward Jesse's car, taking time to look over his shoulder back at the house. He was about twelve, dressed in baggy pants, an oversize shirt, and basketball shoes. His hair was cut low, and he had a small gold earring in his ear. The boy loped along, cool-walking his way to the car. He looked angry, pissed off as though he had a score to settle.

"Hey, Uncle Jesse," said the boy. He smiled a little, his face going from the hard look to one of innocence.

"How you doin', Nikko?" asked Jesse.

"I'm doin'," said Nikko.

"You look like you're ready to kick somebody's butt."

"Gotta look mean or people will try to punk you, know what I'm sayin'?"

Jesse knew. The neighborhood had not changed a lot over the years. "So, how's your sister?"

"Letisha's all right. She wants some kinda school club sweater. Been talkin' about it all day. She's with Mama, trying to cool her out."

"What's Bernice doing now?"

"Cussin'. She's pissed off at you. She said you beat her up and threw her out of your house."

"You know that's not true," said Jesse. "I had to put her out, but I didn't beat her."

"I know. She's mad 'cause she ain't got no money to cop, you know."

"Yeah, I know. So you all got enough food and everything?"

"Yeah, we all right," said Nikko.

"I have some more money for you and your sister." Jesse reached into his pocket and took out some bills. Nikko took them and put them in his pocket.

"Thanks," said Nikko.

There was a long silence between them. Jesse never knew what to say to Nikko. And it seemed that his nephew felt the same way. Moreover, Nikko and his sister seemed afraid of Jesse, like he was somehow passing judgment on them because he'd made it out of the ghetto. It made sense when he thought about it. They were related in blood, but a million miles separated their current fortunes.

Nikko was only twelve, but he was older than his years. The street forced a young boy to grow up early. He talked and acted like a man.

"So, you know what to do with the money?" asked Jesse.

"Yeah, just like always," said Nikko. "I buy food with it and tell Mama I won the money gambling or doing stuff for people. And if she ask for some, tell her I spent it all."

"Cool," said Jesse.

"But, Uncle Jesse, Mama be thinking that I'm selling drugs to get this money. She gets real mad."

"She's got a lot of nerve as much as she smokes." Jesse saw the hurt in Nikko's eyes. "I'm sorry. I didn't mean that the way it sounded. I guess I'm mad at her too."

"Anyway," said Nikko, "it's getting harder to hide the money. One time I caught Mama searching my pants."

"Don't worry. Just keep it from her, or you know what she'll do with it."

"I will," said Nikko. "Bye, Uncle Jesse."

Nikko walked back to the house. Jesse started the car and pulled off.

Jesse's heart was breaking. Nikko and his sister were good kids, cursed with a bad mother. It was like seeing Bernice, Tyrus, and himself again as kids. Doomed. But as strange as it sounded, the kids loved Bernice. They had nothing else in the belly of the dying neighborhood, but a mama was enough to keep them together.

Jesse couldn't even remember the names of the men who had fathered Nikko and his sister. Neither of them came around or helped out. It was a tragedy, and he felt helpless to change it. Kids should not have to live this way. Especially when their parents knew better.

Jesse got onto the I-75 freeway and headed back home. And all that night he could not shake the memory of his sister on her knees in his hallway and Nikko cool-walking his way back to her.

10

Women in Need

Jesse was having an early breakfast with his fiancée, Connie Givens. They sat in a booth of the IHOP on Jefferson. It was a bright and busy restaurant like the others in the chain, only this one was owned by Anita Baker, the famous R&B singer and Detroit native. Her restaurant walls were covered with pictures of soul singers, gold records, and awards, giving the place an added appeal. As usual, the place was packed to the gills, filled with people on their way to work.

Connie nursed her second cup of coffee and looked at Jesse with deep concern. "You look distracted, honey," she said.

"Huh? Oh, I'm sorry," said Jesse. "I've got a lot on my mind today. Didn't sleep well."

"I remember when you couldn't stop paying attention to me." Connie smiled at him over her coffee. She was thirty, thin, and had a head full of long brown hair. She was not pretty, but not homely either, the kind of woman who longed to be the former but was probably destined to be the latter. Connie was also very light-skinned and was often mistaken for white, one of the few things that enraged her.

"Did you see the news last night?" asked Connie. "Someone found a tiger in the basement of a house on the west side!"

"Another one?" said Jesse.

"Don't tell me this has happened before," said Connie.

"Some nut was illegally selling exotic animals around Michigan this year. At least we thought he was. We popped him for trying to sell a big lizard called a Komodo dragon, but he walked."

"How?" asked Connie. "That sounds like the kind of case that's open-and-shut."

"We lost the damned lizard. It got loose, and some guy hit it with his car over on Gratiot."

Connie laughed out loud. "But you still had the body, right?"

"It was just a big red splotch," said Jesse. "We needed the lizard alive. It was no good to us like that, so we couldn't prove anything."

Jesse took another bite of his pancakes. Connie kept laughing. Her voice sounded like a young girl's. Jesse smiled at her amusement; then his face sank into sadness again.

"You wanna talk about it?" asked Connie.

Jesse considered the question; then: "It's my sister again," said Jesse. "Bernice."

"Now what?" asked Connie. She couldn't hide the contempt in her voice.

"More of the same. I had to throw her out of my house."

"Oh, God, Jesse, are you okay?" Connie grabbed his hand.

"Yes," Jesse said. He laughed a little. Connie thought all poor people were dangerous. "I'm dealing with it. Anyway, that's just part of my depression. The other part is the case, the mayor's murder."

"The case you can't talk about," Connie said.

"Right. Something about it has me troubled, and today it's going to . . . well, get worse."

"The rumor is that you have a suspect. Everyone's talking about it."

"Yes, but . . . after the press conference you'll know why I'm so concerned."

"Well, let's not talk about it. Let's talk about us." Connie took another bite of her egg white omelet.

"Okay," said Jesse. "What about us?"

"My friends are bugging me about our wedding," Connie said. She smiled weakly at Jesse.

"You want to set a date?" Jesse asked. He felt irritation creep into his voice. He hadn't meant it to.

"You know I do," said Connie. "The ball's been in your court for some time now."

"Connie, I don't want to have another fight."

"We don't have to if we talk about it civilly."

Connie was a fourth-generation black professional whose family owned three car dealerships. She could trace her family line back through doctors, lawyers, and morticians all the way to a white great-grandfather, who had shocked Virginia society by marrying a freed slave.

Her family was perfect. Rich father, successful mother. A brother who was a doctor and a sister going to Harvard. And they cared for one another with that special kind of love that families have. Jesse could sense it when he was with Connie and her family but could never generate the same love in his own heart, which seemed to be dry when it came to his own relatives.

He loved Connie. She had a bright humor, intelligence, and was a passionate lover. He also admired what she represented: money, class, power, family, all the things that he desired. And though it hurt Jesse to admit it, if Connie had been prettier, she would probably have never looked at him twice.

Marrying Connie had been on his mind a lot lately. Bernice and his own family's jaded past made him leery. He felt that he was destined to be a failure at holding together a family of his own.

"I know you're worried about my parents," Connie said. "But they've treated all my boyfriends like crap. It's kinda their way of weeding out the ones who aren't serious."

"They don't think I'm good enough for you," said Jesse.

"No one will ever be good enough. I won't defend them, but what's important is what we want." Connie caught Jesse's eyes and held them. "That is, if we both still want it."

"I don't need pressure, Connie. I've been down this road before."

Connie's eyes got wider, and Jesse knew he was in trouble. "Don't blame me for that woman, what's her name." Connie was suddenly angry at the mention of Jesse's old flame.

"Karen," said Jesse. He was now sorry he'd brought her up.

"That woman was a nutcase, you said so yourself—"

"Connie, I'm sorry. Look, Karen Bell doesn't have anything to do with this."

"Too late, Jesse. You and that woman were almost married, and she broke it off. That's not my fault." Connie looked around, embarrassed that she'd raised her voice.

"I know," said Jesse. "I just think . . . Connie, you know how I feel about you—"

"I've waited a year, Jesse," Connie said. "I'll be thirty-one on my birthday. All my friends are having their *second* children."

Jesse pushed his plate away. She was right. It was time to step up to responsibility. He had many reservations, but their relationship was solid, and others had built more on less than that.

"You're right," said Jesse. "I'm sorry. After all we've been through, you shouldn't have to even say it to me. Let's get married."

Connie almost jumped out of her chair. She leaned across her food and kissed him. Jesse was embarrassed. He didn't like public displays of affection, but he kissed her back. A few people around them applauded and whistled. Connie sat back down, blushing a little.

"Sorry," she said.

"It's okay," said Jesse. "Let's set a date, any date you want."

"Well, it's October, so how about a May wedding?"

"Great. My case should be over by then. It would be the perfect time to start a new life."

Connie smiled and fought back tears. She was a strong woman and not usually so emotional, but this was something that she'd wanted for a long time.

Jesse finished breakfast, then went in to work. Everyone in the office was happy at the announcement of his wedding. The single guys in the office immediately started making jokes about husband misery and giving a bachelor party. The women seemed glad to see another man go down. But he sensed disappointment from some of them. There were several women who had crushes on him, but he never dated coworkers.

Later that morning Jesse's breakfast rumbled in his stomach as he walked down the long hall in the Frank Murphy with D'Estenne and Dick Steals. They got on the elevator, then went outside, got into a waiting car, and sped quickly over to the City-County Building. D'Estenne didn't want to hold the conference at Frank Murphy. It was always too crowded.

Soon the three men stood at a podium in the lobby of the City-County Building. The lobby was packed. All TV stations and newspapers were represented. The podium had microphones lined around it. Photographers snapped pictures, and handheld TV cameras pointed in Jesse's direction.

The word was out that the prosecutor had a suspect in the Yancy case, and the city was buzzing with the news. Miraculously no one had leaked the identity of the suspect.

D'Estenne was dressed in a navy blue suit with the subtlest shade of gray pinstriping. His crisp white shirt and red and gray striped tie completed his ensemble. His hair had been styled, and he seemed to look younger. He smiled and quieted the gallery.

"Gentlemen and ladies, I guess it's safe to assume in the information age that we all know why we're here. I will make it brief. At ten-thirty a.m., Louise Yancy surrendered to the Detroit police at 1300 Beaubien, where she was formally charged with the murder of her husband, the late Harris Yancy."

The gallery was eerily silent for a second. Disbelief and shock were on their faces. Then the reporters erupted in an explosion of voices and light as photographers and TV cameras captured the moment.

"Hold on, hold on." D'Estenne tried to quite the crowd. "I have a statement."

The gallery quieted; some reporters dialed on their mobile phones. Jesse's stomach tightened. He saw a brief smile on Dick Steals's face. It faded as quickly as it came.

"We have sufficient evidence," said D'Estenne, "to arrest and prosecute Louise Yancy. Said evidence will be revealed in the normal course of prosecution. Ms. Yancy will be arraigned tomorrow. We know this case is volatile, but the high standards of the Wayne County Prosecutor's Office and Recorder's Court will not be affected by the high-profile nature of this case. We will ensure fairness and justice for all parties concerned."

"Sounds like a reelection speech to me," said a female reporter.

It was Carol Salinsky, star TV reporter. After a series of exclusives on a serial killer case she'd been crowned queen of the local news circuit. CNN and all four major networks were interested in her. Though her departure was imminent, she was still on the job as tenaciously as before.

"I don't care what it sounds like, Carol," D'Estenne said. "It's the truth, and it's the way this case will proceed." D'Estenne motioned Jesse and Dick Steals over. "This is our litigation team. Jesse King and Richard Steel. They will be cochairing the matter and will report directly to me."

The questions started to fly again.

"Will the case be televised?"

"Why don't you prosecute it yourself?"

"Will you seek a racially balanced jury?"

"Who is the judge going to be?"

D'Estenne spoke over the crowd. "I will not make this a media case. We've all seen the folly of that. I think we're a little more sophisticated in Detroit. I will not use TV to try this case."

"That is such bull," said Salinsky. She was probably the only reporter who could use those words and get away with it. "You can't just arrest the first lady of Detroit and say no comment. You're using this case to run for reelection against Xavier Peterson. The people have a right to know—everything."

"You'll all get a copy of our statement," said D'Estenne. "Our office will keep the press updated as the case proceeds in the *normal course of business*." His words had anger and power behind them.

D'Estenne left the podium amid more yelling and questions. The reporters accosted Jesse and Dick Steals, but they followed their boss without uttering a word.

D'Estenne, Jesse, and Dick Steals were ushered by a uniformed officer to the crosswalk connecting the City-County Building to Millender Center. From there they went to their car, then back to Frank Murphy.

D'Estenne didn't talk in the car. He only liked to talk around his lawyers, and the driver's presence precluded that. They got to Frank Murphy and went inside. On the elevator D'Estenne adjusted his tie and hit a button hard with his fist.

"I hate that . . . woman." He stopped short of calling Salinsky a bitch. "I will not have this case become a circus and blow up in my face."

"We don't have to worry about her, sir," said Dick Steals. "Our case is strong. It will speak for itself."

The elevator was silent. Then, against his better judgment, Jesse spoke. "She has a point, sir."

There was a silence that felt longer than it really was. Then D'Estenne spoke. "How so?"

"Well, sir," Jesse said, "the case is volatile and no matter what we do, it will be a major bone of contention with Xavier Peterson. If you conduct a lot of media interviews, Peterson will criticize them, nitpicking your choices. If you say nothing, then he gets to set the agenda for how the case should be tried. And you know the media will ask him. But at least if you speak, you get to have your opinions heard."

D'Estenne took a deep breath. He looked up into the dim, fluorescent lights of the elevator, as if looking to God.

"Dammit, you're right, Jesse. I'll call Stan Cramer and ask him if I can have a special segment on the news tonight. And I'll request Salinsky as my interviewer before she butchers me."

The elevator stopped, and D'Estenne got off. He walked hurriedly toward his office, but stopped short. "Good thinking, Jesse," said D'Estenne. "You two get over to 1300. I'll be in touch."

Jesse pushed a button on the elevator, and the doors closed. "I've never seen him like this," Jesse said.

"He's just worried about the election. It'll blow over," Dick Steals said. He had an irritated look on his face. Jesse had upstaged him with the boss, and he didn't like it. "I'm surprised at your advice. I thought Peterson was your man."

"He's my friend," said Jesse. "But I don't work for him."

"You gonna back him in the election?"

"I'm gonna stay out of it, like any smart lawyer would," said Jesse.

"Well, if Peterson does win," said Dick Steals, "I'll resign. I won't work for him."

"Why not? He's a good man," said Jesse.

"But he's just not *my* kind of man," said Dick Steals, "and it has nothing to do with him being black."

"I didn't say that," said Jesse.

"But you were thinking it."

"Okay, maybe I was, but it still shouldn't matter to you."

"Peterson doesn't have any experience," said Dick Steals.

"When D'Estenne was elected, he didn't have much experience either," said Jesse. "In fact—"

"I think you should seriously check out your loyalties, Jesse," Richard interrupted. He had a stern, almost paternal look on his face. "D'Estenne picked you for this case even though he knows you might back Peterson in the election. That's the kind of man he is. He made us both, Jesse. We are both hot young lawyers because of him. He has my allegiance. What about you?"

"My loyalties are with the people," said Jesse. "I want the best man to win, and the voters will decide that."

"That's bullshit, Jesse, and you know it," said Dick Steals. "This is political, and racial, like everything else in Detroit. Look, Jesse, I know D'Estenne comes off like a silver-haired grandfather, but you fuck him and God help you."

Jesse didn't respond. He was tired of the conversation. He forgot the first rule of working for a politician: Never become political. Still, he couldn't tell if Dick Steals's statement was a threat or a warning.

The elevator stopped on the ground floor. The reporters were everywhere. Jesse and Richard slipped out a back entrance where the prisoners were taken out. They walked over to 1300 to question their suspect in the case of their careers.

11

Fast Friends

The drug house on Bristol Street bustled with activity. LoLo stood behind the long table and watched as the transactions were made through a side window of the house. Money was pushed through a slot in the front; then drugs were picked up at a side window. Drugs out, money in, simple and smooth.

Business was good, even after the mess the men had made of the trade. Some fools had tried to reinvent crack but had only managed to poison people and cause their own deaths in the process.

So now the women had finally gotten some play. And it wasn't easy. Even in the drug game men didn't play fair. LoLo's suppliers charged her more, and if a cop shook her down, it was almost double to get rid of his ass. This was the telling tale of life: Even in crime women were not equals.

A young boy ran into the house and went straight to LoLo. LoLo listened intently as he whispered into her ear. Her face turned into a frown. She nodded, then sent the boy away. LoLo ignored the stares of the rollers as she walked into the kitchen.

The room was hot and crowded. The oven as well as several microwaves was baking crack. Six women of various ages made the stuff, working like bees in a hive. They moved as LoLo entered, parting like dutiful servants.

This was her family, LoLo thought. She had never known her own family. Her mother and father both had died when she was five. They overdosed on speedballs while LoLo slept in the next room. With no family left, she went into the system, bouncing from one foster family to another. Always an intruder in someone else's family, longing for her own.

She started out hanging with male rollers, first as one of the many women they kept. But she grew tired of having sex with them and taking their money as payment for it. She became a roller for a dealer named Breeze, a leftover from the old Union. Breeze was a smart dealer, but he stayed high. Eventually the cops got him on possession, and he got life under the three strikes law.

LoLo continued as an independent and soon put together her own crew. She recruited young girls like herself, outcasts, lost and in need of family strength. Life in a crew provided much of what a family did: friendship, safety, even love if you believed in that.

"Earl's foot got infected," said LoLo grimly. "He was lying in a vacant lot all day. He died."

Yolanda sat on an old chair and ate McDonald's. Sheri pushed her food away at the news.

"I'm gonna kill that fuckin' Cane!" Sheri yelled. She slammed her chair into a wall. Earl was Sheri's sometime boyfriend. Sheri was a possessive woman who didn't like anyone tampering with her possessions.

"Chill out, girl," said LoLo calmly. "We'll get Cane, but not now."

"Fuck that," said Sheri. "I want his ass."

Yolanda finished her meal and leaned her big frame back in the chair. "Cane ain't nobody to fuck with by yo'self," she said. Her voice was surprisingly soft. Yolanda didn't talk much, but when she did, she usually had something important to say.

"You damned right he ain't," said LoLo. "The hospital said Earl's foot was chewed up by some kinda animal." She waved a hand in disgust. "Cane. That nigga is crazy."

Sheri pulled a gun. "I'm crazy too. Look, we want to move on him anyway, right? Now we got a reason."

"A reason?" said LoLo. "Just 'cause you was fuckin' Earl and set him up to knock off Cane's house. That don't give me a reason to start a war with Cane."

"But he was my man," said Sheri.

"Fuck men," said LoLo. "They don't mean shit in this crew. You knew that when you joined up. You get the dick; then you get gone." Some of the workers chuckled quietly.

"Don't nobody fuck with my man," said Sheri. "I'm gonna pop Cane. And I don't need your damn help to do it!"

LoLo's face tightened. She walked over to Sheri and stopped in front of her. Reaching back, she unfastened her ponytail and put it in her pocket. "Don't want my hair gettin' dirty." She moved close to Sheri. "You running the crew now?"

"LoLo . . . I didn't say that," said Sheri.

Sheri still had the gun in her hand. LoLo had no weapon. The workers in the kitchen all stopped, sensing danger. A small girl backed toward the door as LoLo passed her. LoLo stopped in front of Sheri, her head tilted slightly, looking up at the taller woman.

"You got the gun, you defying me in front of my people, you must be in charge." LoLo stared at Sheri. "I don't mean shit to you, I guess."

"LoLo, you know it ain't like that," said Sheri. "I just want to—"

"I'm just the one who got you away from that nigga that was pimping you. He had you sellin' ass to his so-called business friends."

"I'm not trying to run the crew," Sheri said awkwardly. "I just—"

LoLo pulled Sheri's gun to her own forehead. "Go on, you a hard-ass bitch. It only takes a second to promote yourself around here."

LoLo could hear the feet of the workers scurry out of the way, getting out of the line of fire. Somebody cursed. Yolanda stood but did not pull her weapon. LoLo didn't take her eyes off Sheri.

Sheri didn't move for a moment. Her hand trembled on the gun. Then she pulled the gun down.

LoLo snatched the gun, then clamped her hand on Sheri's face and shoved her backward into a corner. Sheri fell, knocking over a garbage pail. She started to get up, but LoLo was coming at her, with the gun out in front.

Sheri didn't move as LoLo got to her, then knelt, bringing her face close to Sheri's.

"I would have pulled the trigger," said LoLo. "That's why I'm running this crew. Now, I don't wanna hear no more shit outta you." LoLo stood and stepped back. Then she reached out and helped Sheri to her feet. "You know I don't like to fight with my people," she said in a soft, almost motherly voice. She gave Sheri the gun back and walked out of the kitchen. Yolanda followed.

Sheri looked around the room. The workers were back into it, trying not to look at Sheri. Sheri started to leave, then stopped. She looked at LoLo and Yolanda in the other room, then sat back down at the table in the kitchen.

"What we gone do about her?" Yolanda asked.

"Nothing," said LoLo. "She's still a good roller. She's just young. All she needs is some training."

Yolanda was silent, but LoLo could read her thoughts. Yolanda had never warmed to Sheri and thought her a liability waiting to happen. Maybe she was right. But LoLo didn't want to jump the gun. Good rollers, especially women, were hard to find.

The young boy who'd brought the news about Earl walked in the door and came over to LoLo.

"Some woman outside to see you. She got a big-ass suitcase."

"What's in it, Little Jack?" asked LoLo.

"Don't know," said Little Jack.

"Send her ass away," said LoLo.

"Cool," said Little Jack. "She don't even know who you are. Said she wanted to see the Fast Girls. I told her it was Nasty Girls—"

LoLo yanked the boy closer. "She said Fast Girls?" asked LoLo. Her voice was full of energy.

"Yeah," the boy said, startled. "I told her she was wrong."

LoLo and Yolanda went to the door and flung it open. On the front porch stood Ramona, dressed like a cheap hooker and holding a metal briefcase.

"So, y'all got any food up in here?" Ramona said, smiling.

"Girl!" LoLo hugged Ramona. Yolanda smiled and did the same.

The three Fast Girls went back into the house. The people inside didn't stop doing business as they hugged and kissed one another.

"I can't believe it's you," said LoLo. "I thought you was in the big time now."

"So did I," said Ramona. She took a moment to look around. "Quite a thing you got going here. Took me some time to track you down."

"Pays the rent," said LoLo.

"How you doing, Yolanda?" asked Ramona. "Wait, don't say nothing. I want it to be just like old times."

"Where you get this ho outfit?" Yolanda asked.

LoLo and Ramona laughed loudly. Ramona put the black brief-case on the floor. Her smile faded. "I'm in trouble."

"Figured that," said LoLo. "Well, you know you can hang with us. So, what is it?"

"How about that food first?" said Ramona. "I'm starving."

LoLo called Little Jack over and sent him out to get food. LoLo, Ramona, and Yolanda went back on the porch and laughed, joked, and talked loudly about old times.

In the kitchen Sheri watched the trio celebrate. Her eyes were hard, unblinking. She clicked on her gun's safety and put it into her waistband.

12

Compelling Evidence

As Jesse walked into the interrogation room at 1300, apprehension overtook him. He'd pored over the case file three times and could think of at least ten areas where the prosecution's case was weak. He would have to work hard to plug the holes.

Jesse entered the stuffy room and stopped short. At the big table was Louise Yancy, looking firm and resilient. On her right was Ira Hoffman, one of the three top criminal lawyers in Detroit. Several detectives and members of the Police Commission were also in the room behind them. Jesse had expected these faces. What threw him was his former fiancée, Karen Bell, sitting with them.

Jesse and Dick Steals went to the table and introduced themselves. The bureaucrats made silly statements about fairness and justice, just enough to cover their asses; then they left.

"Jesse," Karen said. Her voice was soft and just ever so husky from her smoking days. She seemed amused at Jesse's shock.

Jesse said something cordial, but his mind was already traveling back through his affair with Karen. The wild sex in offices, cars, and other semipublic places, her divorce from her husband, their engagement (more out of guilt than love), and their nasty breakup, which she had initiated.

Karen looked great. She had a beautiful face. Her skin was the color of cinnamon, and her hair was jet black. Her eyes were hazel, and she had a tiny black mole on the corner of her mouth. But Karen's body was her best feature, full and sensuous from her days as a dancer. Jesse remembered how she'd caused a fender bender on Jefferson Avenue by wearing a short skirt.

Seeing Karen brought back both fond and bitter memories. She was a powerful woman, savvy, independent, and viciously intelligent. They had been doomed from the start. In the end Jesse had been no more a match for Karen than her husband had been.

Karen was also a brilliant lawyer, and Jesse didn't know what was worse: the pain of their past relationship or facing her as an adversary.

"We want to thank you for not incarcerating our client," said Ira Hoffman. He was a small man with quick mannerisms. He had a full head of silver and black hair and was still, for sixty-five, very handsome.

"No problem," said Jesse. "It benefits us both."

"We can make this an easy meeting, Ira," said Dick Steals. "You've heard what we have in proof. I think you should make us an offer."

"No," said Karen.

"Hold on, Karen," Ira said. Then he turned to Jesse and Dick Steals. "I want you to know that I am advisory counsel on this case. Ms. Bell here is the lead counsel. Direct your statements to her."

Dick Steals seemed in shock. Jesse couldn't help but smile a little. Karen was insulted that they assumed Ira was the lead. And if he knew her, she would now be even more nasty.

"I'm sorry, Karen," said Dick Steals.

"It's okay," said Karen. "I know what you're going to say, and the answer is no. We won't deal. My client is innocent."

"Karen," said Jesse, "you have to admit our evidence is compelling. We have a murder weapon with her fingerprints on it."

"My client lived in the house. Of course her prints were on her own kitchen knife."

"We got the toxicology report," said Jesse. "We can prove she tried to poison her husband."

"I've seen that," said Karen. "The amounts of Procan in the blood were not so big as to suggest murder."

"And she had a motive," said Jesse. "Her husband was having an affair."

"Please, I knew about all of them," Louise Yancy blurted out.

Karen and Ira turned on Louise at once. Jesse and Dick Steals shared a look at the admission. Louise Yancy's acknowledgment of the motive was extremely damaging at this early stage.

"Louise, please don't talk!" said Karen. "We have a long way to go."

"That's an admission," said Dick Steals.

"It will never get into evidence, I guarantee you," said Ira.

"I'm just saying for the purposes of our meeting here today, she admits knowledge," said Dick Steals.

"Like I said," Jesse continued, "we have a motive, Karen. The oldest one in the book. Revenge."

"You are so myopic, Jesse," said Karen. "All you ever see is what people tell you to." Karen crossed her legs.

"I see three big, fat fingerprints on a bloody knife that belongs to your client and was used to kill a man. And by the way, myopia is the bread and butter of defense lawyers."

Ira and Dick Steals said nothing. Jesse and Karen were battling each other, and it was obvious that something more than the case was behind it.

"Karen, I know you like to fight, but I am an old man," said Ira. "Gentlemen, excuse us a second." He got up and walked to a corner with Louise Yancy and Karen. He whispered something to them, and they quickly came back and sat down.

"Gentlemen, our client has an alibi witness," Karen said.

Jesse and Dick Steals were unable to hide their shock.

"Was D'Estenne told about this?" asked Dick Steals.

"No," said Karen. "We just found out about it this morning."

"Okay, let's hear it," said Jesse.

"No," said Dick Steals. "We should wait for D'Estenne."

"We can tell him," said Jesse. "Nothing will happen without his say-so." Richard nodded. Jesse turned his gaze back to Karen, who had the look of the devil in her eyes. "Let's hear it, Karen."

"Okay. Ms. Yancy, on the night in question, was with her lover."

Louise Yancy shifted uncomfortably in her seat.

"She was with someone from eight o'clock to the next morning."

"But she said she was out with friends, none of whom could corroborate that story," said Dick Steals.

"All the more reason that she's telling the truth," said Karen. "Why would she give a false alibi unless she had no reason to think she would need one? She was hiding her lover from her husband, not the police."

"Who?" asked Jesse. "Who is the man?"

"It is a man, isn't it?" said Dick Steals.

"You apologize to my client for that fucking remark, you son of a bitch!" said Karen. She jumped out of her seat and got into Dick Steals's face. Her finger was pointed right between his eyes. Jesse wasn't surprised. This was the Karen he knew.

"I didn't mean anything by it," Dick Steals said. "I'm sorry, ma'am."

"No problem," said Louise Yancy.

Karen sat back down. She was breathing hard.

"We'll need a name, Karen," Jesse said. He was mad at what Dick Steals had just said too, but he tried not to let it show.

"We can't right now," Karen said.

"Why am I not surprised?" said Jesse.

"The man is—he's married," said Karen. "And he's prominent. We have to be sure that he won't be exposed."

"This is a waste of time," said Dick Steals. "I'm not going to play this game. You don't want to plead, fine. We'll see you in court for the arraignment."

Karen looked at Jesse. It was a pleading look. She was good, Jesse thought. Help me out, Jesse, show up the white man.

"I agree," said Jesse. "See you tomorrow." The two prosecutors got up to leave.

"Wait," said Louise. "I want to talk to you." She pointed at Jesse. "Alone."

Ira and Karen started to talk to Louise together, but she cut them off.

"No more lawyer games today," said Louise. "I want to talk to him, right now. What do you say, Counselor?"

"Louise, no," said Karen. "Please, at least let me stay with you."

"Why?" asked Louise. "So you can censor my every word? No. You wait outside with Ira. And take him with you." She pointed at Richard.

Ira walked over to Louise and grabbed her arm. "Louise, if you do this," he said, "I'll resign the case."

"Go on," said Louise. She brushed his hand away. "I think I can find another lawyer in this town for the trial of the century."

Ira and Karen looked at each other for a moment. They were at a loss to stop their client. Mrs. Yancy was as fierce and independent as Jesse had heard.

"I don't think Mr. King would feel comfortable doing this," said Karen. She looked at Jesse, her expression begging him to decline. They were lawyers, and this was a matter of principle and respect.

"I represent the people," said Jesse. "Ms. Yancy is one of the people. I'm ready to talk."

Ira and Karen were pissed, but Louise motioned them to the door, and they left with Dick Steals, who smiled at their incredible luck and winked at Jesse.

In the room alone Louise Yancy relaxed. She even smiled a little. "Sit down, Mr. King," she said.

Louise was a tall, elegant lady. She was fifty-five and still a lovely woman. She dressed immaculately and had a fondness for diamonds. Her hands and wrists were covered with them. She had a way about her that made you aware of your behavior, like a strict teacher at an exclusive private school.

Jesse sat down. He was feeling a little awkward. This had never happened to him before. But he knew a little about Louise Yancy. She was by most accounts a remarkable woman. She was cultured, highly educated, and largely responsible for her husband's ascent to power.

"I'd like to thank you for the flowers," said Louise Yancy.

Jesse was shocked. "You're welcome, but how did you . . . I mean, I never expected you to remember."

"You sent stargazers, I think," she said. "I received a lot of flowers from people. All of them a lot more powerful than you. That's why I remember. Most of the stuff from the common folks was separated from the gifts and messages from dignitaries. But your bouquet was sent right along with the senators', millionaires', and the president's. It stood out because I had no idea who you were."

"I'm flattered," said Jesse. "I mean, that you would care at all. He . . . your husband was important to me."

"I know." She looked sad for a moment, then: "Look, I'll make this brief. In spite of my counsel's fears, I believe I can trust you. Anything I say to you here would probably not be admissible anyway, and even if it were, you'd have to resign this case to testify against me."

"You should be a lawyer," said Jesse. "Correct on all counts."

"So I'll tell you a story," said Louise. "My husband and I had a traditional power marriage. He screwed his women, and I had my derivative power, my reward for being married to a man like Harris. Don't get me wrong. I wasn't unhappy. In fact I was very happy. I had my friends, my businesses, and my position. I've traveled all over the world. And quite frankly my days of needing a man between my legs were long gone."

Jesse shifted nervously in his seat.

"Sorry," said Louise. "I tend to be blunt one-on-one. But I was a beautiful woman once. I had men all over the country vying for my attention. And I didn't waste my youth. I had many wonderful lovers, and when I chose to settle down, I chose wisely and got a great life out of it." Louise crossed her legs and leaned to one side of her chair. She seemed to glide in her movements, like a dancer. "I say all this to let you know that I had every reason to want my husband to continue living."

"And you didn't care that he fooled around?" asked Jesse.

"All men cheat, Mr. King. The biggest lie about marriage is that fidelity holds it together. Friendship and respect are what really keep a marriage going." Louise looked away for a second and said, "And I was not always perfect myself."

"So who was this man you were with? The alibi."

"I'll let my lawyers tell you that. I wanted to talk to you because you're black and I know you'll be getting a lot of flak for taking this case. But I feel better knowing that you're here. I've never trusted the white lawyers in your office. I remember when they railroaded black men into prison by the hundreds. I had a cousin that died in the county lockup after being falsely convicted."

"I've heard the stories," said Jesse. "So, if you didn't do it, who did?"

"I don't know," she said. Her eyes looked sad and moist. "Like the wife of any politician, assassination was my nightmare, and now it's here, and it's far worse than I'd ever dreamed."

Jesse leaned back in his chair. He was enjoying this. Louise was honest and forthcoming, and she was not afraid of him. He was impressed by her. She was ready to joust with him to the end if necessary.

"Do you know why the guards didn't come that night?" asked Jesse.

"No," said Louise. "Mr. Nicks takes care of all that out of the mansion."

"We can't find Mr. Nicks. Do you know where he is?"

"No. I never talked to him. He was surly and crude. But Harris liked him, so I never said anything."

"So let's talk about your husband's medication," said Jesse. "I believe it's called Procan SR—"

"I won't be cross-examined, Mr. King," Louise snapped. "I only wanted to do this to appeal to you as a conscientious black man." She leaned in closer. "I want you to look out for me because I'm innocent."

"I would do that anyway," said Jesse. Louise had a steely gaze, and he was drawn to her by it.

"But I had to be sure," said Louise. "Not all black men have the courage of their convictions. And not all of them are black where it counts."

It was obvious that she was not going to give up anything incriminating. He found himself feeling sorry for her. She had a good life, but even the rich and powerful have crosses to bear.

"Well, unless you have anything else to say," said Jesse, "I think we can bring them back before Ira has a stroke."

Louise smiled and nodded. Jesse got up, went to the door, and opened it. Karen and Ira were right at the door, obviously trying to eavesdrop. Jesse was sure that they'd heard nothing. He smiled at them, and they gave him nasty looks. They both thought he should have refused the invitation, but Jesse was glad that he hadn't. Now he was even more concerned about the case. Louise Yancy was a hard woman, but she was not a knife-wielding killer. If he could see it, a jury could too.

"Don't suppose there's any reason to ask what you talked about?" said Karen.

"Ms. Yancy can tell you if she likes," said Jesse. "But I'm taking the Fifth." He smiled a shit-eating smile that he knew would make Karen madder at him. He enjoyed getting the better of her.

"Let's go," said Dick Steals.

Jesse said good-bye to Louise and left with Richard. They walked down a long hallway.

"Did she give up anything?" asked Dick Steals.

"No," said Jesse.

"I didn't think she would," said Dick Steals. "So what did she say?"

"She basically wanted me to look out for her on this prosecution because I'm black."

"She didn't have to throw us all out to do that," said Richard.

"Yes, she did," said Jesse. "She wanted me to know that she trusted me. And now she wants me to trust her. She said she was innocent."

"They're all innocent," said Dick Steals, "until the jury comes in. Man, I thought I'd shit when she threw her lawyers out. The skirt was just dying out in the hall with me."

"Karen," said Jesse. "Her name is Karen."

"Yeah, right. You used to . . . see her, didn't you?" Dick Steals asked, smiling again.

"Yeah. But it was a long time ago," Jesse said. It was a lie. He and Karen had separated only a year and a half ago.

A big man came into the hallway about halfway down. He was under a broken light and looked like a shadow from the distance. He looked in Jesse and Dick Steals's direction and walked their way.

Jesse was nervous for a moment. There was something ominous about the man. 1300 was a spooky building, filled with dark secrets and even darker men. The big man stopped in front of Jesse and Dick Steals.

"Can we help you?" asked Jesse.

"Detective Beletti," said the man. The cop was stocky and had thinning dark hair. "Some people are here to see you."

"What people?" asked Jesse.

"Serious people."

Jesse and Dick Steals were ushered into another interrogation room. Jesse looked at the three men at the table. He and Dick Steals both were shocked.

"Hello, Mr. Mayor," Jesse said.

Richard barely got out his own hello as Lester Crawford, former deputy mayor, now acting mayor of Detroit, motioned for them to sit.

The two lawyers sat down across from the three well-dressed black men. Jesse knew the acting mayor, Lester Crawford, but the other two men were a mystery. One of the men was smallish with freckles and reddish hair. The other was huge and mean-looking, probably a bodyguard, thought Jesse. Crawford looked at Beletti, and the detective left.

"My heart is heavy today," said Lester Crawford. "Detroit has suffered enough without having to go through a trial like this."

"We agree, sir," said Dick Steals.

"Did you want to talk to us about the case, Mr. Mayor?" asked Jesse.

"Yes, I did," said Crawford. "I've already talked to your boss, Mr. D'Estenne, and he assured me that the case would be over soon."

"We certainly hope so," said Richard.

"Good," said Crawford. "Detroit needs to get on with its life. That's why all the local politicians have agreed that there won't be a special mayor's election until next year."

Crawford was in his early forties but looked younger. He was a clotheshorse like D'Estenne, only a lot more flashy. He wore Italian suits and imported shoes and was always immaculately groomed. He was a tall, thin man who was not as good-looking as he thought he was. He was graceful for a man his size and was known to be quite a dancer.

Crawford had also been the leader of the Young Turks in Yancy's administration. He was a Harvard lawyer, with a business degree from Wharton. His family owned a string of McDonald's franchises and other businesses. Both newspapers had run profiles on him over the last year. And when he had been appointed deputy mayor at age thirty-eight, he was officially acknowledged as an heir apparent.

Crawford and his cohorts had quickly assumed power after Yancy's death. The city council chairman had claimed the right to succeed Yancy. But the city charter was ambiguous, and Crawford had quieted the council chair and others who wanted the mayor's job, by promising a special election would be held next year.

Crawford, teary-eyed, announced at the mayor's funeral that he and a committee were going to run the city until an election could be held. But behind the scenes everyone knew Crawford was in charge. He had amassed great power as deputy mayor and made sure everyone knew he was the next in line to the throne. He was known to be a brilliant tactician and a ruthless competitor. Jesse had met him on several occasions and was always left with the feeling that he had just met royalty.

"How can we help you, sir?" asked Dick Steals. "Anything I can do to help, just ask."

Jesse was shocked. He had never seen Richard kiss ass that way, especially a black one.

"Well, I'll just say I want a speedy end to the case," said

Crawford. "The mayor was like a father to me. I want his death avenged."

"We all do," said Jesse.

"If we can get Ms. Yancy to plead, that would help my cause greatly," said Crawford.

"That doesn't look good," said Jesse. "They're trying to prove an alibi."

"Can they?" asked Crawford. He suddenly looked concerned.

"I don't know," said Jesse. "But if they do, and it holds up, I guess—I guess she's not our murderer."

Crawford looked at the man with the reddish hair and freckles. "Of course. Excuse me," he said, and left. The big man went with him. The red-haired man stayed. It was an abrupt departure, and Jesse was a little confused. He and Dick Steals shared a look.

"I'm James Kelly," said Crawford's remaining companion. "What I'm about to say is completely off the record. If anyone says anything about it, we'll deny it."

"Go on," said Dick Steals. He seemed excited.

"I understand," said Jesse.

"We know Louise Yancy killed the mayor," said Kelly. "I won't go into details, but everyone knew they were having a lot of marital trouble. That's why Yancy had so many young women. We know all about your case. If you ever need anything, just say the word."

"Anything like what?" asked Jesse.

"This is Detroit," said Kelly. "In this town the mayor has great influence. That influence can help the cause of justice—or help create it. We'll be in touch." Kelly left, leaving Jesse and Dick Steals alone in the room.

Jesse and Richard took a moment to absorb the gravity of what had just happened.

"Holy shit," said Dick Steals.

"My sentiments exactly," said Jesse. "So do we tell D'Estenne about this?"

"You assume he doesn't already know," said Dick Steals.

"I say we don't talk to Crawford and his men anymore," said Jesse.

"Don't be silly," said Dick Steals. "They can help."

"They were talking about breaking the law, Richard," said Jesse. "Railroading Louise Yancy if necessary. We can *create* justice? What else does that mean?"

"I didn't hear that. I just heard an offer of help," Dick Steals said calmly. He was about to leave when Jesse stepped in front of him.

"We'll prosecute this case by the book, Richard, or I'm gone right now," Jesse said.

"No one's talking about anything illegal," said Dick Steals. "But let's not piss off the mayor. He can help our careers."

"Fuck our careers," said Jesse. The conversation with Louise Yancy and Kelly's statement had made him angry. "Justice, Richard. Do you remember that? Remember your oath? No one can create justice."

"Forever the Boy Scout, huh?" said Dick Steals. "Fine. Be a Boy Scout."

After Richard left the room, Jesse lingered. He fought back his anger. His people had truly achieved equality, he thought. Blacks had gone from being the victims of perverted justice to perverting it themselves.

Jesse walked out of the room into the hallway. It was empty and looked ominous. He made no attempt to catch Dick Steals in the elevator. He was thinking about Louise Yancy's entreaty, Walter Nicks's convenient disappearing act, and Crawford's indecent proposal.

13

Face of Fear

Cane stood in the shadows of the alley as Tico watched the street. Walker was in a car around the corner. Walker was their safety net in case things went wrong.

It was only six o'clock, but it was already getting dark. Cane was happy. The night came early in the fall, and he was going to take apart one of LoLo's rollers. They were on a side street, close to one of LoLo's places of business.

Tico and Walker had wanted to do a drive-by, but to Cane, that was bullshit. Killing was a matter of darkness, best performed up close and personal. He liked to look into a man's eyes, into his soul, when he did it. That's what made Cane unafraid of killing, unafraid of Him.

"I don't know why I let you do this," Tico said. He stood on the sidewalk about ten feet in front of Cane. He was dressed in shabby clothes and held a crumpled-up paper bag with a bottle in it.

"Do you see them yet?" asked Cane.

"Not yet," said Tico. "This shit is fucked up."

"It has to be this way," said Cane. "When this is over, we'll have this city beneath our feet. We'll be able to enjoy our hard work, while other people take the risks. But to do that, we have to get rid of these bitches."

Cane raised his hand to Tico. On it he wore a black leather glove covered in metal spikes. Cane had seen it in a kinky little sex shop on Eight Mile. He'd sharpened the dull little spikes himself. It was heavy, pointed, and nasty. Just what he needed.

"You are crazy *and* full of shit," Tico said, pointing to the glove.

"Maybe, but I will beat these women," said Cane. "You got anything on Jaleel yet?"

"Not yet," said Tico. "But I got one of his people watching him for me. If he's stealing, we'll find out." Tico looked down the street, then back at Cane. "Someone's coming."

Tico pulled his skullcap down around his face and leaned back against a telephone pole, doing his best drunk imitation.

Sheri and Little Jack walked down the side street, closer to Tico. They slowed when they saw him. Sheri said something to Little Jack, then went out in front, moving closer to Tico.

"You can't be standing here, pops," said Sheri. She had her hand behind her back. Tico said nothing. He just pretended to take a drink, keeping his face from them.

"Get yo drunk ass outta here, nigga," said Sheri. "We rollin' up in here."

Tico was silent. He moved closer to the alley's entrance.

Little Jack took out a gun but held it to his side. "Look, old muthafucka, you gotta go," said the boy. He moved next to Sheri.

The rollers stood side by side. Tico just looked down and away from the pair. Little Jack took a step closer, and Tico grabbed the boy and wrestled him into the alley. A shot went off into the ground.

Sheri was lifting her gun when Cane emerged from the shadows. She almost screamed at the sight of the one-eyed man and the thing on his hand. Cane grabbed her and carried her off into the alley.

Tico was holding Little Jack on the alley floor. The boy struggled, striking out at Tico. Tico picked him up and put Little Jack's own gun to his head. At the feel of the gun's barrel Little Jack stopped his fighting.

"Say one word and you dead," Tico said. "Where's the damn money?" Little Jack reluctantly pointed at his jacket. Tico felt it. The lining was leaden with money.

Cane had Sheri's mouth covered with the spiked glove. He had grabbed her gun. He tossed it aside. He stared into her eyes. Even in the dimness he could see the fear in them.

"The gun fired, Cane," said Tico. "Somebody might be comin'."

"Don't worry," said Cane. "This won't take long. Hold him up so he can see this."

Tico brought Little Jack closer as Cane took the spiked glove from Sheri's mouth. It left angry red marks around her lips.

Sheri drew a breath to scream as Cane curled the glove into a fist and brought it swiftly into her face.

Ramona sat with LoLo and Yolanda in the drug house on Bristol Street, eating greasy takeout from a local restaurant. Her silly red wig was gone, and she was now dressed like the other Nasty Girls in baggy jeans and a big plaid shirt. Her braids fell in a cascade down her back. For the first time in days Ramona was not worried. Ironic that in the bosom of criminals, she felt safe.

They'd had no luck opening the metal briefcase. It was solid and strong, but they'd promised to break it open later. Ramona didn't know what was inside but thought it might be valuable.

"So, two big dudes in masks killed the mayor?" asked LoLo.

"Right," said Ramona. "They were serious too. They did Yancy, and they were gonna get me too."

"But it's all over the news. The mayor's wife did it," said LoLo.

"Well, that's bullshit," said Ramona, " 'cause I was there."

"So, you gonna tell the cops how it was?" LoLo asked. Yolanda turned to look at Ramona. She was interested in the answer.

"Are you crazy? They will put my ass *under* the jail," said Ramona.

"You know, a lot of folks don't believe the mayor's wife did it," said LoLo. "They're even offering a reward for the killer."

"Well, I'm not turning myself in," said Ramona. "I don't know who these muthafuckas are who tried to kill me. They could be cops. I go in, and they got me for sure."

"Ms. Yancy's got money," said LoLo. "She'll buy her way out of it. Anyway, I'm glad to see you, girl. You lookin' good. I like them braids."

"And it's all my hair," said Ramona. "None of that fake shit, like you."

LoLo pulled off her ponytail. "Hey, this is my real hair. Wanna see the receipt?" She and Ramona laughed. Yolanda chuckled softly.

"Well, you can lay low with us, make some money," said LoLo.

"I don't wanna deal, LoLo," said Ramona. "I just need to get away. I don't need to get back in the life."

LoLo's face turned sour. "Yeah, I guess rollin' is a step down from sellin' pussy, huh?"

Ramona stopped eating. "I ain't no ho."

"Right," said LoLo. "I guess the mayor and your other men just gave you money 'cause you was cute and your hair is real. I know you always thought you was fine, but sellin' ass is sellin' ass."

"He cared about me!" Ramona said with anger. "My name—my name was the last thing he said before they killed him." She was fighting a wave of emotion.

"Really?" LoLo laughed. "I thought his last words would have been 'Swallow it, bitch.' " LoLo laughed loudly and high-fived with Yolanda.

Ramona was furious. She grabbed LoLo by the collar and pulled the smaller woman to her. LoLo jerked to get away, but Ramona held her.

LoLo pulled her gun and put it under Ramona's chin. "Turn me loose—now."

Ramona looked LoLo in the eyes for a second, then let her go. LoLo kept the gun leveled at Ramona, the smaller woman's eyes cold. Yolanda quickly moved between the angry women.

Ramona and LoLo just looked at each other with anger and hurt. Ramona now remembered the reasons she had left the Nasty Girls in the first place. LoLo was a good friend, but she was also jealous, evil, and loved to hurt people.

Ramona and LoLo each backed away, not speaking. Ramona sat down in a chair and stared out the dirty window of the house.

Little Jack ran into the room. His face was moist with sweat; his eyes were wild. "Cane hit us!" Little Jack said. "He caught me and Sheri over by Nevada!"

"Damn that mother—" LoLo said. She slammed the table and for a moment didn't know what to do. "Where's Sheri?" LoLo asked.

"Gone," said Little Jack.

"What the fuck do you mean, gone?" asked LoLo. "He killed her?"

"Yeah, real bad too." Little Jack was still scared.

"What about the money?" asked LoLo.

Little Jack shook his head. "He got it all."

"Fuck!" LoLo said. She threw her food against the wall. She grabbed Little Jack by the collar. "You let him take all my money?"

"Her face . . . Sheri's face . . . it was all gone." Little Jack choked out the words.

"Stop talkin' stupid, boy," said LoLo.

"No, for real. Cane beat it off with some kind of glove with knives on it."

LoLo let the boy go. Her face showed her anger, but there was hurt in her eyes, too.

"Damn," said Ramona quietly.

"Crazy muthafucka," said LoLo. "All right. This is what he wanted. Yolanda, get our people together."

Yolanda sprang up and started to the door.

"It's what he wants you to do," said Ramona.

"What?" asked LoLo, wheeling on her.

"Moving on him now," said Ramona. "He wants you to act out now. That way he can get you all."

"Wha—" said Little Jack. "You just showed up here yesterday, woman. You don't know shit."

Ramona ignored Little Jack. Her gaze was fixed on LoLo. "He'll be waiting for you to come, and you know it," said Ramona.

"Fuck her," Little Jack cried. "Let's go. I know where his main place is. We can burn that muthafucka to the ground!"

LoLo slapped Little Jack on the side of his head. "Shut up. You lucky I don't cap your ass for losing my money. Ramona's right," she said finally. "If it was me, I'd do the same thing. Hit my enemy, then hope they try something. We're supposed to be stupid-ass women. Yolanda, get the word out to my people to crank up production. Little Jack, you talk to my main rollers on the street. Call in some debts. I won't be able to pay them white boys if I'm low on cash."

Little Jack was about to protest but didn't. He left. Yolanda followed him without a word.

Ramona walked over to LoLo. She looked at her old friend. Ramona could see in LoLo's face the apology that her friend would never bring herself to say.

"Come on," said Ramona. "I'll help you make a plan. Just like the old days."

14

Arraignment

The courtroom was packed. D'Estenne had been unsuccessful at banning TV cameras, and they lined the walls. Louise Yancy's family filled the first row, their faces somber, angry. The mayor had two grown children, a son and a daughter. They had come into town on short notice to be with their mother. Reporters, politicians, and leaders of community groups filled in the other seats.

The same old faces, thought Jesse. NAACP, the Urban League, national black this and neighborhood that. Whenever there was an event, they would all come out for the party, seeking to be seen and eventually to become a part of the process.

Jesse was happy to be in court at last. Since the press conference he'd been dodging reporters and trying to ignore all the angry phone calls and threats he'd gotten. In the eyes of some, prosecuting Louise Yancy made him the ultimate traitor to black people.

Jesse sat at his table with Dick Steals. Richard was in a good mood. He lived for this kind of thing. And just coincidentally the morning paper had a profile on him calling him "a new breed of prosecutor." Dick Steals again, Jesse thought.

Ira Hoffman and Karen were opposite them in the courtroom, flanking Louise Yancy. Jesse tried not to look at Karen. She was striking in a blue suit with a tight skirt. Her hair was down, falling to her shoulders. And her breasts looked good under her shimmering pearl blouse. Karen had turned heads when she entered the courtroom.

D'Estenne was in his office, watching the feed on TV. He'd

wanted to come and even to sit at the table, but Jesse had convinced him that his presence would be too distracting. D'Estenne had not argued much. His guest appearance with Carol Salinsky had gone on live and garnered the station's highest ratings that year. D'Estenne was a happy man.

Karen and Hoffman were rushing the case for some reason. They'd waived the twelve-day rule that mandated that a defendant have a preliminary examination twelve days after being arraigned.

A preliminary examination, or prelim, as the lawyers call it, is a hearing wherein the court decides if there is sufficient evidence to warrant probable cause that a defendant committed the crimes he is charged with. Most of the time this proceeding is routine. The court will find probable cause, and a defendant is bound over for trial. But in this case Jesse knew that Karen and Ira would try to spring Louise Yancy, using everything they had.

And so they insisted on a preliminary examination the same week of the arraignment, which gave Jesse only a few days to prepare. D'Estenne and Dick Steals both had eagerly agreed.

Jesse wanted to wait. He wanted more time to contemplate a strategy and plug the holes in the case. But he was a lone voice. Everyone was in a big damn hurry to end this one.

"Thirty-six District Court is now in session," said the bailiff. "The Honorable Mason Johnson presiding."

Judge Johnson took the bench. He was from Mississippi but had come to Detroit and married into one of the city's most powerful families. "Well, let's get to it," said Johnson in his southern drawl.

"People versus Louise Monroe Yancy," said the bailiff.

Counsel introduced themselves, and Karen took the podium next to Louise Yancy.

"Ms. Yancy, how do you plead in this matter?" said Johnson.

"Not guilty," said Louise Yancy.

Six black women in the back of the courtroom burst into cheering and applause. Bailiffs went to them and began to usher them out. The TV cameras got it all for posterity.

"Black women, unite!" they chanted. Several bailiffs rushed to their seats. Others put their hands on their weapons. The women were then physically removed from the room.

The courtroom settled down after a while. But Jesse was upset. This case was already becoming a circus.

"Okay, anyone else want to watch from the local bar?" said Johnson. He was enjoying his moment in the public eye. "All right, counsel, now the moment we've all been waiting for. Bail. I've read the briefs submitted, and I'm ready to make a decision, but I will hear argument first. Mr. King."

Jesse stepped forward. "The people request no bail be given, Your Honor. This is a first-degree murder case. Ms. Yancy is a wealthy woman. She has access to many means of—"

"Your Honor, the people didn't see fit to—"

"I'm not finished, counsel," Jesse snapped. He and Karen stared each other down. Jesse wanted her to know that she would not be allowed to take over this case.

"Let him finish, Ms. Bell," said the judge.

"Thank you, Your Honor," said Jesse. "Ms. Yancy is a flight risk. And this is first-degree murder, where as you know bail is not normally granted. I refer the Court to the cases cited in our brief. Our office will take every precaution to insure Ms. Yancy's safety while incarcerated." Jesse sat down.

"Your Honor, this is ridiculous," said Karen. "Ms. Yancy is not a threat to society. She's not some stickup man. She's the first lady of Detroit. She's involved with at least twenty charitable and community organizations and has extended family and businesses in the city. She is a woman of honor, and she'd be running away from her life if she left town. Bail's only purpose is to guarantee the appearance of the defendant. But money doesn't tie Louise Yancy to this city. What binds her is three decades of love, service, duty, and family. For her that is the ultimate bail." Karen stepped back from the mike. The gallery applauded loudly.

Jesse took a deep breath. Karen was as good as ever. "Murder, Your Honor," said Jesse, standing up again. "Society's most heinous crime. Harris Yancy was a leader, a legend in this city. And he was killed like an animal. It's like Dr. King or JFK being assassinated. We understand that a defendant is innocent until proven guilty, but the scrutiny of the people has fallen upon Louise Yancy, and *the people* deserve the security of knowing that she will be here to see justice done to the memory of her late husband."

Jesse was surprised at a smattering of applause in the gallery.

"Ms. Bell?" said Judge Dixon.

"A fine speech, Your Honor, but the fact is the prosecutor's office allowed my client to remain free after they knew she would be charged with this crime."

"Sidebar, Your Honor!" Jesse said.

All the lawyers walked to the judge's bench. Johnson turned off his microphone.

"Your Honor," Dick Steals said, "that was a matter of courtesy extended to Ms. Yancy for one day!"

"But it was extended," said Ira Hoffman.

"It wasn't in their brief on bail, Your Honor," said Dick Steals. "I think that it shouldn't be allowed at this late stage."

"I can't believe you would use this, Karen," said Jesse.

"After what you did with my client?" said Karen. "Be for real."

"Enough, children," said Johnson. "Look, I've read the briefs and now I've heard argument. I'm ready to rule on the matter. Step back."

This was going to be a hard-fought trial, Jesse thought. Karen was resourceful and ruthless. She was going to come at him from all angles, fair and unfair. Jesse went to his table shooting her a nasty look.

"Does counsel have anything further?" asked Johnson.

"No, Your Honor." Jesse and Karen overlapped in response.

"Well, the court is ready to rule," said Johnson. The reporters all perked up. "Bail is not normally granted in murder cases. It is within my discretion. Mr. King makes an excellent point about our system of justice. The scrutiny of the people is a powerful force and must be respected. However . . ."

Jesse's heart sank. Dick Steals cursed.

". . . notwithstanding any deals or courtesies extended before today, I find that Ms. Yancy is neither a substantial flight risk nor a threat to society. Therefore I will set bail accordingly. Bail is set at one million dollars—cash."

"We are ready to post bail, Your Honor," said Karen. She was smiling.

"Okay," said Johnson. "The court appreciates your speed, Ms. Bell. Preliminary exam will be this Friday unless anyone objects."

Jesse looked at Dick Steals, who shook his head. Jesse sighed. "No objection, Your Honor," Jesse said.

"Defendant is free on bail," said Johnson. "This matter is adjourned."

Jesse and Dick Steals tried to keep civil faces for the cameras. They started out of the courtroom but opted instead to follow Louise Yancy and her lawyers, who left out the rear through the judge's chambers.

Jesse was already feeling the pain of the tongue-lashing they would get from D'Estenne. He averted his eyes from Louise Yancy's family, who were giving him nasty looks.

Suddenly Karen pulled him aside. Jesse was surprised at the force with which she yanked his arm. She pulled him inside a little secretary's room off the judge's chambers. She was close to him, and her scent was wonderful. Jesse looked at her, and for a second he was lost in her beauty.

"Eleven o'clock tonight, our place, and don't bring the white boy."

Before he could respond, Karen walked away, catching up with her client.

Jesse waited in a dark corner of Mario's, an Italian restaurant in the heart of Detroit's Cass Corridor. The place was busy, so he had requested a table in an empty banquet room.

This had been his and Karen's favorite place. The hushed atmosphere, sweet wines, and exquisite pasta had been their foreplay on many an evening. Jesse couldn't stop a smile from spreading across his face. He and Karen once had a good thing, but he confessed that it was mostly lust.

The affair had started almost the moment he first saw her in the lobby of the courthouse. He remembered how Karen had flirted and fidgeted with her wedding ring. They talked about the law and her weak relationship with her husband. She laughed at his jokes, and he boyishly complimented her. Even now Jesse was excited by the memory of that night, knowing that it might happen but not completely sure, waiting for her to open each door of opportunity, then carefully step through. Finally, when they made love, it was in his car, like two high schoolers.

Jesus, Jesse said to himself as he felt an unmistakable swell in his pants, I'm acting like a goddamned kid. He forced the memories from his head, but they were soon followed by even worse thoughts.

His breakup with Karen had been one of the juiciest stories in their circle. Karen had left her husband, Fred, an amiable accountant, and moved in with Jesse. There were rumors that she was pregnant, but that had not been the case.

They were quickly engaged, trying to stop the sting of gossip. But Jesse soon found that Karen was a more remarkable woman than he'd ever imagined. She was brilliant and knew it. She was commanding, powerful, and required a lot of maintenance. Jesse was a capable man but not used to such a dynamic woman. He wanted to hold her, keep her, but by her very nature she would not be held. After the sex had cooled, they were left with only their personalities to build on. It was over within a month.

Karen walked into the secluded room at Mario's. She was still in the blue suit, but the jacket was gone, and the shimmering pearl blouse danced as her breasts swayed underneath. Jesse let out a deep breath. He was still taken by her.

"This had better be good," he said.

"It is." Karen sat down. A waiter came, and she ordered a glass of red wine.

"I won't go into that shit you pulled in court today," said Jesse. "Just tell me what you want, so I can get out of here."

"All right," said Karen. "I want to take you into the men's room and fuck you," she said seriously.

Jesse was exhilarated but managed to hide it. In his mind, however, he was already seeing it. "Get to it, Karen, or I'm outta here—now."

"That was it, really," she said. "I want you, right now."

"You never know when to quit, do you?"

"Okay," Karen said, laughing. "I was hoping you'd developed a sense of humor, but I can see some things never change."

"I was thinking the same thing about you," said Jesse.

"Okay, I want you to promise—"

"It's all off the record, Karen," Jesse said. "You have my word. Go on."

"Louise Yancy is innocent."

"Yeah, I know. She told me," Jesse said sarcastically.

"No, really. I wanted to come here because I'm going to give you her alibi and some other info that's strictly off the record."

"Tick, tock," Jesse said impatiently.

Karen took a moment as the waiter brought her wine. She took a deep drink and licked a drop from her lips. "I needed that," Karen said. "Okay, Louise Yancy was with Seth Carson the night of the murder from eight until the next morning."

"Seth Carson?" said Jesse. "President of BoldCom, wannabe mayor of Detroit? Married-for-twenty-years Seth Carson?"

"The same."

"Okay, when can we take his statement?" he asked. He couldn't hide the interest in his voice.

"Well—"

"Don't even think about it, Karen. Just because Carson is powerful doesn't mean that we're gonna drop this case."

"I don't want you to."

"He makes a statement, or no deals whatsoever," Jesse said. "You and Ira started playing dirty in this case, so you don't get anything unless it's by the book from now on."

"I don't believe this. You're pissed 'cause I kicked your ass this morning," Karen said.

"And I am not falling for that one either," Jesse said. "You will not get me to 'be a man' and forget how you sandbagged me."

"Look, you know I play to win. Try it sometime."

"I play to find justice," said Jesse. "It's my job, and unlike a lot of black people in this town, I take it seriously."

"Oh, please." Karen crossed her legs. "You need to drop that conservative nigger shit. God knows that's the thing I disliked the most about you. Black conservative. That's a goddamned oxymoron."

"I am not gonna let the prime suspect in the biggest murder case in Detroit's history quietly walk away because she's having an affair with a wealthy man," said Jesse. "They're adults. People know what they're getting into when they cheat on their spouse, right?"

Karen winced. Jesse let the thinnest of smiles rise to his lips. He'd hit her below the belt, and it felt good.

"I can see that you'd rather hurt me than try to make headway in this case," she said softly. She looked hurt, but Jesse wasn't sure. It was difficult to know when she was serious and when she was acting.

"Don't wait for an apology," Jesse said. "I have changed in some ways."

"Well, if you're not willing to deal," said Karen, "we can go our separate ways."

"Wait. What about this other information you promised me?"

"No way," said Karen. "I'll only say if you deal."

"Will Ms. Yancy go to jail to protect Carson?"

"Yes," said Karen flatly. "I don't recommend it, but as you know, Louise is a strong-willed woman. And in case you forgot, I plan to have her acquitted."

"Okay. But how do you know I won't subpoena Carson?"

"Because you're honest, Jesse," said Karen. "Everybody knows that you'd rather be shot than break your word."

Karen downed her drink and got up. Jesse rose and reached for his jacket. He was putting it on and thinking about the drive home when Karen turned to him.

"I felt you watching me today," Karen said. Caught off guard, Jesse was about to deny it, but Karen waved him off. "It's okay, I was watching you too. Only us women are too slick to get caught."

"Well, you were looking good," Jesse said. He felt a confession was appropriate.

"It was more than that," said Karen. "At least it was for me. I was thinking . . . that we never really knew why we were together. We thought it was love, then sex. Then we thought it was a mistake. Finally we became friends. People stay married on less than that, Jesse."

"Karen, I don't think we should—"

"I was thinking today that if I had done one thing differently back when we were together, we might be married right now. I'd have a life outside the law." She took a step toward him. "I haven't had a real boyfriend since you. There aren't as many good men out there as I thought. I've had old rich men, up-and-comers, who like me on their arm, and pretty boys, looking for someone prettier than they are. And I rolled over all of them, just like I did you and my ex-husband. I came here to make a deal, but in my heart I was wondering about my chances with you."

Karen looked sad and beautiful standing there before him. Jesse was barely holding himself together. He was fighting the urge to embrace her. He found himself stronger than he thought.

"Sorry, but I can't get involved with you again, Karen," said Jesse.

She quickly closed the distance between them and kissed Jesse. He never thought about stopping her. He grabbed the back of her head and inhaled the scent of her hair, perfume, and the wine she'd drank. Karen pushed her body into his and hugged him tightly. He felt her breasts under the silky blouse. They moved in unison, hands roving, enjoying their transgression. She pulled her tongue out of his mouth, lingering a moment to plant a kiss on his lips.

"Needed that more than the drink," she said.

And then she was gone.

15

Florence

"You gotta fuckin' be shittin' me, Jesse!" said the woman. She leaned back on her wooden chair in a cramped office in the basement of Frank Murphy. Jesse had just told her what Karen Bell had said to him the night before. "She's a lying sack of cow shit, and you know it."

"Florence, I just need you to ask a few questions about what Crawford and his people are doing," said Jesse, "and do a little checking on Seth Carson."

"Man, Karen Bell musta spread 'em for you right in the goddamned parking lot," said Florence.

Florence Connor was a former cop. She was forty-five, white, and very ornery. She was now an investigator for the prosecutor's office because her drinking problem had driven her from regular active duty. She hadn't completely kicked the habit, and desk duty kept her from being on the street waving a gun.

Florence and Jesse had first met on a murder case a few years back. He had been losing badly when Florence found the murder weapon. The defendant had taken the gun apart and hidden the pieces. Florence had known the model of the weapon and found a piece sticking out of the dirt in the backyard. A search revealed the rest of the weapon hidden in various places. She was a mess socially, but when it came to the job, she was sharp, methodical, and, most important, trustworthy.

A picture of a younger Florence stood on her desk. In it she was a beautiful young woman with red hair. Florence's face was now etched with lines from too much worry and too much drinking. Her eyes were world-weary, her red mane was streaked with gray, and she'd added a few extra pounds.

Jesse didn't even think of Florence as a woman. She had a way about her that was like a guy. A lot of women cops were like that. It's what it took to fit in sometimes.

"I just need you to look into this for me, okay?" said Jesse.

Florence lit a cigarette. "Louise Yancy and Carson, two old farts, fuckin' like kids. It's too far-out, Jesse."

"Hey, old people do have sex, you know. And if I add that to the holes in this case, I get something really big."

"A cover-up," said Florence. "I'm way ahead of ya. Take my advice, Jesse, let this shit go. You know how Detroit is. When it gets like this, you step aside or you get fucked."

"We're talking about obstruction of justice at the least, Florence. I can't ignore that."

"Aw, fuck that motherfuckin' garbage. Sometimes you just gotta piss on that legal shit."

"You eat with that mouth?" asked Jesse.

"Comes with the badge," said Florence. She liked her foul mouth for some reason. For her, cursing was almost an art form.

"Maybe," said Jesse. "But I tell you, that kind of language is not very ladylike. I mean, you are a woman, you know."

"Suck my dick." Florence laughed, and Jesse couldn't help but join her. "Hey, you know I'll help you," she said. "But these kinds of things can be fucked if you get caught."

"But you're gonna do it, right?"

"Yeah, yeah, but if this thing blows, I don't know you."

"Cool," said Jesse. "And another thing. I need to find a cop named Walter Nicks."

"That crazy bastard?" Florence's eyes widened. "What for?"

"He might have been at the scene of the crime."

"Hell, if Nicks was there, he probably *did* the crime," said Florence. "Fuckin' Vietnam whack job."

"Then he should be easy to find," said Jesse. "I looked over the mayor's phone records, and his calls all seem innocent. Yancy made hundreds of calls every day, but on the day he was killed, he only made six calls—the whole day."

"No shit," said Florence. "To who?"

"He made one to his wife; that figures. He made one to a

minister. I'm gonna meet him today. He made one to the Chapel, Swiss law firm. The lawyer he called, Louis Franklin, is on vacation."

"Conveniently," said Florence.

"The others were made to Manoogian Mansion. And he made one to the infamous Michael Talli."

Florence straightened in her chair. "Talli. The mob guy? That's where I'd be looking."

"No one's ever proven that," said Jesse. "But I know Talli had millions invested in bringing casinos to Detroit. And Yancy was trying to distance himself from him. Talli's alleged underworld connection made getting casinos that much harder."

Detroit's leaders had been thinking about bringing casinos to the city as a way of saving the ailing economy. But time and time again community leaders, especially ministers, had thwarted the effort. While the debate raged, Windsor, a city across the river in Canada, had put in a casino, and it raked in the cash—Detroit cash. Every weekend the hardworking people of the city went across the river and lost their shirts.

Yancy, envious of the half billion in gaming revenues generated by a city just across the river, had turned up his efforts to get casinos before his death.

Jesse got up. "I gotta go. I only have a few days to prepare my preliminary examination."

"Shit, they are rushing it, aren't they?" said Florence. "Wanna drink?" She pulled out a bottle.

"I need one, but I'll pass," said Jesse. "Too early."

He walked to the door as she poured a drink. Florence was good, but Jesse was worried. He feared for her safety. They were chasing shadows, but in Detroit even a shadow could be dangerous. They'd even been known to kill.

"Florence?"

"Yeah, Jesse?"

"Watch your back."

16

MACs & Manoogian

Jesse walked through the big church. It was a huge tabernacle richly appointed with expensive wood and stained glass, but he hardly noticed the opulence. He'd been in the Church of God before.

COG, as it was sometimes called, was a political church. In the black community political and economic power had always rested heavily in the church. And COG was as big as they came. Every politician in the state as well as several presidents had spoken there. The who's who of Detroit's black elite all belonged. Jesse remembered that Ellis and his wife, Penny, had been married there. His fiancée, Connie, was a member too.

Jesse followed an old black woman through the sanctuary into the back of the building. COG was a complex with three buildings that took up an entire city block.

Jesse was led into a large conference room. It was beautiful, decorated in redwood. It could have been the den of a wealthy businessman or a celebrity, but it was the conference room of the pastor of COG, Oscar Paul, Jr., called Reverend Junior by everyone.

Reverend Junior sat at the head of a long wooden table. A medium-built man, of about forty, he was average-looking with light brown skin marked by a nasty-looking patch of acne. He wore nerdy black-rimmed glasses and sported a small Afro.

Reverend Junior had a degree from Harvard and had studied divinity at Princeton. He was on every list of prominent young leaders in the country. In a business that was crowded with self-ordained and suspect men of God he was the real deal.

Reverend Junior was seated with three other black ministers of various ages. They looked imposing in their dark suits and white collars. They were the members of MAC, Ministers against Casinos. When Mayor Yancy and prominent businessmen tried to bring gambling to Detroit, Reverend Junior had put the MACs together and stopped them. And as the casino plans continued, the MACs foiled each try, building power and support in Detroit's communities.

"Gentlemen," said Jesse.

"Have a seat, counselor," said Reverend Junior.

Jesse sat down. The old black woman rushed in with a tray of soft drinks. She set down the tray and left.

"These are Reverends Turner, Hunter, and Washington," said Reverend Junior. "We've been anxious about your visit, counselor."

"Really? Why so?" asked Jesse.

"We know who killed the mayor," said Turner in a raspy voice. He was an old man of about seventy with wispy white hair.

"Excuse Reverend Turner," said Reverend Junior. "He thinks God killed the mayor."

"He did," said Turner. He drank his drink.

"What Reverend Turner means is that Yancy was a sinner and he paid the price for it," said Washington. Washington was big, muscular, and couldn't have been more than twenty-five or so.

"He was a sinner, and God took him!" yelled Turner.

"We're all sinners," said Reverend Junior. "Reverend Turner, please try to control yourself."

"What is it we can do for you?" asked Hunter. He was a big, overweight man of about fifty. He was handsome with a head of dark, curly hair.

"Just following up leads," said Jesse. "The mayor called here the day he died." He took out a notepad and pen.

"I took that call," said Reverend Junior. "He just called to tell us that he was planning another casino initiative. He asked me to meet him to talk about it. I agreed to meet him, but you know the rest."

"Is that all?" asked Jesse, taking notes.

"Yes," said Reverend Junior. "Yancy was always firm in his belief that we should have gambling. He was fearless about it."

"Did you ever hear of anyone who might have been upset about the mayor's casino plan?" asked Jesse.

"The people were upset," said Reverend Junior.

"We've defeated all the referendums," said Washington, "one charter proposal, and countless actions in the state capitol. The power of the people's values is with us."

"Casinos will only bring sin to Detroit," said Reverend Junior. "And there's enough sin to go around already. Harris Yancy was wrong about trying to bring them in."

"See, politicians think prosperity flows from business," said Hunter. "But we know that it flows from God."

The other reverends all said amen to this.

"You believe in Jesus?" Reverend Junior asked Jesse.

Jesse was somewhat thrown by the question. He did not want to let the reverend get him off the subject. But the power of the black church was strong. He felt guilty for even thinking about not answering the question.

"Yes," said Jesse. "I'm a Christian."

"Good," said Reverend Junior. "Then you understand that our society is in trouble because we've turned our back on Jesus's example. Jesus was a revolutionary, a man who lived to show the world what His father, the living God, wanted them to do in life. We've turned away from that example of love and sacrifice. Instead we're concerned with self-pleasure and sin. Casinos don't want people to gamble with money; they want them to gamble with their souls. I can't allow that. We are nothing less than the sword of God, and we will strike at all attempts to bring more evil to this city."

"I won't disagree with that," said Jesse. "But aren't you all afraid that the new mayor will just bring them in anyway?"

"No," said Reverend Junior quickly. "We will fight Crawford if we have to."

"Have you talked to Crawford about this?" asked Jesse.

Hunter leaned over the table and gave Reverend Junior a look, holding up a hand.

"It's okay, brother," said Reverend Junior. "I'll answer. Reverend Hunter is an attorney. He worries. Yes, I talked to Crawford about casinos. He wanted to help us in our fight against them."

"Was this before or after the mayor died?" asked Jesse.

Hunter gave Reverend Junior another look.

"So, just what is your business here again, counselor?" asked Reverend Junior.

"Just following up leads, like I told you before," said Jesse.

"This organization had nothing to do with the mayor's death," said Hunter. "Your questioning here is inappropriate."

"Sorry," said Jesse. "I didn't mean to offend anyone." Now he was fired up. These men were obviously hiding something.

"No offense taken," said Reverend Junior. "I'd like to know how you think talking to us will help. I thought you had your suspect."

"I don't want to leave any stone unturned. They'll say it was a rush to judgment, that sort of thing. We want to be able to say that we followed every lead, no matter how ridiculous it was."

This made Hunter relax. As a lawyer Hunter knew that there was truth in Jesse's statement. Any good defense attorney knew that sometimes police and prosecutors ignored leads. Some would say that alone was reasonable doubt.

"Well, we all want Ms. Yancy to get a fair trial," said Reverend Junior. "She is a member here, you know."

"Yes, I do," said Jesse.

"She didn't kill him," said Turner. "God did."

Reverend Junior gave Reverend Washington a look. Washington stood and went over to Turner. He whispered something to the old man, then took him out of the room.

"I wonder why COG didn't come out in Ms. Yancy's defense," said Jesse. "I mean, she is prominent and, as you said, a member."

Hunter frowned. He shot a look at Reverend Junior, but it was too late.

"I made that decision," said Reverend Junior. "COG doesn't like to inject itself into these kinds of matters. And everyone is not so sure about Ms. Yancy's innocence. Hell hath no fury, Mr. King."

"We have members in high places in the police department, the city government, and on the bench," said Reverend Hunter. "We cannot show favoritism. It puts us in the position of having to do it all the time."

Jesse knew that was not the truth. COG was the most political church in the city and could do anything it wanted.

"I see," said Jesse.

"I'm afraid we have an urgent meeting," said Reverend Junior. "But before we leave, we'd like to offer a prayer for you and for Ms. Yancy."

Jesse didn't know what to think. Reverend Washington came back into the room. The MACs stood and bowed their heads. Jesse instinctively did the same as Reverend Junior spoke: "Heavenly

Father, we ask you to bless our sister Louise Yancy. Do not let her fall if she is innocent, and forgive her if she is not. And watch over this young lawyer. He is your instrument against the evil that took our brother Harris Yancy from this earth. Bless him as he strives to find the truth. And protect him from those who would deter him in his mission. We ask these and other blessings in Jesus' name. Amen."

Jesse raised his head and stared directly into the eyes of Reverend Junior. "Amen," said Jesse.

Jesse entered Alex Manoogian Mansion on Dwight Street just outside downtown. The mansion is the official residence of the mayor of Detroit.

Jesse was greeted by an old black man in a suit. "I'm Jesse King. I'm from the prosecutor's office."

"Samuel Jackson," said the old man. He was about seventy and had lost most of his hair. He was very dark, and his mouth was filled with perfect white dentures.

"Oh, like the actor," said Jesse.

"Come in," Samuel said, not responding to the comment. The old man ushered Jesse into a spacious living room, decorated with fine furniture. The house had the air of a palace. He tried not to look overwhelmed. The walls were lined with portraits of past mayors: Gibbs, Cavanaugh, Young, and Yancy. In the middle of a big wall hung a picture of Lester Crawford.

Jesse sat on a big sofa. Samuel stood over him and asked, "Would you care for a refreshment, sir?"

"No, thanks," said Jesse. "Hey, have a seat."

"I'm the house director. I do not sit on assignment."

"Okay," said Jesse. "Then I'll stand."

"As you wish, sir."

Jesse stood up with his notepad, then: "Sam, I wanted to know if you—"

"It's Samuel, sir," said the old man. "My name is Samuel."

"Sorry," said Jesse. This guy was certainly one for formality, Jesse thought. Many old blacks in service positions found their dignity in the forgotten etiquette of yesterday. Jesse suddenly felt embarrassed for being so uncultured. "I need to know, Samuel, if you know why the mayor called here on the night he was murdered."

"Yes, I do. I took that call for Mr. Crawford," said Samuel.

"Really?" Jesse said, unable to hide his excitement. "What was he doing here?"

"There was a procasino meeting here. A lot of wealthy men."

"Was there a Michael Talli here?" asked Jesse.

"Yes. He was at the meeting," said Samuel. "Mr. Crawford—" He cleared his throat. "Mayor Crawford presided over the meeting."

"I see," said Jesse. Even though Crawford was personally against casinos, Yancy had obviously made him support the city's plan to get them. "So, did Crawford seem upset when he took the call?"

"I didn't watch him, sir," said Samuel. There was a tinge of irritation in his voice.

"Sorry," said Jesse. "Who took the other call?"

"There was no other call from the mayor that night," said Samuel.

"Are you sure?" asked Jesse. "I have verified phone records."

"I am positive," said Samuel.

"All right. Can I have a list of the people at that party?"

"Yes. We keep a list of everyone who comes to the mansion," said Samuel.

"That's great. Please let me have a copy," said Jesse.

"Very good." Samuel started off.

"Why do you keep such a list?" asked Jesse. "If you don't mind my asking."

"Mayor Yancy liked to know who was here in his absence. He especially wanted to know when his wife was here."

"Why was that?"

"You know," said Samuel. "I see no need to soil his memory further."

"I see," said Jesse. "But if you can tell me, were they happy, the Yancys?"

"Happy is a relative term. They fought quite a bit, but it was common. But they had moments when they were like newlyweds." He looked a little sad at this memory. "I'll get that list."

Samuel walked out of the room and returned in a few minutes with several stapled pages. He handed them to Jesse. Jesse looked at the list and sighed heavily. Talli had been there that night. And during the day of the murder the mansion had been visited by many others. Crawford, D'Estenne, Walter Nicks, Reverend Junior, and Richard Steel had all come by at various times. Even his old friend

Ellis Holmes had been there. Ellis had mentioned that, hadn't he? Jesse couldn't remember.

"Why were there so many people here that day?"

"I think it was the New City Project. The mayor had just gotten the brochures on the proposal, and he didn't want to have them delivered. He made everyone come here to get them. He liked to summon people sometimes."

"Well, thank you," said Jesse. "I think that I have everything I need."

Samuel showed Jesse to the door, but Jesse hardly noticed the old man. He hurried out of the big house holding the list, feeling that he was getting closer to some hidden truth.

17

Old Days

LoLo stretched her arms in a big yawn. It was late, and she and Ramona had been up a long time. They had discussed Cane's strength and weaknesses and where it would be best to hit him. Cane's operation was tight. His system was complex and efficient. He'd recently gotten his rollers to deliver their goods on bikes. That way, if they got busted, the cops couldn't take their cars under the forfeiture laws.

Cane's people were too loyal or too scared to turn on him. Tico and Walker were fierce, ruthless, and as tough as Cane himself. They had discussed getting to him through a woman, but Cane wasn't known to have one.

Ramona had always been the brains of the crew, always had a scheme to get money, avoid the cops, or take down an enemy. They had made a good team: her brains and LoLo's ruthlessness. LoLo was hot-tempered and crude, but she had the mettle to make things happen.

"Maybe Sheri was right," said LoLo. "Maybe we should just hit him, burn down one of his houses."

"You think that's good enough?" said Ramona. "He'll just get you back, nip and tuck. Naw, you wanna devastate him. One blow."

"Yeah, maybe do like the Mafia, kill his whole family," LoLo said.

"Does he even have a family?" asked Ramona.

"Everyone has a family," said LoLo.

"What makes you think he cares about them? He's in the

life. They probably don't even talk." Ramona was speaking from experience.

"Let me tell you something, Mona," said LoLo. "Rollers may be evil, murdering bastards, but they all love their mamas."

Ramona thought about that. Even to those in the life, family was important. It was your basis in the world, like it or not. She had lost her family because of her fast friends, who had become her new family, a sorry substitute.

"So, you and me can find out who they are, then we pop his old lady," said LoLo.

"I can't do that," said Ramona. "I can't kill somebody's mama."

"What the fuck is it with you?" said LoLo. "You know, you've never smoked anybody as long as I've known you. You down with me in this or not?"

Ramona looked a little hurt. "When we got into this, we always said we wouldn't be crazy and destructive, that we was just out to get paid. What happened to that?"

"Things change," said LoLo sourly. "People change."

"I haven't," said Ramona.

"Then forget it," said LoLo. "You still all messed up over what happened to your sister. That's so fuckin' weak. Just get your stuff and go then. I don't have time for you."

"Look," said Ramona, "we don't have to do this. If you can turn one of Cane's men, you might be able to get to him. Cane may not like women, but I bet the others do—"

A police siren uttered a short blast. To LoLo and Ramona, it sounded like the voice of the devil. LoLo jumped up and went to the window.

"Damn!" said LoLo, grabbing her gun. Then realization washed over her face. "Cane," she said.

It suddenly hit them that while they had been planning, so had Cane. They were looking for a way to move on him, but his hit on their rollers had been just the start of his plan.

"I can't let them take me," said Ramona.

"That muthafucka," said LoLo. "I got some drugs in here. So, if they pop us, we go down hard."

"There's only one car out there," said Ramona. "We can do like we used to, split and run— LoLo, where's my briefcase?"

There was a hard knock at the door. Ramona and LoLo broke for the back door. The two women hit the back door together, knocking the officer on the other side of it to the ground. They jumped over him and ran like hell, going in opposite directions.

Ramona didn't look back. She pumped all her energy into running. She saw herself shooting at the dealers, then her sister, Sarah, being hit with a bullet, her mother crying, yelling at her. . . .

"Stop!" yelled a voice from behind her.

A shot rang out. Then another. Ramona couldn't tell if they were shooting at her or LoLo.

"Stop or I'll drop your ass!" The voice sounded closer.

Ramona looked over her shoulder and saw a male police officer after her. A jolt of adrenaline shot through her. Just as she rounded a corner, she slammed into an old shopping cart parked haphazardly on the sidewalk. Ramona fell as the cart rolled in the street. Her leg twisted, and a sharp pain went through her leg as she hit the pavement.

Ramona struggled to get to her feet but was kicked back down. Hard fists slammed into her side and back, and angry curses followed. She was pulled roughly to her feet, and a nightstick was placed over her throat. The cop choked her, cursing and punching her in the side. Ramona struggled to speak but couldn't.

Finally the cop let her go, and she fell to the ground, unable to get up.

18

Riverfront

Jesse sat with Connie in the banquet hall of the River Front Ballroom in the Westin Hotel in the early-morning sun. The breakfast meeting was filled to the rafters with Detroit's elite. Across the room, through a huge picture window, Jesse could see the Detroit River, rolling along peacefully.

Connie was drinking coffee and nibbling on a croissant. She was in heaven. She loved places and events like this. She was perfectly at home among these people. She was gracious, funny, the perfect social companion for a professional man.

Steven Brownhill was giving a dull speech about urban renewal. Crawford and his minions were seated at the dais, as were several prominent ministers and politicians. Jesse only half listened to the speech. The Brownhill family, called the Kennedys of the Midwest, was extremely wealthy and everyone knew they wanted one of their sons in the governor's mansion. This was really a disguised fundraiser for the election.

Brownhill had formed a committee called the New City Commission. It was planning a big renovation of the east side of Detroit. He was stomping around the metro area, looking for investors.

Brownhill's partners in New City were Margaret Blue, the CEO of Blue Pipe, a plumbing and construction firm. She was a hard woman, called Icewater behind her back. Rounding out the commission was Willie Gibbs, a black retired NFL star and owner of a profitable real estate and construction company. Gibbs's company specialized in urban renewal. Gibbs was a big, loud man who was fond of cigars and young girls. The New City Project was certain to increase their already vast fortunes.

Jesse hardly noticed his fiancée or Ellis and his wife, Penny, a pencil-thin woman with an annoying needle nose. Ellis and Penny had been ecstatic when Connie told them they were getting married. Ellis had immediately told Jesse that he had to have the wedding at COG. Connie was a member, so it was the socially correct thing to do. Jesse was noncommittal. After talking with the MACs, he doubted he would ever want to go there again.

Jesse glanced around the room at the celebrity crowd. His eyes stopped suddenly at a table on the far side of the room. A group of white men sat quietly in a corner listening to the speech. Jesse recognized one of them as Michael Talli, a contractor and casino proponent. Talli was a bulldog of a man. He was about fifty, overweight, and eternally angry-looking. Talli had a head full of thick black hair that made him look younger but no less menacing.

Talli was surrounded by four men in dark suits. They should have just had a sign that read MAFIA. Jesse couldn't take his eyes off the men. Talli was a local businessman, but why did he care about Brownhill's thinly disguised political campaign? Mob guys always care about politics, he reasoned.

Talli's construction company had been the target of a RICO suit several years back. The feds thought that Talli had engineered a hit on a rival contractor and forced several others to work under him, sharing profits and contracts. The case fell apart when key pieces of video and audio surveillance magically disappeared.

Jesse tore himself away from Talli long enough to notice that Brownhill was finishing his speech.

". . . it's no secret that Detroit is in financial trouble," said Brownhill. He had a strong, commanding voice, with just a hint of tight-jawed East Coast influence. "We need to stop dreaming up fly-by-night ways to fix the problem and look at long-term solutions. The New City Project, revitalizing the east side will be the start of that solution."

The room was filled with mostly white people, all well heeled and intelligent-looking. But there was a good number of black people there too. Ellis had done a fine job darkening up the place, Jesse thought.

Brownhill finished, and the crowd applauded wildly, standing. He descended the podium with Blue and Gibbs at his side, hand-shaking his way out of the room. The big bodyguards followed them closely. Brownhill, Blue, and Gibbs went over to Mayor Crawford and took several photos.

Jesse watched Talli and his men get up and wade into the crowd. No one knew for sure if Talli was a real criminal, but he seemed to enjoy the infamy the rumors brought. Talli and his men cock-walked around the room, swaggering like made men.

Jesse went cold as he saw Brownhill, Gibbs, and Blue come his way, followed by a throng of reporters. The group stopped at Jesse's table. Ellis fell all over himself shaking their hands.

"This is my friend Jesse King," said Ellis. "But I guess everyone knows him by now."

The three partners shook Jesse's hand, each complimenting him and wishing him luck. Gibbs almost choked on his words. As a black man he didn't like the fact that another black man was prosecuting the first lady of Detroit.

The three partners flanked Jesse, and the cameras exploded with flashes. Ellis quietly slipped into the shot, making sure to be close to Brownhill.

The flashes stopped, and Brownhill hurried away, pressing more flesh on his way out of the door.

"Thanks, Jesse," said Ellis. "This will mean a lot to my career." Then Ellis grabbed Penny and hurried behind the partners as the crowd moved on.

Talli and his men intercepted Brownhill in the middle of the floor. Brownhill's bodyguard went up to Talli and said something. Talli turned red and did an abrupt about-face. He walked back to his table.

"Now I know why Ellis wanted me here," said Jesse. "Just a photo op to boost his presence at the firm."

"Oh, you loved it," said Connie. "You'll look great in tomorrow's paper." Jesse and Connie sat back down. "So, did you ever resolve that situation with your sister?" asked Connie.

"What?" said Jesse. "Oh, that. Yes, I did. I'm giving her kids the money."

"Is that wise?" asked Connie. "I mean, those kids might use it for something bad too."

"*Those* kids? You said it like they're criminals or something." Jesse was mad.

"Are you okay?" Connie looked at him with concern.

Jesse caught himself. Connie was too sweet ever to be condescending to him and his family. He suddenly felt guilty about snapping at her.

"No. I'm not okay." He waited a moment, then said: "I had a drink with Karen Bell last night."

"Oh?" Connie said.

"Yes, she met me at Mario's and—" Jesse looked around. There were too many people within earshot. He walked Connie over to a window, away from everyone. He noticed the jealous look on Connie's face. Karen was an eternal sore spot. "Karen made an offer in the case. I refused it, but when I think about it, it all makes sense. I think maybe Louise Yancy is innocent."

"Jesse, are you sure?"

"No, but it's a strong feeling. I've done so many cases I can tell when something is not right. Louise Yancy wasn't sleeping with her husband, but she had no reason to want him dead. My boss wants this case closed yesterday, and Crawford, the acting mayor, has offered to railroad Ms. Yancy if we need it."

"What?"

"You didn't hear that, please," said Jesse. "I shouldn't have said it. Look, if I'm on edge, just bear with me, okay?"

"Of course I will, Jesse," said Connie.

"I'm sorry," he said. And he kissed her, a deep, loving kiss.

"Well, that sure was nice. You, kissing in public. I think I like it." She smiled and wiped lipstick off his face.

They walked back to their table and made small talk with several of their colleagues. Jesse was tempted to tell Connie about Karen and the passionate kiss, a full confession of his sin, but he thought better of it. There were some things a fiancée didn't need to know.

Jesse took a drink of water and looked across the room for Talli and his men. But they had disappeared.

19

Custody

LoLo was pissed. She had barely escaped the cops. She'd run like hell and lost her pursuer, then jumped a fence and hid in a garage. The cop had run right past her and never come back. While crouched in the foul-smelling garage, LoLo had heard shots fired. So she waited awhile; then, against her better judgment, she doubled back and saw the cops arresting Ramona. Ramona was bent over as she was pulled into the police cruiser.

Cane was smarter than even she'd thought. He'd set them up but good. Never would she have imagined that he'd call the police. It was an unwritten law between rollers, but apparently Cane didn't give a shit about that street code.

LoLo sat with Yolanda and a roller named Marly in a motel on the far east side. LoLo had told her people to tighten up all operations and carry extra firepower until further notice. It was dangerous for them all to be strapped and risk a weapons charge, but she was planning her next move, and this time there would be no waiting.

Marly was a pretty young woman with a baby face and an hourglass figure accented by a large chest. She looked older but was only eighteen. She was a new street dealer in LoLo's crew.

LoLo had lured her away from her boyfriend, a wannabe rapper who called himself Bugsy. LoLo got close to Marly and talked her into joining her crew part-time. Bugsy found out and went postal. He came to one of LoLo's houses brandishing a gun, screaming about killing "all them bitches." LoLo and Yolanda beat him so badly that he was in the hospital for over a month. Marly joined the crew full-time after that. She was another hothead, but she was tough, and that was what LoLo needed right now.

"So what if she drops on us?" asked Marly.

"Mona won't do that," said LoLo. "Besides, she don't know anything to tell about us."

"I don't trust her," said Marly. "For all we know, she brought the cops down on you."

LoLo had already thought about that, but it didn't make sense. Ramona was a prissy little bitch, but she was loyal and part of the family. "Ramona ain't dirty. And the cops beat her ass good when they picked her up."

"How we gone do it?" asked Yolanda. She seemed to be upset about recent events.

"I don't know," said LoLo. "Ramona gave me an idea, though, and I'm gonna need you for it, Marly. I'm gonna need that gunman, the white boy, what's his name?" asked LoLo.

"Pierre," said Yolanda.

"Right," said LoLo. "I want some special gear for this."

The killers tore the room apart. They broke the old, faded furniture and ripped gaping holes in the walls with a sledgehammer. The drug house was deserted, and they were searching for the black metal case Ramona Blake had carried.

The Blake girl was associated with the drug-pushing women called the Nasty Girls. They also knew that she had stayed in this house, but so far there was no sign of the case.

The man who'd worn the red mask breathed audibly as he worked. His chest wound was wrapped in thick bandages that inhibited his breathing. He rubbed his ravaged face, then pulled open an old storage door and peered inside. Nothing but cobwebs and dust inside.

"It's not here," he said.

"Fuck!" said his partner, the larger of the two. He tossed the sledgehammer to the floor.

"She's gotta have it with her," said the wounded killer.

"The cops got her ass. She probably hid it somewhere before they got her. Don't be so fuckin' stupid."

"Fuck you," said the wounded man. "I got cut by that bitch. And I ain't forgot that you stabbed me the second time."

The larger man looked at his partner with rage. Then he picked up the big hammer and walked over to him. He was a full four inches taller and dwarfed the other man. "You looking to get me for that?" he said. The heavy hammer hung in his right hand.

"You don't wanna be walking up on me with that thing. I'll shove it up your goddamned ass."

"We're only in this mess because you couldn't kill one little skinny ass bitch."

"I suppose it was just luck that she coldcocked your stupid ass with that briefcase."

The bigger man took a half step toward the other. The wounded man jumped back, reaching for the gun in his waistband. The big man stopped, letting the hammer fall on the floor.

"Okay," said the big man. "No need for us to get on each other over this thing. We're both on the hook here."

"All right by me. Just watch your mouth."

The big man walked away, and the two men stood in silence for a moment. Each of them knew the consequence of failing again. Yancy's execution had been botched, but that situation had been calmed down. The Blake girl was in prison, and no one was the wiser. The only missing element needed to close the matter was the black case and its contents.

Ramona was a smart and resourceful woman. She had eluded them twice. But now the law had her, and to get away from them, she needed cold, hard evidence. The contents of the black case were the only thing that could set her free. She was going to have to go for it sooner or later.

"It's not in here," said the big man. "I'm afraid we're gonna have to take her."

Ramona hurt all over. Her skin was bruised badly, and the cops had done a nice little number on her ribs. She groaned as she sat up in her cell at 1300. They'd at least taken the time to have a doctor fix her up. The cops would deny ever beating her, or they would lie and say she resisted arrest.

Ramona understood the gravity of her situation. Though she'd been brought in on drug charges, after they ran a check on her fingerprints, it was only a matter of time before they came up with her name. Her criminal record had never been expunged, so she was sure that they would ID her. After that happened, she was in deep trouble.

A tray of food had been placed in the cell, but Ramona had no appetite. She just wanted to get out. She was sure that whoever killed Yancy and tried to kill her would find out where she was and finish the job. In prison she was a sitting duck.

And she had never gotten a chance to open the briefcase to see if whatever was inside could help her. The case. Good thing LoLo had hidden it in the house under the floorboards. No one would ever find it there. She had instructed LoLo to take the case and keep it with her if anything ever happened to her.

Footsteps. Coming her way.

A uniformed officer led the way, and behind her was a big white cop dressed in plainclothes. Ramona looked at his jowly face. It was unfamiliar, yet she hated him all the same.

"Well, Ms. Blake," said the plainclothes cop, "looks like you've saved us the trouble of finding you."

20

The Hidden Truth

Jesse's little office was filled with charts, reports, and forensic manuals. He had a preliminary examination coming, but he wasn't too worried about it. They'd pulled Judge Victor Power. He was a good judge, who never compromised his ethics. Jesse didn't think Power would spring Louise Yancy in a prelim.

But the trial would be a different matter. Their case was weak. Louise Yancy was a beloved woman who seemed credible. And they had a lot of things to explain, things that would not get by the watchful eye of Karen Bell. On one chart Jesse listed the areas where the defense would try to take their case apart:

> Unknown blood sample
> Immaculate murder scene
> Alleged woman—unknown
> Mayor's bodyguards gone

"We're in trouble," Jesse mumbled to himself. He could see reasonable doubt right there on the board. Even if they could use all the evidence they had against Louise Yancy in court, a jury could take any one of those elements and think that someone else had killed the mayor.

Jesse went to the board and wrote in:

> Louise Yancy alibi?
> Karen's "Unknown Information"

Crimes follow certain patterns, he thought. Whenever something deviates from the pattern, reasonable doubt looms.

Reasonable doubt was a logical hesitation to convict. If a juror found something in the case did not make sense and it made him or her stop and think that the defendant could be innocent if it were true, then that juror was lost to the prosecution. The burden to convict was heavy, but that was the system, and now it was leaning on Jesse like dead weight.

Jesse sat down and looked at the board. He was going to have to pull a rabbit out of his hat. Then he remembered his own credo: "My job is not to convict. My job is to find the truth, no matter how terrible it might be."

Jesse went back to the board and quickly wrote in:

Casinos
Crawford: anticasino
MACs: anticasino
Talli: procasino—forced out by Yancy?

The phone rang. Jesse grabbed it. When he did, he heard a static hum, a light buzzing that came and went quickly. He ignored it.

"King," he said.

"Fuckin' shit's hitting the fan, Jess!" said Florence.

"What's up, Florence?"

"I got nothing on Crawford and Seth Carson so far, but a drinking buddy of mine at 1300 told me that they caught the woman from the Yancy murder scene last night."

"Okay, thanks. I'll call you later." Jesse hung up. He buzzed Dick Steals's office but got no answer. Then he tried D'Estenne. He was not in either. Jesse thought for a moment. Where were Richard and D'Estenne?

"Shit," he said. He quickly called another number, then ran out.

"I want a lawyer," said Ramona to the man in the dark room. Both her hands were handcuffed to a table.

"We want answers," said the detective. "You talk to us, and we'll get you a lawyer."

"I've seen enough TV to know you can't do that," Ramona said.

Oscar Beletti sat across from Ramona in the interrogation room of 1300. There were two men behind him that she could not see. Ramona had been taken from her cell and brought to the room. She had not been allowed a phone call, and they made sure that no one saw her in the hallways.

"Talk to me or you'll be one sorry-ass bitch," said Beletti.

"Why ain't y'all talkin'?" Ramona asked to the men in the shadows.

"Don't worry about them," said Beletti. "You just—"

One of the men held up a hand. He whispered something to Beletti. Then he and the other man walked out of the room. Ramona never saw their faces.

Ramona tightened in the seat. Beletti got up and adjusted his pants. Then he just walked out, leaving her alone.

"Jesse King!" he yelled to the uniformed officer at the reception desk. "I'm an assistant prosecutor. I know you picked up a suspect in the Yancy case, and I want to see her—now!"

"I don't know what you're talking about," said the officer, a young woman about twenty-five.

"I don't believe this shit!" said Jesse. "If she's here and we're withholding information, we are in some serious—"

"Jesse," said a voice.

Jesse turned and saw Dick Steals behind him.

"Richard, where the hell have you been?"

"In court, but I heard about the arrest. News travels."

"So where is she?" asked Jesse.

"Hey, I just found out myself. I left D'Estenne a message." To the female cop, Dick Steals said: "We want to see a young lady named Ramona Blake."

"Sorry, don't got nobody here by that name," said the young cop.

"There's obviously a mixup here, Jesse," said Dick Steals. "Why don't we go back to the office."

"Fuck that," said Jesse. "Let me go to the holding cells and see for myself."

"I can't do that," said the young cop.

"Why the hell not?" said Jesse. "I go visit defendants there all the time."

"Got orders just today. No civilians of any kind in the back," said the young cop.

Jesse bolted for a door leading to the holding cells. The young cop jumped from behind her desk and followed him. She instinctively had her hand on her weapon.

"Come back here!" she said.

But Jesse was gone. He went through the door and down the hallway. The cop was right behind him, yelling for help.

Dick Steals, still in the lobby of 1300, turned, cursing under his breath, and walked out.

Ramona tensed when Beletti walked back into the room. Something bulged under his rumpled jacket. She stiffened all over.

"Time to stop fuckin' around with you."

"I want my lawyer."

"Who helped you kill the mayor?"

Ramona said nothing.

Beletti walked her way, hand inside his jacket.

Loud voices sounded from the hallway. Beletti stopped. He went to the door, where Ramona saw him whisper to a uniformed young black cop. Beletti looked upset, then left. The young black cop came in. He stopped and looked at her with hatred. Then he took off her handcuffs and led her back to her cell.

Ramona sat down hard on the bench that was supposed to be a bed. She was hungry, and someone had taken the food away. She wondered for the first time if LoLo and the others were okay. That Cane person was obviously a smart man. He'd hit them, then called the police as part of an elaborate setup.

Now she fully recalled why she'd gotten out of street life. It was dirty, dangerous, and— She stopped herself. She'd given up dealing for what? Sleeping with rich men, and look where it got her. In jail with a murder charge hanging over her head.

They would drag her through the system, vilify her in the media, then send her to prison, where she would be killed by some crusading fanatic out to avenge Yancy's murder.

Ramona perked up as the familiar scent of perfume reached her. It was an expensive scent, but she couldn't remember the name. Too good for some streetwalker, she thought.

Then she saw an attractive woman walk up to her cell. A black plainclothesman was with her. The cop was tall and very good-looking. He opened the cell. The woman looked at the cop and smiled. He smiled and took several steps back. The woman stepped inside.

"I'm Karen Bell," she said. "I hear you need a lawyer."

21

First Chair

"Obviously the police got carried away," said D'Estenne. "They loved the mayor, and they wanted to squeeze her."

"So they violate her civil rights and blow the case to hell?" Jesse asked.

He was in D'Estenne's office with Dick Steals. The cops had been holding Ramona Blake for almost a day and had told no one. Now Karen Bell was on the case, and all hell might break loose. Karen had gotten to Ramona and was now her lawyer. It was a conflict of interest, but one that disappeared if Louise Yancy was released.

"You act like you're mad at me, Jesse," D'Estenne said.

"I'm sorry," said Jesse, "but we should have been notified. In any event we have a problem. This case could be over before it begins."

"Why?" D'Estenne asked.

"Because her rights were violated."

"Jesse," said Dick Steals, "there's no way we're not going to get a chance to prosecute this Blake woman. Everyone wants blood for this murder. We can cop to what the police did, and no judge on the bench will kick the case."

"But we won't," said D'Estenne. "Let the defense whine about it. No one will care."

They were right, Jesse thought. The infraction was minor even by big-city standards. He took a seat. His anger was not with the cops but with D'Estenne and Dick Steals. He didn't like their quiet, secretive manner and their quickness to downplay a constitutional violation. He tried to forget that they were white and he was not.

"Okay," said Jesse, "let's say the case doesn't pop. What do we do with Louise Yancy?"

"We let her go," said D'Estenne. "I've already started the ball rolling."

Jesse was floored. Louise Yancy was going to walk because they now had another body to fry for the murder of the century?

"Well, I'm glad I was consulted," he said.

"I still run this office," D'Estenne said sternly. "Besides, her alibi witness stepped out."

Jesse and Dick Steals both looked shocked. "When did this happen?" said Dick Steals. He seemed upset that D'Estenne had not let him in on this secret.

"Last night I got a call from Ira Hoffman. Seth Carson and his wife are divorcing. Carson saw no reason to let Louise Yancy go on suffering. Louise is quite a lady. I called her and personally apologized."

Jesse was shocked but relieved. Louise Yancy didn't belong in jail. But he was still unsettled by the shadowy way D'Estenne was handling the case.

"Forget all that, Jesse," D'Estenne said. "I have good news. The Yancy case is now yours. This young girl looks good as the killer now. I need Richard to work that corruption probe out in Dearborn. You can choose your own second chair."

Jesse didn't know what to say. On the one hand, it was good to be free from Dick Steals. On the other, it was typical of D'Estenne to pull a white prosecutor from a case that no longer had race card potential. Prosecuting Ramona Blake was not nearly as sexy as prosecuting the mayor's wife.

"Thanks, Frank," Jesse said, choking on the words.

"No problem," said D'Estenne. "I know you'll do a great job. My only order is that you keep me informed at critical stages, and I want a list of all evidence obtained."

Jesse didn't know how to respond to that last request. It was unusual, but the case was still important. "No problem," he said.

"Good luck with Karen Bell," said Dick Steals. "She's a real ball-buster."

Jesse got up and left, not bothering to look back. Something smelled really bad here, and he was afraid that it was coming from his own house.

Once in his office he sat down and reached for his phone. He had put the receiver to his ear when he heard the static hum again. It was faint, a whisper, but noticeable enough that he stopped dialing. Jesse hung up the phone and picked it up again. This time he was sure he heard it.

Jesse got up and went into the offices of Pete Saunders and Peter Janowski, across the hall. Pete & Pete were on a trial as usual, and the office was empty. Jesse picked up their phone and heard only the dial tone. He hung up and listened again. Nothing.

Jesse went back to his office and listened to his phone. No, he hadn't imagined the noise. The static hum was there. Jesse's heart started racing. Was this real or was he paranoid? After today's events he didn't feel like taking chances. He picked up his briefcase and left the building.

"I owe you one," said Karen Bell on the phone.

"Think nothing of it," said Jesse. After becoming sure his phone was bugged, he'd gone to a local restaurant that had a nice, secluded phone booth in the back. "How'd you get in to see her?"

"This cop I used to date got me in," said Karen. "He's an inspector now."

"When Richard couldn't be reached, I got suspicious. These guys will never learn. You can't fuck the system like that."

"My little Boy Scout," said Karen. "Hey, thanks for letting my other client go. Ms. Yancy is comfortably free of charges."

"Well, she has an alibi now," said Jesse. "I bet tonight is the first night in weeks her boyfriend, Seth Carson, won't shit his pants."

They both laughed. There was a silence on the line, then: "I dreamed about you last night, Jesse."

"Karen, don't start."

"I did. We were in Mario's. I offered to go down on you and you said yes."

Jesse sighed. He was visualizing it and couldn't stop. "Karen, why do you do this to me?"

"You want me to, and you know it."

"No, I don't," said Jesse. "I'm spoken for, and *you* know it."

"Oh, that's right. You have a girlfriend. How is old plain Jane what's-her-name?"

"Fine," said Jesse. He waited a second, then added, "Actually, we just set a date."

More silence on the line. Jesse had not thought before saying it. A woman never likes to see a former lover going on with his life. It makes her feel used, old, and sad. Jesse felt bad having to tell her on the phone like this.

"Congrats," said Karen a little flatly. "So, I need a favor for my new client, Ms. Ramona Blake."

Karen was all business again. Jesse could tell she was hurt.

"Wait a minute," he said. "I need you to tell me what Louise Yancy's 'information' was."

"Oh, that. Well, it's all very cryptic, actually. She told me that her husband was up to something big before he died. She thinks it had something to do with that casino thing they keep bringing up."

"Gambling?"

"Right. But she had no names for me," Karen said. "And apparently Mayor Yancy was going to propose a new business coalition for casinos. He included a lot of influential Michigan business people."

"Michael Talli on that list?" asked Jesse.

"No," said Karen. "He was not part of it anymore. Talli and his crooked-nosed men were shut out."

"That's useful," Jesse said almost to himself. "Did Yancy change his mind about casinos? Because if he did . . ."

"No," said Karen. "But he was determined that blacks share in the wealth."

"I see," said Jesse. He took a moment, then: "So, Karen, I suppose your new client, Ramona Blake, is innocent too."

"Of course," said Karen. "I don't have the whole story yet, but I'll get it. Which brings me back to my favor."

"What is it, Karen?"

"I need Ramona Blake out of jail."

Jesse almost laughed. "This is a joke, right?"

"I wish it were, Jesse. She's not safe in there. Word has already gotten around that she killed the mayor. And in case you didn't know, the cops beat her, threatened her life, and violated several parts of a little document called the Constitution."

"Okay, Karen," said Jesse. "I know we fucked up, and if you say that in court, I'll deny it. Anyway, what do you want me to do, get her into Club Med?"

"No, a security hospital. She's got injuries, so it's legit. I don't care if you put a hundred cops on her room. In fact I'd like that."

Jesse hesitated, thinking this over. He didn't want to show weakness this early on, but he knew that Karen was right. The Blake girl was in danger.

"Okay," he said. "I'll see what I can do. But if she tries to run, you know they'll shoot her dead."

"You're a saint," said Karen jubilantly. She waited a moment, then: "I hope you're very happy with your new wife." She hung up before he could say anything.

Jesse hung up still a little upset that he'd told Karen about his impending marriage over the phone. He walked out of the restaurant and headed back to work. He'd given in to Karen rather easily, but he had to. If he didn't help protect Ramona Blake, she might not be alive much longer.

22

Island Games

LoLo looked over the long table of weapons in the basement of the old house. Glocks, Smith & Wesson's mini .357, a Taurus .45, and other assorted weapons were all assembled in a neat row. She was using a little house on the east side as a temporary base until she could finish with Cane.

Pierre Reed stood proudly next to his arsenal. He was a thin white man with wild blond hair and a little mustache. He was a licensed gun dealer, but this part of his trade was strictly off the books.

"This ain't shit," said LoLo. "I can get this anywhere. I need something that's gonna fuck people up when I use it."

"I just got the regular shit," said Pierre. "Handguns, shotguns, double-action—"

"Stop fuckin' with me, boy," said LoLo. "I know you carry special stuff. You sell it to the men. I wanna see it."

Pierre didn't seem to care for LoLo's demand, but he was not about to say anything back to her. "Okay, okay," he said, relenting. "Be prepared to pay, though."

He went outside and returned shortly with a little case. Yolanda said nothing as she stood behind LoLo watching the white man. Pierre pulled out a black gun with a short barrel and two twisting metal cylinders on the end. It was a nasty-looking weapon with a thick trigger and a red seal on the stock.

"This is a mini Mack-10. We call it a Stiletto."

"Now you talkin', goddammit," said LoLo.

"Hold up a second," said Pierre. "Lemme tell you somethin'. These things are special. A group out West developed them for urban assaults. I got them while they were being tested."

"I don't want the shit if it don't work," said LoLo.

"I didn't say that," said Pierre. "They wanted a machine gun that could fire more shots at a faster rate. This little baby can shoot its magazine of thirty in about ten seconds."

"Get the fuck outta here," said LoLo.

"If I'm lyin, I'm flyin'," said Pierre. "I only got one right now. They are hard to come by." He reached into the box and pulled out a clip. He put it in the Stiletto, then handed it to LoLo.

The weapon looked like a toy with its shiny black snout and fiery red seal. Pierre cocked it for her. "Now it's hot," he said.

"Stand back," said LoLo.

Everyone moved aside, and LoLo looked for a target. She aimed toward a wooden wall. She pulled the trigger, and the Stiletto jumped in her hands. The kick actually pushed her back a few inches. The barrel blazed red and yellow as the gun spit out the bullets. In a few seconds the gun was empty.

"Damn!" said LoLo. She went to the wall and examined it. There were holes all over it. Big ones. "How much?" she asked.

"Thing ain't safe," said Yolanda.

"I don't give a shit," said LoLo. "Cane dropped on me to the cops and killed Sheri and stole my money! Fuck him. I'm gonna take him out, and I don't want no doubt about it!"

"Ten big," said Pierre.

"Ten!" said LoLo. "So, you just gonna jack me, right? You wouldn't charge a man ten big for this piece of shit."

"Lemme tell you somethin'," said Pierre. "I'll give you a special price if you throw in that." Pierre pointed to the black metallic briefcase sitting at LoLo's feet.

"No," LoLo said. "That belongs to a friend."

"You don't even know what you got there, do you?" said Pierre.

"I don't care what's inside," said LoLo. "It's not for sale."

"It's not what's in it. That's a government briefcase, real secret agent–type shit. See how it has no seams?"

"Can you open it?" asked LoLo.

"No," said Pierre. "But I might know someone who can. So what do you say, ten percent off for the case?"

LoLo thought a second. Pierre was a smart businessman. If he wanted the case, then the damned thing was worth ten times what he was willing to pay.

"No deal," said LoLo. "I'll have to get that ten to you later. Until then I'll give you a thousand and you hold this gun for me. And if you sell it, I'm coming to find your ass. Yolanda, give him the money." Yolanda stepped forward and counted out some bills to Pierre.

"Okay," said Pierre, "but my offer for that case is still open if you change your mind."

LoLo didn't answer. She picked up the Stiletto and aimed its black barrel, looking down its angry red sight.

Cane was thinking about sex. After setting up the Nasty Girls, he wanted to indulge himself, kind of a celebration. It was not like him to get aroused by violence, but this was special, a particularly sweet occasion.

After he had killed the female roller with the spiked glove, a story started that he was a maniac, a monster. The story mutated, and in its current incarnation he was peeling the girl's face off with his bare hands.

Cane heard on the street that crackheads all over town were paying off debts and young rollers were joining his crew. Fear was working. The streets were buzzing with his name. Cane was becoming a legend, larger than life. Soon the mere mention of his name would frighten people.

So he was thinking about fucking somebody, a christening to his legacy. But he decided against it. Sex could be a clumsy and vile undertaking. It depleted a man's power and wasted valuable time. It also gave your sexual partner personal information that tended to humanize a person. And he didn't want that.

Cane was with Tico on Belle Isle. They were parked by the shore, watching the river. It was evening, and the October sun was setting, its edges turning orange and red. God was leaving the earth, and Cane had won yet another day of life.

The young folks were just starting to come on the island. Cane loved Belle Isle. Coming there as a boy was one of the few fond memories he had as a child.

"Island's fillin' up," said Tico.

"Yeah," said Cane.

"Shouldn't we be gettin' on? The Girls still own this place."

"Fuck them," said Cane. "Their shit's finished."

"LoLo didn't get picked up by the cops," said Tico. "She's still out there."

"Only a matter of time. Her people are freakin'. They don't wanna go against me. And when we take her house, it's all over for them bitches."

"Cane," said Tico, frowning, "I still don't know about that shit. Why do we need to do that?"

"She won't expect it," said Cane. "That's why. Tico, you got to remember: Always do the unexpected, no matter how dangerous it is." Cane put his hand on Tico's shoulder. "I got some business, but you and Walker can take the house. It's small-time, but it's in her territory."

"We should wait awhile," said Tico. "Wait for them to move, then—"

"You the man now, Tico?" asked Cane. He turned to face Tico and moved closer to him. His bad eye blinked quickly.

"Come on, Cane, you know it ain't like that." Tico was scared but held his ground.

Cane turned back to the river. "Then we cool. You and Walker take that shitty-ass little house, while I deal with my new connection. Did you check out Jaleel yet? Is he stealing from me?"

Tico hesitated a moment. "Now don't go do no crazy shit, okay? Jaleel is skimming. The house is making money like never before, but he's holding back. Jaleel is hitting the pipe a lot and acting crazy. He even bought a gold collar for that little mutt-ass dog of his."

"Okay," said Cane calmly. "We hit the Girls again; then we deal with Mr. Jaleel."

"All right," said Tico. He was glad that Cane didn't get angry.

"I like it here," said Cane. "This is the best place to watch the sun go down, to watch Him leave."

Tico didn't respond. He hated when Cane got into this God and sunset shit. Cane was scary enough on the job, but this screwy philosophy of his was terrifying.

Three young men on ten-speeds rode up to them. Tico reached for his gun until he saw familiar faces. Cane glanced at them, then quickly climbed into his car. He never liked to talk with street rollers.

"Wha'sup, nigga?" a young man said to Tico.

"What you doin' down here, Nickel?" Tico said.

The young man got off his bike and went up to Tico. He was about nineteen. Two other men were on bikes also.

"We been rollin' here," said Nickel.

"Since when?" Tico looked shocked.

"Since the cops slammed the Girls, this place has been wide open. You said take some initial, remember?"

"That's *initiative*, dumb-ass, and I didn't mean invade the damn island with your crew!"

Tico glanced at his own car. He didn't want to get Cane involved in this. Cane would go on talking about visions and philosophical shit.

"Get the fuck outta here," Tico said. "Don't roll up in here until I say so."

"Yeah—" said Nickel. "I'm out."

Nickel was about to ride off when a bullet slammed into his chest. Nickel fell forward, his legs tangled in the big ten-speed. Tico pulled his gun and jumped behind his car's front end.

The other two rollers left their bikes and scattered, running in opposite directions. Several other people screamed and ran. Car engines started. Someone burned rubber.

The sun was almost down, and Tico could not see very well. He had no idea where the shots came from.

Cane had been sitting quietly in the car. Now he opened the door and stepped out.

"Cane, get the fu— Get down!" Tico yelled.

More shots were fired. Tico shot in the general direction he thought they came from. As bullets flew, Cane just stood there, looking into the twilight.

"There, over by those Dumpsters," Cane said, pointing.

"Crazy ass—" Tico pointed his gun in the direction Cane pointed and fired. Cane got back into the car on the driver's side.

Tico put another clip in his gun, cursing, then fired several shots and hopped in the passenger seat.

Cane started the car and sped off, away from the dead body of Nickel. Shots were fired at them as they drove. Cane knew that they had to get off the island now. The gunplay would be reported to the police, and they would search every car as it went off the Belle Isle bridge.

Cane pulled the car safely onto the island's bridge. Tico was sweating and looking at Cane angrily.

"You know what?" said Tico. "You are crazy."

23

The Lexington

Jesse avoided the media circus that surrounded St. Paul's Hospital, an old facility on Detroit's east side. He had allowed Ramona Blake to be placed in the building's security wing. He was on his way there to meet Ms. Blake.

Ramona had claimed indigence, so Karen had taken the case on judicial assignment. There wasn't much money in it, but it was still a high-profile case.

Jesse and Marcia Daniels, another black prosecutor, walked into the building through the rear entrance of the hospital. Workers loaded food and laundry on a platform while a fat guard half watched them. An officer had been assigned to let Jesse and Marcia in. The officer walked them into the lobby, and they headed for the elevator.

Marcia was a "book lawyer." She was competent in the court-room, but her real skill was in legal interpretation, an area where Jesse was deficient. Marcia had committed the evidence rules to memory. And as every lawyer knew, evidence was the real battle-ground of trying criminal cases.

"Damn reporters, they make my ass hurt," said Marcia as they stepped in an elevator car.

"Yeah," said Jesse. "This case is still hot, even though we don't have Louise Yancy."

"So, you think Ms. Bell will cop a plea for her client?"

"Karen Bell has never pleaded a client to my knowledge," said Jesse.

"I can believe it," said Marcia. "She's kicked my butt on several occasions, most recently an armed robbery last month."

"Well, this is my first time against her," Jesse said.

"She's never lost a murder case, you know."

"And neither have I," said Jesse defiantly.

"Oh, this is going to be *real* nasty," Marcia said. She laughed.

The two stepped off the elevator on the seventh floor. Jesse immediately noticed the cops guarding the wing. He and Marcia showed their IDs and were escorted into a room.

Inside, Ramona sat with Karen Bell and Ira Hoffman. Ramona was wearing a prison jumpsuit. Her braids hung over her shoulders. She had some bruising on her face, but Jesse was still awed by her beauty. She was even more striking than Karen.

"*That's* a murderer?" Marcia whispered to Jesse. "Looks like a goddamned fashion model."

Karen was talking with Ira and turned to face them. "Come on in, Jesse," said Karen.

The prosecutors walked over to a small table that had been set up in the room. Ramona looked suspiciously at Jesse as he approached. Her face was cold and angry.

"Good to see you again, Marcia," Karen said.

"Wish I could say the same," Marcia said. She and Karen laughed.

Jesse heard a muffled thumping sound. He looked toward a wall in the room. "What the hell was that?"

"Elevator," said Ira. "This hospital is very old. It used to be the Lexington Hotel back in the fifties. The old service elevators still run inside the walls here."

"Sounds like this place is falling apart," said Marcia.

"Man, the Lex used to be hot," said Ira wistfully. "Had a mean jazz band, Duke Brown and the Starlights. I used to come here after trials to celebrate. . . ." He trailed off. "Excuse me, I'm getting old. All I have are my memories." He laughed a little.

"Let's get down to business," said Jesse.

"I didn't do it," said Ramona.

"Ramona, please," said Karen.

"I don't like all this meeting shit," said Ramona. "I just wanna get out of this."

"It takes time," said Karen. "I thought we agreed to that, remember?"

"I didn't come all the way down here for this," said Jesse. "Do you want to deal or not?"

"No, we don't want a deal," said Karen.

"Then why are you wasting my time?" Jesse asked.

Karen sighed. "Actually I don't know." She looked at Ramona, who nodded in reply. "My client feels she's in danger."

"Only as far as the law is concerned," said Jesse, starting to get annoyed.

"It's more than that," said Ira Hoffman. "She feels that if she tells what she knows, she will be killed."

"Should I pull out my tape recorder for her statement?" Marcia said.

"My client hasn't told us what the story is yet," said Karen.

"Why not?" said Jesse. "It's all privileged."

"Apparently she doesn't trust us either," said Ira.

"Damn straight I don't," said Ramona. She rubbed a bruise on her cheek. Ramona stared at Jesse, searching his eyes. Jesse was confused but did not look away.

"And she wanted to meet you first, Jesse," said Karen. "I told her that I know you and we can trust you on this."

Jesse was surprised by what he saw in Karen's eyes. There was sincerity in them, but that was not what startled him. He saw fear.

"I'm flattered," he said. "But you're still wasting my time. We can place her at the scene. So unless she can give us a name—"

"It's not that simple," said Karen. "At least I don't think it is."

"Look," said Jesse, "if there's a story to tell, let's hear it. I'm sure our office will take the entire situation into consideration before it decides what action will be taken."

Karen turned to Ramona who kept staring at Jesse. Then she stopped and focused on Karen.

Jesse was embarrassed. He was excited by the sight of the two beautiful women so close together. He saw Ira looking nervous too.

"What do you say, Ramona?" asked Karen.

"I'm not talking to him," said Ramona. "He's full of shit."

"Ramona!" Karen said.

Ira Hoffman sighed heavily.

"That's it. I'm out," said Jesse, shooting Ramona a steely look. "I only did this out of respect for you two."

"She didn't mean that, Jesse," said Karen. "I apologize for her."

"Save it," said Marcia. "This is all the cooperation you'll get from us."

"I see the white man still likes his niggas loyal and dumb," said Ramona.

"Hey," said Jesse, "I didn't come here to take crap from a—" He caught himself. "Karen, Ira, from now on we meet only on official terms."

Jesse and Marcia walked out into the hallway. They heard Karen cursing behind them. They started back to the office.

"What the hell was that?" asked Marcia.

"I'm not sure," said Jesse. "But I know Karen pretty well—"

"So I've heard," Marcia said too quickly.

"Yes, everyone has," said Jesse. "I don't know what they're up to, but one thing's for sure, Karen was scared back in there."

"She did seem a little apprehensive," said Marcia.

"I think she knows something already," said Jesse. "And whatever it is, we should know it too. Let's call on Florence. She should have something by now."

Jesse left the old hospital a little worried about his ex-flame. Karen was a hard woman, and it would take a lot to frighten her.

"That girl was sizing you up, Jesse," said Marcia.

"I know. Apparently, she didn't like what she saw."

"I was thinking more like she hated you."

"A defendant hates me. So what else is new?"

The October wind had a chill in it as they stepped outside. Jesse got into his car and headed for Frank Murphy. Even with Louise Yancy out of the picture, he was still puzzled by the case. Ramona Blake was an idiot, but she didn't seem like a cold-blooded killer. If she knew anything about the murder, she was obviously not going to give it up. He reasoned that whatever she knew, she would have a lot of time to think about it after he put her ass in the penitentiary.

24

Things That Cities Do

"Opa!" yelled the waiter and the diners as the former put a lighter to the saganaki. The Greek kasseri cheese was set on fire, and the yellow flame shot into the air.

Florence was drinking heavily, scotch and soda, her favorite. Jesse sat with her in a booth at Pegasus, a restaurant in Greektown. The place was crowded for lunch. The smell of onions and lamb permeated the air. Jesse just stared at the sandwich he'd ordered, waiting for Florence to tell him what she'd uncovered.

"I need to get back to my case. What do you have for me?"

"Wait a fuckin' minute," said Florence. "Gimme a chance to unwind here. I had a hard coupla days."

"Sorry, it's just that the case was dropped in my lap by D'Estenne, the media is all over me, and the defendant told me to go fuck myself yesterday."

"Really?" said Florence. "I like her." She emptied her glass, signaled for another, then took a big breath. "Well, on the case, all the witnesses check out; they're mostly cops who knew the mayor was banging this chick. Her other trampy friends are probably gonna rat on her too. The defense ain't got nothing up her sleeve. Although I imagine you're interested in what's up her other garments."

"No need for that shit, Florence," said Jesse.

"You cursing? Man, you are stressed. Anyway, I checked out the crime scene," said Florence. "It was pretty tight, just like you said it was, nothing out of the ordinary. That Yancy bastard lived like a king. Nice place, even with the bloodstains. So all in all I think we got a good case on this babe. We can place her at the scene, and she's got a record."

"That's good to know," said Jesse. "So, did you ever find my lost cop Walter Nicks?"

"Nope. Man's gone. No one's seen him. I heard a rumor that he had a lady friend in Southfield, but it was a false lead. Don't know where he could be."

"Question is, *Why* is he gone?" said Jesse. "Okay, Florence, what about the other things I wanted checked out?"

Florence sighed and looked at the ceiling. Jesse stirred with interest. That always meant Florence was on to something big.

"Okay, Jesse," she said. "There's some funky-ass shit goin' on around here."

"Fill me in."

"Before I tell you, I want you to promise that you won't do any silly-ass cowboy shit like you did on that Patterson murder last year."

"Sorry, but I can't promise, Flo," Jesse said.

"Then I'm sorry too," said Florence. "And don't call me Flo. What am I, an old woman or some shit?"

"Look," said Jesse. "All I can promise is that I won't do anything without talking to you first."

"That's bullshit." Florence adjusted in her seat. "But I guess I'm feeling like a sucker today. All right, here's the deal, Yancy was formalizing a plan to bring casino gambling to Detroit—soon. He had the business people behind him, the minister do-gooders and suburbanites on the other side, but he was also dealing with some very bad people."

"Mafia?"

"Please," said Florence, taking her drink from a waiter. "Let's not insult our Italian brothers, but yes, that's what I hear. My sources tell me that Yancy took several clandestine meetings with men known to have those kinds of ties."

"Talli?"

"That was one of them. Also, Yancy supposedly met with that Reverend Junior from the MACs at least three times before he was killed," said Florence.

"He called him the night he died too," said Jesse. "Yancy was trying to get them to back off most likely."

"Yancy also saw that asswipe Crawford a few times. Apparently he was about to fire him."

"Yancy was always about to fire him," said Jesse. "What was Yancy's beef with Crawford this time?"

"Same shit, Crawford and his young assholes taking liberties, acting like they were in control. I got a spy over there in his office. I'll be gettin' more as time goes on." Florence took a deep drink.

"Well, I can't question Crawford, but I can talk with the good reverend again," said Jesse absently.

"And one more thing," said Florence. "Your man Yancy was going to back Xavier Peterson in the race for county prosecutor."

"He was?" Jesse was shocked. "Yancy always backed D'Estenne. I just assumed that he would again."

"Well, he changed his mind this year. Apparently he wanted a county prosecutor he could control with the casinos coming."

"Damn," said Jesse. "Xavier Peterson is a minister. If Yancy supported him, then it would have gotten the MACs off his ass too. So, did D'Estenne know about this?"

"I don't know. But I'd bet that he did."

Jesse looked off for a moment. Louise Yancy was right. There were many reasons to want a mayor out of the way. Mayor Yancy switching to Xavier Peterson was a brilliant political move, but it was also an out-and-out betrayal of D'Estenne.

"I think my office phone is bugged," said Jesse.

"No shit," said Florence. "Well, don't call me on that thing if it is. So, what are you gonna do about all this?"

"I'm going to try this case and win it," said Jesse. "The other stuff is interesting, but Ramona Blake is still the prime suspect. Maybe she knows who did it, or maybe she helped them do it."

"Don't make sense to me. She's fuckin' Yancy, so she pops him, for what?"

"There could be a lot of reasons; drugs, money, extortion, who knows? I guess I won't know until we get into this thing."

"Well, I gotta go, Jesse," said Florence. "You let me know if you need anything else and I'll keep you posted."

"All right, Florence."

After she left, Jesse finished his lunch, then returned to the office. He went back to work on the Yancy case. He stopped only once to plea-bargain a second-degree murder case down to manslaughter.

By the time he left work, he still had plenty to do. He was mulling over the case as he walked to the parking lot. It was dark and quiet. The evenings were getting colder. Winter was coming and soon.

Jesse had got to his car when he heard someone walking behind him. He turned and saw a woman coming his way, holding something in her clenched fist. Jesse tensed, straining to get a better look as the woman came closer. Finally he saw her, and it was Karen Bell, holding her car keys and still looking afraid.

"We need to talk," she said.

They went to Karen's house in Rosedale Park on the northwest side. Jesse had agreed to come along, thinking that Karen might try to seduce him and vowing not to be seduced. But she didn't try anything. She only said she needed to talk to him. Jesse was already formulating a story to tell Connie about where he had been.

Karen's house was spectacular. Immaculately decorated, a pool in the back. Apparently freeing scumbags paid well.

They stood at Karen's little bar while they talked. She was dressed in a dark green skirt and a light green blouse. Her hair was tousled and ran over her face.

"Karen, if you want to talk, I'm here. If not, I have to go."

"My client doesn't trust you," she said.

"I gathered that."

"She says you're a sellout, an Uncle Tom because you put black people in jail."

"Heard it all before," said Jesse. "But that's not what you called me here for, is it?"

"No," Karen said. She hesitated a moment before going on. "Jesse, I know we've had our bad times, but I know you're my friend. So I have no fear that you'll report me to the state bar for what I'm about to say."

"You know I won't do that," said Jesse.

"All right. Ramona Blake told me that Yancy was killed by two men who also tried to kill her—hit men, Jesse. Now, before you say what I know you're thinking, let me tell you that she has proof."

"Good, I'd love to see it," said Jesse.

"It's at your crime scene," said Karen. "I'll need you to get it."

Jesse stared at Karen. She was serious. "Okay, Karen. I can wait and see if this is real. But right now I want you to tell me why you're so scared."

Karen reached into her purse and pulled out a tiny silver object. "I found this in my office today."

Jesse took it and examined it. It was a small transistor of some type. "Jesus," he said. He was thinking about his office phone and the funny sound he'd heard. "It's a bug."

"Right. I'm not an FBI agent, but I know that's a fucking listening device. It was under the rim on my desk. I bumped into it, and it fell."

"It wasn't on the phone?" he asked.

"No. And something else. I swear someone was following me all day. I kept seeing these dark vans. When I went to see Ira, there was one parked by his office too."

"Are you sure about being followed?" asked Jesse, growing uneasy.

"No, but I wasn't taking any chances. I called Ira from my mobile and told him to meet me."

"So why are you telling me this?"

"Whatever else is going on, Jesse, Ramona Blake is innocent."

"Karen—"

"I know you can't do anything now, but I need your help. If Ramona is telling the truth, then this is big, and whoever did it is watching me—and you too." She grabbed Jesse's hand. "You're in the government. You can help me go to the cops and do something."

"Of course I'll help you, Karen," said Jesse, trying to take this all in. "I don't want that woman to go to prison for something she didn't do."

"There's one other thing," said Karen. "Ramona escaped the murder scene with a black metallic briefcase. She said when she went into the bathroom, the case wasn't there, but Yancy and the killer were fighting over it when she came out."

"What was in it?" asked Jesse.

"She doesn't know. She said it had no latch or seams or something like that. Whatever it is, it was worth murdering the mayor."

"Jesus." Jesse sighed. "So did she give it to you?"

"No, why would I—" Karen's face paled. Realization washed over her. "My God, they think I have it."

"It makes sense, Karen," said Jesse. "You're her attorney, and it's evidence."

"Shit, why didn't I think of that?" She slammed her fist on a table. "Damn, I'm stupid. I was so weirded out by that bug that I never thought of it. Fuck!"

Karen was a perfectionist. Another of her annoying qualities. She hated it whenever she didn't know everything. It made her feel weak, which was the only thing she hated more.

"Don't blame yourself," Jesse said. "Where's the case?"

"Ramona said she left it with some friends. I took it these friends were on the wrong side of the law."

Jesse had never seen Karen look so desperate. Behind all the bullshit she was a good friend, and she was right on the mark about that bug.

"Okay, what is this evidence at the murder scene?"

"It's a tape," said Karen. "Yancy used to audiotape their love-making. He was too afraid of video. He had a tape player hidden in the headboard of his bed."

"So the murder might all be on tape? That would certainly be exculpatory evidence," said Jesse.

"Yancy didn't think Ramona knew about it," said Karen, "but she did. So, unless somebody got to it, it's still there."

Jesse thought a moment. It was unlikely that Karen was leading him on. Either the tape was there or it wasn't. If Ramona Blake was innocent, then a lot of troubling things about the case made sense.

"Okay, let's go get it," said Jesse.

25

Wetwork

The dark blue van cruised along the freeway headed downtown. The big man was glad to be rid of his meddlesome partner for a while. He was getting tired of his partner's bitching about being hurt and getting back at Ramona Blake for cutting him. He was a weight, and this would be their last time working together.

He'd sent the injured man off into the neighborhoods to see if he could find out if Ramona's drug-dealing friends had the black case. It was a lead that he'd forgotten about, and at this point he could not leave any stone unturned.

He was upset that Louise Yancy was free, but they had lucked into another suspect for the murder. The Blake woman was in prison and had been moved to a security hospital. That was good. Security at the hospital was minimal, so it would be easier to get to her.

But Ramona was not his primary concern these days. It was her lawyer, Karen Bell, who interested him. Lawyers always get their clients' property, and if the lawyer had the black case, he was going to get it and close this worrisome matter forever.

Jesse King, the prosecutor, was seeing a lot of Karen Bell for some unknown reason. He could be fucking her, but it didn't seem likely. He'd been counting on King to force Ramona Blake's lawyers to move for the case. Jesse looked like he might be trouble. He was smart and obviously weak for that lady lawyer. He would bear watching.

His mobile phone rang. He picked it up and turned it on. He heard a series of clicks, then: "Status."

"Nothing else yet," said the big man.

There was a silence as the mobile line crackled. The big man held the little phone to his huge face, waiting for his employer to respond.

"I'm growing impatient."

"I know. Everything is under control."

"How can that be? I don't have my property."

"I'm on the case. That's all I can say right now."

"You'd better say a hellofa lot more than that, goddammit! I've put my life on the line for this. The girl is still alive. Double dead. That was the contract."

"Yes, but things went wrong."

"Understatement is really a talent of yours. I want the matter closed."

"It will be, but there might be more casualties along the way."

"I don't want any more killing! Just bring me the case. I don't care if you kill the Blake girl, but no one else, do you hear me? People will become suspicious if more deaths are recorded. We need to operate undercover. Things have to be discreet, like military wetwork."

"I got it."

"You don't sound like you got it. I want to hear you tell me."

The big man pulled the little phone from his face and cursed. He hated this treatment, but it was part of his job.

"No more killing," he said, but he knew it was a lie.

"Now get me that black case. The sooner you get it, the sooner you can get the rest of your fee and get out of my life."

There was more silence on the line as the big man cursed again under his breath.

Then his employer spoke again. "You fail, and you're dead, you know that, don't you?"

"Yes, I know."

The line went silent.

26

Last Words

The throng of media had gone. Only police surrounded Yancy's house now. The affluent neighbors were probably pissed about all the action. Rich folks like their privacy. The beautiful colonial was draped in yellow "Crime Scene" tape. The big, shadowy house looked haunted as the two lawyers approached it. Jesse was thinking that only weeks before, the killer had walked these same steps.

Two uniformed cops let Jesse and Karen into the house. It was dark inside. Jesse turned on lights and went upstairs.

The bedroom was still filled with evidence markers. The body outline was even still there. Jesse and Karen both were apprehensive. They'd been in the room before, but now it was different. They were looking for the first clue to a cover-up.

Jesse went to the ornately carved headboard. He noticed that in the middle there were several tiny holes, holes that didn't fit the carved pattern in the mahogany. He pulled out the bed and looked behind it. Karen peeked over his shoulder. He put on rubber gloves and felt the back of the headboard. He stuck one arm behind the big piece of wood.

"There's something here," he said.

Jesse struggled with the compartment he felt in the headboard. Karen looked on impatiently. She couldn't see behind the headboard, and it was driving her crazy.

"What's wrong?" she asked.

"There's a compartment, but it's stuck." Jesse continued to

struggle. He shifted his angle and put both hands behind the headboard.

"Want me to take a crack at it?" Karen asked.

"No . . . I got it," Jesse said as he pulled out a small microcassette player. "Holy shit," he said. "She was telling the truth."

The gravity of the moment fell upon him. He was about to open the door on the biggest scandal in the history of Detroit.

"Give it to me," said Karen.

"Wait," said Jesse. "This is evidence for the state's case."

"Jesse, I told you where it was, so it's mine."

"I don't believe you, Karen." Jesse waved the recorder, gesturing. "We are on the verge of something like this, and all you can think about is glory. You will never change." Jesse looked closer at the cassette. The life drained from his face. "Dammit. The tape is gone."

"What! Let me see. . . ." Karen looked at it. "Shit! They must have known it was there."

Jesse and Karen took a moment, cursing under their breaths. Karen sighed heavily.

"Why would they leave the recorder?" Jesse asked, almost to himself.

"I would," said Karen. "I'd put it back just in case anyone knew about it. That way they wouldn't suspect anything. The tape is all that matters."

"Is it possible that your client took the tape?" asked Jesse.

"Anything's possible, I guess. But why would she do it?"

"Maybe it incriminated her," said Jesse.

"I don't think she's that smart," said Karen. "I know it sounds elitist, but she's a very simple girl. And she's scared."

Jesse put the recorder into a Baggies. He'd have the cops dust the headboard for prints again, but he knew that it and the recorder were clean. If there was a conspiracy, these were not dumb people.

"Now what?" asked Karen.

"I guess we find that black case," said Jesse. "So, you gonna be okay tonight?"

"Yeah, I guess."

"Good, I'll call you tomorrow."

They walked out of the room, then the house. Jesse made sure to hide the recorder in his coat as they passed the patrolling cops.

★ ★ ★

Jesse dropped Karen off at her house, then headed home. Karen fought with him about the tape recorder and managed to talk Jesse into letting her have it after he ran it for fingerprints. Jesse did not put up a big fight about it.

Because he had the tape that had been inside it.

He'd removed it in his fake struggle behind the headboard. Karen had been so frazzled that she didn't notice when he put his other hand back there and removed it. Jesse had slipped the tape up his sleeve, then pocketed it when she looked at the empty recorder. He used to steal candy like that when he was a kid. Old habits die hard, he thought.

It was dishonest given the circumstances, but Jesse knew Karen. She would have broken the story to the press and covered herself in glory, making him look like a fool. If there was exculpatory evidence on the tape, he'd let her client go, but he was not about to hand her control of the case on a silver platter.

Jesse pulled the car into a Rally's parking lot. The place had about ten cars in it, and the drive-through was packed. The smell of burgers reminded him that he had not eaten dinner.

"First things first," Jesse said aloud. He rummaged through his briefcase in the car, took out his gun, a .38, and carefully placed it to one side of the case. Prosecutors were allowed to carry guns, and he wanted his close. If there was indeed a conspiracy, he was not going down easy.

Jesse removed his own microcassette recorder. He carefully removed the cassette from his pocket and put it in.

Jesse rewound the tape, then hit the button. Soon he heard the sound of a couple making love. A woman singing. The voices rose as orgasm was achieved. There was silence, then: *"I can feel your heart,"* a woman said on the tape.

"The whole state can hear that bum ticker going," said a man.

"Yancy," Jesse whispered. It was sad and eerie hearing his voice.

There was more talk, then: *"You taking a shower, Ramona?"* Yancy said.

"Bingo," Jesse said. Now he knew that Ramona Blake had been at the murder scene.

Just then a van pulled next to Jesse. Swiftly he turned off the tape. The door of the van opened, and a family came out. The father and mother were arguing loudly, their kids following behind them in silence. Jesse started the car and drove into a far corner of the parking lot before turning the tape back on.

Jesse heard more noises, a door closing, then a very loud rattling and banging. The noises stopped, and the tape went silent. He kept listening, but the rest of the tape was blank.

"Damn," Jesse said.

But at least Ramona Blake was telling the truth about the tape. The fact that it was there meant that she wasn't lying, he thought.

"Unless she was the one who turned it off," he said out loud.

At trial the tape would be great evidence, provocative and sexy, but ultimately it was inconclusive. All it did was put Ramona Blake at the scene, and they already knew that. Jesse would argue that Ramona Blake could have easily turned off the tape, then killed Yancy. Karen would argue that the killers turned off the tape.

All he really knew now was that he was in extra-deep shit with Karen. If he told her about the tape, she would swear that he'd erased the part that proved her client innocent. If he hid the tape, he'd be guilty of nondisclosure. Either way he was screwed.

Jesse pondered this for a moment. Then he decided that Karen would just have to believe him. He was putting his neck out for her, so she damned well better trust him on this one.

Jesse forgot about his hunger and started the car. He pulled onto the street and headed for home. The existence of the tape might not prove Ramona Blake's innocence, but it didn't prove her guilt either. He was back where he started, with a weak case and his gut telling him something was terribly wrong.

Jesse pulled up to a traffic light and stopped. He put the tape in his briefcase, then took the .38 and placed it under the armrest.

27

Encroachment

Tico didn't mind killing the people in the house. It was taking it over and trying to run it that scared him. Cane was off checking out some new supplier from the East Coast. But before he left, he'd finalized their plan to start a takeover of the Nasty Girls' territory. The house in question was just across Woodward close to the Davison Freeway. It had only been doing business for a month or so. They were small-time, but taking a house in their territory was symbolic, or so Cane thought. Tico might have been able to talk him out of it until LoLo's women hit them at Belle Isle. Now it was in Cane's blood to get them back.

Tico and Walker sat in a car at the corner from the house. Two other men were positioned behind the house. It was dark, and that cover would serve them well.

Cane had been specific that no one was to be killed. He rambled on about its being more scary now not to kill after what he had done to that girl's face. But Tico was sure it could not be done that way. A dealer never wanted to go out like a punk. And even though the house had only one armed guard, that was enough to make bullets fly.

Their plan was simple. The house had a guard, who stood out in front. The other rollers would enter from the back and take the house. Then they would pop the guard.

Hitting the house made some sense, but Cane wanted them to take it over and run it after they did. The Girls would come down on them hard. Cane had even said that he'd come there himself to work. He was not one to shy away from danger.

"Let's get this thing done," said Walker. His Jamaican accent was thick with his excitement. He cradled a big Colt .38 Python in his lap. "I'm gonna hit a reggae club tonight."

"Reggae," said Tico with disdain. "I hate that shit. It all sounds the same."

Walker shot Tico a nasty look. "I'm gonna take you to Jamaica one day," said Walker, "and you will sing a different tune."

The men sat in silence for a while. They kept watching the house and the guard posted outside it.

"Cane must be crazy making us do this," said Tico.

"Too late for complainin' now," Walker said. He looked out of the window. "And Mr. Cane hasn't put us on the wrong track yet."

"I don't like this shit," said Tico. "These bitches are not to be taken lightly. They kill just like we do. I gotta talk to his ass about this."

"Talk after we get this thing done," said Walker.

"You gonna back me up?" asked Tico. "You know how Cane can be."

"Against Cane?" Walker asked, laughing. "He is your boy. You know how he is. You can fight that one alone, my friend."

"Sorry-ass nigga," said Tico. Suddenly he saw a light flash from a window in the house. "The shit is on," he said.

Tico and Walker drove up to the house. They heard several shots from inside. The guard pulled her gun. Walker shot at her but missed. To their surprise the girl ran away.

Tico and Walker ran into the house, guns out in front of them. When they got inside, they saw their men, dead on the floor. There were about ten women rollers, with guns pointed at Tico and Walker.

Tico lifted his gun, only to feel Walker's .38 at his temple.

"No future in workin' for a crazy man." Walker took Tico's gun away from him.

Tico took a swing at Walker and missed, as the latter sidestepped the punch. Walker hit Tico hard in the stomach. He doubled over from the blow.

"That's for dissin' Jamaica, you little bitch," Walker said. He moved over to the women, and Marly stepped out to meet him. She was wearing a low-cut top, and her ample chest bulged out of it. Walker kissed her hard on the lips.

"You dead, Walker, you hear me!" Tico yelled.

LoLo stepped from the crowd. Yolanda followed, carrying a gun. They looked strange together, the big woman and her short, mean-looking boss.

"This just ain't your night, my brotha," LoLo said.

"Go on," Tico said. "Do what you gotta do."

"Sorry, but killing's over for tonight," said LoLo.

Yolanda stepped forward and hit Tico in the ribs. He fell to one knee, grunting loudly. The second punch to his head dropped him cold.

28

Messages

Jesse returned home, feeling less nervous about the tape inside his briefcase. He considered waking up D'Estenne at home and bringing him the tape. But if he did, that would be the last he saw of that tape. D'Estenne would take it and hold a big press conference announcing that he'd solved the case. D'Estenne wanted to win reelection so badly that he'd screw anyone at this point.

No, he needed to wait awhile. First he had to make a copy of the tape, then log it into evidence under his name to have a record. After that he could give it to his superiors.

Jesse parked and walked into the lobby of his building. After the night's activities he was ready for a hot shower and bed.

As he entered the lobby, he noticed a big man in a dark coat and a black fedora standing next to the guard in the lobby. The big man was black, hard-looking, like he was fresh from beating someone down. Jesse knew that look, a cop look. The big man's gaze locked on Jesse. He slowed down as he walked up to him.

"Jesse King?" asked the big man.

"Yeah, that's me," said Jesse.

"I'm from the police. I need to talk with you."

"Really? Well, let me see some ID first," said Jesse.

"He wanted to go in your apartment, Mr. King," said the guard named Renaldo. "But after that thing with your sister, I said no."

"Shut the fuck up and earn your minimum-ass wage," said the big man. He shoved a badge in Jesse's face.

"Nicks? Walter Nicks?" asked Jesse.

"Right," said Nicks.

"I've been looking for you," said Jesse. He walked to the elevator. "Come on."

The two men got into the elevator. They said nothing as the car rose. Nicks had been Yancy's personal bodyguard and had a reputation for being unstable. Nicks had also disappeared when the investigation started. A lot of the missing pieces resided in his head, Jesse thought, and now all of a sudden here he was. Something was not right, and Jesse did not feel safe around the cop.

The elevator stopped, and they got out and went into Jesse's apartment.

"I need to talk to you about the mayor's death," said Jesse.

Nicks pulled out a big .44. "We need to talk, all right," he said.

Jesse was shocked but stayed calm. He met Nicks's stare and held it. "Okay. But put that thing away first or I'm not telling you anything."

Nicks kept his stare and the big gun on Jesse. Jesse looked back into his eyes, not looking at the gun. He knew the classic cop intimidation. Most people were afraid of guns and violence. They lost their composure, thinking only of safety. If he broke, Nicks would have an advantage. It was times like this that he was glad that he was from the wrong side of town.

Finally Nicks slowly lowered his gun. Jesse put his briefcase on the floor and walked away from it.

"Got balls for a lawyer," said Nicks. He seemed a bit distracted now as he put the gun away.

"Wanna tell me what this is all about?" asked Jesse.

"I wanna talk with that woman you're holding for the murder," Nicks said. "Get me to her."

"I'm not gonna do that unless you tell me what you want."

"Why isn't she in the county lockup?" asked Nicks.

"Did you look for her there? How'd you get in?" Jesse asked. Nicks didn't respond. "Look, you ain't getting anything out of me unless you tell me what's going on here. So get to talking or get out of my house. I'm tired."

Nicks took this in, then said, "That bitch you're holding can't know anything, or she'd be dead by now." He walked to Jesse's little bar. He reached for a bottle, then changed his mind.

"You were there that night, weren't you?" asked Jesse.

"I was there, but not when it happened. If I had been"—Nicks paused a moment, and Jesse heard the faintest trace of regret in his voice—"the mayor would still be alive."

"So you don't believe Ramona Blake killed him?" Jesse intended to cross-examine Nicks and get as much out of him as he could.

"She was just a piece of ass," said Nicks. "The mayor liked his whores young, pretty, and stupid. I checked her out before Yancy took up with her. She was small-time, sold drugs for a while, then got into fucking rich guys. But she never did anything like this."

Nicks was not telling him anything he didn't already know. Jesse thought about sharing what he knew with Nicks, but this was a man who definitely could not be trusted.

"I'd like to help you," said Jesse. "But I'll need you to tell me everything you know. What happened that night?"

Nicks chuckled. "Fuckin' lawyers. You think you got power." He pulled back his coat, showing his guns. Two .44s were nestled under his arms. "All your legal papers and talk don't mean shit. This here is the only thing that counts in Detroit."

Jesse wasn't impressed. He kept up his line of questioning. "Why have you been avoiding the prosecutor's office?" he asked. "If you're so bad, why have you been running?"

"I've been *chasing*," said Nicks. "Big difference. And when I find what I'm looking for, a whole lot of people are gonna be fucked, big time."

Jesse took a second, then decided to do some intimidating of his own. It was risky, but men like Nicks could not be coddled. Jesse moved closer to Nicks; his face was hard, angry. "Why the fuck didn't your men get the assignment that night?"

Nicks's face darkened. He turned to Jesse, and for a second Jesse thought Nicks would hit him. "Fuck if I know," said Nicks. "They should have been there. I left the assignments in the security office at Manoogian like always, but they never got it. Broadhurst and Reed were supposed to be there."

"Well, they never got the goddamned assignment," said Jesse. "And they were accounted for at the time of the murder."

"I know, I talked to them," said Nicks. "They were scared, said they just didn't get the assignment, and I believe them. My men are incorruptible. I guess maybe I fucked it up somehow."

"Why do you want to see Ramona Blake?" asked Jesse.

"I'm looking for something," said Nicks, "something I got from another damned lawyer and gave to the mayor that night."

"You're only making matters worse by withholding information," Jesse said. He wasn't about to tell Nicks that he knew anything about that black briefcase.

Nicks just looked at him with contempt. "Stay outta my way. And don't try to have me picked up, or I'll come back for you."

"Do you know who killed the mayor?" Jesse asked.

Nicks opened the door and walked into the hallway. "No, but I will," he said. Nicks walked quickly down the hall and jabbed the button for the elevator.

Jesse closed the door. Nicks was on the trail just like him. He was a nut, but Jesse didn't think he had killed the mayor.

Jesse took the precious tape out of his briefcase and put it in his nightstand. He was going to sleep with it close by.

He started to undress and caught sight of his answering machine. Seven messages. He thought about listening to them tomorrow, but he was never one to wait on information.

The machine's mechanical voice started: *"You have seven new messages. Message one."*

"Jesse . . . Damn, I hate machines. This is Marcia at the office. I need to talk to you tomorrow about our preliminary witness list. I'll be in at eight."

"Message two."

"Hey, Uncle Jesse. This is Nikko. Just callin' to say whassup. We all cool here at home. Talk to you later. Peace."

"Message three."

"Jesse . . . this is your fiancée. Where the hell are you? You stood me up! Did you forget?"

"Jesus, I'm getting married," said Jesse.

"Message four."

There was silence; then someone hung up the phone.

"Message five."

"Jesse. Ellis. How's the case going? Look, Penny wants to do the dinner thing. Some partners from the firm will be there, so this is your big chance. Call me, okay? Talk to you later."

"Message six."

"Jesse, this is Connie again. Call me as soon as you get in. We need to talk."

"Message seven."

"Jesse, Karen. Don't get too excited, but I think I found that item we were looking for. Listen, I think we should go get it tonight. If you're not here in the next hour, I'm going to get it alone."

"No more messages," the machine's mechanical voice said.

Jesse played Karen's message again. She'd found the black briefcase. But she never said those exact words. Knowing Karen, he'd show up at her place, and she'd be there in a negligee or naked. He hated to admit it, but the thought of that wasn't all bad. Still, Karen had been right about the tape.

Jesse took the tape out of the nightstand, got his gun, then left.

He left the building again and went to his car in the garage. On the way he checked his rearview mirror every so often. Karen's story about being followed and meeting Nicks had made him paranoid.

Jesse rolled down Jefferson. It was cold out, and people were dressed in their winter coats. Soon it would be winter, then spring, then marriage to Connie. He confessed that part of the reason he was going to see Karen was to avoid having to talk to Connie tonight. He'd completely forgotten about their appointment. He was going to have to make it up to her somehow. He drove his car onto the Lodge Freeway and headed uptown. In a few minutes he was pulling in front of Karen's house.

Jesse walked up to the house. The lights were on inside. He pushed the doorbell and heard the soft music sound inside. No one came. He tried the doorbell again. Nothing.

"Shit," he said. She was playing games again.

He knocked on the door and found it open. In the moment he stepped inside, it struck him that he should have taken out his gun first.

Jesse was grabbed by a shadow and yanked inside the house. He fell to the ground, and the shadow smashed him hard in the face. Jesse swung at the dark air and connected with something. A man's voice groaned. Jesse struck out again and again but hit only the air. Then he felt another pair of hands on him. The new hands held him, and the first attacker struck him hard in the side. He fell to his knees. Before he could recover, something hard hit him on the side of the head, and Jesse fell on his face. He was vaguely aware of the men above him as the darkness crowded his murky vision and descended.

★ ★ ★

Jesse's head pounded as he opened his eyes.

"Holy shit," he said. He rubbed his temples, but it only made the pain worse.

He struggled shakily to his knees. A draft blew across him, and he realized that he was wet. He looked down at himself and saw he was naked and streaked with sticky, dried blood. A wave of panic overtook him. He ran his hands over his body, looking for wounds. All he felt was a big knot on the side of his head. The bleeding had stopped, but it still hurt like hell.

Jesse looked around at the ransacked bedroom and realized that he was no longer in Karen's living room. Where was he? Whose blood—?

Jesse looked at the bed in the middle of the room and saw his answer. Lying in the bed, naked and bloody, was Karen Bell.

"Oh, my God . . . oh, no . . . no . . ." He was almost yelling. His head throbbed, and he fought the intense pain. He went to Karen's body. She'd been beaten and stabbed. Her beautiful face was streaked with blood, her mouth clenched in pain, and her eyes were still wide open.

Terror coursed through Jesse. He had seen death before but never like this. This was worse than anything he'd ever seen. She'd been slaughtered.

He ran into the bathroom and put a cold rag on the back of his head. Then he jumped into the shower and scrubbed himself so hard that it hurt. Jesse quickly analyzed his legal case:

One: He was being framed for murdering Karen.

Two: He was in the victim's house.

Three: There was physical evidence, blood, DNA, fibers, and probably fingerprints in the house.

Four: He and Karen had been seen together by cops earlier that night at the murder scene. And there was a message on his machine at home from the victim.

Five: They had also had a prior sexual relationship, and it had ended badly.

Six: He was fucked.

He quickly got out of the shower and looked for something to wear. He was terrified as he scrambled around the room. Being arrested and put through the system was his personal nightmare. He'd been through it before as a kid. But now he had so much more to lose. He felt he was an interloper, granted a brief passage in the middle class, and could be sent back to hell at any time. And this was it: He was set up for murder. His life was over.

Karen must have been forced to call him before she was killed. Or had she really known where the black briefcase was?

But why did they do this? he wondered. Why not kill him too? It was because they need someone to take the rap, he surmised. They were smart. Just like when they killed Yancy, they needed his wife to take the blame. Otherwise there might be embarrassing questions.

Jesse found his clothes. They were partially covered by blood but didn't look too bad. He searched for the tape, but it was gone. He cursed.

Jesse gathered his wits, then left the nightmarish room, trying not to track blood on his shoes.

If the men were as smart as he thought, they had already called the cops as part of the setup. It was about ten when he was knocked out. Karen's clock showed ten-twenty. He had to move.

Jesse walked down the stairs into the living room. He stopped. If he left now, no one would ever believe him. Then again, no one believed a black man in this situation. When he prosecuted cases, he sure didn't. He could not bring himself to stay and face the system.

Jesse stared out the front door, then thought better of it. He sneaked out the back door. He tried to look casual as he walked around to the front of the house, got in his car, and drove away.

29

Heart of the City

Ramona was feeling better. The hospital was a hole, but it was better than jail. She'd actually had a decent meal tonight. She watched television from her bed. It was late, but she couldn't sleep. She was worried about Karen. She hadn't called about the tape yet, and Karen was a very reliable person.

The guards kept her up too. They were always bothering her, flirting, trying for a quickie between shifts. Ramona actually didn't mind that so much. The guards were sleazy creeps, but it was nice to know she still had it.

The wall thumped again. Those damned elevators were too noisy. This old place never stopped making noise. She turned off the TV and lay down.

She'd been in deep shit before, but this was the worst yet. They had her for killing the city's father, and there was no way they'd ever let her go. Jail. Ramona had never been to a real prison. She'd been in lockups, detention, holding cells, and, of course, county, but a penitentiary: That scared her. She knew quite a few people, mostly men, who'd been to the penitentiary. Prison was hell no matter who told her the story. Violent inmates, sadistic guards, perverted sex, and hopelessness.

LoLo and her friends couldn't help either. She'd seen the war starting between LoLo and Cane on the news. The shooting at Belle Isle was just the beginning. But even if LoLo wasn't occupied, what could she do? Nothing.

Ramona sighed. Maybe she'd call Karen and tell her to cut a deal. Maybe if she got a lesser charge and did a few years . . .

"No, no, fuck, no!" Ramona said out loud.

She couldn't do time. She was young, beautiful. She didn't belong in jail. She wasn't a common criminal. She was meant to be on the arm of a rich, powerful man, spending his money and having a good life. She had to think of something. There had to be some way out of this mess.

There was a knock at the door. Ramona put on her robe and went to it. She looked at the clock. It was almost twelve. These damned guards needed to be cursed out. She didn't mind their trying to get some, but they could at least do it at a decent hour.

"Who is it?" she asked.

"Someone to see you," said a guard.

"I don't wanna see nobody."

"It's me, Ms. Blake," said a man.

Ramona recognized the voice but couldn't remember who it belonged to. She opened the door and frowned as she saw Jesse King, standing in front of a policeman with a skullcap on his head. Jesse said something to the officer, then closed the door behind him.

"What do you want?" Ramona said, going back to the bed. "Hey, can you be here without my lawyer?"

"No. It's illegal for me to be here," said Jesse. "I told the guard I came here to trick a confession out of you. That's illegal too. And it's also illegal for me to help you escape, but that's what I'm gonna do." Jesse looked tired and serious.

"What the hell are you talking about?" asked Ramona.

"You and I have to get out of here tonight, or we'll both be dead."

"Is this some kind of cop trick? I try to escape, you all shoot me?"

"I wish it were," said Jesse. "I'm serious." He pulled off the hat and showed her the bruises on his head. "They came after me tonight, the same men who killed the mayor. We don't have a lot of time. I told the cop outside that I wanted you put in a room down the hall because we're bringing a dangerous prisoner in tomorrow."

"Sorry, but I don't trust you," said Ramona. "You work for the enemy. You been bought, my brotha. Unh-unh." She walked back to the bed.

"I have the tape," Jesse lied.

Ramona stopped. She turned and walked back to him. "You found it?" she asked.

"That's what I said."

"Then why do I need to escape? I'll just stay here and—"

"Karen's dead. They killed her," said Jesse.

Ramona showed shock and sadness. "Dead? I just talked to her this morning."

"I'm sorry," said Jesse. "She was my friend too. They tried to kill me, but . . . they failed. They've set me up as Karen's killer. I don't think right now either of us can trust anybody."

Jesse decided not to tell Ramona everything until she agreed to come with him. It was a tough decision to take her with him. For all he knew, she had killed Yancy. But if she was right about the tape, then the infamous black briefcase existed too, and she was the only one who could get it. And that was the only thing that could exonerate him now, he hoped.

"Okay then, where's the tape?" asked Ramona.

"You have to come with me if you want it," said Jesse.

"I see. So you're gonna blackmail me." She was angry.

"Let's just say I need the case first."

Ramona sat down on the bed as if the weight of the world were on her. Jesse knew that feeling. He didn't envy her.

"Okay, I'll go with you," said Ramona. "But how are we gonna get out?"

"Let me worry about that," said Jesse. "You just go into the new room and wait for me."

"But they got cops all over this place."

"I know. It won't be easy, but the one thing we need to do is get started. Time is not on our side."

Jesse and an officer took Ramona down to the other end of the hall and put her in the room. Jesse talked to the officer for a moment. They shared a laugh; then he left.

Ramona sat on the bed in the new room and waited. She'd packed her bag full of everything that she could. Clothes, makeup, and the little money Karen had given her. She was ready to go.

This Jesse guy was fucking with her, she thought. He was not going to give her that tape until she did what he wanted. Well, after they got out of this place, she'd get the tape, and then he could kiss her black ass. He was right about one thing, though. If the killers were after him, they would find him. They'd almost gotten her twice. Suddenly she felt better about the idea of escaping.

Soon Ramona heard the familiar sound of the elevator thumping in the wall. It was then she realized that the two rooms she'd been in were at opposite ends of the hall. The elevator shafts ran next to the end rooms. The thumping stopped. Then it started again, then stopped, started, then stopped. He was in there, she thought. Jesse was in the elevator, playing with it. Then she heard other noises. Ramona turned on the TV and turned up the sound.

After a few minutes the wall facing the elevator began to crumble at the base. A small hole appeared in the wall and began to expand. Soon the hole was about the size of a baseball. Jesse's hand began to carefully pull away the thin plaster and old wood, dropping the waste inside the wall.

"I'll be damned," Ramona said.

"Get something to hide the hole," Jesse said. Ramona picked up a tall wastebasket and placed it by the wall. The wastebasket was tall and extra wide. The hospital's name was printed on it in blue.

When the hole was big enough, Ramona grabbed her bag, ready to crawl through. She pushed the bag inside the opening, then struggled to get her body in. Jesse had to pull her. She started to go in, but it was hard.

"The hole isn't big enough," she muttered. Her braids swung back and forth in her face.

"If I make it any bigger, they'll see it, and we need the time it will take for them to look for you inside the hospital."

"Shit," Ramona said. She struggled, inching farther inside.

There was a knock at the door in the room.

"You asleep, beautiful?" said a guard's voice from outside.

Ramona and Jesse panicked. Jesse began to push her back through.

"I'm not supposed to come in, but if you ask me, I can," said the guard.

Jesse pushed harder, and plaster crumbled around Ramona's torso.

"Not so hard, it hurts," Ramona said.

"Get in the bed, and don't forget to put something over this hole," Jesse said.

Ramona wiggled out of the hole and put the tall wastebasket

against the wall to cover the hole. She got into the bed and pulled the covers up to her neck. She lay there for a few minutes; then the guard pushed the door open and peeked inside. He walked in and looked at Ramona asleep in the bed.

"Damn, what a waste," he said. He touched her breast lightly, and Ramona grunted and turned over in bed, away from him. The guard stepped back, afraid. He took a step to her, then backed off. He turned off the TV and left.

After a few minutes Ramona got out of the bed and went back to the hole in the wall and got inside.

"What happened?" Jesse asked.

"Fuckin' pervert felt me up," Ramona said.

She crouched down, determined to get in the hole. She threw her little bag inside and squeezed in on the first try. Jesse held her up and helped her get her footing on the elevator car's roof. He had left the car just under their floor so that he could access the wall near its base.

"Okay," he said. "Pull that basket against the wall; then drop through that door on the roof of the elevator. We'll go out the basement through the alley. There's only a few people working tonight."

Ramona pulled the big wastebasket over the hole, then got into the elevator with Jesse. The elevator lurched as Jesse lowered it toward the basement, thumping all the way down. From there they easily made their way out to Jesse's car.

Jesse sat in the car and took a moment to settle down. Just a few hours ago he had been a lawyer with a bright future. Now he was a criminal who'd committed at least four felonies in the last two hours. This was his last logical chance to turn himself in and hope someone would believe him.

"What are you waiting for? Let's get the fuck outta here," said Ramona.

"After this point there's no turning back. I'm just making sure I know what I'm doing."

"Wasting time is what you're doing. I'm not goin' back in there no matter what you say. So drive, or I'll get out right now."

Jesse put the car in gear and glided past the police cruisers parked around the hospital. He drove away from the hospital and got onto the freeway.

"I know a place for us to stay out in Eastpointe," said Jesse.

"Fuck that," said Ramona. "We'll stick out in whitey land.

Eastpointe," she said with contempt. "That city used to be called East Detroit, until those racist-ass white people changed it."

"You have any ideas?" said Jesse, glaring at her.

"Yeah. We need to go where the cops never go. Just follow my directions," said Ramona.

Jesse turned onto a freeway headed east. He knew then where he was going. He was going to the one place he'd thought he'd never go again, the place the police would have the most trouble finding them, the heart of the city.

PART TWO

FUGITIVE

1

On the Run

They were mesmerized by the little television in the dim motel room. The TV was cheap, old, and bolted securely to a chest of drawers. They'd gotten to the Groundling Motel on the east side late in the night. Jesse was sure that the clerk, who appeared to be drinking, hadn't noticed them. Just another couple headed for a quickie.

Overnight the murder of Karen Bell and their escape had been discovered. It was now the media event of the year. Their faces were plastered on the front page of every newspaper and local TV news show. It was a nightmare for Jesse. This had been his fear since the day he stepped out of the ghetto. He was a criminal again, a nigger, whose long journey had come to a predictable end.

Jesse went cold as his picture flashed across the screen. "Jesus," he said, "we won't be able to go anywhere if this keeps up."

"At least your picture looks good," said Ramona sourly. "That mug shot of me is not happening at all."

Jesse looked at her with disdain. Here she was, in a life-and-death situation, and she was worried about how she looked on the damned tube.

In the hours since their escape Jesse had sized her up. Ramona was nothing more than a cheap little criminal just like that cop Nicks had said. But she was street-savvy, and it had come in handy.

She had suggested that they switch license plates on Jesse's car. He agreed and watched with amazement as Ramona easily stole the plates from another car and switched them.

Jesse had no faith in the woman, but she was the only one who knew where that black briefcase was. At least she was not hard on the eyes, he thought. Even tired and disheveled, she was beautiful. Under ordinary circumstances he would have been thinking really nasty thoughts, but that sort of thing was low on his list of priorities.

He'd seen her type before, a rough neighborhood girl blessed with good looks. They were like angels until they opened their mouths; then they turned into typical undesirables. Ramona's every mannerism bespoke her history in the ghetto. Jesse actually envied her that. He was uncomfortable with his history. Since he'd become a professional, his past followed him like a specter.

It took the cops an hour to discover their escape route. Carol Salinsky, a local reporter, had called the escape "brilliant" and "dynamic." Lucky was what it was, Jesse thought.

Ira Hoffman had given a teary interview stopping up just short of calling Jesse the devil. Ira had no doubt that Jesse was guilty and had posted a reward. In closing, he had appealed to Jesse and Ramona to turn themselves in.

Salinsky also recounted Jesse's affair with Karen Bell in detail, even interviewing Karen's ex-husband, who cried as if he were still married to her.

Jesse became suddenly sad. He'd been so worried about getting caught and going to prison that he had not mourned for Karen. She'd had everything to live for, and someone had snuffed out her precious light. He felt grief for her family and himself. He made a promise that he would find whoever was responsible for her death and lock them away forever.

Jesse was pulled from these thoughts as he saw Ellis's face on TV.

"We're here with Ellis Holmes, a prominent attorney and one of Jesse King's best friends," said Carol Salinsky. *"Mr. Holmes, did you have any idea that Jesse King was capable of this kind of act?"*

"Nothing's been proven," said Ellis. He looked upset as the cameras closed in on him. *"Jesse was a good lawyer and friend. Let's not be so quick to judge him until all the facts are in."*

"This must be a double shock to you after the suicide death of Louis Franklin," said Salinsky.

"Yes," said Ellis. He looked even more upset, almost sad. *"Louis was . . . a good man. Excuse me."*

As Ellis walked away from the cameras, Jesse smiled a little. At least someone was standing by him.

"That was Ellis Holmes, Jesse King's best friend," said Salinsky. *"He is reeling from the King-Blake murder and escape as well as the suicide of his law firm's only African American partner, Louis Franklin, who hung himself in the basement of his home."*

"Harris Yancy called Louis Franklin the night he died!" said Jesse to Ramona. She didn't respond.

". . . and earlier today," said Salinsky, *"King's fiancée, Connie Givens, had this to say."* After a moment Connie's face appeared on TV.

"I know he didn't do this," she said. Several microphones were in her face. *"And that's all I have to say."* She went into an office building saying *"No comment"* to the mob of reporters.

"Jesse King's embattled fiancée," said Salinsky. *"She maintains her belief in his innocence, but from where I stand, I'd say the wedding's off."*

The report ended, and Jesse turned down the TV.

"Figures," Ramona said with a trace of contempt.

"What?" asked Jesse.

"You being engaged to a white woman. You brothers all get a little money and you lose your damn mind."

"Connie is not white," Jesse snapped. "She's black."

"Black?" said Ramona. "Damn, the color must be really fucked up on this TV." She laughed, then waited a moment before asking, "So, did you kill Karen?"

"No," said Jesse harshly. He held back the anger he felt at her for even asking the question. "Did *you* kill Yancy?"

"You know I didn't," said Ramona. "You heard the tape."

Jesse felt trapped for a second. He forgot that he was hiding what he knew about the tape. "Yeah. Sorry," he said.

"I only asked," said Ramona. "Because a girl likes to know what kind of man she's hanging out with. You know, is he sensitive, funny, or a cold-blooded killer?"

"I don't appreciate your humor," said Jesse. "These people, whoever they are, are not joking. They're smart, ruthless, and they will kill us to get what they want."

"So, did Karen tell you my story?"

"Yes, she told me most of it."

"Then I'd like to hear what you know," Ramona said.

Jesse told her everything he knew.

"Shit," she said. "The men who attacked you sound like the same ones who tried to kill me." Ramona suddenly laughed. She had one of those faces that made you happy when they smiled. It caught Jesse off guard, and he smiled a little.

"Now what's so funny?"

"I beat those men, but they kicked your ass. I guess that means I can whip you."

"I wouldn't test that theory if I were you," said Jesse. "Besides, they ambushed me," he added a little defensively.

"So, where's the tape?" asked Ramona.

Jesse took a moment. The tape was gone, and he needed her to exonerate himself. But if he told her he didn't have the tape, she'd fly, and then he'd be in really deep shit.

"Before I give it to you," he said, "I need to find the black briefcase."

"A friend of mine has it," she said. "If I lead you to it, I want that tape."

"Deal," said Jesse. "Who is your friend?"

"Never mind, but I'll tell you right now. She's a dealer."

"Okay," said Jesse. "I just hope it's not one I put away."

"For your sake, I hope not too," said Ramona. "So, what's in that black briefcase?"

Jesse turned off the TV. "I don't think you wanna know that." He was putting on an act, but he had to keep her believing that he knew something about all this that she didn't.

They decided to leave the Groundling. It wasn't safe to stay in one place too long. Jesse cut his hair down low with scissors and his electric razor and pulled the skullcap he'd worn over his head.

For her disguise Ramona wrapped her braids around her head and pulled a cap over them. It didn't fit, so she cut the sides of the cap until it did. Then she put on a lot of makeup.

They went into the parking lot. There were six cars there. Edging open the cheap door, they both jumped in horror when they heard the short blast of a siren. They moved back behind the door into the motel room, until they saw an ambulance roll by. They breathed easier.

"Man, that scared me," said Ramona. "Okay, we can't take any more chances in your car," she said to Jesse. "After a day the cops will stop any car that looks like yours."

"You're right," said Jesse. "Okay, how about that Lincoln?"

"You crazy?" asked Ramona. "The cops always look for new cars first," she said. "And he probably has a Lojack on that bad boy. I think we need that one." She pointed at a dark green Ford.

"That piece of crap?" said Jesse. "It might not make it out of this parking lot."

"But the owner won't care if we take it," said Ramona. "And neither will the police."

They walked over to the car and found it open. It was littered with beer cans and cigarette butts. And the steering column was busted. Wires hung from it.

"Damn, someone already stole this car!" said Ramona.

"Only in Detroit," said Jesse. "Okay, this makes our job easier. I have to get rid of my car. You follow me, and after I ditch it, we go together."

Ramona got into the car, rubbed two wires together, and started it up. Jesse jumped in his car and drove away. He pulled the car onto a side street and left it. The police would find the car soon. The kids who would inevitably steal it would be questioned. That would buy them some precious time.

Jesse got into the car with Ramona and roared off in search of her criminal friends. Jesse watched her as she drove. Her face was determined, strong-looking. She was a good partner to have if you were a criminal, he thought darkly. He just hoped that her friends still had that black case.

2

Bait

Cane watched without emotion as they brought the blindfolded boy closer. There was a time when he might have felt sorry for a kid like Little Jack, but those days were long gone. Two of Cane's men stood behind the boy in the living room of one of Cane's houses.

One of the men was a thin roller everyone called Q. He had been in the crew for only a short time, but he had a long reputation on the street. Q never combed his hair and wore an unusually long earring shaped like a chain.

The other man was a huge roller named Turk. Turk was a freelancer, muscle for hire. After Tico had been taken, Cane needed more muscle. Turk was fresh out of prison, where he'd done five years for an armed robbery. He still had the smell of prison on him and was eager to get back into the life.

"Here he is," said Turk. His voice was high-pitched, a contrast with his massive frame.

Cane didn't know if Tico was still alive. He was a hostage of the Nasty Girls, and Walker had betrayed them both. The thought of Walker enraged him. There was nothing worse than a man who was not loyal.

When Cane heard the news, he was about to go to Jaleel's house and take him out. Tico's spy there had confirmed that Jaleel was stealing. But with Tico gone, Jaleel was not a priority. Tico was like family, and family always came first.

And so LoLo had sent this boy, Little Jack, as a messenger to him with her demands. Demands. The very thought of the word made him want to choke somebody.

"Nigga just walked up to the crib," said Q. "Hard little muthafucka, ain'tcha?" He slapped Little Jack on the back of the head. Little Jack tensed like he was ready to fight.

"All right, take off that rag," said Cane. Turk took off the blindfold.

Cane watched as Little Jack's eyes adjusted to the light. The boy had a look of pure terror on his face. Cane liked that. He had the upper hand already. Cane recognized the kid. He had been with LoLo's roller Sheri when Cane and Tico hit them. Cane had spared the boy in order to spread the news to LoLo's crew.

"Make it quick," Cane said to the boy.

"The Girls want . . ." Little Jack's voice cracked. "They wanna stop all this madness, killin', and shit. LoLo say, if you give back what you took from her, she release your man and everythang's even."

"And if I don't?" Cane asked.

"She kill your boy Tico," said Little Jack.

Cane walked to a dark corner in the room and grabbed something. He stepped into the light and revealed the spiked glove that he'd used to kill Sheri. Little Jack took a step back, only to be pushed forward by Turk.

"Hey, man, killin' me won't help your boy!" said Little Jack.

Cane just stared at the young boy for a moment. "Are you a man?" Cane asked.

Little Jack seemed thrown by the question. He couldn't take his eyes off the spiked glove and the man holding it.

"Yeah, I'm a man." He tried to fill his voice with courage.

"Then why are you working for bitches?" Cane asked. "Men don't put themselves under women. So you must be lying. You must be a bitch."

"I ain't trying to hear all that," said Little Jack. "I just came to deliver a message."

Cane put the glove in the boy's face. "Don't you wonder why I killed that bitch but not you the other day?" he asked.

Little Jack looked confused for a moment, as if he had never thought about it. "Guess I got lucky."

"I don't kill men who don't deserve it," said Cane. "But bitches, they have no business in a man's game. That's why I let you live."

Cane took a step back from the boy. "Do you think you'll ever get any real money from those bitches?"

"Hey, I'm gettin' paid," said Little Jack.

"You're a fool," said Cane. "All the leaders of that crew are women, and it's always gonna be that way. They're using you."

Little Jack turned angry at that remark. "I didn't come here to hear this shit."

"I know why you came, messenger *bitch*!" Cane yelled. "What I'm doing now is trying to help your sorry little ass. You are a man working for bitches. That makes you a bitch whether you like it or not! If you want to be a man, you'll listen to me. You keep interrupting me, and you'll never leave this house."

Cane brought his face closer to Little Jack's. The blind eye was grotesque, but the good one seemed to frighten the little boy even more.

"You get pussy, boy?" asked Cane.

"Yeah," Little Jack said immediately.

"You a damn liar!" said Cane. "The only time you been in a pussy is when you was born." Turk and Q laughed loudly. Little Jack turned quickly to look at them, having forgotten they were there.

"Fuck all y'all!" said Little Jack.

Cane's hand shot out, and he grabbed Little Jack by the shoulder with the spiked glove. The boy winced. Even through his coat he could feel the spikes digging into his body.

"Your man Tico," said Little Jack, "he be dead if you mess with me." His voice trembled.

"Watch your mouth." Cane pulled the glove away. "You already dead, boy," said Cane. "LoLo won't trade Tico for your ass. And she don't want peace. She wants me. Tico is a man, and he's been ready to die since we got into this. But your bitch-ass boss LoLo don't know that. See, she thinks men are dumb asses, like you. I'll negotiate for Tico, but not to save his life. I'll do it because when LoLo comes to trade Tico for her money, I'll kill her tiny ass. You go back and tell her that I'll meet her in Greektown this Friday at eleven p.m."

"What?" said Little Jack. "Greektown be full of cops at night."

"Just tell her," said Cane. "And if she don't agree, she can kill Tico. I don't give a shit."

"Why you telling me what you gonna do?" asked Little Jack. "You know I gotta tell LoLo."

"No, you won't," said Cane. "I've been calling you a bitch, I know you ain't one." His voice was softer now. He knew that this boy, like so many others, had no father, no male role model. And no matter what women did for Little Jack, he'd rather follow a man. The young boys in the neighborhoods were lost and without any focus on the elusive prize of manhood. Little Jack was young, but he was old enough to have learned the contempt that all men have for women. It was a risk, but one Cane had to take if he was going to save Tico.

"I know you're a man," Cane continued. "You watched me tear that girl's face off, and you didn't flinch. And after that you walk in here to bring me a message, knowing what I am. Takes a man to do that. You just young. And when the time comes, I know you gone be with me against them bitches because you know in your heart this is where you belong."

Cane walked away from the boy. He waited for a moment, knowing that Little Jack was not sure if he would leave the house alive. Cane took a deep breath. Then, with his back still to Little Jack, he said: "Let him go."

3

Fame

They went deeper into the neighborhoods, and Jesse saw the face of Detroit he'd forgotten. On his trips to see his sister and her kids, he had not stayed long and never got the full impact of what the city was. The hard, ugly visage of the street stared at him, into him, from every abandoned house, vacant lot, and hopeless young face. It mocked him. He had walked out of the ghetto a winner and a symbol of something. Now he was back in shame, and the neighborhood seemed to be saying, "We knew you'd be back."

The two stopped on a plain-looking street called St. Aubin and entered a big two-story house. LoLo's favorite house on Bristol had been shut down after the raid, but this one was still going strong. The place was actually very nice inside with furniture that looked new. All the business was transacted outside through a window, a trademark of LoLo and her crew.

Jesse looked around the drug house with dread and disgust. This was what he'd dedicated his life to stopping, and now he was here, inside this place, seeking help.

They both were patted down by a roller, then led to a back room. Inside were a man and a woman. The man was heavyset and hard-looking with dyed red hair. The woman was dark and attractive with a head full of braids with beads on the ends. They looked at Jesse and Ramona with mean, stoic faces; then they started to clap and laugh.

"Girl, you famous!" said the man. He clapped Ramona on the back.

"Hey, Dell," said Ramona to the man.

"This him, baby?" asked the woman. She pointed at Jesse.

"Yes, Cat," said Ramona. "That him."

Cat and Dell looked at Jesse, smiling. "You one of us now, huh, baby?" said Cat.

Jesse remained silent. These two dealers sold death to children, caused the birth of crack babies, and they stood here joking and laughing at him like *he* was the criminal. He looked at the dealers and wanted to haul them both off to jail.

"You talk or what, nigga?" asked Dell.

"I talk," said Jesse tersely

"I need to find LoLo," Ramona announced.

"Wait a minute, baby," said Cat. "I wanna know how y'all beat the cops like that."

"Yeah," said Dell. "What's the four-one-one on the great escape? That was like some movie shit."

"Just like the news said," Ramona explained. "We busted through a wall and snuck out."

"So y'all fucking like the news said too?" asked Dell.

"What?" said Ramona. "When did they—"

"They didn't say that, Dell," said Cat. "They said *possible romance.*"

"That news talk for fuckin'," said Dell.

"That's bullshit," said Ramona. "He got me out because people are tryin' to kill us."

"Well, he look pretty good to me," said Dell. "I'd give him some—or vice versa." Dell and Cat slapped five.

Jesse saw now. Dell was a big, fat, crack-dealing homosexual. Jesse thought of himself as a liberal when it came to gays. But he was nauseated by Dell's suggestion.

"I'd give him some too," said Cat. "In fact I got time right now, baby. Whatcha say?"

Dell and Cat laughed, slapping five again. Ramona just shook her head. "You two are still the same," she said.

Jesse was tired of the duo and their nonchalant attitudes. "We don't have time for your shit."

Dell and Cat stopped laughing. Silence fell on the foursome. Ramona looked at Jesse with unbelieving eyes. Cat and Dell looked at each other. Then Dell pulled a gun.

"Dell, no!" said Ramona.

"Shut the fuck up," he said. He stepped over to Jesse and put the gun in his face. "Excuse me," he said. "What did you just say?"

Jesse stared into the face of the big man. He saw Cocoa and Kelvin dead, his sister clinging to her addiction and the life he'd thrown away. At this moment he was frustrated and angry but not afraid of the man before him.

"I said, we don't have time for your silly-ass bullshit."

"Cap his monkey ass," said Cat.

"LoLo won't like that," said Ramona. "She needs to see this man. It could mean lots of money. You do anything to him, and you'll have to answer to her."

Dell contemplated this. He scowled at Jesse, then pulled the gun away. "Lucky-ass nigga," he said.

"We need to find your boss," said Jesse.

"Fuck you," said Cat. "You killed that woman, then come up in here giving orders. Find her the best way you can, muthafucka."

"*I'm* asking, Cat," said Ramona.

"Hey, I never liked your prissy ass neither," said Cat. "Fuck you too."

"Okay," said Ramona. "We'll go. And when LoLo gets the money this man has to give, I'll be sure to mention that you-all didn't help get it to her when she gives everybody a taste."

This statement grabbed their attention. "How much money?" asked Dell.

"Never mind," said Ramona, heading for the door. "But you see how the police is after his ass, don't you?"

Jesse turned and followed, playing along with her. Ramona was good, he thought. Money was something even these lowlifes understood.

"Wait," said Dell. "LoLo is on the DL, you know."

"DL?" asked Jesse.

"The down low, dumb ass," said Cat.

"She's hiding out because of this thing with Cane," said Dell. "LoLo grabbed Cane's boy Tico and wants to trade him for some money Cane took."

"Dell, do you know if LoLo still has my case, the black case?" asked Ramona.

"I don't know nothing about that," said Dell.

"Yeah, you do, baby," said Cat. "That white boy who sells the guns said something about wanting to buy it off LoLo."

"Oh, yeah, Pierre," said Dell. "Yeah, I guess she still got it."

"Thank God," said Ramona.

"Where can we find LoLo?" asked Jesse.

"Ain't nobody talking to you, murderin'-ass nigga," said Dell.

"I didn't murder anyone," said Jesse.

"I didn't murder anyone," Cat said, mocking Jesse's proper English. "You talk like a damn white boy. Mona, you'd better watch your back. I think this nigga's one of them sick muthafuckas. Probably cut you up and eat you."

"He can eat me," said Dell. "You like sausage?" He and Cat laughed again.

"Dell, Cat, please," said Ramona.

"All right," said Cat. "Last time anyone saw LoLo she was over by Roxanne's."

"In general, she be 'round the way, you know," said Dell.

"Thanks," said Ramona. Ramona studied the duo a moment, assessing them, then asked, "Look, I need a few. I'll get it back to you."

Dell contemplated it a second, then pulled out a wad of cash and peeled off some bills. Jesse looked at the money with a mixture of disgust and need. Money was precious to them right now.

"You can have some too," said Dell lightly to Jesse. "But you know what I want for it."

"Fuck that. Mine is free," said Cat.

"Since I'm a murderer, aren't you afraid I might fuck you to death?" asked Jesse.

Dell and Cat roared with laughter.

"I think I like this nigga now," said Dell. "Hey, I'm sorry about that gun in your face thing. Let's make up."

"You don't want none of that," said Cat. "His shit is toxic." They both laughed again.

"Dell, was LoLo hurt when she grabbed Cane's man?" asked Ramona.

"Naw, it was clean," said Dell. "LoLo turned one of Cane's men, that Jamaican. Why you ask that?"

"No reason," she said. "Just worried about her, that's all."

She and Jesse left, hearing Cat and Dell catcall to Jesse. The moment they walked outside, they were hit by a cold, biting wind.

"Damn," said Ramona. "We gonna need some bigger coats."

"Well, we struck out on that," said Jesse, ignoring the cold air. "We're right back where we started."

"How you figure that?" asked Ramona, annoyed.

"Those two laughing hyenas don't know where your friend LoLo is."

"You don't speak the language no more, do you?" asked Ramona. "Dell said LoLo's would be 'round the way. LoLo has a few places she always goes to, areas she hangs out in. All we have to do is check them and we'll find her."

"You know these places?" asked Jesse. Doing criminal cases, he had heard many slang terms, but he never remembered them. He had no use for such things anymore.

"I know all her places," said Ramona. "That's why I asked if LoLo was hurt. She's got a place she goes when she gets hurt. Only me and Yolanda, her best friend, know where it is."

"Where is it?" asked Jesse. "We could go there and wait for her."

"No," said Ramona. "LoLo won't go there unless she's racked up."

"Let's go anyway," said Jesse. "We might get lucky."

"Sorry," said Ramona. "I'm not giving up her secret unless I'm sure she's there."

"Are you kidding me?" asked Jesse. "This is important. It's my life." He was angry. This criminal code of honor shit was stupid.

"Okay," said Ramona. "We can go, but if LoLo finds out, she might get really pissed off."

"I'll take that chance," said Jesse.

The wind whipped up, and Ramona wrapped her arms around her chest, shivering. "Damn," she said. "Let's get in this car."

They walked to the beat-up Ford and got inside. Jesse played with the wires sticking out from the steering column of the stolen car. Struggling with the wires, he glanced over at Ramona. She was calm. It was as if they were going to find a school buddy and not a drug dealer who could save their lives. She was either the coolest customer he'd ever met or a fool.

"You don't really think I killed Karen, do you?" asked Jesse. He needed to prove his innocence to somebody, even Ramona.

"If I did," said Ramona, "I would have let Dell shoot you."

"Nice to know I have your confidence," said Jesse sarcastically. The car's starter caught, sputtered, then went silent. He kept trying.

"You know," said Ramona. "I should go back and ask them to give us a gun. We might need one where we're going."

"No need," said Jesse. He reached behind his back and pulled out his gun. "I got it covered."

"I see," said Ramona. She was impressed. "I guess you still got a little of the 'hood in you."

"What do you mean?" asked Jesse.

"Nothing," said Ramona. She shivered.

Jesse put the gun between his legs. He tried the wires again, and the old car started up. He drove away, turning up the heater.

4

Blue Feet

Florence needed a drink. She'd been in this little room filled with cops and prosecutors for over an hour. They'd come to her house and pulled her out of bed that morning. What the fuck was Jesse trying to do?

Florence believed in him. Jesse was as straight as they came. He'd bent the rules a few times, but he was honest about it. He'd done a little more than bending this time, though, and it did not look good for him.

The interrogation team was headed by D'Estenne, Dick Steals, and a good-looking blonde named Denise Wilkerson. D'Estenne was dressed in a beige suit with a brilliant white shirt and geometric tie. Florence didn't usually notice men's clothes, but he looked nice. He was also a wreck. He seemed like *he* was the wanted man.

The other two men and one woman were cops. Florence knew them, but they were basically grunts. This was D'Estenne's show.

"So did Jesse call you at any time yesterday?" asked D'Estenne.

"Shit, no," said Florence. "We'd met a few days earlier, but since then nothing."

"What did you talk about at that meeting?" asked D'Estenne.

"The Yancy case. I was trying to dig up info on that girl. But I didn't find jack shit we didn't already know." She was a little scared, but she was not about to turn Jesse. This D'Estenne asshole was just looking for anything to stop the embarrassment of what Jesse had done. He was running for reelection against some black guy who was using this Jesse thing against him.

"So has he contacted you since he ran?" asked D'Estenne.

"I told you already, no. I ain't seen Jesse in a few days. Look, I know this is bad. But I don't know nothing about this crazy fuckin' stunt he pulled."

Denise Wilkerson seemed bothered by Florence's language. Florence smiled at her. She liked upsetting little Suzie homemaker types like her. The other people just stood there like idiots. Dick Steals was jumpy, like he wanted to say something but was afraid to speak up.

"We know," said D'Estenne. "But you're the only one he had contact with recently. We don't suspect you. It's just that we need to know where we stand."

"I know how it is," said Florence. "Fuck, I'd do the same shit myself." She smiled as Denise Wilkerson cringed again.

"But if he contacts you, I'd like to know that you'll come to me first," said D'Estenne. He smiled ever so slightly at her.

He was a handsome devil, Florence thought to herself. He'd be the perfect man if he had a dick that dispensed scotch.

"Sure, I will," said Florence. "I think Jesse will turn himself in," she lied. "He's just scared, so if he calls, we should hook up and try to help him. Can I go now?"

"Yes," said D'Estenne. "And please don't forget your promise to me."

"I won't." Florence got up.

"An officer will escort you out," said D'Estenne. "And please don't talk to the media."

As Florence left, the other people in the room all huddled together and talked. She thought that they might put a tail on her, but if they did, she'd shake it in three seconds. She had to get to Jesse, to help him, before he completely fucked up his life.

Florence walked out of the little room in the long hallway of 1300 with a big uniformed cop behind her. She saw the faces of all of Jesse's coworkers at the office sitting on a wooden bench against a wall. D'Estenne was going to grill them too.

It suddenly occurred to Florence that D'Estenne hadn't bothered to put any of Jesse's black colleagues on his little interrogation team. He'd picked two white prosecutors. These guys were all alike, she thought. Sexist, racist, typical bullshit politicians playing the odds that anybody who was not white wasn't worth a damn.

Florence walked to the big front doors of 1300. At the bottom of the steps was a mob of reporters. She'd passed them coming in. They'd yelled questions at her and pushed big microphones in her face. The cop turned and led her to the side entrance. They had the side blocked off so the media couldn't get to it. That way they could bring in whomever they wanted. Florence had no sooner walked out of the door than a reporter started to yell at her beyond the barricade.

Florence stopped in her tracks. This was what she needed. Reporters. Cameras.

"Something wrong?" asked the uniformed cop.

"Naw," she said.

They walked on. Florence was approaching her car when a big black limo pulled up. A crowd of reporters trailed it. They were stopped as the barricade opened and the limo went in. Florence and the cop instinctively looked at it. Lester Crawford, the acting mayor, got out and ran inside with his aides.

Florence snorted a laugh. Everybody was feeling the heat of this thing. She got into her car and was let out. She promptly circled to the front of the building.

"Okay, Flo," she said to herself. "You're on."

She pulled past the reporters. They yelled questions at her and took pictures. She crossed an intersection, then turned off her car. She coasted to the curb. She faked trying to start the car twice more again. Then she got out and popped the hood.

The reporters descended upon her. They ran to her, cameras and microphones out in front.

"Jesus H. Christ!" Florence said. "Can't ya see I'm stalled out here?"

The throng didn't hesitate. They yelled and pushed one another trying to get next to her.

"Did you work with Jesse King?"

"Do the police have any leads?"

"Is he in love with the girl who killed Yancy?"

"I don't know nothing, all right," Florence said. "Just go away before I shoot you."

"Do you think he's guilty?" asked Carol Salinsky.

"Like I said, I don't know nothing. I'm just a cop. I got blue in my heart just like the next guy. Now move, before I put a blue foot in your ass." Florence pulled something under the hood.

"What did the police ask you?" asked another reporter.

"You want this blue foot in your ass too?" asked Florence.

Pushing her way through the crowd, she got into her car, started it after a moment, then drove away. The reporters immediately calmed down, like machines running out of power. Cameras and tape recorders were turned off, and they trudged back to the entrance of 1300.

As Florence drove away, she had to laugh a little at her acting. It wasn't half bad. She just hoped that Jesse was near a TV or a radio.

5

The Chair

Tico was hurting but still alive. After beating him, the Girls had tied him up to a heavy wooden chair in a dark room. He was out for a while, so he had no idea where he was. The house seemed old, and the room had boarded-up windows and a musty smell. It could be anywhere in Detroit. Below him he heard the muffled sound of a rap tune. He was in an upstairs room, maybe an attic, he reasoned.

Squirming, trying to get an angle, Tico struggled to get free. The ropes were too tight, and the damn chair weighed a ton. It was no use.

There was no way LoLo was going to let him live. He understood that he was still alive only because she needed him for some reason. He reasoned that she was trying to use him to lure Cane out, then kill him. She was smart. Cane was crazy, but he and Tico were tight, like brothers. Neither of them was close to his family. Tico was probably the one person in the crew that Cane would not forfeit.

The door to the room opened, and two figures came in. Tico strained to see them. One of the figures reached out and touched a wall. A dim light sprang on, and the flood of weak light hurt Tico's eyes. When his eyes adjusted, he saw Walker.

The Jamaican had a young girl with him. Tico recognized her as the one Walker had kissed when LoLo had captured him. She was young and very voluptuous. This was what Walker had betrayed the crew for? A piece of ass he could have gotten anywhere.

"Make it easy on yourself," said Walker in his heavy Jamaican accent. "Come on over to our side."

"Fuck you, dead man," said Tico.

"Don't talk to my man like that," said Marly.

"Young Marly here don't like you," said Walker breezily. "And she's an excellent judge of people." Walker gave her a wet kiss and felt her up. "Yes, she is."

"I don't care about your little bitch," said Tico.

Walker hit Tico viciously across the face with the back of his hand. "Watch yourself, boy."

"Big man," Tico said, his face stinging from the assault. "Big-ass man."

Marly walked over to a little sofa by the boarded-up window. She was dressed in black jeans and a white top that showed off her large endowment. She was nice-looking, Tico thought, but not worth risking your life for. And that's what Walker had done. Cane had to know by now, and he would kill Walker for sure.

"Here's the deal," said Walker. "You tell me where Cane's money house is, and we won't kill you. Simple."

"Fuck you," said Tico. "This is the reason he never told your island ass. I'm already dead, and you know it."

"LoLo left it up to me," said Walker. "And I say, if my boy Tico is down, then we should let him live."

"That's right," said Marly. "I heard him say it."

Tico laughed. "You two must think I'm stupid. You think I'd fall for that? You stupid Rasta trash and some ho."

Marly jumped up and started for Tico, but Walker held out a hand.

"Cool yourself, honey," said Walker. "We're talking business now." Marly went back to the sofa, pointing a threatening finger at Tico.

"First of all," said Walker, "I ain't no Rasta. And second, you'd better believe me, if you want to live." He moved closer to Tico and knelt next to him. "Just tell me where the money is, and after I get it, I'll let you go. But you have to leave town altogether, out of Detroit."

"Even if I knew where Cane hid his cash," said Tico, "I wouldn't tell you."

"All right," said Walker. He pulled out a knife and flicked it open. "Maybe if I took off one of your fingers, you'd remember," he said.

"Now you talkin'," said Marly. "Fuck his ass up, baby."

Tico's hands were tied down, and he couldn't protect his fingers if he wanted to. He looked Walker in the eyes. He was going to let him do his worst, but he would not turn on Cane. Not if he had to lose all his fingers.

"I feel sorry for you, man," Tico said. "You can cut me up, but it's nothing compared to what Cane will do to you."

Walker grabbed Tico's right hand and pulled up his baby finger.

"You know how Cane is," Tico said. "You know *what* he is. He'll take you somewhere and torture you for days. Remember the tiger? That's nothing compared to what's gonna happen to you."

Walker put Tico's baby finger down and took his middle finger. He put the blade on it.

"I'm gonna take it off a little at a time," said Walker. "Where's the money?" Walker turned the knife.

"Go to hell," said Tico.

Walker raised the knife, then brought it down hard between Tico's fingers. It stuck into the hard wood of the chair, but Tico was unharmed.

The door opened again. Tico, Walker, and Marly all looked toward it. LoLo and Yolanda walked into the little room.

"What's up?" said LoLo.

"Just talking with my boy here," said Walker.

"Get away from him," LoLo barked.

Walker got up, snapping the knife closed.

"Wait. Gimme that knife," LoLo said.

Walker gave her the blade. LoLo opened it. She lifted the point of the knife to Walker's eye. LoLo was so much smaller that she almost had to stand on her tiptoes.

"What the fuck is this?" Walker said. His eyes blinked rapidly.

"I told you to leave him alone. Anything you did to him, I'm gonna do to you," said LoLo. She lowered the knife to his belly. "What did you do?"

Yolanda walked over next to Walker. She had a 9 mm in her hand.

"No, LoLo," said Marly, bouncing off the sofa. "We was just trying to get some information out of him."

Yolanda shot Marly a look. Marly backed down.

"Nothing," said Walker. "I didn't do nothing to him. Just talkin'."

"He cut my dick off," said Tico. He laughed, enjoying Walker's humiliation.

Walker stared down into LoLo's eyes. He was angry but aware that Yolanda was next to him with a loaded weapon.

"Get your ass over there, and sit down," said LoLo.

Walker smiled, throwing up his hands in surrender. LoLo closed the knife and tossed it to Walker. He caught it, then went over to the sofa with Marly. LoLo moved over to Tico.

"This is some Mickey Mouse shit, you know that?" Tico said. "Go on and shoot me 'cause I know that's what you're gonna do. But you ain't gettin' nothing outta me. Nothing."

"Your boy Cane made the deal," said LoLo. "Just thought you should know that." To Walker, she said, "Don't let nothing happen to him." She walked out of the room, Yolanda on her heels.

Tico watched them leave, then looked at Walker, smiling. "It's all over for you now," said Tico. "All over. Cane will kill you and these bitches as sure as I'm sittin' here."

Walker got up slowly from the little sofa. He moved over to Tico, his eyes full of mischief. "Tell me, boy, you ever see Cane with a woman?"

"What?" said Tico. He was thrown by the question.

"A woman, boy. You ever see him get some?"

Tico said nothing.

"No, you've never seen him with one, and you know why? Because he's a faggot."

Marly laughed, slapping her leg loudly.

"Bullshit," said Tico. "Cane is a man. He's just crazy."

"No," said Walker. "What's bullshit is you thinking he's some kind of nut because he don't like pussy." To the girl, Walker said, "Cane don't even look at women. All he cares about is this man right here."

"We're friends, a crew," said Tico. "But you wouldn't know nothing about that, would you?"

"Fags!" said Walker. "I think he's fucking you, boy. That's why he's gonna risk his neck to save you."

Tico struggled violently against the ropes that held him to the chair. "I'm gonna kill your ass!"

"When you gonna do that?" Walker asked lightly. "Before or after Cane gives it to you up the ass?"

The Jamaican went to Marly on the little sofa. "Hey, boy, see this woman here? This beautiful woman. This is what people like you and Cane don't want."

Walker unbuttoned Marly's blouse and kissed her. Marly rubbed Walker's leg, then moved over to his crotch, pulling at his zipper. Walker soon had her blouse open, exposing Marly's ample cleavage.

She unsnapped the bra, and her breasts tumbled out. Walker's face soon covered them. Marly threw her head back, then looked at Tico, blowing him silent kisses.

"I don't fucking believe this," Tico mumbled. He was disgusted but couldn't take his eyes from the couple.

Walker stood up and dropped his pants. Marly got on her knees and took him in her mouth. Walker looked over at Tico. "Want some of this, boy? I don't think so."

"Sick son of a bitch," said Tico.

Marly continued to work on Walker for a while; then she stood up and wiggled out of her pants. She got on the floor on all fours, and Walker knelt behind her. He slipped himself inside her. As the couple rocked back and forth, Walker looked over to the bound man, laughing at him.

Tico closed his eyes, but he was unable to control the erection in his pants. And he swore if he got out of this alive, he would kill Walker, kill him with his bare hands.

6

Roxanne, Roxanne

Jesse and Ramona sat in the back of Roxanne's Nail Salon. The outer room was filled with black women getting their nails done or waiting. The room was loud with talk and laughter. Toni Braxton crooned on a radio.

These places were a new cultural phenomenon to Jesse. Young black women had grown fond of wearing long, colorful, elaborately decorated fake nails. They were striped, polka-dotted, lined with glitter, and curved at the ends. Jesse personally found them grotesque, but Roxanne was doing a brisk business.

They had left Dell and Cat's drug house and gone east to LoLo's safe house. It was a little one-story building on the far east side, right on the border. They got there, but no one was home. Ramona wrote out a note, then decided that it was too dangerous to leave any evidence that they'd been there.

Roxanne was a friend of LoLo's and had sneaked them in the back, hiding them in the little storage room. They sat on stools behind a plastic curtain in Roxanne's. The room was dark and filled with boxes stacked high and covered with sheets.

Jesse had always disliked these places. When he was young, he used to run errands for his mother and her friends, and he had to come to joints like Roxanne's, dirty, shady little places with shady people in them. It was all coming back to him now. He wanted out all over again.

"Maybe we should have just waited for your friend to come to that safe house," said Jesse.

"No," Ramona said curtly. "LoLo might not go there for weeks, and the man who lives there wouldn't let us hang around without her."

"Who is he?" Jesse asked curiously.

"Never mind," said Ramona. "But he would run us off—or worse."

"Can't we call her or something?" said Jesse, growing frustrated.

"LoLo don't like cellular phones. One of her friends is in jail because she had one. FBI busted her doin' a deal."

Smart girl, Jesse thought. The airwaves are not protected. It was no wonder they had such a hard time at the prosecutor's office. Damn dealers were almost lawyers themselves.

"So how long do we wait?" asked Jesse.

"Why you sweatin' me?" asked Ramona. "I know as much as you do."

Jesse fell silent. He did not want to get into an argument with Ramona. They had enough trouble already. He wondered what the people in his life were doing, what they were thinking of him now. His coworkers, Connie. Poor Connie. Jesse was sure her parents were using this to try to break them up. Hell, how hard could it be? he thought. Murder, flight with a young woman. He was surprised that Connie had defended him. He found himself missing her, wanting to be with her.

Jesse reached for the little TV Roxanne had in the back room. It sat on a wooden crate.

"Roxanne said no noise," Ramona said.

"I'll keep it down," said Jesse. "Besides, they'll never hear us with all the racket they're making." He turned the TV on.

He grabbed a newspaper that Roxanne had been reading. Jesse skimmed the stories on Ramona and himself. A reporter had even interviewed his sister, Bernice, or at least, he tried to. Bernice refused to talk to the reporter. Thank God for small favors, he thought.

Jesse dropped the paper. There was nothing on the TV stations so far. He looked over at Ramona, who was watching too. She was such a pain in the ass, he thought, but he was stuck with her. Ramona was like so many of the criminals he put in jail. She didn't grasp the gravity of her situation.

Jesse went back to the newspaper. In the back was an obituary on Louis Franklin, Chapel, Swiss's dead partner. The article showed a

Jesse heard a noise from the alley behind the little shop. "What was that?" he asked. "Did you hear that?"

Ramona didn't answer. She ignored him.

Cautiously Jesse got up and went to the back door. He looked into the alley. There was nothing back there. He sat back down next to Ramona just as Florence appeared on the TV.

"Florence," said Jesse.

"Who?"

"My investigator." Jesse turned up the TV a little. A group of reporters was harassing Florence in front of the police station.

"Do the police have any leads?"

"Is he in love with the girl who killed Yancy?"

"What? Why are people saying that—" said Ramona.

"Quiet!" Jesse said.

"Just go away before I shoot you," Florence said on the little TV.

"Do you think he's guilty?" asked a reporter.

"Like I said, I don't know nothing," she said. The camera was shaky as Florence looked under the hood of a car. *"I'm just a cop. I got blue in my heart just like the next guy. Now move, before I put a blue foot in your ass."*

"What did the police ask you?" another reporter asked Florence.

"You want this blue foot in your ass too?"

Jesse's face broke into a broad smile. "That's my girl!" he said. He turned down the TV as the segment on Florence ended. He took out a pen and looked around the stacks of covered boxes until he found a piece of paper. He began to write on a paper bag.

"I suppose she's black too," said Ramona.

Jesse didn't respond. He was immersed in his writing.

"What are you writing?" asked Ramona.

"I just got a message," said Jesse. "Florence knows I'm innocent, and she wants to meet me."

"Wha—when did she say that?" asked Ramona.

"Just now, on TV. I guess *you* don't speak this language," Jesse said. "When we worked together and we needed to talk in private, we used to go to this old bar downriver called Packer's."

"So? She didn't say nothing about no Packer's," said Ramona.

"The first time we went there, I had just started at the prosecutor's office. Packer's is a working-class bar, and I came dressed in a blue suit. I had on blue shoes. The guys there ragged on me all night about my blue feet. After that it was our code for the place. And no one knows that except us."

"Downriver. That's all the way on the west side," said Ramona. "A lot of shit can happen between here and there. It's too dangerous."

She had a point, Jesse thought. They were on the east side of Detroit. Packer's was a good forty miles away. They could be stopped for traffic, have car trouble. Hell, in the city there was always the chance they'd get jacked by some punk.

"I know it's far away, but we have to chance it," said Jesse. "Your friend ain't coming here today."

"You don't know that," said Ramona. "And the word is *isn't*."

"Listen, we have to—" Jesse stopped short. He was facing the dirty plastic curtain that separated the two rooms. A tall woman in jeans walked into the shop and sat down. "Holy shit," he said in a whisper.

"What?" said Ramona.

"We got trouble." He went back to the back door and looked through the window. Nothing. He opened the door and carefully peeked down the side of the building. Just as he thought, there was a nondescript car parked across the way. Two men in plainclothes were inside.

Jesse closed the door and began to pace back and forth, cursing to himself.

"What's going on?" asked Ramona in alarm.

"A woman just walked in. Her name is—" Jesse searched for the name. "Nell, Nell Parker. She's a cop, an undercover officer. She did her first trial testimony as a cop with me. I think she's on the job here right now."

"Maybe she's getting her nails done," said Ramona. "A cop can have class, you know."

"I don't think so. Besides, there are two cops sitting in a car in the back, waiting. This place is being set up."

"But . . . how did they find us?"

"They didn't. At least I don't think so. If they thought we were in here, they would have made their move by now. No, they're after someone here."

"Probably Roxanne," said Ramona. "She sells stuff out of here."

"Stuff?" asked Jesse, his eyes widening.

"You know, stolen stuff."

Jesse sighed heavily. He pulled back the sheet that covered the boxes in the little room. TVs, stereos, VCRs, radios. "Why didn't you tell me that before?"

"What difference does—"

"Fuck—forget it," said Jesse, determined to keep his cool. He paused for a moment, thinking about their options. "We've got to get out. And I've got to sneak past Nell. The car's down the street. If they're still doing this the same way, a big-ass cop will bust through this back door, and some other cops will come in the front door. Nell's their plant inside, so all they need now is their other undercover man. He's probably been working the place for a while."

"What do we do?" asked Ramona. She suddenly looked scared.

"Okay," Jesse said. "We have to move. Somebody's gonna be coming through that front door any minute now to buy something from your friend Roxanne. Then—"

"We have to warn Roxanne," said Ramona. She started for the curtain.

Jesse grabbed her arm. It was soft and warm, and he held it a little longer than he should have. Ramona gave him a look, and he let her go.

"We can't do that," he said.

"Look, where I come from, we don't leave our people hangin'," she said. "Another rule you forgot when you was black."

Jesse was unmoved. "You tell her and we're dead. When a bust like this breaks down, the cops will raid the place just for the hell of it, trying to get anything they can. In this case that's us."

Ramona didn't move. She just looked at Jesse, and he could tell she was trying to see if he was lying to her. "Okay," she said. "We'll do it your way this time."

"All right," said Jesse. He went to the door and looked around the plastic curtain into the shop area. "If we go out the back, the backup cops will get suspicious and hold us. So we'll have to walk right out of the front door."

"You gotta be kiddin'."

"I'm afraid not. And we have to get past Nell. She'll never recognize me in this hat and glasses, but let's not take any chances. Nell is on the left side of the room. You walk on my left so she can't see me. We get to the door and keep going."

"Maybe we can get Roxanne to distract her."

"No time," said Jesse, his voice suddenly growing intense. "I think the undercover man just arrived."

In the store a man had come in and hugged Roxanne. Jesse could tell he was a cop. He was laughing, joking, and trying to put everyone at ease. Nell read a magazine and pretended not to notice him.

"Okay," said Jesse. "Let's go now."

Jesse had started out when Ramona hooked her arm in his. "Let's hit it," she said.

As the two walked out of the back room, Jesse drained all expression from his face. The door was ten feet or so away but looked like a million miles.

They surprised Roxanne, who put her arm around the cop and led him toward the back room. Jesse had passed them when the cop's hand shot out and grabbed his arm.

"Got a light?" the cop asked. He held a cigarette in his other hand.

"Naw," Jesse said. He tried not to look directly at the man. He jerked his arm away and moved on.

Nell stood up. She put down her magazine. She looked at Ramona, then reached for another magazine.

As they reached the door, Jesse could see another nondescript cop car across the street. It was going to get hot in a few seconds, he thought.

Just get out, Jesse told himself. He put his hand on the doorknob. His palm was sweaty, and it slipped. Then he tried to pull the door, and it wouldn't move. A wave of panic came over him. Somehow the door had been locked. Then he noticed the sign that said PUSH. Cursing, Jesse pushed the door, and they walked outside onto the street.

"Okay, we're doing good," said Jesse, letting out a breath. "Let's get to the car."

"Damn, that was tight," said Ramona.

Jesse looked at her. Cool as ice. He'd fucked up at the door, and she never made a sound. Despite her funky attitude, he was beginning to admire her.

They walked down the street to their car. It wasn't far away. There were people around, and he didn't know who was a cop and who was just a street person. They got to the old Ford, and Jesse realized that Ramona had never let go of his arm. She released him, and he felt the coolness where her arm had been.

They were getting in the car when the street was flooded with police cars. The police ran into the nail shop and secured the front door. Jesse hurriedly started the car and drove off. He rolled down the street and stopped at a traffic light. Police sirens wailed. A cruiser flew right past them and screeched to a halt.

Jesse waited for the light, then pulled away from the bust. Turning a corner, he began to put distance between them and the police.

"Okay," said Ramona. "There's another place that LoLo hang—"

"Forget that," said Jesse. "Not after this close call. We're going to Packer's."

7

The Princess of White Castle

Florence finally shook the tail that the cops had put on her. It wasn't hard. She could have lost them right after she'd first seen them, but that wouldn't do. She had to play it cool and lose them without letting them know she'd done it on purpose. That way they wouldn't get any more suspicious and lay some heavy surveillance on her.

She hoped Jesse had gotten her message. But before she tried to meet Jesse, she had to keep her date here with her snitch in the mayor's office.

Florence entered the White Castle restaurant on Nine Mile Road and Telegraph. She would have picked a location in the city, but she was afraid that someone might see them. The dining area of the building was relatively empty. White Castle sold tiny, inexpensive hamburgers heavy on the onions.

Florence ordered four burgers and a coffee and sat at a booth in the back of the restaurant.

Yancy's murder had smelled bad from the very beginning. She figured that Jesse had just gotten too close to the truth and paid for it. Poor bastard. Doing the right thing was never a healthy occupation in the city.

Florence waited for a half hour before her man showed up. Randall Wallace walked into the restaurant with a sour look, but once he spotted Florence, the grimace faded. He went to her. She stood and smiled. Randall hugged Florence and leaned in to kiss her lips. Florence turned her head to the side, offering her cheek.

"Good to see you again," Randall said. His voice was deep and husky from many years of smoking.

"Likewise," said Florence.

"So, why did you want to meet here?" he asked. He took her hand and stroked it gently with one finger. "I don't like the food here."

Randall was a very handsome black man of fifty with graying hair and a thin beard. His eyes were light brown and jumped out at you in contrast with his darker skin. He wore an expensive coat, designer glasses, and a big gold Rolex.

"You know I like this place, Randall," said Florence. She gently freed her hand, and they sat down.

"Yeah, I remember," said Randall. "I could never keep you out of here, princess."

"You still can't," she said. She tried to hide her reaction to the name he called her. He smiled brilliantly at Florence, and for a second she betrayed her resolve and smiled back.

Randall was a tireless flirt, a man whose sexiness was manifested in looks, subtle physical moves, and vocal intonation. His every mannerism bespoke his need to be with you. That's how he had gotten her so many years ago. Randall cast a spell on women. But she was older and much wiser. Randall's magic had no effect on her now.

Florence and Randall had been lovers. She was a uniformed cop back then, brash and pretty. He was an assistant to a councilman and recently married. Their transgression had been long and passionate. It was filled with last-minute trysts, sex in other cities, and too many hotel rooms to remember.

Randall always called her princess because of her background. Florence had been born in a trailer park downriver. She and her friends were rough, ill mannered, took drugs, and drank too much. She often referred to herself as a trailer park princess. Randall thought it was cute, and he used the word as a term of affection.

Randall's wife found out about the affair after three years and went ballistic. Sleeping with another woman was bad enough, but his wife seemed to be bothered most by the fact that Florence was white. In the end Randall went back to his family, just as Florence always knew he would.

A long time ago, she thought, thirty pounds and a truckload of scotch ago. She could hardly think of herself as a young woman anymore.

It was uncomfortable sitting with him like this, but Randall was a high-ranking mayoral assistant. She desperately needed information to help Jesse, and he was the one person in that nest of vipers that she knew she could trust.

"How's Michelle and the kids?" Florence asked, lighting a cigarette. She thought she could stop his impending flirtations by reminding him of his family.

"Everyone's good," said Randall. He smiled as if he knew what she was trying to do. "The kids are all grown-up now. How about you?"

"I'm okay," Florence said.

"Well, you look great," Randall said.

"Thanks for that lie. Denial is my best friend these days." She smiled and hated herself for it. Maybe he still has a little magic left in him, she thought.

Randall pulled out a big manila envelope and placed it on the table. Then he took the cigarette from Florence's mouth and put it in his own. "Don't have any smokes, princess," he said, and smiled at her.

Florence wasn't surprised. Randall was always working. The cigarette goes from your lips to his lips, a connection of flesh. And now, if he were still the old Randall, he would touch her in some way, completing the promise of physical contact.

On cue Randall reached out and took her hand, rubbing the back with his thumb. Florence pulled her hand back and took another cigarette.

"I've missed you now and then," he said. His voice was soothing.

Florence looked in his eyes, and for a moment she was twenty-five again. Her hair was shimmering red, her hips were thinner, and her heart beat faster. "We have business," she said.

"Okay, princess," Randall said. "The info is in that envelope, but there are some things I can't verify because they're only rumors."

"What's in the package?" asked Florence.

"Just memos on the circulation of money in the city treasuries," said Randall. "Crawford is moving money around like a madman. He even pulled several accounts from a bank when they gave him shit about it."

"So what's he up to?"

"Don't know," said Randall. "But the rumor is that it has something to do with muni bonds."

"Municipal bonds?" said Florence. "But the city hasn't had a major bond issue for years."

"I only know what I heard," said Randall, shrugging. "Yancy, God rest his soul, was trying to cover up the money problems too. He was pushing hard on that casino business. I think he really thought it was our salvation."

"This is all very vague," said Florence. "Don't you have anything concrete?"

Randall raised his eyebrows. "Yeah, sure, the mayor is gonna tell me the city's most important secrets. I'm lucky I know the rumors. When Crawford got in, he issued a gag order. I could be fired just for talking to you."

This wasn't getting her anywhere. "Hear anything about Michael Talli?" she asked.

"The Mafia guy? Well, he's been chasing Crawford and Steven Brownhill and his partners trying to get a meeting. Think he wanted in on that new neighborhood renovation thing. Looks like he got what he wanted because I hear he's been added to the committee."

"Hmm," said Florence. "Anyone else chasing down Crawford?"

"Uh, no," said Randall. "Well, except the prosecutor, D'Estenne. He's looking for an endorsement in the election. I hear Crawford's going to do it. Against a brother, can you believe that?"

Florence opened the manila envelope and looked at some of the contents. "So, money's moving around?" she said.

"I've never seen anything like this," said Randall. "Crawford managed to stave off the special election for a new mayor, and while no one is looking, he's cooking the books."

"Any rumors on who killed the mayor?"

Randall grinned wryly. "Man, all anyone is talking about is how that woman got Jesse King to help her escape. She must have the best stuff in the world." He laughed. "I saw her picture. She's fine, but not that fine. I heard the cops picked up a witness, a cop who was there that night, but they're keeping it hush-hush."

"Nicks?" asked Florence. "They found Walter Nicks?"

"Yeah, I think that's the name I heard," said Randall. "He was Mayor Yancy's bodyguard."

"Where'd they find him? How?"

"I don't know. I just heard people talking. He must not be a suspect, or it would be in the papers."

Florence said nothing. It would be easy enough to check out. "Well, I'd appreciate a call if you find out anything else."

"You wanna tell me what you're working on?"

"Do you really wanna know?" asked Florence.

Randall laughed. He took her coffee cup and drank from it. Then he took her hand again. "How about you and me getting together again, princess? For old times."

"Now why would I want to do that?" Florence asked.

Randall played with her hand, shifting it in his own. He smiled slyly at her. "Well, you know, once you've been intimate with a person, you just want to remember what you were, you know, feel like you used to feel when you were younger."

Florence pulled her hand away again. Years ago it would have worked. The young Florence with the mane of fire on her head would have melted. But now she was too old and too jaded to feel romance. She wondered how many young girls Randall had seduced with those eyes and that voice over the years. The thought that she was perhaps the first in a long list of conquests made her suddenly angry. He didn't want her; he just needed to seduce women. But right now she needed him.

"I'll think about it," she said.

"Teasing," said Randall. "I like that. You were never easy, princess. So, you need to know anything else?"

"Who were Yancy's biggest opponents on the casino thing?" asked Florence.

"The usual suspects," said Randall. "Baptist Church, Catholic Church, community groups, neighborhood this and that. Self-righteous assholes. Oh, and of course the MACs."

"The ministers at that big church."

"Yeah, COG, the designer church," said Randall. "Reverend Junior was a holy terror, excuse the joke. He even threatened Mayor Yancy with a recall if he went through with bringing in casinos. But it doesn't matter anymore. As soon as he got in office, Crawford killed all Yancy's casino plans."

"I didn't read anything about that!" said Florence. She raised her voice and then lowered it.

"Because Crawford is a smart bastard. The mayor can run his house any way he sees fit. Yancy set up that casino commission to study how to bring casinos to the city. Well, Crawford took office and immediately said the casino task force was no longer a priority. He diverted all his attention to Brownhill, his partners, and the New City deal. That means attention, time, and, most of all, money are diverted from the casino task force. So without ever taking any official action, the kind of action that draws attention, he's killed it."

"Something's rotten here," said Florence. "I can smell it." She made the statement not to Randall but to herself.

"Princess, you know that woman killed Yancy," said Randall. "Just like the newspapers said. And for some reason Jesse King helped her get away."

"That's not what my instinct tells me," said Florence. She was sorry she'd said anything to Randall, but she had to trust someone. "This city has always been full of slick men. Black or white, they're all greased up with the same slime. Jesse King was one of the good ones. And so was Harris Yancy. Yancy was too smart to get knifed by some whore."

"Don't go chasing ghosts, princess," Randall said. He was suddenly stern, like a parent. "Don't go screwing around with things that are beyond you." He gazed at Florence with deep affection and said, "If anything ever happened to you, I swear, I'd never forgive myself."

And for the first time since he came, Randall's eyes held real sincerity. Now Florence remembered his real magic: Underneath all the BS he had a heart.

Randall got up. "Gotta get home. It was good to see you."

Florence stood up and folded the manila envelope. Her mind was processing all the information she'd just gotten. Then Randall leaned in to kiss her on the lips again. Florence was caught off guard and couldn't stop him.

8

Maintenance

The big man popped the gun's magazine and caught it in his hand. He placed the clip on the table as he prepared to clean the big gun. He pulled the slide catch and moved the slide itself off the long barrel of the 9 mm Smith & Wesson.

Things were completely out of hand. The botched contract had now escalated into a full-scale manhunt. No one was in prison for the murder, and the heat was on everyone in town.

The lady lawyer and Jesse King had gone back to the crime scene. That was highly unusual. They were up to something, and the killers just had to know why. They were closing in on that black case, and they could not afford to let it slip through their hands. They had to take her. They put on masks and caught her just as she stepped into her house.

It was bad from the start. She had fought them, throwing things and screaming. The big killer had hit her, but that only made her more defiant.

They tied her up and questioned her but got nothing. She was a tough chick, but they had to get something out of her. They had exposed themselves, so there was no turning back. He had pulled his gun and forced her to make that call to Jesse King. Maybe he would know something. His plan had been to make them both talk and find that case.

Then he made the fatal mistake of leaving the woman with his partner. He went to the bathroom, and when he returned, his partner was cutting up the lady lawyer in a mad frenzy. He pulled the sick bastard off her, but it was too late. Karen Bell was dead.

His mobile phone rang loudly, startling the man. He looked at the phone but did not answer it. It kept ringing, a sound that sounded like angry thunder. He knew who it was. His employer was probably enraged by the new murders. A few more rings, and it stopped.

The killer went back to cleaning the weapon. He slid the barrel out and removed the recoil spring and its guide. He dropped the pieces into a cleaning solution and wiped his hands.

He had chosen the wrong man for this mission. His partner was a nutcase. Ever since the Blake woman had injured him, he had a short trigger and was looking to do some damage.

"How long do we have to stay here, North?"

"I told you never to use my fuckin' name! What if this hotel room is bugged? Huh?"

"Who gives a pissy wet fuck?" said the smaller man.

"Say it again and I'll kill you," North said seriously.

He glared at his partner, and the smaller man walked away into the other room.

North cursed. He would have to kill his partner, but not yet. He needed him until he could close out the case. Two men were better than one. But when he got his hands on that black case, his next action would be to put a bullet into his big, stupid head.

When Jesse King arrived at Karen Bell's home, they'd had no time to interrogate him. They set him up and left the scene, praying that the frame would take. It did, but it was a mixed blessing. King was on the hook for the kill, but he'd sprung the Blake woman. North thought King would be like most people and panic, then run to the police with a crazy story. But King had a big set of balls. He busted her out right under the cops' noses. He was smart, that one. It would be a shame when they killed him.

Now King knew what the girl knew, and that was not good. He had to find them and the black case. It was his life or theirs now.

9

Gas 'N' Food

The old Ford rolled down Seven Mile Road. The street needed paving, and it was a rough ride. It was dark, and Jesse was having trouble seeing as the car lights jumped on.

Jesse and Ramona were traveling due west and making good time, but the car was acting up. It wasn't in very good shape, and they needed gas.

Jesse had an all-news radio station on, listening for anything that might help. The police were saying only that extra patrols were out, and all access to get out of the state was covered.

The car jerked hard to the right. Jesse compensated, grabbing the wheel tightly. A moment passed; then the car sputtered and jerked again.

"Damn, something's wrong," he said.

"We probably should be getting a different car anyway," said Ramona. "It takes them awhile, but the cops will be stopping all suspicious vehicles pretty soon, and this car has crime written all over it."

"Speak of the devil," Jesse said ominously.

He was looking down the road. A half mile away he saw a Detroit police cruiser, and on the other side of the street, farther down, he saw a state trooper's car. The troopers had been patrolling traffic for a long time, but they almost never sat on the street like this.

"Shit," said Jesse.

Suddenly changing lanes, he cut off a car whose driver hit the horn loudly.

"Hey, what the—" said Ramona.

"Sorry, but they're laying for us."

Jesse turned a corner a few blocks before the two police cruisers. After pulling onto a side street, he traveled south for a while. Finally he spotted a gas station on a corner and headed for it.

"What was that all about?" asked Ramona.

"The cops. The state troopers and the Detroit police. When there's a manhunt, they work together. They sit on the road with space between them and stop any car that looks suspicious."

"So?"

"So they probably have this car on a list. We can't take the chance that they'll pull us over."

"This is whack," Ramona mumbled. "Look, let's ditch this car and I'll cop us another one."

"When the time is right. Until then we have to make do," said Jesse. He pulled into the service station with the catchy name of Gas 'N' Food.

"Food," said Ramona. "I'm starvin'."

Jesse was too. They had not eaten all day. It wasn't a priority right now. He could only think about getting to Packer's and seeing Florence. He hoped she could shed some light on what was going on.

Jesse pulled the old car next to a pump. He and Ramona got out. At the pumps there was a Mustang with a young black man in it. Behind him was an old Volkswagen van. Two white men were inside. The black kid's stereo loudly pumped a rap tune.

Ramona walked toward the gas station's ministore. Jesse stopped her before she went inside. He looked in. Behind the counter, surrounded by thick bulletproof glass, was a Chaldean clerk. The place was filled with big mirrors to deter theft, but he spotted no cameras.

"Good," he said. They went in. The clerk walked to one side of the counter so that he could watch Ramona as she took items from the shelves.

Jesse had forgotten how the influx of Chaldean businessmen had affected the city. Many of the black small-business owners had sold their businesses to the Chaldeans, who were Iraqi immigrants. They'd come to Detroit and immediately opened businesses in the all-black neighborhoods.

In the corner of the store was a little door with a small mirror in it. Jesse knew from prosecuting robbery cases that there was a man with a gun back there, just waiting for anyone to do anything wrong.

Ramona walked up with an armful of junk food and soft drinks.

"Okay, let's get out of here," she said. "I hate these damned camel jockeys."

Jesse looked at her with disgust as she went to the counter and paid for the items. Not only was she a pain, but she was prejudiced to boot.

"Hey, don't add the shit up but once," Ramona said to the clerk. "I'm watching your ass."

"I watch you too," said the clerk. He smiled at her.

"And give me five dollars of gas on number five," Ramona said.

The Chaldeans and blacks had an uneasy relationship at best. Blacks resented yet another minority group coming into their community, opening businesses selling alcohol and cigarettes and charging high prices when blacks could not even get loans to start a business.

Ramona had probably grown up learning anti-Chaldean sentiment. She turned to Jesse and shook her head as the clerk pushed the food through a big bulletproof glass door.

Suddenly a shot rang out. It came from outside. Ramona and Jesse stopped in their tracks. Behind them the little door in the corner burst open, and a big Chaldean man holding a semiautomatic gun ran to the door. The clerk pulled out a huge handgun.

"Down! Get down!" yelled the clerk.

Jesse and Ramona moved to a window. Outside the Mustang roared off. On the ground the young black man lay facedown on the pavement. The white van sat where it was, doors open.

The big man ran back in, holding the gun, and said something in his native tongue. He went behind the counter with the clerk and yelled at him frantically. The clerk picked up a phone and dialed.

"Shit, let's get out of here," Ramona said. "These fuckin' people are crazy."

"We're taking that van," Jesse said to Ramona.

"What? Those guys—"

"Just follow me."

Jesse walked out the door and crossed over to the van. He got in but immediately saw there were no keys. "Fuck," he said.

"Let's go," said Ramona. "Before the cops—"

"Hey, what the fuck are you doin'?" the big man yelled out of the store window. He moved from behind the counter.

"Shit, that guy with the gun is coming," said Ramona.

They ran back to their car and got in. The big man charged out of the front door with the gun. Jesse pulled off then, but the big man stood in his path. The gun was pointed right at Jesse.

Jesse hit the gas, and the old car jerked forward. The big man tensed and realized that Jesse was going to ram him. He jumped out of the car's path. Jesse pulled the car onto the street and zoomed through an intersection.

"Damn, I ain't never seen a brother get jacked by some white boys," said Ramona.

"Why did they take those damned keys?" asked Jesse to himself.

"They didn't know we needed a car, you know," said Ramona.

Jesse shot her a nasty look. "Is nag the only thing you know how to do?"

"It was stupid," Ramona replied fiercely. "We didn't have time to grab that van. I could have popped it, but I'd need at least four or five minutes."

"Well, we have to get rid of this car," said Jesse equally as angry. "I know the cops. They're looking for this thing by now."

Tension hung in the air as they rolled along. Silence fell upon them as they each stared out of the dirty windshield.

"Okay, turn here," said Ramona. "I know somebody who can help us."

"No," said Jesse. "I'm tired of your network of criminal screw-ups. Unstable crack dealers and nail-polishing fences. We can risk it."

"You know anybody who can help us?" asked Ramona.

"Florence. That's why we're going to Packer's."

"Fuck Packer's," Ramona protested. "This car ain't gonna make it downriver, and you know it. Besides, we never got the gas we stopped for."

Jesse pulled the car over. "You're not in charge of this thing," he said grimly.

"Yes, I am," said Ramona. "You just don't know it yet."

"I'm making the rules here. You follow my lead or we'll both end up in prison."

"Follow *your* lead? Like you almost led us into getting shot by that camel jockey just now?"

"He's a *Chaldean*, you stupid—" Jesse stopped.

"What?" said Ramona. "Go on and say it: *bitch*. Stupid bitch! You men. It's all you know with your simpleminded asses. And by the way, fuck you."

Jesse gritted his teeth. She was completely juvenile. He wondered for a moment if he could find this LoLo person without her. He knew, though, that it was not an option. "Look," he said, fighting for a calm tone, "I'm sorry."

"Like hell," said Ramona.

"I'm just upset, and I'm taking it out on you," said Jesse levelly. "I'm serious. Let's just forget this and start over, okay?"

Unexpectedly Ramona laughed. Jesse didn't know what was so funny, but he was glad to see she wasn't mad anymore.

"Is that your best rap?" she asked. "Is that how you get them high-class bitches in bed, with that weak shit?"

Jesse was pissed all over again. She was truly a child. "I'm not trying to get you in bed. I'm just apologizing."

"Boy, I bet you didn't get any pussy when you was in the 'hood." Ramona laughed at him again.

"And I bet everybody got some of yours—if they had the money." The taunt came out before he could stop it.

Ramona shot daggers at Jesse. "I told you, I'm not a ho!"

Her face was a paradox. Her anger was grown-up, but her face was cute, like a little girl pouting. Men were prejudiced by beauty, he thought. Beautiful women couldn't be angry or hard. But Ramona was shattering that myth for him with every passing moment.

"I'm not gonna tell you about that ho shit again," Ramona said. "Next time I'm jumping your ass."

"I look forward to that," said Jesse.

It was obvious that Ramona cut a fine line between her occupation and the world's oldest. Jesse reasoned that she had to have some self-esteem, and this was her way of getting it.

When Jesse pulled away, the car rattled louder. He wasn't a mechanic, but he could tell that it wasn't going to last much longer. He glanced at Ramona. Even in the silly disguise she was stunning. He wondered how someone so beautiful could be so crass and hard. Then he realized that the ghetto is the same as any other place. It has beauty and ugliness like mainstream life. And just because God graced you with a pretty face didn't mean you were better than the place you grew up. None of us were, he thought.

"You're right about one thing," said Jesse. "We can't make it to Packer's tonight. Not the way this car is running."

"Well, we can go to a motel, spend the night," said Ramona. "I'm tired anyway."

"Can't," said Jesse. "By now every motel owner in the tricounty area has a description of us. And even with our disguises, they'll be looking out for anything suspicious."

"So you wanna sleep on the street or something?"

"Yeah, quite frankly," said Jesse.

"Fuck, no," said Ramona. "It's too damn cold."

"We don't have a choice," said Jesse. "This car is on its last legs."

"I know where we can get another one," said Ramona.

Jesse sighed heavily. He didn't want to face any more of Ramona's friends. "Okay," he said. "Can we get there tonight?"

"Yeah, but it'll be late," said Ramona.

"Then we should wait until tomorrow," said Jesse. "Late at night there are less people out, which gives the cops a better chance of finding us."

"Damn, did you used to be a dealer or something? You know an awful lot about the cops."

"I worked with the cops," said Jesse absently. "I know how they operate."

Jesse drove along until he saw a big church on a corner. He turned off the lights, then pulled the old car into the church's parking lot. A big sign proclaimed: LAMB'S BLOOD TABERNACLE. There were church buses and vans in the parking lot. Jesse pulled the car between two buses.

"I don't like this," said Ramona.

"Me neither," said Jesse. "But if we park anyplace public, we could get busted."

Ramona looked angrily at the buses, then settled into her seat, leaning back. She looked almost innocent now, staring out the window. She seemed to be lost in thought, dreaming of better times and places, he guessed.

Suddenly Jesse felt responsible for her. If he was a better prosecutor, maybe he would have proved she was innocent and he could have protected her. She was no saint, but she was still mostly a kid, fresh out of a bad situation and in way over her head.

"I'm sorry," Jesse said in a low voice. Ramona was silent. After a moment he tried again. "Well, do you accept my apology?" Jesse asked.

"Say I'm not a ho first."

"Are you serious?"

"Say it or you can stick your apology up your ass," said Ramona.

Jesse breathed deeply. She really was angry. He didn't particularly care one way or the other, but he had to stay on her good side, at least until he got that briefcase. "Okay," he said. "You are not a whore."

"The word is *ho*," Ramona corrected.

"Damn," said Jesse. He took a breath then. "You are not a ho. Okay?"

Ramona considered his words for a moment, then said, "Thank you." She closed her eyes.

The car was already growing cooler, and Jesse could feel the cold air around his ankles. He would start the car now and then just to keep it warm. They had enough gas for that.

"You know, I really don't like fighting with you," he said. "It's just that . . . I feel responsible for all of this, you know, and I have to make sure— I can't let anything happen to you." He didn't know why he said that, but it was too late.

Ramona opened her eyes. She looked at him, her head cocked to one side. She smiled crookedly, one corner of her mouth rising before the other.

"Well, that was nice," she said. "Now you could get laid with a rap like that." She laughed softly and closed her eyes again.

10

Minnesota

Even in the dark basement Cane knew where the sun was. It was gone, and the night had risen. It was Cane's victory at each sunset. Another day gone. Another day of life for him.

These thoughts occupied Cane as he listened to the fat white man talk about their drug deal. Cane hadn't planned on the invasion of LoLo's territory going wrong. He had been talking with the white men for several months now about doing business. He needed more power to defeat the Nasty Girls. He needed product, and there was only one place to get it: the white man.

Cane and the fat man sat at an old card table in the middle of the basement in a house on the west side. He had friends who lived there. It was not a drug house. He had been moving around a lot, and when doing this kind of business, he needed special places like this.

The fat man was called Minnesota, probably because of that pool player, Cane thought. Minnesota was a big boy, six feet three and about two-sixty. He had a head of thin blond hair and a face filled with tiny pink holes. Minnesota also had a terrible habit of belching in the middle of sentences. He obviously ate a lot, and over the years it had done him in. It was so second nature for him that Minnesota actually spoke around his burping.

". . . so, after their family was [burp] taken out, my man took over," Minnesota said. His accent was unmistakably East Coast. "So, we need to make a big move. I gotta lay off at—[burp] at least thirty keys."

"Thirty is a lot," said Cane. "That will wipe out all of my cash."

"Yeah, I—[burp] I know," said Minnesota. "But we're gonna extend some credit. Heroin is making a big comeback [burp]. With this shipment this city will be yours."

"I don't like to be in debt," said Cane. "Especially to men who kill for a living. What's to stop you from getting me over a barrel, then moving in yourself?"

Minnesota laughed and burped loudly in the middle of it. "I like you, man. Listen, we don't deal on a street level. My people have been [burp] out of that for a long time now."

"I don't know that. I don't know anything about you."

"Sure, you do. You've been asking about me all over. Look, we're not unreasonable men. And we don't kill our friends. We need you, and we'll [burp] do whatever it takes to make this work."

Cane considered this. Here was his chance finally to become a real player in Detroit. After the Union there were no real big-time dealers. No one had the money or the muscle to make a major move.

Heroin was becoming the drug of choice again. From Hollywood to the inner-city projects people were going back to the needle or snorting it, which was just as dangerous. It was now called names like Redrum, Homicide, Super Buick, but it was definitely back in style.

While the other dealers were still selling crack, he would bring in heroin and cut them all out. He would get all of the high-end clientele and make mad money. He saw himself standing atop all of the other small-timers, but once again LoLo was an obstacle, right in the path of power.

"You have a deal," said Cane. "But give me some time to get the money together."

"No pro—[burp] problem," said Minnesota. "Give you until the beginning of November, next month."

"Not enough time," said Cane. "I'll need at least three months to get the money together." He didn't want to tell Minnesota that he had to deal with Jaleel. If Minnesota knew he had a thief in his ranks, the fat man might not think he was worthy of being their man in Detroit.

"Sorry," said Minnesota, "but we gotta get this shit on. We have people in [burp] other countries to answer to. Nasty people. And they don't take no for an answer."

"Then I can't do it," said Cane.

Minnesota's face hardened. Suddenly the fat, jolly salesman for killers was gone. Minnesota's pockmarked face turned sour. "Then we'll go to [burp] your competition. Straight up. And your death [burp] will be the beginning of our business."

"That's what I thought," said Cane. "I think I like you people already."

Minnesota laughed. "Smart. That's why we picked you."

"How will the product be delivered?" asked Cane.

"The less you know, the [burp] better right now. We have a new and [burp] proven way of getting it in."

"I've heard that shit before."

"No, no, really," said Minnesota. "It's—" He had an almost violent series of burps. He covered his mouth with a handkerchief and held up his hand as if asking Cane to wait for him.

Cane watched, thinking that maybe this man was actually very ill inside. He wondered if Minnesota had some contagious disease. It would be just like God, Cane thought, to try to kill him by bringing a sick man close like this.

"Oh, man," Minnesota said. "Sorry. Like I said, our new method is a pain in the ass, but it works."

"So what do we do?" asked Cane.

"Wait. We'll let you know right [burp] before it's time. So you'll need to be ready at a moment's notice. Our window of opportunity will be small."

"I don't like it," said Cane. "I'm used to knowing how and when my suppliers bring in their shit. I don't like being in the dark about these things."

"Then you'd better learn to," said Minnesota. "Because this is the way it's gonna [burp] be from now on." He covered his mouth with the handkerchief again, but nothing happened. "I gotta jet," he said. "But I'll be in touch."

Minnesota got up and shook hands with Cane. Cane felt something cold and hard in the fat man's hand. Minnesota pulled his hand away, and Cane saw that Minnesota had put a straight razor in it. It was gold and bigger than the ones barbers used. Cane opened it. The blade shone dully in the dim light.

"We checked you out," said Minnesota. "It's a gift from my people and me."

"Gold?" asked Cane, clearly pleased with the gift.

"Gold-plated," said Minnesota. "After all, we just met you. Use it wisely."

Minnesota walked up the stairs and was soon gone. Cane could hear the big man's heavy footsteps on the ceiling above him grow softer as he left the house.

In the dimness of the cellar Cane admired the razor once more, then closed the weapon and placed it gently in his pocket.

11

The Missing Flower

They drove slowly down the street. Jesse was stiff from sleeping in the car all night. Ramona seemed irritated for the same reason.

On the radio they heard that the police had found Jesse's car and arrested two young kids joyriding in it. The kids had been taken downtown. That had bought them some time. The cops were probably interrogating the hell out of the kids, trying to get anything they could.

They had spent most of the day hiding, taking side streets, stopping and resting, trying to stay away from the police. Jesse was hurting at what he saw. Since leaving the ghetto, he had kept himself in solid middle-class circles. Downtown, Indian Village, Palmer Woods, Rosedale Park, and of course the suburbs. He'd forgotten how the city gets inside you, holds you, until it is indistinguishable from your identity. Seeing it again up close and personal was breaking him down. He was reminded of that terrible feeling that he would never get out alive.

And so he felt even more sorry for Ramona. She'd made it out, in her own way, but not far enough. She must be feeling a lot of what he was, he thought. But you wouldn't know it to look at her. She seemed thoroughly in control.

The old car was noisy as they moved along. It had just about given up, and if they didn't replace it soon, they would never get to Packer's.

The October wind was cold, but the afternoon sun was strong

enough to fight it off. The trees were shedding, and their leaves were swept across the street by the wind.

Jesse hoped that Florence would not give up on him. She had to know that since he hadn't made it last night, he'd be there tonight. He needed to talk to her, to find out what was going on. If he was going to get out of this in one piece, he had to have help on the inside.

Jesse was still trying to put his case together. Whoever had killed Karen Bell had also killed the mayor. They had to be in a position to benefit from the deaths. That could be almost anyone, Jesse thought.

"It's that little house there," Ramona said.

"Huh?" Jesse said, jerked from his thoughts.

"That's the house there," Ramona said. "We need to get in as fast as we can."

Jesse regarded the house. It was old and in need of repair. The street itself was in pretty good shape, though. There were only two vacant lots on the block.

"Wait," said Jesse. "You still haven't told me who these people are. We don't want a car if it's hot."

"Just come on," said Ramona. "I know what I'm doing."

"No. I'm not walking into the unknown here," said Jesse. "I want to know what kind of house this is. Drugs? Stolen property? I don't want to get into something we can't get out of."

Ramona opened the door and got out. "You don't have to go. You can stay here if you want."

"I'm not going to let you go in there by yourself," Jesse said. And as soon as the words were out of his mouth, he wished he hadn't said it.

"I don't need protection from my sister," Ramona said coldly.

As she walked toward the little house, Jesse jumped out of the car and grabbed Ramona by the arm.

"We have to go right now!" he said. He was looking up and down the street, panicked.

"Why?" Ramona asked.

"Your sister. The police will be watching her house."

"They don't know Cheryl lives here," said Ramona, shaking off his hand. "She got pregnant and ran away from home a few years ago. She moved back recently. No one in the family knows she's here but me." Ramona walked on.

"But the police have resources that—" It was too late. Ramona was already at the door knocking. Jesse ran up to her. "Let's at least go to the back," he said.

They moved off the front porch and walked through thick weeds to the back of the house. Jesse noticed for the first time that bars covered all the windows and the house was dark inside.

They got to the back door, and Ramona knocked again. After a moment the door opened, and a face peered at them.

"Who is it?" asked a woman's voice.

"Cheryl, it's me," said Ramona.

"Jesus!" said the woman.

The door was opened, and dim light flooded the small wooden back porch. Jesse could see the woman inside. She was younger than Ramona, heavyset and dressed in a faded blue housecoat. He could see the resemblance, but Cheryl was not nearly as good-looking as her big sister.

They went inside. The back door led to a little kitchen and storage area. Ramona and Cheryl hugged tightly. Ramona smiled, and Cheryl tried to stop her tears. Jesse noticed that Cheryl was holding a little .22 pistol.

"I been seeing you on the news, Mona," said Cheryl. "I was so worried about you."

"You should watch that thing," said Jesse, pointing at the gun. "If it's loaded."

Cheryl looked down at the gun in her hand. Then she put it in the pocket of her housecoat. "Sorry, gotta be careful around here these days. You must be that lawyer guy."

"Yes," said Jesse. "And we can't stay."

"They keep saying that you two are like Bonnie and Clyde, that you're—"

"Cheryl," said Ramona, "I need you to give us your car."

"My car? But it's not legal. The plates are from Texas and close to expired."

"That will be the least of our worries," said Ramona.

"Okay, okay," said Cheryl. "I just have to find the keys. I don't drive it. I've been waiting to get some money to make it legal." Cheryl walked out of the kitchen.

Jesse and Ramona followed Cheryl as she moved into the dining room. The house was run-down but homey. The furniture looked secondhand, and the place needed a new coat of paint. Cheryl went to an old bureau and rifled through a mess of junk in a big drawer. Jesse watched the street through a window.

"So, how are you?" asked Ramona.

"Good. I'm gettin' along fine," said Cheryl.

"We have to be going," said Jesse. He saw the looks on Ramona and Cheryl's faces, then said, "Sorry, but we do."

Ramona ignored Jesse's interruption. "Find any work yet?" asked Ramona.

"No, I—I haven't been looking lately," said Cheryl. She glanced nervously at Jesse. "Nothing out there. I'm on the aid right now." Cheryl didn't look at her sister.

"No need to be ashamed," Ramona said. "You had it tough. Tony was an asshole. He broke his promise to you. You just need some time. And hey, you're doing better than me."

"You always know what to say," said Cheryl. She fished out a ring of keys. "It's one of these, I think. It's the red Toyota outside."

Ramona took the keys. "Thanks. So, can I see him?"

Cheryl walked into the bedroom off the dining room and quickly returned with a sleeping child.

"He's been kinda sick lately, so be careful," she said. "You know how baby germs are."

Ramona took the baby boy in her arms. He was only about one. Jesse saw her face light up. Ramona kissed him and rocked him in her arms. She was serene and happy. Jesse envied her.

"How old is he now?" asked Ramona.

"He'll be one in two weeks," said Cheryl.

"Happy birthday, Anthony," Ramona said. "Too bad you got stuck with your daddy's name. I'm gonna come back and see you after I—"

Her voice cracked, and she sat down with the baby, looking misty. Cheryl comforted her. Jesse went to the window and looked away, not wanting to embarrass Ramona more than she already was. He got the feeling that there was a lot of history here that he didn't know about. He thought about his own sister and her kids.

"It's okay, Mona," said Cheryl. "You'll be fine."

"We got some family, don't we?" Ramona said. "Another generation coming and look at us. Just look at us, Cheryl."

Cheryl didn't say anything; she just kept hugging her sister.

"Car!" said Jesse. He was still looking out the window.

Cheryl rushed to the window. "It might be my neighbor, Alice. She gets off work about now."

"It's not a police car," said Jesse.

"Damn," said Cheryl, her voice tensing. "It's Mama."

"Mama?" said Ramona.

"I thought no one knew she was here," said Jesse.

"When did you start talking to her?" Ramona's voice was tinged with anger.

"Just a few days ago," Cheryl said. She looked away from Ramona's stare.

"You promised," said Ramona. "We promised."

"That was a long time ago," her sister protested. "Tony left me. I had the baby, and I was back here. I got lonely. So I called her. But she promised not to say anything to my friends here."

"You broke your promise," said Ramona angrily.

"We gotta go—right now," said Jesse.

Jesse began to walk to the back door, but Ramona just stared at her sister, not moving.

"I'm not leaving. I want to see her," Ramona said.

"Are you crazy?" said Jesse.

"Yes," said Ramona. "I'm completely crazy right now." She stared angrily at her sister.

"We can't," said Jesse. "If your mother knows your sister is here, she could have told anyone. We don't know if the police have found out."

"He's right, Mona," said Cheryl. "You should go."

"I don't want to talk to her," said Ramona. "I just want to see her. I'm not leaving." To Jesse she said, "And I've got the keys to the new car."

"I don't believe this," said Jesse.

"Give Anthony to me," said Cheryl. "I'll put him back into bed." Cheryl took the sleeping boy and went into the bedroom.

There was a knock at the door.

"Don't be silly," Jesse whispered. "We've got to leave now."

"No." Ramona was defiant. She went into the bedroom with Cheryl. Jesse threw his hands up and followed. The knocking at the door continued.

"She's always been stubborn," said Cheryl to Jesse as she came out of the room.

"That's not the word I was thinking," said Jesse.

"You'd better go in there with her," said Cheryl.

Jesse slipped into the little room with Ramona as Cheryl went to the door. Cheryl collected herself, then opened the door. Her mother walked in carrying a bag.

"What's wrong with you, girl?" asked Bethel Blake. "It's cold out there." She walked in like she owned the place and headed for the kitchen. Cheryl followed.

"I was putting the baby to bed, Mama," said Cheryl.

In the bedroom Ramona and Jesse stood in darkness. Ramona was close to the door, listening. Jesse stood behind her, fighting off the urge to ram her head in the wall. The baby slept peacefully in the bed.

"You've seen her, okay?" Jesse whispered. "So let's slip out of this window and get the hell out of here."

"No, I want to hear what that woman says about me," said Ramona. "And in case you didn't notice, the house has bars on all the windows. Damn, I can't hear them in that kitchen."

"We don't have time for this," said Jesse. "I don't want to have to take those keys from you."

Ramona turned to face Jesse in the little room. He could barely see her face, but he was aware of her body so near him, and it made him uneasy.

"Here," she said. "Take them and leave me here." She held up the keys. "You can run right now. My mother will just think you were some man Cheryl was shacked up with."

Jesse reached out and took the keys from her. Ramona walked back to the door. Jesse waited a moment, then walked up behind her and put his hand on her shoulder.

"You know I'm not going without you," Jesse said.

"You probably guessed we don't get along with our mother," said Ramona in a low voice. "When I left home, Cheryl stole some money and gave it to me. When she got pregnant and left a few years later, my mother tried to have her get rid of the baby. When Cheryl said no, she tried to send her away. I helped Cheryl get away. We promised that we would never speak to Mama again. But I see how much she cares about that promise," she ended bitterly.

"You can't really blame her, can you?" said Jesse.

"Yes, I can," said Ramona in a hushed voice. "It was a promise between us. But Cheryl was never the strongest of us."

Jesse's eyes were adjusting to the dark, and he could see the pain in Ramona's face.

"I don't mean to belittle all this," said Jesse, "but we do have other things to do right now."

"Quiet, they're coming back in," said Ramona.

Bethel Blake and Cheryl walked into the dining room carrying soft drinks. Bethel was a tall, thin woman. She had salt-and-pepper hair and a face accented with wrinkles at her eyes and the corners of her mouth. She seemed elegant as she walked; you could see that in her day she probably turned the head of every man in town.

"Those groceries were heavy," said Bethel. "I knew you didn't have any food here. My grandson will starve to death if I leave it up to you."

"Don't start, Mama," said Cheryl. "I didn't get a chance to go to the market today. And I thought I asked you to call if you were coming over."

"I was visiting Sister Helen from the church. I didn't think about it. She practically lives right around the corner from here."

Bethel sat at the small dining room table and crossed her legs. Cheryl flopped down across from her. An awkward moment passed between them.

"So, your sister, the murderer, was on the news all day today," said Bethel.

"Mona didn't kill anyone," said Cheryl.

"I knew she'd end up like this. She was never no damn good."

"Mama, if you're just going to sit here and dog Ramona, you might as well leave."

"Sure, you feel that way. *You* didn't have the police drag you downtown. *You* didn't have reporters all over your house when you came home. And *you* didn't get calls from every member of Holy Grace Church asking why *your* daughter killed the mayor!"

"I don't want to get into it with you, Mama," said Cheryl wearily.

"I'm just telling you what I've been through. Every day it's something new about your sister," said Bethel. "Once again she's managed to bring tragedy on our family."

"Why do you come here to punish me like this?" asked Cheryl. "Okay, I messed up my life, but I'm trying to get it back together. Can't you ever encourage us?"

"I'm not punishing you," said Bethel. "I'm talking about your sister. After all the things she's done to this family, you could at least see my side of this."

Cheryl laughed. "I knew it. Always the same. You against Mona. You know, some mothers would be sad about what's happening to Ramona. But not you, Mama. You gloat, happy that you were right about her. Happy that you finally beat her. But you know what? You're wrong. Ramona may be a lot of things, but she's not a killer."

"How can you say that when you know what she did to your sister," said Bethel.

"I don't want to hear that again," said Cheryl, exasperated. "Let Sarah rest in peace."

"This is your problem, Cheryl," said Bethel. "You don't like to face up to the truth. The truth about Ramona, that man who got you pregnant, and yourself." Her voice rose and gained righteous conviction. "The Book says—"

"Please don't quote the Bible, Mama. I can't take that tonight."

"The Word is the way, Cheryl. You been reading that Bible I gave you?"

"No. I'm tired of all that stuff," said Cheryl.

"You'd better hope a lightning bolt don't come down and strike you dead for saying that," said Bethel. "Blasphemy."

"I don't care," said Cheryl. Then she added: "And neither does God."

Bethel reacted as if she had been smacked in the face. "Well, you finally got what you wanted. I'm leaving. I'll just kiss my grandson and I'll go."

"Anthony is sleeping in there, Mama," Cheryl said. She raised her voice a little so that Jesse and Ramona could hear.

Something shuffled inside the bedroom.

"Sounds like he's up to me," said Bethel.

Cheryl went to the bedroom door first and pretended to have trouble opening it. There was a closet in the room, and she prayed that Jesse and Ramona had heard her and gotten inside it.

Cheryl and Bethel started to walk inside the dark room when suddenly the lights went on. Ramona stood next to the light switch, glaring at Bethel. Jesse stood next to her, looking like a deer in the headlights.

"Hello, Mama," said Ramona calmly.

Bethel screamed.

Cheryl quickly clamped her hand over her mother's mouth. Jesse ran over and held Bethel with Cheryl.

"I'm sorry, ma'am, but you have to stop that," said Jesse. "Please don't make us have to do something we'll regret."

Bethel's eyes were wide with fear. She stared at Ramona, who smiled like the devil at her.

"Okay," said Jesse, "we have a situation here. Okay, Ms. Blake—"

"Her name is Bethel," said Ramona. Her tone was nasty.

"Okay, Bethel," said Jesse. "Your daughter is going to take her hand away from your mouth. And you will not scream again, okay?"

He looked at the woman for a response. She nodded her head. Cheryl slowly took her hand away. Ramona walked past her and into the dining room. Bethel stood dumbstruck. Jesse put his hand on Bethel's shoulder and guided her out of the room. Cheryl followed.

Ramona sat at the table and took a sip of Bethel's soda. She stared at her mother over the rim of the cheap glass. Jesse kept a close eye on Bethel as she sat down with Ramona.

"What are you going to do to me?" Bethel asked Jesse.

"We're not going to do anything, ma'am," Jesse said. "We're just trying to clear our names."

"They need help, Mama," said Cheryl.

"How could you let her suck you into this?" Bethel hissed at her younger daughter.

"No one sucked her into anything," said Ramona.

Bethel was frightened, but she didn't seem to be getting ready to scream again, Jesse thought. If she did, well, he would have to incapacitate her. He couldn't take the chance that someone would call the police.

"That was my drink," said Bethel to Ramona.

"Didn't have a name on it," Ramona said. She took another swallow.

"Ms. Blake," said Jesse, "I want you to know that we didn't do anything. This whole thing is a big conspiracy." He looked at her for a response, but he almost didn't believe what he had just said himself. "Look, we have to go, but we have to have your assurance—"

Ramona laughed. "She'll call the police as soon as we hit the door. And if Cheryl tries to stop her, she'll just leave and call them, right, Mama?"

Bethel was silent. She just kept staring at Ramona.

"I'll get you another drink, Mama," Cheryl said. She went into the kitchen.

"I don't know what to do about this," said Jesse. "But I do know that we have to get going here." The situation was unnerving him.

"There's no end to the misery you cause this family," said Bethel.

"I could say the same thing about you, Mama," said Ramona.

"That's comical," said Bethel. "And just like you. Diverting your sin to others."

"No. That's what you do," said Ramona pointedly. "You forced your bullshit upon us, disguised it as religion, and when we got hip to it, you beat us down like it was our fault."

"You were a bad seed," said Bethel. "You corrupted your sisters with your willfulness and indecency."

"Bullshit!" said Ramona. "This whole thing was always about you. You had a life until you started having kids, and you blame us for losing Daddy. And what you never realized is it all started because you couldn't keep your legs closed."

At this insult Bethel jumped out of her chair. Ramona stood up with her, defiant and angry.

"Who the hell do you think you're talking to?" said Bethel. Her face was different now. It had hate and violence in it. It was as though she'd become another person, and for a second Jesse was scared of her. He watched the two women, afraid that the police were coming but fascinated by their hatred for each other.

"Go on," Ramona taunted. "Hit me like you used to. Make me believe that I have to respect you."

"You killed your sister," said Bethel. She said it slowly and with conviction. "You shot at those drug dealers and killed your own flesh and blood. You brought your filthy street friends into our life, and she died."

"I didn't kill Sarah," said Ramona, hurt by the statement. She began to tremble as she faced down her mother over the cheap wooden table.

Cheryl came back in with another soda. She stepped between

Ramona and Bethel and put the drink on the table. "Here, Mama," she said.

Bethel took the drink and sat down. She took a drink of her soda and grimaced a little. "This pop tastes funny," she said.

"It's generic pop, Mama," said Cheryl. "You bought it. What do you want for fifty cents a quart?"

"Look, we have to go now," Jesse said to Ramona. "Mrs. Blake, we can't let you go to the police."

"So are you gonna kill me like you did the others?" said Bethel, sneering at him. "Go on, I have faith in the Lord." She took another drink.

"Nobody's gonna kill you, Mama," said Cheryl.

"Look, we'll just disconnect the phone or something," said Jesse. "That will at least buy us some time."

Ramona had not given up the argument. "Even with all the trouble I'm in," she said, "I'm glad I'm not you, Mama. My life may not be the best, but I don't blame anyone for that but myself. We had a family, and you ruined it. Family, Mama. That never meant anything to you." She turned to Jesse. "Come on, let's get the hell out of here."

"You can say anything you want," said Bethel. "But you still killed your sister. You know it, I know it, and God knows it."

Ramona turned to her mother defiantly. "I know it was part my fault she's gone. I accept that. It's part of who I am now. But if it wasn't for the way you treated us, she might still be alive. We both did it, Mama. Only I take the blame for what I did."

Ramona headed for the door. Jesse stood and, not knowing what to do next, watched her.

"You know what I see every day?" said Bethel. "Each morning before I go to work, I see a vase by the door. Those drug dealers shot it to pieces when Sarah was killed. After we buried your sister, I sat for weeks gluing that vase back together. I found every piece except one, a piece with a little green flower on it. I loved that vase so much that I didn't care, so I put it back on the table, but you can see the piece that's missing. Every day I see that vase, I think about Sarah and the life that I'll never get back. I think about how I could have stopped it by stopping you. But I didn't bring sin, evil, and bullets into our house. You did."

"Whatever makes you happy, Mama," said Ramona. She walked toward the door. Jesse followed.

Bethel stood up. "You're going to hell, Ramona. Straight to—" Bethel dropped her drink to the floor and put her hands to her head. "What—I feel—" she said.

Then Bethel fell to the floor with a thud. Ramona took a hesitant step toward her mother, then stopped. Cheryl helped Bethel up and led her to the sofa.

"Oh," said Bethel, "what's—what's wrong?"

"It's all right, Mama," said Cheryl. "Just put a few sleeping pills in your drink."

"You drugged her?" said Jesse. He took a moment to think about it, then said, "Nice move."

"I couldn't let her turn you in," said Cheryl. "She would have too. Listen you two, she'll be out all night, so go, run and don't come back here. It'll be too dangerous after this."

Ramona hugged Cheryl tightly. "I love you."

"Me too," said Cheryl. "Now go on."

"Thanks," said Jesse.

Bethel was out cold on the sofa. Ramona looked at her mother, and her face filled with sadness.

They left the little house, got into Cheryl's red Toyota, and drove away. Ramona drove the car toward the freeway entrance.

"Don't go on the freeway," said Jesse. "The cops will have double patrols at night. We need to stick to the smaller streets. Even the avenues will be dangerous. It will take awhile, but it's safer."

Ramona obeyed mutely. They drove without talking for a few miles. Then Ramona turned to Jesse and said, "I know what you're thinking."

"Do you?" he asked.

"What you're thinking is, no wonder I turned out so fucked up," said Ramona. "My family is fucked up too."

"Well," said Jesse, "for once you're right. That's exactly what I was thinking."

"Screw you," Ramona said. She managed a smile.

"Look, everybody's family is messed up," said Jesse. He knew what he was talking about. He wondered what Bernice and her kids were thinking about him through all this.

"If I hadn't shot that gun, my sister would still be alive." Ramona's voice was filled with regret and pain.

"You don't know that," said Jesse.

"Sometimes it's all I can think about," she said. "I can barely look at a gun now. I was never like my friends. They were really hard, tough, you know. I was the brains, the planner. I had no business with a gun. I don't know what the hell I was doing."

"I thought you and your mother were going to have a knock-down-drag-out fight," said Jesse.

"Wouldn't be the first time," said Ramona. "After Daddy left, I got tired of her beating us, and we fought all the time."

Jesse did not reply right away. He had something on his mind, but he didn't know if he wanted to share it with her. "My old man cut out on us too," he said. "But my mother never raised a hand to us," said Jesse. "It wasn't her way."

"Lucky you. We got it all the time. Wooden switches, extension cords, leather belts."

"You go to jail for that these days," said Jesse, a little disturbed by what she was telling him.

"My mother blamed me for being born," said Ramona. "Like if she had aborted me, she would have had a better life or something. I don't mind paying for my mistakes, but I'll be damned if I'll pay for being born."

"She's just weak," said Jesse. "My sister, Bernice, is the same way." Jesse hesitated, then added: "She uses." He had to force the words out of his mouth. Even now he felt ashamed of her.

"I'm sorry," said Ramona.

"Me too. Bernice took the breakup of our family harder than I did. We were both on the wrong track, but she started partying, doing drugs, anything to forget her pain. Eventually she went out and found men like our daddy to sleep with. She was trying to change them, the way she couldn't change our father, but they left her too."

A car approached them slowly down a dark street. The street was narrow, and Ramona veered over to the right to make room. The other car moved in front of her. She slowed down.

"Is it a police cruiser?" asked Jesse anxiously.

"Can't tell," said Ramona. "It's too dark."

The other car rolled toward them, then turned into a driveway on the right side of the street.

Ramona sighed. "Damn, this is making me old." She drove to the end of the street and turned left. She crossed an avenue and went back to the side streets. "So you think maybe she's right?" asked Ramona. "My mother, that is?"

"About what?" asked Jesse.

"About my sister dying?"

"Don't do that to yourself," said Jesse. "It was an accident."

Ramona took her eyes off the road for a moment, looking at Jesse with great seriousness. "Don't ever leave your family," she said. She drove on without another word.

As they headed downriver, Jesse's heart was leaden with the turmoil of Ramona's family. It reminded him of his own family and how much he had already lost. They headed toward Packer's, and he promised himself that he was finished losing things. He was determined to get his life back.

12

Trapper's Alley

Cane loved his new sunglasses. They covered his bad eye in public, and they darkened the world around him. This was the way life should be, he thought, tenebrous, a night world.

He walked the streets of Greektown, waiting for LoLo to show herself. It was night, and Greektown's sidewalks were thick with people of all races.

Cane walked along with Turk, who was carrying a leather backpack on his broad shoulders. Behind them walked two young rollers. A few blocks away Q was in a car with the engine running.

Greektown was a few city blocks filled with Greek restaurants, shops, and businesses. At night, when most cities came to life, Detroit died. Businesspeople, black and white, left, headed out of the city to their homes. It was almost like a daily "white flight" each evening. But Greektown and a few other places downtown defied that rule. People flocked to the area as darkness settled.

And so did the police. For Greektown to prosper, it had to be safe. 1300 was right around the corner, and so there was always an abundance of uniformed cops around. You couldn't go very far without seeing a couple of uniforms on foot or a cruiser making the rounds. And you never knew if there was a plainclothes undercover cop lurking in the smiling faces of some crowd.

This made Cane feel good. LoLo would not try anything here. And she probably felt that he would not either. But she did not know him very well. He desperately needed to do business with Minnesota before they decided he wasn't worth it. Cane had to raise some fast cash and get rid of her and her meddling bitches for good. This was a desperate situation, and he had to go to extremes.

Cane signaled, and the two young rollers broke off. Cane and Turk walked on, circling the block several times. He was about to try a different area when he saw LoLo. She was walking along with a big woman. They were headed toward Trapper's Alley, a sort of minimall of stores and restaurants.

Smart, Cane thought. A contained space lessened the likelihood that he would try anything. And she might already have a setup in there, he reasoned. Cane signaled to his men. Then he walked inside.

Trapper's Alley bustled with activity. The smell of food permeated the air. Laughter, music, and chatter bounced off the brick walls. Cane spotted LoLo and Yolanda at the back of a big crowd in the lobby.

Three jugglers were putting on a show for a large crowd, a comical distraction that happened once an hour or so. The crowd was in a big semicircle around the show. They laughed and applauded the jugglers, and they threw pins in the air. LoLo and Yolanda were stone-faced, keeping to the back of the crowd.

Cane moved over toward them, carrying the backpack on one shoulder. He watched the faces in the crowd, looking for LoLo's plants in any. As he did, Cane noticed a uniformed cop in the crowd. He was on the other side of the jugglers, by the door. Cane continued to move toward the two women.

Marly was mingling in with the crowd. She saw Cane. As Cane passed her, Marly moved out of the crowd and circled behind him. She opened her big red purse, putting her hand on the weapon inside.

Cane's men, the two young rollers, entered the building and spotted their boss. They moved away from Cane, going closer to the uniformed cop.

Cane was excited but unafraid. The sun was gone, and so he was stronger. These women could not harm him, he thought. He would take them just as he had planned.

Cane and Turk moved closer to the women. Cane turned and pretended to say something to Turk while quickly slipping the gold razor he'd gotten from Minnesota into his hand. Turk shoved his hands into the pockets of his jacket.

LoLo and Yolanda stared fiercely into the black lenses on

Cane's approaching face. LoLo's arms were folded across her waist. Yolanda stood behind her boss, towering over the smaller woman. Yolanda's hands were shoved into the pockets of her big down-filled jacket.

Cane stopped about two feet in front of the women, close enough to see there was no fear in their faces.

"Where's my man?" he asked.

Tico sat motionlessly in the heavy wooden chair. Walker sat on the old sofa, holding a cellular phone. Tico knew something was up. The women were all gone, including Walker's girlfriend, Marly, and the house was unusually quiet.

"Tonight's the night, boy," said Walker. "Tonight you'll learn all the mysteries of life."

"Kiss my black ass," said Tico. "Let me out of this chair, and I'll show you a mystery."

Walker got up and walked over to Tico. "When this phone rings, I'm gonna put a bullet in your brain."

"Do it now," said Tico. "Don't drag this shit out any more than you gotta."

"Gotta wait," said Walker. "The ladies have to make sure your boy Cane takes the bait. If I kill you and he don't take it, then it's my ass."

Tico got the picture. They were trying to set up Cane. If they could lure him out in the open and hit him, then Walker would get the call. With Cane gone, he might as well give up the info on the money house or Walker would kill him.

"You can still save yourself," said Tico. "Let me go now, and I'll square it with Cane."

"Oh," said Walker. "I hear a little desperation in your voice. Not so full of courage to die now, are you?"

"I should've known better than to trust a damn foreigner like you. You fuckin' Jamaicans ain't got no integrity whatsoever. You for sale to the highest bidder."

"Watch your mouth now," said Walker.

"I've been to Jamaica," said Tico. "It ain't nothing but a second-rate, bullshit, backward-ass hole in the ground."

"You don't know the island, dead man," said Walker, growing tense. "It's a paradise."

"That's why you left, right?" asked Tico. " 'Cause it's a paradise.

It's a shit hole, and you know it. People living in grass huts, eating dead dogs, living in their own piss and shit, that's Jamaica!"

Walker walked over to Tico and slapped him hard in the face. "You gonna learn not to disrespect my home," said Walker. "You gonna learn to respect your betters. You lousy niggers here don't know nothing. Don't even know what you are. You're mostly half-breeds, the white man's seed running all through your race. You got no heritage, no history. All you got is sorrow, pain, and death."

"Better than Jamaica, a third-rate country where women sell their babies for a loaf of bread," said Tico.

Walker pulled his gun and put it to Tico's head. Tico closed his eyes and took a deep breath.

Enraged, Walker cocked the gun. A long moment passed. Then Walker laughed. "Nice try, boy," he said. "You wanna go out easy, don't you? No. I'm gonna make sure you feel it when you die. I'll give it to you in the gut, so you bleed to death inside, drowning in your own blood. Or maybe I'll suffocate you, let you die while your eyes bulge and your lungs burn." Walker turned his gun around and hit Tico hard in the face with it. Tico's lip split, and blood sprayed from his mouth. "Or maybe I'll beat you to death," said Walker.

The door to the little room opened. Walker spun around quickly, raising the gun.

"Whatcha doin' here, boy?" Walker asked.

"Just chillin'," said Little Jack.

"Where my damn money?" asked LoLo.

Yolanda's eyes were locked on Turk, looking for any sign of dangerous movement. Around them the crowd buzzed and laughed.

"My man Turk here got it right in that bag on his back," said Cane. Then he added: "You little bitch."

Two young girls, twins, in black leather jackets were standing nearby. One had braids dyed a bright blond; the other had short, spiky dreadlocks. They heard Cane's statement, then walked away from them, looking disgusted.

Cane edged back from the crowd. Turk followed, careful not to take his eyes off the women. Cane moved a few feet to an area next to a shop that was closed for the night. LoLo and Yolanda followed carefully. Turk took the backpack off and set it on the floor.

When Marly saw this, she walked over to where Cane and the twins had just been. She made sure not to make eye contact with

LoLo and Yolanda. She took her place at the back of the crowd next to the twins in the black leather jackets. Marly pretended to watch the show. She was about ten feet away from Cane.

"Gimme my money," said LoLo.

"We can just stand here and jack each other off," said Cane. "Or you can show me Tico."

Cane's two men were still near the uniformed cop on the other side of the crowd. They started to talk louder, pretending to have an argument. The cop noticed them but did not stop the exchange.

"I'll take you to him," said LoLo, "as soon as you show me what's in that bag."

"Bitches," said Cane. "I was killing men when you were still trying to figure out how your pussy worked."

"Punk ass," said Yolanda.

"I got your punk ass, you fat bitch," said Turk.

"We can stand here and dog each other all night," said LoLo. "Or we can do some business—"

A cop with a thick mustache walked in the back entrance and blended into the crowd next to Marly and the leather-jacketed twins.

LoLo's eyes darted over to the cop, and for the briefest moment she showed concern.

Cane saw the look on LoLo's face, and now he knew that she had a plan as well. A plant in the crowd. He was glad they could not see his eyes behind the dark glasses. That was his advantage. LoLo was scared because she had not expected that cop to come in. This was his chance to strike, when she least expected it.

"Okay," Cane said. He lifted his arm into the air and scratched his head. "Gimme the bag, Turk."

Seeing the signal, the two young rollers immediately began to fight. One of them pulled out a knife. The cop by the two men pulled his gun and rushed over. Someone screamed.

LoLo was distracted for a moment. When her eyes returned to Cane, she saw the blur of Cane's swinging arm and a flash of gold.

Then things happened fast.

Little Jack walked over to the old sofa and sat down. Walker paid him no attention. Walker turned back to Tico and slapped him again in the face. Tico's face was bleeding and starting to swell around the lips.

"Damn," said Little Jack. "Why don't you just shoot his ass?"

"I will," said Walker. "I can't wait until this phone rings." Walker put his gun away and walked back to the sofa. "Why you not down at Greektown with the women, boy?"

"Because I'm a man," said Little Jack. He whipped out a gun, moving so fast that Walker was still in the process of sitting when the gun was pressed against his thigh. Little Jack pulled the trigger and blew a hole in Walker's leg. The Jamaican screamed and fell to the floor. Walker reached for his gun, but Little Jack was on him, putting his gun in Walker's mouth.

"Don't move," Little Jack said. He reached into Walker's waistband and pulled out his gun.

"Yeah! Yeah!" said Tico with elation. "Come on, little man, get me out of this chair!"

Little Jack backed away from Walker, who put his hand over his wound, trying to stop the bleeding. Little Jack walked up to Tico and put the gun barrel in Tico's face.

Tico looked into Little Jack's eyes. For a moment his happiness subsided. The young boy's face was grim, like a tiny, world-weary old man.

"You see what I'm doin' here?" asked Little Jack.

"Yeah, I see," said Tico. It was okay, he thought. The young boy was just making sure Tico knew that he owed him. "Now cut me loose."

"You remember this when we get back to your man," said Little Jack.

"They gonna kill you, boy," Walker said. His voice was covered in pain.

"Shut up, you funny-talking nigga," said Little Jack. Then he put Walker's gun in his pocket, pulled out a knife, and cut Tico's binds.

Tico got up slowly. His joints were stiff from sitting for so long. He looked over at the little boy and found him holding up Walker's gun.

"Cane said you'd be wanting to get rid of him yourself."

Tico took the gun, then put it in his waistband and picked up the heavy wooden chair he was sitting in. He had to strain to get it up.

"No, no," said Walker on the floor. He tried to crawl away.

"Told you I was gonna kill you," said Tico.

He smashed the heavy chair on Walker's back with all his might. The chair cut Walker's skin and broke bones. Tico struck again and again, until Walker's head was bloody and one of his arms was broken and disjointed. Tico was spotted with blood and breathing heavily.

"We gotta get goin'," said Little Jack.

"Right," said Tico.

Tico pulled off a wooden leg from the chair. "Shoulda stayed your ass on the island," he said to Walker. Walker groaned something that Tico couldn't understand.

Tico moved over Walker's body. Walker was broken, bloody, and shaking. Tico noticed teeth lying next to his head covered in thick blood.

Tico raised the heavy wooden chair leg with both arms and brought it down onto Walker's head.

Cane lifted the big straight razor toward LoLo's throat. Seeing it, LoLo moved back, raising her arms. Cane caught LoLo on her right forearm just above the elbow. The razor cut through her coat and her sweater and opened a long gash. LoLo shrieked in pain. Cane pushed himself backward, toward the crowd.

Turk pulled his weapon before Yolanda could get to hers and fired at her. His shot missed. Yolanda heard the bullet whiz by her ear. Before Yolanda could return fire, Turk was hit in the upper chest by Marly from across the way. Turk fell on his back, dropping his gun.

The cop with the thick mustache pulled his weapon and put it to Marly's head. "Drop it!" he yelled.

The advancing crowd heard the new gunfire and stopped. Someone screamed again, and the crowd surged in the other direction.

Cane was in the crowd, moving toward the door. People ran in all directions, yelling and darting for cover.

In the confusion Yolanda remembered to grab the backpack.

"Damn!" said the cop with the mustache. He pulled out a pair of handcuffs and was about to handcuff Marly.

"Let her go," said one of the twin girls in black leather. She held a gun to the cop's head, her braids swinging in her face.

"What the—" said the cop. He dropped the handcuffs. Marly snatched the cop's gun and threw it out of reach. Then she ran with the twins toward the back entrance. As they got to the exit, three cops, two male, one female, came in the entrance. Their guns were out in front of them.

Marly and the twins stopped in their tracks. For a moment the three cops and the three women held their weapons on each other. Then:

"I got 'em," said the cop with the thick mustache from behind the women. He had his gun trained on them. "Give it up—now!" he yelled.

Marly and the women hesitated. The twins looked at Marly for direction.

"Fuck it," she said. She dropped her gun and put her hands up. The twins did the same. The cops arrested them.

"There are two more somewhere outside," said the cop with the thick mustache. He pointed at the back entrance. "One of them was cut by a man."

The two male cops ran out of the back entrance, talking into their walkie-talkies. The policewoman stayed behind and cuffed Marly and the two young girls. The cop with the thick mustache walked to the twin who'd put her gun to his head and reared back to hit her. The policewoman grabbed his clenched fist.

"Not here," she said. The cop dropped his fist, shooting the girl a nasty look. They took the women away.

Cane was by the entrance, watching as people ran out around him. LoLo had the place packed with her people, Cane thought. A lot of damned good it did her. Cane saw Turk on the floor in a pool of spreading blood, unmoving. He was gone.

Cane went outside in time to see his men who'd started the fight being put into a police cruiser. They smiled at Cane as they were arrested. They'd be all right, Cane thought. They were too young to be kept in jail, and he'd make sure they were rewarded when they got out.

Cane looked down Monroe Street. He saw no sign of Yolanda and LoLo. The street was filled with people and police. Cane turned into a brisk October wind. It chilled his face. He had not gotten LoLo like he wanted, but the razor was new, and he wasn't used to it yet, he reasoned. LoLo would be really pissed when she discovered the backpack was filled with paper.

Cane hurried down the busy street, out of the area to the I-75 freeway service drive. A car pulled up, and Cane jumped in with his man Q behind the wheel.

"Let's get the fuck out of here," said Cane.

The car rolled away as more cops poured into Trapper's Alley. If everything had gone according to plan, Cane thought, he and Tico would be having a beer tonight.

13

Packer's

The country music was loud in the background. Jesse put one hand over his free ear as he listened on the pay phone at the 7-Eleven. He'd been put on hold by the man who answered the phone, which at Packer's meant the phone was dropped on a counter while the man made drinks. It sounded lively at the bar, loud voices mixing with Travis Tritt's racy music.

Ramona was in the car, probably still laughing at him because he couldn't remember where the hell Packer's was. Jesse glanced over and saw her with a big smile on her face. Women. They loved it when men screwed up.

They were in the city of Taylor, a little town downriver from Detroit. Taylor was jokingly called Taylor-Tucky, as in Kentucky, because of its rural atmosphere and abundant population of trailer parks and self-proclaimed rednecks. It was actually just a working-class town, the very soul of America.

A dirty-looking white man walked by the car. He looked at Ramona for a moment. Jesse watched nervously until the man moved on. He walked to a brick wall by the 7-Eleven and pulled at his pants. Jesse saw the stream of urine as the man pissed on the wall. Jesse breathed easier. Just a local drunk.

Jesse turned up the collar on his jacket. It was getting colder, and he'd worn layers of clothes to keep warm. But the Michigan wind had a way of finding the one crack in your cover and going inside it.

Jesse got the directions over the loud music and hung up the phone. He turned and saw Ramona getting out of the car. She looked at Jesse and pointed to the 7-Eleven. She held some money in her hand. She intended to go inside. Jesse shook his head. He was about to say no when the dirty white man moved toward Ramona. He was coming up behind her, and she didn't see him.

"Move!" Jesse yelled as he ran to her. The man saw Jesse and pulled out a knife. Jesse cursed himself for leaving his gun in the car.

Jesse got to Ramona just as she turned toward the man. He was bigger than Jesse first thought and mean-looking. The man swung a knife at Ramona as Jesse stepped between them. He caught the man's wrist as the knife struck him. It cut through Jesse's jacket and two shirts and hit his belt. The blade went up and cut Jesse just above the waist. There was a sharp sting, and Jesse could feel the blood come.

Instinctively Jesse brought his knee up into the man's groin. The man yelled loudly and fell to one knee. Before he could do anything, Ramona's foot smashed the man on the side of the head, and he fell backward.

"Are you okay?" Jesse asked Ramona. He held her shoulders and looked at her like a parent who catches a kid after he falls.

"Yeah," she said.

"I saw him coming at you and I—"

Ramona stared at him strangely, like he was crazy. Her eyes fell. Jesse followed them and saw that the knife was still hanging out of his clothes. He pulled it out and hurled it as far away as he could. The man groaned. Ramona kicked him again. The would-be robber struggled to his feet and ran away.

"Is it bad?" she asked.

"No, it just cut me a little, but I'm bleeding."

Before Jesse could stop her, Ramona ran into the store. Jesse got in the car on the driver's side. Ramona came out of the store and pushed Jesse to the passenger side of the car. She settled into the driver's seat and stared at Jesse again.

"What?" he asked.

"Nothing," she said. They drove away.

Another semi pulled into the parking lot. Like most of the others, it pulled no cargo trailer, just the cab. Jesse had forgotten that Packer's was a trucker hangout. The parking lot was unpaved and filled with semis, older model cars, pickups, and assorted sport-utility vehicles.

They sat in a dark corner of Packer's huge parking lot. They'd been there for three hours, looking for Florence. So far they had not seen her. Only five women had gone into the place.

"You okay?" asked Ramona.

"Yes," said Jesse. "The bandage is fine, really. He didn't cut me too bad."

"I didn't even see him," said Ramona. "I'm usually more on the ball, but we're not in Detroit, you know."

Jesse laughed. "Hey, they have robbers out here too, you know."

"I know, I know. I was—I wasn't thinking," Ramona said. Her expression softened. "You know, if you hadn't stepped between us—"

"I don't wanna think about it," said Jesse. "I just . . . you're welcome."

"I didn't say thank you."

"You don't have to. I'm not asking you to." He inhaled sharply and shifted in his seat, trying to stop the pain from his bandaged wound. "He might have killed you, you know?"

"You just had to say it, didn't you?" Ramona said, hiding the fear from her near miss. She turned up the radio. A rap tune came out.

"Please," Jesse groaned. "I'll start bleeding again."

"I should have known you don't like rap," said Ramona.

"Sorry, but it rubs me the wrong way."

Ramona turned off the radio. "So what we gonna do if she don't show?"

"We keep coming here until she does," said Jesse.

"Well, you can, but not me."

Jesse sighed. "I'm too tired and hurt to argue with you."

"Good," said Ramona. "We'll give her until midnight; then we're outta here."

A few minutes later a car pulled into the parking lot and rolled slowly over the unpaved ground of the lot. It looked like Florence's car, but Jesse wasn't sure. The car stopped, settling in across the way from Jesse and Ramona.

"Well, is it her?" asked Ramona.

"Not sure," said Jesse.

The woman inside the car didn't move. She turned off the engine and sat there.

"Maybe I should go over and see," said Jesse. He started to get out of the car.

"No," said Ramona. She grabbed his arm.

"Why not?" asked Jesse.

Ramona hesitated, and he could see that she was concerned. "Take out the gun first, that's all," she said.

"Right," said Jesse. He pulled out the gun and put it in his waist-band behind his back.

Jesse walked over to the car, keeping the gun behind him. His wound flared up with renewed pain, and he winced a little.

Halfway there the woman in the car flashed the lights. Jesse smiled. When he got there, the window rolled down, and he saw Florence's face behind the wheel.

"About goddamned fuckin' time," Florence said.

Jesse signaled to Ramona, and she walked over and they got into the car.

"You got heat," asked Ramona. "Good." She slipped into the backseat.

Jesse got into the front seat. Florence kicked up the heat a notch. Jesse was so elated to see her he wanted to give her a hug. But it was too weird. It would be like hugging a guy.

"Good to see you," he said instead.

"Yeah," said Florence. "You look like shit, Jess."

"I know you don't have a lot of time," said Jesse. "So tell me, how bad is it?"

"Shitty," said Florence. "The cops were all over me. It took me a half hour to lose them tonight. Fuckers. Don't even trust one of their own."

Jesse laughed at the irony, then said, "Okay, Florence, I know you believe in me, so here's the truth about what happened."

Jesse told her the whole story. Ramona filled in whenever he was missing information.

"Holy shit in the blue morning," said Florence when they were done. "So who—"

"You got me," said Jesse. "But I do know a few things. The mayor was calling in favors all over the state to get those casinos in the city. And he was not going to back D'Estenne in the election."

"Crawford is backing him," said Florence. "Just came out this morning."

Jesse was quiet. He was thinking about D'Estenne's secretive manner during the case and the bug he'd found on his phone.

"I see," he said at last.

"I know what you're thinking," said Florence. "D'Estenne is an asswipe, but I don't think he'd kill to stay in office."

"All depends on what he had to lose," said Ramona.

Florence looked back at her with surprise in her face. "Yeah, I guess so," said Florence. "And you'll be happy or sad to know that the cops picked up Walter Nicks a few days ago. They're holding him in a special cell for 'questioning.' That's all I could get out of anyone. They don't think he did it, but he ain't talking, and they're making sure he don't get bail."

Jesse thought about Nicks and the look of loss in his eyes. "He was there that night, and he feels responsible," said Jesse. "But they won't get anything out of him." Jesse felt good that Nicks was on ice. He was looking over his shoulder enough right now.

"Well. I got a few things on Crawford," said Florence. "They tell me that the city needed money."

"So what else is new?" said Jesse. "All cities need money."

"Not like this," said Florence. "Apparently Detroit is in really deep shit. I don't know the details, but people are plenty scared. The acting mayor, Crawford, is moving money around, robbing Peter to pay Paul. He calls it restructuring in his memos, but he's really putting up a big smoke screen for something."

"Makes sense," said Jesse. "If the city is really strapped, he won't be able to pay his bills, and he'll never be officially elected mayor if his house isn't in order."

"Anyway," said Florence, "while everyone is worried about you and your friend here, Crawford is trying to put out a big fire."

"And what is Crawford doing about the casino issue?" asked Jesse.

"He killed it," said Florence. "He very quietly disemboweled the task force."

"I'll be damned," said Jesse. He considered what this might mean. "We got something here, Florence. Yancy was trying to save the city with those casinos, and he was willing to betray long-held confidences to do it. Maybe someone didn't like that, and they had him killed."

"Who?" asked Ramona, wanting to be part of the discussion and to know who had tried to kill her.

"The answer is in that black briefcase," said Jesse. "We gotta find that thing soon or we're dead."

"Oh, and a couple of other things," said Florence. "The reward of fifty thousand for you two is up to a hundred thousand now."

"Who put up the new money?" said Jesse.

"Anonymous," said Florence. She waited, struggling with the difficulty of what she had to say. "And you were disbarred, Jesse."

"What?" said Jesse. "They can't—not without a formal hearing."

"They did," said Florence. "Some asshole in the state bar, trying to make a point. Says if you want to defend your license, all you have to do is show up. It was in the newspaper."

"Must have missed it," Jesse muttered. "It's just a gimmick anyway. It doesn't mean anything." Still, he was disturbed. His law degree was his certification that he had changed his life. Now he was a criminal and out of the bar. He was truly right back where he had started from.

"So now I've committed a felony for your ass," said Florence.

"I appreciate it," said Jesse.

"This is gonna cost you more than overtime," said Florence. To Ramona, she said, "Look in that green duffel bag back there."

Ramona opened the canvas bag. It contained clothes, money, snack foods, and a big envelope. "Where are my clothes?" she asked.

"I don't know you," Florence said. To Jesse, she said, "There's also a phone number. I want you to call me at it every night between eleven and midnight. If I don't answer, hang up and keep calling until I do."

"Right," said Jesse.

"I don't like your attitude," Ramona said to Florence. "I was just kiddin' about the damn clothes."

"Boy, you really got your hands full with this one," said Florence. She and Jesse shared a laugh.

"Don't laugh at me, bitch," said Ramona. "I'll kick your old white ass."

Florence turned in the seat and looked at Ramona. "You know, I just started liking you," she said. "Okay, you two, get lost. I got things to do. And use that number, Jesse. We gotta keep talking."

Jesse and Ramona got out of the car. Jesse leaned in the window and shook Florence's hand. Florence's normally hard visage softened a little. It was the first time Jesse had ever seen anything but her business face. He felt strange but was moved by the gesture.

As Florence drove away over the bumpy ground, Jesse felt lost and alone again. His link to the real world and his innocence was gone. Suddenly his dilemma rose like a mountain before him.

"Let's go," said Ramona. "It's cold as shit out here."

They got into the car and drove away. Jesse was thinking about all that Florence had told him.

"I wonder if my mama will bust on us," said Ramona. "I bet the police are looking for this car."

"I don't think your mother will say anything," said Jesse quietly. "If she does, then she'll have had to turn in your sister. I don't know your mother, but I don't think she'd want her grandson's mother to get locked up."

"Yeah, maybe you're right," Ramona said softly.

"But still, we might wanna get rid of this car just in case," said Jesse. "I'm sorry I didn't think about that earlier."

They drove away from Packer's, taking the streets. They were near I-75 south, and Jesse could see the Porter Street exit sign. Eventually he had to get on an avenue as they headed back to Detroit.

"I'm sleepy," said Ramona. "Where we gonna crash tonight? And I don't wanna sleep in this damned car again."

"I don't have any idea," said Jesse. "If you have another place where we might find your friend LoLo, we can head in that direction and see what comes up—"

Just then a shot rang out. Jesse turned the wheel hard, and the car swerved to the right.

"What the—" yelled Ramona.

"Get down!" said Jesse. He pushed Ramona toward the floor. In the rearview mirror he saw the headlights of a car speeding toward them.

Another shot rang out. Jesse heard a metallic clang and a loud pop as it struck the car's frame. Ramona raised herself up.

"Get back down!" said Jesse.

"Just drive the damn car!" yelled Ramona.

Jesse slammed on the accelerator, and the car took off down the street. Behind them their pursuer's car sped up.

"It's them," said Ramona with fear.

Jesse hung a sharp right onto a side street. He prayed that there was no one in the street.

"Gimme your gun," said Ramona. "I'm gonna shoot back."

"Don't be silly," said Jesse. "You stick your head out the window and you'll be shot."

Another shot rang out, and Jesse heard another, smaller explosion. Immediately he felt the car pull to one side.

"I think they hit a tire!" he cried. Jesse moved toward a traffic light. It turned red, but he kept going. Jesse went through the intersection, barely avoiding an accident. The car that was trailing him screeched to a stop.

Jesse jerked the car right at the first intersection. He quickly pulled the car over on the residential street; as they slowed, the sound from the flat tire grew louder. "Get out," Jesse said to Ramona. Ramona grabbed Florence's bag, and they darted away from the car.

As they moved between a row of houses into an alley, they could hear their pursuer's car roaring down the street behind them. The alley was dark, and it stank to high heaven.

"Shit, who died back here?" Ramona said.

"Please, don't say *die*," said Jesse.

A car pulled into the alley. Its headlights flooded them. Jesse and Ramona took off running. Two quick shots rang out.

"This way!" yelled Jesse. He jumped over a weather-worn fence and ran through a yard. Ramona followed. He headed for the front of the house. They heard the car slide to a stop on the gravel of the alley behind. A door opened.

"Don't look back!" Jesse said.

They bolted into the front of the house and kept going across the street into the backyard of a small wood-framed house, painted a dirty brown. The backyard was dark and filled with thick grass. Jesse and Ramona went over to the small wooden garage.

"We can't keep running," said Jesse. "Sooner or later they'll hit one of us." His heart raced, and he was out of breath.

"In here," Ramona said. She pulled the garage door open. There was no time to discuss it. Jesse and Ramona went inside. The garage was dark, but light from a streetlamp seeped in, cutting the room into light and shadow. Ramona grabbed Jesse's hand and searched out a place to hide. Jesse felt awkward holding her hand, being led by a woman, but he didn't dare get into the macho argument about that now. Ramona inched across the darkness. Her foot hit something, and it clanged softly.

"Dammit," Ramona whispered.

"Careful," said Jesse.

Finally they discovered a tall wooden crate at the back of the garage. They got behind it. Ramona pulled the green bag in front of her. Jesse moved in as far as he could get. In the tight space they were shoulder to shoulder.

Through his fear Jesse realized that Ramona was squeezing his hand like a vise. He felt her body next to him, and he could feel her shaking. He put his arm around her, pulling her in front of him. He pulled her near protectively, and she did not resist. She nestled into his body, and her trembling subsided.

Jesse could feel her warmth, the texture of her hair, and her heart, beating wildly. He was frightened by the killers and excited by the woman with him.

"I hear them," Ramona whispered.

Outside, he heard the sound of men moving. The killers seemed to be in the yard next door to the dirty brown house. Jesse heard something fall on the ground with a soft thump.

"Shit!" said one of the men.

Ramona's eyes widened. Her heart beat faster. "It's them, one of the killers," she whispered.

"Shut the fuck up," said another voice from outside.

The two men came closer to them. Soon Jesse heard the sound of the men moving through the thick grass in the same yard they were in. It was an awful sound, swishing, like a knife being pulled across coarse fabric.

The door to the little garage opened. A man stepped inside.

Then Jesse heard the sound of another door open, only farther away.

"Get the hell off my property!" said a woman's voice.

"Kiss my ass," said one of the men.

"I'm calling the police!" said the woman. Then a door slammed shut.

"Fuck, let's go," said one of the men. "We'll catch 'em on the street." The man in the garage with them left.

After the man left, Ramona's heart slowed. She took a deep breath, then let it out. Her grip on Jesse's hand loosened, and suddenly he was aware that he was wrapped around her body. He stood behind her, his arms around her torso, their bodies pressed tightly together.

They waited a full ten minutes before they dared move out of the dark corner.

Ramona moved away from Jesse. He felt the coldness wash over the places where her body had been. He mentally admonished himself for being so taken by her. He had to keep his mind on business.

They left the garage, moved through the thick grass in the backyard, and went to the street. It was dark and deserted.

"Now what?" she asked.

"They'll be waiting by our car, so we can't go back to it," said Jesse. "We need to get away from here right now."

A big semi rolled down the street. It was covered with a heavy tarp. From the other end of the street, coming toward the truck, a police car turned the corner. Jesse's heart bounded into his throat.

Ramona quickly dashed behind the rolling truck and jumped inside with the duffel bag. Jesse didn't have time to think. He followed her.

Inside the semi he felt big metal cylinders. The police cruiser rolled down the street and stopped by the dirty brown house.

Ramona found a little patch of floor and sat down. Jesse leaned against the back of the truck's flatbed.

They sat in darkness, bouncing with the load. No one could see them, but they had no way of knowing what was going on outside. They had moved along for several minutes when the semi came to a halt. After a few moments the truck was still not moving.

"Why'd he stop?" asked Ramona.

"It's not a traffic light," said Jesse. "I don't know."

They sat for another ten minutes. The sound and smell of truck and car exhaust were all around them. The truck jerked along for a moment. Then they heard: "Where you goin'?" said a man with a raspy voice.

"Leamington," said the driver. He had the high, semimelodious tone of a Canadian.

"Purpose?"

"Carrier for construction."

"What you totin'?"

"Piping," said the driver. "Just like it says." The driver waited a moment, then added: "Hey, I'm really running late. Can you cut me some slack, eh?" Now Jesse was sure he was Canadian. They always said "eh?"

"You been by here before, right?"

"Yeah, two days ago. You did me before, eh?"

"Right, I remember you," said the guard. "We're really backed up tonight."

"Tell me about it," said the driver.

"Goddamned cops are all over the place since that thing."

"That black guy, killed a woman."

"Yeah. He's a lawyer too. Just goes to show you. Don't matter where they end up, huh? Look, I'm gonna let you through."

"Appreciate it."

The truck started to move. It gained speed; then it bumped as the surface changed. Suddenly they could hear the tires moving over metal ridges. It sounding like a big electric razor.

"Lord," said Jesse. "We're on the bridge."

Ramona sighed as recognition washed over her. "Damn," she said.

The truck moved faster. Jesse and Ramona were tossed by the big truck as it sped along. They heard engines roaring around them as the big truck rolled across the Ambassador Bridge into Canada.

PART THREE

DOUBLE DEAD

1

O, Canada

Windsor is a city in the province of Ontario. It is a scant few miles from Detroit, but worlds apart in the way people live. Canada's strict gun laws make violence a rare occurrence, and Windsor has few of its American neighbor's racial ills.

Jesse and Ramona slipped quietly out of the big truck as it stopped for gas. Crossing the border on the Canadian side of the bridge had been less harrowing, but they were still left with a dilemma. They were in another country. A half mile from Detroit, but a million from their goal.

As they headed down a dark street, the Detroit skyline looked mean and distant.

"Damn," said Jesse. "The border patrols will be a bitch to get past." He walked along hurriedly. It was even colder by the river. "Come on. If we're spotted here, our little adventure becomes a federal matter. We don't want that."

"So what?" said Ramona indifferently.

"Federal police don't fuck around like these local boys," Jesse snapped. He was angry and frustrated. "Forget it. Just be quiet and listen to me for once, and I'll get us out of this mess."

She looked at him incredulously. "Who the hell are you talking to? You know, I shoulda dumped you like I wanted to."

"And go where?" asked Jesse. "You would have been caught inside a week."

"Not if I didn't have to carry your ass around," Ramona shot back, walking past him.

"You carry me?" Jesse said. "That's funny. I just saved your— Forget it."

"You're not gonna hold that over me," said Ramona, getting louder. "So you took a cut for me. So what?"

"I'm not holding anything over you," said Jesse. She was right in his face and looked angry, as angry as she could with a face like hers.

"This whole fucked-up mess is your fault!" said Ramona. "If we didn't have to meet that white woman, they never would have found us. She probably led them to us."

"Florence wouldn't do that. I swear, you are so damned juvenile," said Jesse. "Like a kid who blames her mama because she can't have a toy."

Ramona winced at the mother reference. "You know what, fuck this," she said. "I want out. You get back the best way you can. I'm going my own way—right now." She walked off defiantly, flinging down the duffel bag.

"Go on," Jesse said. He picked up Florence's duffel bag. "I'll be going back across tonight." He didn't think about the fact that he needed her to find LoLo and the black case. He was pissed at her and didn't care.

Ramona walked quickly away from him, her arms swinging up and down. She muttered something to herself that he couldn't hear. Jesse started to go after her but could not bring himself to do it. Ramona hesitated at an intersection, then kept walking, rounding a corner and moving out of sight.

A half hour later Jesse sneaked in the back of the Windsor Casino. It was a huge place, but a far cry from the glitzy glamour of Las Vegas. Windsor Casino was strictly blue-collar, a trucker's version of a gaming temple.

Windsor had a long tradition of gambling and nightlife. Jesse used to think of it as a city of bingo parlors and strip bars because its downtown streets were filled with both.

Windsor Casino was also a wake-up call to Detroit's leaders, who had been thinking about building their own casinos for over a decade.

Jesse entered the back of the casino carrying the duffel bag on his shoulder. Activity was thick, and he blended in with the working-class crowd. He nestled into a corner, away from the action.

He tried not to think of Ramona as he walked over to a courtesy phone on a wall by the rest rooms. How would he find her when he got his transportation together? Would he be able to? First things first, he thought. He picked up the receiver.

"Hello, I need you to page a Velane Johnson," said Jesse. He waited, and a moment later he heard the name repeated over a loudspeaker. Another moment, then: "This had better be important," said a man's voice on the phone.

"It's me, Jesse," said Jesse. "And it's *very* important."

Silence, then: "Holy shit," said Velane. "Where are you?"

"In the casino."

"In the casino!" said Velane. "Jesse, you're hot, man." Velane's voice was quavering. "Man, you're all over the news."

"I know," said Jesse. "I need your help."

"Jesse, I can't—"

"Sure you can. Just remember what I did for you."

More silence, then: "Meet me at the McDonald's over by the bridge in twenty minutes. Twenty minutes sharp, Jesse."

"Got it," he said. As he hung up, he breathed easier. Velane had connections that could get him back safely to America. Now all he had to do was find that stubborn woman.

Jesse grabbed the green bag and turned around—right into the face of Dick Steals.

Ramona stood by Cheetah, a strip club close to the river. There was a small park nearby on the waterfront. Several people sat on benches and watched the boats and Detroit city skyline.

Ramona looked out across the water and wondered bleakly how long it would take to swim across.

That damned Jesse had a lot of fucking nerve blaming her for anything. She'd saved his ass ten times in the last two days, and this is how she's treated? It suddenly occurred to her that she was acting like a scorned lover. "Bullshit," she mumbled to herself, yet she had to admit she was attracted to him. He was handsome, in that rough kind of way that she liked. And better yet, he had no idea how good-looking he was, always a nice quality in a man. Jesse was a poor boy who'd made something of himself too. Their shared background in this regard made her feel closer to him. He had changed, the way that she had always wanted to but couldn't. Jesse also had a sense of refinement, education, and class that she definitely lacked.

He had probably saved her life when the dirty white man tried to stab her at the 7-Eleven. That knife would have gutted her good, and he took it for her. And on top of it, after he was cut, Jesse stood there, knife hanging out of his clothes, asking her if *she* was okay. She had been struck by something at that moment. She couldn't believe that he'd sacrifice himself for her so willingly. All the men she had known were selfish or something close to it. Their affection for her had always been some twisted extension of their own love for themselves. But Jesse was different. He appreciated her for what she was. Ramona could not remember anyone feeling that way for her.

Her thoughts drifted to the dark garage where they had hidden from the killers. She had been terrified but felt safe when he embraced her. He was afraid too, but she knew at that moment that Jesse would have given up his life for her. It was a comforting feeling in contrast with the great danger they were in. It was ironic that she'd found this great devotion in a man who thoroughly pissed her off.

She hadn't had a man affect her like this in a long time. Maybe that was why he enraged her so much. She was weak for him, and she detested weakness. She tried to deny it, but the truth of this fact lingered in her heart. It was frightening to think that anyone had control over her this way. She had made it a long way with-out falling for some man and his bullshit. But Jesse had gotten to her somehow. She wanted him, and it thrilled and angered her to admit it.

She dismissed these thoughts as she watched a big yacht pass by on the river. She had to get back to Detroit. Once there she would get the case, find Jesse, and get that tape. He was nice, but he was holding her back with his nonsense. And she always did work better alone.

Ramona heard people coming out of the strip club. A group of men in business suits were talking loudly and drunkenly as they left the club. Too old, she told herself. Two women then walked out, laughing and lighting up cigarettes. "Two weird," she said out loud.

She had gone back to gazing at the river when a Windsor police cruiser rolled onto the street behind her. Ramona saw it, and fear leaped into her heart. She calmed herself, then turned her back on the cops. The cruiser went right by her.

A few minutes later the sound of loud voices made her turn back to the club. She saw a group of four young men coming out of the bar. There were three white and one black. They were probably barely old enough to go into the place. Many young kids came to Windsor to drink because the drinking age was lower than in Detroit.

Ramona decided to make her move. She was a little scruffy, but she still looked good. Her jeans were tight enough, and she'd draped her braids over her shoulders.

As she walked over, the men stopped instantly. Ramona could see the lust from watching the naked women still in their eyes. She had them.

"Excuse me, fellas," she said, "but I need some help."

Jesse knew that Dick Steals recognized him. Even with his hair cut short and a scruffy beard from not shaving, Richard had made him. Dick Steals was coming out of the bathroom and was still tugging at his zipper. He looked at Jesse, and recognition flashed in his eyes. It was quickly masked by fear, then resolve. Dick Steals turned away and started to move on.

Jesse started to run, but he didn't. Instead he stepped in front of the attorney.

"Richard, you know it's me," said Jesse.

"I don't know you."

For a moment they stood facing each other, saying nothing. Then Dick Steals reached into his jacket, and for a moment Jesse was about to go for his gun. To his surprise, Richard pulled out a wad of bills. "Here, take it," he said. "It's all I got."

Jesse was too shocked to answer. He barely noticed his own hand extending for the cash. As he took the money, he noticed the look of sadness on Dick Steals's face. It was almost apologetic.

"Whatever you're doing, Jesse, be careful," said Dick Steals. And he walked away.

Jesse watched him narrowly, expecting him to run to the nearest cop and rat him out. But Richard returned to a craps table and quietly settled in with a crowd. Jesse watched, waiting for him to make a move, but he didn't. Suddenly Jesse wanted to know what Richard knew. Why would Richard help him?

Then Jesse became aware of other familiar faces at the table.

Frank D'Estenne and Jesse's old friend Ellis Holmes were also there, drinking, laughing, and gambling. Jesse watched them for a while, then shoved Richard's money into his pocket and left the way he came in.

2

Me and the Boys

The music of Parliament pumped loudly from a boom box as a rapper's lyrics flowed over it. Tico raised another bottle of beer to his still-swollen lips and drank deeply. About ten of Cane's men danced and drank in the living room of the old house.

Little Jack had delivered Tico just as Cane had hoped. Tico had smiled and hugged Cane and everyone in the house when he got there. He was happy. It was the little things, like not getting killed, that made you happy in the life, Cane thought.

Tico regaled everyone with Little Jack's ruthlessness. The boy proudly accepted the accolades of his new male peers. He was filled with new bravado and courage.

The men drank, danced, and stomped loudly on the floor to the tune. They all raised their bottles and sang with the chorus:

> If you hear any noise,
> it's just me and the boys . . .
> gettin' it—

There was electricity in the room. It wasn't often that a crew celebrated life. The young black men's hearts were filled with light and hope. It was as if Tico's escape from death had made them all forget that they were going to die.

Cane stood by the front door, bopping to the beat. He wasn't much of a dancer. In fact he had very little natural rhythm, blasphemy for a black man in the 'hood.

The door to the house opened, and Q stepped inside. He walked over to Cane, his long chain earring swinging with his steps. Over the music he said, "Big man's here."

Cane nodded, then went outside. This house on Daniel Street had two vacant houses on either side. The two empty houses were rather nice, and Cane and his men routinely chased squatters out of them. The street itself was perfect, only five families on a short block, and none of them foolish enough to talk to the cops. Cane bounded down the steps and went to the dark green car at the curb. Q was behind him.

The car's dark-tinted window rolled down, revealing Minnesota's chubby, smiling face.

"Hop in," said Minnesota.

Cane glanced at Q. The roller nodded. Q walked a few feet away but kept his attention focused on the car. Cane got in the backseat. It was a new car, and it still had that smell in it. The backseat was empty. The driver was a black woman about twenty or so. She smiled at Cane, showing her perfect teeth. Minnesota got in the back with Cane from the other side.

"The woman has to go," said Cane.

"Why?" said Minnesota. "She's [burp] cool."

Cane just stared at the fat man until he got the message and turned to the woman. "Step out for a minute, baby," he said.

"No problem," said the woman. She got out of the car.

"Cool?" asked Minnesota.

Cane said nothing. Minnesota shifted on the leather seats. "Our thing is on. Three [burp] days from tonight. It's comin' in on the river. [Burp] By boat."

"Boat?" said Cane. "How the hell did you do that? The feds locked down all that shit years ago."

"Didn't you hear? We [burp] won the War on Drugs?" Minnesota laughed. "The man got his headline, and we got the system back."

"Okay, gimme the details," said Cane.

He listened as Minnesota told him the plan. Minnesota repeated it twice. Cane didn't commit anything to writing. Memory was the smart dealer's file.

Cane was always impressed by the ingenuity of white dealers. They seemed to have all the answers, and why shouldn't they? he reasoned. This was their game.

Minnesota finished up and rolled away with his woman. Cane walked back to the house. Q remained on the street, standing guard. The house's door opened. Slowly Tico stepped out, holding a forty-ounce beer. The door closed, muffling the blare of music.

"Hey, man, whatcha doin'?" said Tico. "Come on back inside."

"Had to talk to Minnesota," said Cane. "It's on. The heroin is coming in by boat. We need to get our shit together now. It's time to call on Mr. Jaleel about the money he's been stealing from me."

Tico's face darkened, and he lowered the big bottle in his hand. "Look, man," he said, "I don't know about this no more."

"Minnesota's cool," said Cane. "I had him checked out. Brothers in Philly, Harlem, and Chicago say he's cool. What I want to do now is get everyone together. We need to work this thing like clockwork. No one's selling H here. We can own the whole damned thing."

Tico walked over to a railing on the porch and sat on it. The weak railing gave a little, and he jumped away from it.

"Cheap-ass house," he said. "Look, man, after what happened, I—I don't know if I wanna keep doin' this shit."

Cane saw the fear in his friend's face. Almost dying in the pit in that juvenile prison had made Cane a stronger man, but Tico had been broken by his ordeal. Now Tico was going to punk out on him, leave him and go the other way. But Cane knew the answer to this kind of fear: a bigger one.

"Tico, you're like family," said Cane calmly. "So if you want to, go on."

"I knew you'd understand," said Tico, relieved. "I thought I could die for the crew, but in the end I wanted to live, you know."

"And what are you going to do now?" Cane asked.

Tico looked at him blankly. He had not even considered that prospect.

"You gonna get a job? With your record? All you can get is shit-shoveling work, breaking your back to make some other fool rich." Cane sneered a little. "You gonna get married? Lay up with some bitch, sittin' on her fat ass, asking where you going every night? You gonna take care of some crumb-snatching kids?" Slowly Cane closed the distance between himself and Tico. "How you gonna get the life you want, Tico? Who's gonna give you the money, the fine women, the cars, the right to do *what the fuck you wanna do*? The white man?" Cane uttered a short laugh. "Only thing he givin' away free is jail time. The rich-ass niggas downtown? They ain't got nothing to give away but lies and more misery. So go on, quit, you'll be dead anyway. But at least my way you're in charge of your own shit." Cane moved closer and put a hand on his friend's shoulder. "And maybe, just maybe you might live to tell."

Cane motioned to Q, who left his post and went inside the house. Cane turned to Tico, who was stunned by Cane's statements.

"If you outta the crew, then don't come in. We all picked the life we want in here." Cane walked inside and shut the door.

Tico stood on the porch, facing the door. The street and freedom were behind him. He turned and looked out at the old houses on the block. He could see two streets over through the vacant lots that dotted the area. A darkness filled the windows behind their cheap curtains. It was deep and menacing, like doom.

The closeness of death was still with him, but it did not seem as bad as the world he looked at now, a world no bigger than the block he stood in. The crew was his family, and without it he would be alone.

Tico took a long swig of the beer, then walked back into the house.

3

The Tunnel

Velane Johnson was a small man, only about five feet two. He had a thin body and light brown skin. Even though he was thirty-five, he looked like a man of twenty or so. Those boyish looks helped Velane run an insurance scam that had almost landed him in prison. Jesse had prosecuted the case and got Velane a misdemeanor deal and probation in exchange for testimony for the bigger fish. Jesse then helped Velane get a job in the casino when his probation was over. If anyone ever owed Jesse big, it was Velane.

Jesse smiled a little as the small man walked up to him by the busy McDonald's. Velane, however, did not look happy. He was scowling, and he looked nervously over his shoulder and around him.

"Long time," said Jesse.

"If you want money, I got some," said Velane. "Otherwise I can't help you." He was scared.

"Sure you can," said Jesse. He moved away from the restaurant, taking Velane with him. "All I need is a ride back to Detroit."

"Oh, is *that* all!" Velane said sarcastically. His voice was high-pitched from his nervousness. "Just help a fugitive and commit a crime. What is that, ten to life?"

"Actually it's probably only five years, depending on the judge," said Jesse dryly.

"Jokes," said Velane. "You're so quick with the jokes. Well, here's one, why did Velane cross the road? To get away from your red-hot ass!"

Jesse grabbed Velane by the arm. He put a nasty look on his face and stared into the thin man's eyes. "You were on your way to prison and a felony record. If the faggots didn't butt-fuck you to death in the joint, you would have certainly had no life when you got out!"

"That's over and done with, man," said Velane, weakening. "I don't wanna face that again. Did you know I'm getting married soon, Jesse? Well, I am. We have a kid, a little girl. I have a lot to lose here."

"Like I don't. I helped you because a black prosecutor hates to see one of his own go down unnecessarily. You've got to believe that I didn't do the things I'm accused of."

"Then why did you run?" said Velane. "You believe in the system, so why didn't you stay and face it, man?"

The question hurt Jesse. And Velane was right to ask it. But he didn't understand the system. It only works when things are fair, and the setup Jesse had been put in was hardly fair.

"I can't go into that," said Jesse. "You'll just have to trust me, like I trusted you. I helped you get this life you have now. Help me get mine back."

"Let go of my damned arm." Velane pulled away from Jesse. Jesse remembered that Velane had not lasted a minute before he confessed to the insurance scam. He was the nervous type, dangerous under these conditions, but he was all Jesse had right now.

"I got a friend who goes across all the time," said Velane finally. "She's a stripper. She always travels with a bodyguard, and they all know her at both borders. She's going over tonight. You can substitute for her regular man. That should do it."

Jesse went to Velane and put his hand on the small man's shoulder. "Thanks for this, Velane," he said.

"Yeah, but now we're even," said Velane. "Forever."

An hour later Jesse was standing on a street corner, waiting for a light blue car to come. The night was chilly, and he kept moving to stave off the cold. He kept thinking about Dick Steals and the look of compassion in his eyes. *"Whatever you're doing, Jesse, be careful."*

It made no sense. Why would Richard help him unless he knew he was innocent? And something else troubled him. What were Richard and D'Estenne doing there with Ellis? D'Estenne's presence meant politics of some kind. Chapel, Swiss was a big contributor to political campaigns, but it had no criminal practice to speak of.

He was also worried about Ramona. Letting her walk off like that had been stupid. He imagined terrible things happening to her. This was his fault, he reasoned. He was supposed to be looking out for her. She was smart, but she was a hothead, and she might find herself right back in jail. He had to find her.

A light blue sedan pulled up to Jesse and stopped. He went to the car and opened the door. Inside was a young white woman with the biggest breasts he'd ever seen. She had a blond wig and was dressed in a nurse's uniform that was barely a uniform at all. It was short, tight, and he could almost see everything she had to offer.

"Get in, honey," she said.

"I don't know about this," said Jesse. "I don't need to attract attention. If you're dressed like that—"

"Look," said the stripper. "I go through the tunnel sometimes three times a day. They all know me. I could ride through with an elephant, and they wouldn't stop me. It's cool, eh?"

Jesse hesitated. There were two ways to get to Detroit. The bridge over the river or the tunnel that ran under it. Going through the tunnel was usually faster and safer because of the volume of cars and the generally harmless nature of the people.

"Okay," said Jesse. He got in the car.

"I'm Sula," said the stripper, putting the car in gear.

"Nice to meet you," said Jesse.

"What's your name?" asked Sula.

"You don't wanna know," said Jesse. "The less you know the better."

"Dangerous man, eh?" said Sula. "I'm all tingly."

Jesse smiled a little and tried not to look at her. She had probably been an attractive woman until she put in giant breast implants. Now she looked grotesque. He glanced at her chest. It shook as the car hit bumps in the street.

"Can you do me a favor?" asked Jesse.

"Besides this?" asked Sula.

"Yes, I came here with a friend, and she and I—we had a fight, and I need to find her."

"Lover's spat, eh?" said Sula. "Okay, I'll circle downtown a few times before we go."

They drove around for a half hour. Sula talked about how she planned to have the implants removed after she got enough money to go back to school. Jesse listened politely, but he didn't believe a word of it.

They didn't spot Ramona, so Jesse decided to head for the tunnel. He didn't know what else to do. He'd be lost without Ramona at his side, but maybe she was already back over. She was not one to sit around on her ass. What he had to do now was find her on the other side.

Sula pulled up to the Windsor side of the tunnel. The cars coming from Detroit were on their left. There were a lot more people going to Canada than vice versa. Windsor was definitely getting the best of this bargain. They approached the toll booth. Jesse tightened all over as he saw the toll taker and his uniform.

"Hey, Sula," said the toll taker, a man of about fifty or so.

"Hey, Walter," said Sula.

"Got the day off tomorrow," said Walter. "How about coming over to give me a private show?" He laughed.

"Yeah," said Sula. "I'll do your wife first, then you." Sula and Walter laughed. Jesse sat nervously as Walter looked at him and then back to Sula.

"Where you dancing tonight?" asked Walter.

"Got a private party in Bloomfield," said Sula.

The car behind them blew its horn loudly.

"All right!" said Sula to the man in the car. "See ya, Walter."

"Okay," said Walter.

Sula took off and got into the tunnel lane. Inside the tunnel it was narrow with only one lane in each direction. Jesse eased back into the seat a little as the car moved along briskly. The line coming the other way was backed up and not moving at all. Car horns sounded, making discordant echoes off the tunnel's thick walls. The din only made Jesse more nervous. Sula leaned on her horn, adding to the clamor.

Soon they were out of the tunnel and entering a line for customs to Detroit. This was the hard part. They let you out of Canada easily, but getting into the other country required a check at the border. Sula slowed down as they approached the guards. Suddenly she veered to her right.

"What are you doing?" asked Jesse. He was jumpy and looked around for danger.

"I was in line for that woman guard. The women all hate me. I do better with the men." Sula guided the car over to a fiftyish black man.

"Sula, baby!" said the black guard.

"How's it goin', Clarence?" said Sula. She handed Clarence some papers.

The guard took the papers but hardly glanced at them. "You're the best thing I've seen all night," he said.

"You bet your dick I am," said Sula.

Though Jesse's heart was racing, he had to admire Sula. She was a real pro. She didn't rush her normal routine of flirting so as not to arouse suspicion. All the same, the waiting was killing him.

"I'm coming to see you at the club next week," said Clarence. "Bringing some of my relatives from out of town."

"Then I'll have to do something special for you, eh?" said Sula. "How about the shower?"

"Yes!" said Clarence, pumping his fist. "Sula, I love you."

"Just bring plenty of money," Sula said.

The guard never even looked at Jesse. He handed Sula the papers back and motioned her ahead. Jesse calmed as they passed through the border into Detroit.

"You okay?" asked Sula. "You look like shit."

"That was intense," said Jesse. "I've been over and back a hundred times, but never has—"

Jesse stopped. His heart leaped into his throat. Their car was passing the customs holding room. Inside he saw four young men being ushered in—and Ramona standing with them.

"Stop," said Jesse.

"What?" said Sula. "What for?"

"Stop the damned car!" Jesse yelled.

"Okay, okay," said Sula. She pulled over into a service parking spot.

A young security officer started walking over to their car.

"Tell me what's up before he gets here," said Sula. "You're not supposed to park here."

"The woman I'm looking for is in there with a customs cop," said Jesse. "I need to get her out. If they find out who she is, she'll go to jail."

"Shit," said Sula, "once you're in there, you never—" She didn't have a chance to finish. The officer was at the door. He was young with sandy brown hair. Sula stepped out. "I need to get some information from an officer in the holding room," she said. The young officer looked admiringly at her chest and smiled. She flirted with him, and like magic, he walked Sula to where Ramona was being held.

Jesse watched as Sula stepped inside the customs room. Ramona and the young men were lined up on a bench. The customs cop had several driver's licenses in his hand. Sula went over to him and said something. Jesse's heart sank when the man didn't smile at her. Maybe the magic was gone. Sula pulled the man aside and began to talk urgently to him.

Out of the corner of his eye Jesse saw the young security officer walk toward him. Jesse slowly turned his face away from the window. The officer walked over to the other side of the car, still trying to get a look at Jesse. He couldn't figure out why the cop was so interested in him. He suddenly remembered that Sula was white and he was black. A black man traveling with a woman like that was always suspicious to a cop. Jesse pretended to cough and covered his face. The cop had moved toward Jesse's door again when Clarence, the old black cop, ran up, said something, and took the young cop away.

"I'm gonna have a fucking heart attack," said Jesse out loud.

He almost cheered when he saw Sula walking out with Ramona at her side. They got to the car, and he got out and rushed Ramona inside.

"You okay?" he asked. "I saw you in there and—"

"I'm okay," said Ramona without emotion. "Let's get out of here." Ramona got inside the car's backseat.

"You're welcome," said Jesse sarcastically.

Sula started the car, then waited. To Jesse, she said, "You're lucky. Old Bob just got back from a vacation tonight, and he's in a nasty mood."

"Then he doesn't know who we are," said Jesse.

"Didn't have a clue," said Sula. "But neither do I."

"Can we get the fuck out of here, please?" asked Ramona curtly.

"Sure," said Sula. "God, I'm gonna be late." She drove toward the street; then to Jesse she said, "How much money you got?"

"I don't know." He reached for the money Dick Steals had given him. He'd never bothered to count it. Sula grabbed the money.

"That's enough," she said. "You don't know what I had to

promise Bob back there, but you just paid for it." She looked at the money. "A lot less than I usually get, but it'll have to do."

Sula drove away from the border onto Jefferson Avenue and into Detroit.

Sula pulled into the little motel on Eight Mile. She got out of the car and headed for the business office. "Be right back," she said. She looked at her watch. "Oh, I am so damned late!"

Jesse and Ramona sat in silence. They were each full of hamburgers from Rally's. Sula had stopped on the way to the east side.

Jesse could feel Ramona boring a hole in the back of his head. He heard her take a deep breath. He thought that she would speak, but she didn't.

Ramona was a proud woman, Jesse thought. Too proud to admit that she'd screwed up tonight. He wondered if she would have stopped to save him. He supposed that she had to. She needed him as much as he needed her.

Sula came back with a room key on a cheap plastic key chain. "Here you go, kids," she said. "Enjoy."

The two got out of the car. Jesse pulled the duffel bag from the car's floor. He could use a shower and a change of clothes, he thought.

"Thanks," said Jesse as he shook Sula's hand. "I can never repay you."

"I'll remember that if I ever need something," said the stripper.

"Thanks for everything." Ramona extended her hand.

Sula leaned in to Ramona, grabbed her hand, and whispered something to her. Then she walked back to the car and drove away.

"What did she say to you?" asked Jesse.

"Nothing," said Ramona.

C-3 was a nice little room, clean and comfortable. The bed looked great, but Jesse knew he'd never be in it. Even if Ramona would let him, he'd never get any rest with her body so close.

Jesse closed the door and turned on the TV. He dropped the bag and sat on the little sofa against the wall. His body eased at the softness of the old sofa.

"Thank you," said Ramona.

Jesse was surprised. He caught her eye and said, "No problem. I wasn't about to leave you there."

"Thanks for taking that knife for me too," said Ramona. "I'm used to taking care of myself, you know."

"I understand," he said. "It was my pleasure to get stabbed for you."

"You know, your rap is gettin' better all the time." She smiled, and Jesse smiled back. "I'm gonna take a shower and wash these clothes. They should be dry by tomorrow."

Ramona went into the bathroom, and soon Jesse heard the shower running. He turned up the TV and searched for reports about them, but there were none.

Then he heard a strange sound from the bathroom. He went to the door and he heard it again. Ramona was moaning softly. The hot shower must have felt good after so long, he reasoned. He heard her sigh. He thought of her inside the shower, naked and wet.

Jesse moved away from the door. He could no longer deny that he was taken with her. She was everything that men wanted. She was beautiful, sexy, and she had a vulnerability that lived just underneath her womanliness. He wanted her, and given her recent gratitude for saving her life, he thought he had a chance. And then he thought about Connie, his promise to her and the faith she'd shown in him. Life was a bitch, he thought.

The shower stopped, and he heard Ramona get out. She came out of the bathroom in a towel. He saw clearly the outline of her breasts. Her long legs made the towel seem very short.

"It's all yours," Ramona said.

Jesse went in the bathroom quickly, not wanting to look at her or think about the suggestive words she'd just said. He took a hot shower, and it did feel good. He finished up and dried off.

Jesse stopped to check himself out in the mirror. The white bandage on his wound stood out against his dark skin. Not bad, he thought. He had a pretty good-looking face; his chest was broad with just enough hair on it. He was muscular from his workout regime, and although he didn't like to brag, he was sufficiently endowed.

Maybe Ramona was attracted to him too, he thought. Maybe she was out there, listening to the door as he had. You could never tell with women. He pulled a pair of shorts from the duffel bag. He put them on, then put on a pair of pants.

Jesse walked into the room shirtless, hoping that Ramona was still up. She was perched on the edge of the bed watching TV. The white towel was pulled up to the top of her thighs, and she struggled to keep it down.

"You can have the bed," Jesse said.

"Hey, listen to this on the news." Ramona turned up the volume.

"*. . . that was Police Inspector James Cole. And so there are still no arrests in the violent incident at Trapper's Alley in Greektown that left one man dead,*" said the reporter. "*Police say their suspects, three young women, are not talking, and it appeared to be a confrontation between young black men and women. . . .*"

"LoLo and Cane," said Ramona.

"Yeah," said Jesse. "But what good does it do us?"

"If she was hurt," said Ramona, "she might be back at that safe house we went to the other day. Remember, she goes there when she's hurt. She's got a man there."

"Right," said Jesse, brightening at this prospect. "That's our first stop tomorrow. Let's go to sleep and get an early start. Fewer cops out then."

"Okay." Ramona got up from the bed. "I have to wash my clothes in the bathtub." She went back into the bathroom.

Jesse sat back on the little sofa. Not much of a bed, but it beat sleeping in a car or on the street.

"You know, I bet we'll be laughing about this when it's all over," Ramona called from the bathroom.

"Assuming we're not in jail," said Jesse.

"You're so down about everything," said Ramona. "We'll get that black case, then we get my tape, and we'll both be free."

Jesse didn't respond but listened to her scrub her clothes in the bathtub. The tape— He had forgotten all about it. He got up and went to the door.

"Ramona—I lied about the tape," he said.

She stopped scrubbing. She rose from her crouch and walked to him, her hands covered with wet soap. "Lied?" she said. "What? You didn't find it?"

Jesse regretted telling her, but now it was too late. "No, I did find the tape," he said. "But I lost it. The killers must have taken it when I was knocked out. And anyway, it didn't prove anything. Someone cut it off before the killers got him."

"And when were you going to tell me?" asked Ramona, her voice rising. "After I helped you and they took me back to jail? You sorry-ass bastard!" She was right in his face.

"Look," said Jesse, trying to diffuse her anger. "I've been think-ing about this a lot. The black case is the key here. All of this has happened because of what's inside it. I'm sure that once we get it, it will exonerate you too."

"You mean, you don't even know what's in it?" she yelled.

"No," Jesse confessed. "But whatever it is, it was worth killing the mayor for. Listen, if I had told you I didn't have the tape, would you have still come with me?"

"That's not the point," Ramona said. "How could you lie to me about something like that? I thought we . . ." She trailed off in her anger. "You men, all you do is hurt people. All my life, whenever I trust one of you, you treat me like shit."

"Just listen to me for a second, will you?" said Jesse.

"I'm just another ghetto bitch to you," she said. "Something to be used to get what you want. Then you go back to your little world of rich people, niggas with suits, and your white woman who thinks she's black. Well, you know what? Fuck you, Jesse. Tomorrow I'm outta here." She went back into the bathroom and slammed the door.

"Ramona, I won't let them put you in jail, I swear!" he said. "I— I was wrong for lying to you, but I know I can help you."

"Go to hell!"

Jesse turned away feeling miserable. After the fight with her mother, and hearing her bare her soul about her dead sister, he could see that he'd betrayed Ramona in the worst way. Jesse was now her mother, her father, and every other person who'd let her down.

He sat on the sofa for ten minutes, listening to her scrub her clothes and curse. Then it grew quiet. At length the bathroom door opened.

Jesse looked up and saw her standing by the door. He stood up and moved toward her. Her eyes were red, and her face was sad, like a child. She walked over to him and took off the towel, revealing her naked body to him.

Her wet hair hung over her shoulders and dripped water on her breasts, which stood up, full and perfect. Her flat stomach flowed into her narrow waist. The curve of her hips was slight, moving into her long legs.

Jesse was overcome. She was even more beautiful than he'd imagined. Even the motel's cheap soap was perfume on her. He felt an erection build, and he was powerless to stop it. Ramona came closer to him. She stopped just in front of him, her hard nipples brushing his bare chest.

"Don't touch me," she said. She stared up at him with her teary, hurt eyes. "You see," she said to him. "See what you did to me?"

"I'm sorry," Jesse managed to say. "I swear—"

Ramona pushed him aside gently and walked to the bed. She got under the covers and rolled onto her side.

Jesse realized that she had exposed herself to him to let him know that she had intended to make love to him. But not now. She was showing him what he would never have. He went to the bed and sat on it next to her.

"I won't let anything happen to you," he said. "I lied to you before I knew you. . . ." He trailed off. He had to find some way to make her believe him, see that he was not going to hurt her again. He grabbed her hand and squeezed it tightly. "Please don't leave me," he said.

Ramona sat up sharply. The cover fell from her, exposing one of her breasts. "You don't care about me," she said. "You just want your lucky-ass life back."

"How can you say that after—" Jesse didn't want to bring up taking the knife for her. "You know I do. Maybe not at first, but after being with you, I do." He paused again. He sounded like a boy professing his love at recess. He had to make sense now or he would lose her. When he continued, though, his thoughts were still a jumble of emotions. "When you left me in Canada, all I could think about was if you were safe. Then when I saw you being held, I had to help you. If I didn't care—"

"It was the case," said Ramona. "You just need the case."

"No, no!" he said loudly. "I wanted to get you out of there." He stopped, frustrated. Jesse slid off the bed and got onto his knees so he could look her directly in the face.

"If I can't clear you, I'll help you get away," he said. "I'll break the law again, but I won't let you go back to jail." Then softly he added, "Even if I have to go in your place."

Ramona didn't respond for a long time. She just stared past him, thinking and looking at a wall. He sat next to her on his knees, his face a picture of his emotion and frustration.

"You know, men say the nicest things when I'm naked," she said finally.

"A chance," said Jesse, "that's all I'm asking. You don't have to be with me. Just let me prove I'm not out to get you."

The sadness and anger started to fade from her face. Ramona put her hand on his chest. "You want me, Jesse?"

"You know I do."

"I mean, do you want *me*, the real me, just like I am?"

Jesse hesitated. He was thinking about Connie.

"It's just you and me in this room right now," she said as if sensing his thoughts. She moved her hand to his cheek. "Just you and me."

Jesse felt his body ease. He was not thinking rationally, but right now nothing was rational. All he knew was that this woman was a part of him now, and he didn't want to lose her. "Yes, I want you."

"I never ask men that question until it's too late," she said, "until I'm broken down and scraping my heart off a wall." She smiled her crooked little smile. "You have a good heart, Jesse. That is the only thing in the whole world I'm sure of right now. And if I'm really in your heart, you'll never be able to betray me."

She took her hand from his face and pulled back the covers, revealing herself to him. "Come on," she said. "I'm all ready for you now."

Jesse leaned over and kissed her. He struggled out of his clothes, careful not to rip off his bandage. He climbed into bed with her. They embraced and kissed for a while, feeling each other. He rolled on top of her, and she parted her legs. He settled between them, then slipped inside her. The warmth surrounded him and took his breath away.

He savored the moment, their connection, then felt her moving under him. Jesse started his rhythm, catching up to hers. Ramona pulled him close to her, clutching him tightly, as if she would never release him.

4

All Hallow's Eve

The sun woke Jesse the next morning. He stirred, then grumbled when he realized that his night of rest and peace was over. He had to get back to the job of solving his problem.

Ramona slept peacefully next to him. One long braid lay across her face, and she looked like innocence itself. Jesse slipped his arms around her and kissed her cheek. She moved, then hugged him softly.

"Good morning," she murmured.

Jesse felt her hands move over his body. She kissed him, and he returned it. She rolled on top of him, and they made love again.

When it was over, they lay next to each other, staring at the motel's old, cracked ceiling. Ramona hummed her tune.

"Why do you hum like that, you know, after you have sex?"

"Sex, music, they're the same," she said. "So, when I feel like sex, I feel like music. You got a problem with that?"

"What do you think?" said Jesse. Then he kissed her again. "I have a better question. Where in God's name did you get the condoms we used?"

Ramona smiled a little. "Your friend Sula gave them to me last night. She pressed them in my hand and said, 'He's cute, give him one for me, eh?' " Ramona imitated Sula's voice.

"Women," said Jesse, chuckling. "So damned sneaky." He ran a finger down her hair as he grew serious. "I meant everything I said last night."

"I don't wanna talk about that anymore," said Ramona. She adjusted her body and propped herself up on one elbow.

"I'll have to tell Connie about us as soon as this is over."

Ramona didn't respond. She got up and went to the bathroom. She took her dry clothes from the shower rod and got in. Jesse joined her, and they showered together.

After they got dressed, they peeked out into the motel's parking lot. Only two cars there. One was a new Toyota, and the other, a Chrysler, had a big red antitheft bar on the steering wheel.

"Damn," said Jesse. "We can't get either one of those."

"We have to get moving," said Ramona. "These little motels have early checkout times." She pointed at a woman knocking on a door and going inside a room with a passkey.

"We can't walk the street," said Jesse. "Someone will notice us for sure."

"I say we get on the bus and chance it."

"Too dangerous," said Jesse. "Let's stick to the neighborhoods. Once we get there, something will turn up."

"I know you don't wanna hear this," said Ramona. "But I know some people that way." She pointed south.

"Me too. I used to live over there," said Jesse. Painful remembrance settled in his face, then quickly faded. "Okay, let's check them out."

Jesse packed up their stuff in the green bag and left the room. They headed to Dequindre and went south. The day was beautiful. The sun was out, and it felt warmer than previous days. Ramona walked next to Jesse, holding his hand. He surged with energy. His passion for Ramona had lifted his spirits. He felt a little strange at his newfound emotion, but he did not betray his joy to her. He gripped her hand tightly and smiled at her.

They walked for an hour, taking side streets and hiding to avoid the occasional police cruiser. Soon they had crossed Six Mile Road when Jesse stopped short at a corner.

"What?" asked Ramona. "You tired?"

"No," he said. "I grew up not too far from here."

They looked around the area. It wasn't a pleasant sight. The neighborhood had definitely seen better days. The streets were in need of paving. Billboards touted the joys of malt liquor and cigarettes, overshadowing a small antidrug billboard. In the middle of the despair, bright, shining fast-food joints stood in bitter contrast with their surroundings.

"You come a long way," she said.

"Not today I haven't," he said woefully.

"What's the deal on the McDonald's and the KFC?" asked Ramona. "Seems like they wouldn't come here."

"Neighborhood's bad," said Jesse. "But the families here probably feed their kids on that stuff."

A car horn sounded, and they jumped at the sound. Looking over, they saw an old Pontiac with three black men in it at the corner.

"Yo, y'all need a ride?" asked a man in the passenger seat. He was about thirty or so, big and bald-headed. His teeth were yellow and jagged.

"Naw," Jesse said. He grabbed Ramona's hand and swiftly walked away. The Pontiac turned the corner and followed them.

"What's their problem?" said Ramona.

"I don't—"

The Pontiac pulled over, and the doors opened up. The three men were getting out.

Jesse and Ramona took off running. They ran up the street and didn't look back. The green duffel bag jumped and tossed as Jesse ran with it on his back. He looked over his shoulder. The men were closing on them. Jesse turned a sharp right and went down a street.

Suddenly they heard a train whistle blasting in the distance. Jesse remembered that there were train tracks nearby. "This way," he yelled as he pulled Ramona across a street.

"You can't run, nigga!" said one of the men.

The crossing arm was down as the train approached. Jesse and Ramona sped up. The engine's whistle blew a warning. They ran harder and crossed the tracks just before the big train roared into the intersection, closing off their pursuers.

The couple stopped and caught their breath. They turned toward the three men. They could see them in flashes as the train rolled by. Jesse looked down the tracks. The train was long, but the men would probably get in their car and go around it.

"Those busters—" said Ramona. She was still out of breath. "They tried to jack us."

"I think maybe they recognized us, or they were going to rob us," said Jesse. "Come on, we need to lay low for a while."

They walked down a long, narrow street with an abandoned factory on the corner. Jesse found a house that looked empty. They went inside through a broken window. The train rumbled in the distance.

It was cold in the basement of the vacant house. Jesse could hear the wind gusting outside. They had been hiding out all day. Moving from one house to the next, one street to the next. They'd seen the three black men riding around the neighborhood looking for them once but had kept out of sight.

Jesse knew this part of town well. A family named White once lived in the house he was in now. They had a little boy who made kites out of newspaper and old shopping bags. Jesse had a strangely good feeling in his heart. He'd had some good times here. There were not many, but over time the good memories always outlasted the bad.

Ramona was huddled next to Jesse, her arm wrapped around his waist. Jesse could feel her body expand and fall as she breathed.

"I think maybe it's safe to go now," he said.

"We're a long way from that safe house," said Ramona. "How are we gonna get there?"

"I don't know," said Jesse. "But it's dark, and we'll have a better chance of moving around."

They got up and went to the window they'd climbed in. The staircase to the upper part of the house was rotted away. Jesse moved to the window and was about to lift Ramona up when he heard something crash above them.

"What was that?" asked Ramona.

"Sounded like glass breaking," said Jesse. "Come on, let's get out of here." He grabbed her by the waist and started to lift.

"Jesse," said Ramona, "something's burning. Smell."

He stopped for a moment. Faintly he smelled the odor of burning wood. "Jesus," said Jesse. "Let's get out of here."

He lifted her through the window, then climbed out after her. Outside, they saw smoke, and the yellow flicker of a fire behind the house's boarded-up windows.

"Oh, shit," said Jesse, checking his watch. "It's Devil's Night."

"Damn," Ramona said quietly. "Then we have to get away from here now. People will be coming soon." They hurried down the street.

Detroit had a long and infamous tradition of arson on Devil's Night. Many fires were set in the city's most impoverished areas, causing destruction and further tainting the city's image. But recently the city and community groups had taken to the streets to stop the arsonists. If the patrols were out, the fire would attract a swarm of firefighters, police, and volunteers.

Like clockwork, as they got to a street corner, they saw three cars with civilian volunteers racing down the street. Soon they heard the sound of fire engines and police cars. The people were very organized. The area would be full of volunteers, looking for the kids who'd started the fire.

"We need a place to hide," said Ramona.

A police cruiser rounded a corner several blocks away. Its siren and lights were on. It was coming right toward them.

"This way." Jesse pulled Ramona across the street and between two houses. They waited until the cruiser passed, then ran up Victoria Street.

"Where are we going?" asked Ramona.

"No time," said Jesse.

A few streets away they ran into the backyard of a small house. They now heard the fire engines coming. Jesse and Ramona went through the house's backyard, across an alley, and into the backyard of another house that was painted a faded blue.

On the street a car rolled up, and they heard the car doors open, then close. The patrol always checked the nearby streets, looking for the arsonists. That was bad news. Jesse knew that if they were spotted, the volunteers would call the police.

Jesse went to the back of the house and knocked on the door. Nothing.

"Jesse," said Ramona nervously, "we have to go."

Jesse said nothing. He could hear the patrols coming closer. He knocked again, and after a moment the door opened.

Bernice, Jesse's sister, looked out through the dirty screen door of the faded blue house. She regarded Jesse with shock, then anger. She started to say something, then shut the door in his face.

"Bernice! Bernice!" Jesse said in a hushed voice. "Open this goddamned door."

Ramona saw a flashlight beam flicker across a tree in the backyard.

"Let's run," she said, pulling at Jesse's arm.

286 / Gary Hardwick

He just stood there, looking at the door like it had betrayed him. Then the door opened, and Nikko opened the screen door and let them in. Jesse and Ramona ducked inside, locking the door behind them.

Inside the house Bernice sat on the sofa in the living room watching TV. She ate from a bag of potato chips. She didn't look at Jesse as he sat in the dining room with Ramona.

"Damn, Uncle Jesse," said Nikko. "What you doin' here, man?"

"We need to stay here for a while."

"Jesse, we can't stay here," said Ramona. "If this is your sister's place—"

"It's okay," said Jesse. "The police probably sat on the house for a while until they found out that me and my sister . . ." He trailed off. "They know that this is the last place I'd go."

"The cops are down the block," said Nikko. He went to the window. "Damn, they're gone. They used to sit three doors down in an ugly green car, but—"

"The fire," said Jesse. "There was a fire three streets over. They probably got a call to go to it. The mayor hates bad press the day after Devil's Night."

"Niggas messin' up," Nikko muttered. "Won't be nothing left 'round here if they don't stop."

Jesse looked at Bernice. She continued to stare blankly at the TV.

The house was well kept, but Jesse knew it wasn't Bernice's doing. Letisha probably kept house for them all.

"Where's your sister?" he asked.

"She went out with some dude," said Nikko.

"A date?" said Jesse. "She'd not old enough to go out. How come you let her—"

"None of your fuckin' business what she's doing," Bernice snapped. She got up and walked into the dining room. "I should call the police on your ass. Mr. Big-Time Lawyer, running from the cops with some ho."

Ramona started to say something, but Jesse stopped her as he stood up and walked over to his sister.

"Call the police if you want to," he said. "I won't try to stop you."

"You *can't* stop me," said Bernice. "I should throw you out, sorry, murdering—"

The front door opened, and Letisha King walked in drinking a Coke. She was a young girl with big eyes and short black hair.

"Hey, y'all, there's a fire out—" Letisha's eyes widened when she saw Jesse. She dropped her Coke on the floor, then picked it up. "Uncle Jesse," she said in a whisper.

Nikko rushed to his sister. "He just came. We gotta hide him."

"No, we don't," said Bernice angrily. "We don't have to do shit. You threw me out of your house like a dog, Jesse, and now you come here. Well, I got your ass now." She moved over to a phone on a table.

"You won't do it," said Jesse.

"Like hell I won't."

"You know why I threw you out," he said. "And you know I didn't kill anybody, Bernice. You wanna scare me? Well, I'm already more scared than I've ever been in my life."

"Good," Bernice snapped. "You need to get taken off your damned high horse."

"I put you out of my house because I couldn't support you hurting yourself," said Jesse. "And you know what? I don't regret it. It was what you needed."

"And maybe this trouble you're in is what your ass needs." Her voice was losing its edge.

Jesse backed down a little at the truth in her words, then: "Maybe it is," he said. "Go on, call if you want to. I don't give a shit." He sat back down next to Ramona.

"Want me to stop her?" Ramona whispered. Jesse shook his head.

Bernice looked at her brother, the phone shaking in her hand. She started to cry and put the receiver down. Then she walked up the stairs without a word.

Nikko moved over to the phone and hung it up. "Phone don't work anyway," he said. "We can't pay the bill."

"She went to the hospital and signed up for that drug program today," Letisha explained. "That's why she's so cranky. So, Uncle Jesse, did you kill them people?"

"No, Letisha," Jesse said. To Nikko, he said, "Your mother checked into rehab by herself?"

"Yeah," said Nikko and Letisha together. They smiled like it was Christmas.

Jesse stood up and turned to Ramona. "I'll be right back." He went upstairs.

Jesse entered the small bedroom where his sister slept with Letisha. The house had only two bedrooms, and Nikko had one to himself. One side of the room looked normal, but Letisha's side had a big poster of TLC and other singing groups. There were also rows of cheap-looking shoes lined up against a wall. He remembered that Letisha loved shoes.

Bernice was sitting on the bed with her face in her hands. "I went to the hospital today," she said.

"I know," said Jesse, sitting next to her. "Nikko and Letisha told me. Life ain't easy for nobody, you know. I thought I'd made it away from all this, and look at me."

Bernice got up off the bed and moved over to a dresser. She didn't look at him. "Sometimes I look in the mirror, and I don't even know who that woman is on the other side," she said despondently. "She's nasty-looking and sad. I just want to kill her for ruining my life."

"Funny. I felt the same way this morning," said Jesse.

He stood and hugged his sister. He felt his problems fade away. This was all the family he had left, he thought. He just hoped that after this was over, they'd still have him.

He heard footsteps coming his way. Ramona poked her head into the room. Jesse and Bernice broke their embrace, feeling a little embarrassed.

"Hey," said Ramona.

"We're okay up here," said Jesse.

"Your nephew says he can borrow a car and take us to LoLo's safe house."

"But Nikko isn't old enough to— Forget it," said Jesse. "I keep forgetting where I am."

"He can drive pretty good," said Bernice. "I taught him back when we had a car."

"I'd like to stay, Bernice," said Jesse.

"I understand," said Bernice. "Y'all can't stay the night anyway. Those reporters come by every morning bothering me."

"We can go out the back," said Jesse. "Nikko can circle around and pick us up on another street."

"I'll tell him," said Bernice. She put her hand on Jesse's face, leaned in, and kissed him on the cheek. "Be careful."

When his sister had gone, Jesse went to a window and looked out on the street. The community patrols were gone, but he could see the lights of fire engines two streets over. Ramona appeared beside him and put her hand on his shoulder.

"You were right," she said. "Everybody's family is messed up."

He smiled and kissed her.

5

Healing

LoLo had spent the day taking pain pills and sitting on her ass. Her bandaged arm throbbed where Cane had slashed her. If she hadn't reacted so fact, he would have cut her throat.

Marly and the twins were in prison, and Walker was dead. That damned Little Jack. She should have known never to trust a man, no matter how young he was.

Cane had played her but good. He was bold and didn't care about his own safety. How did you fight a man like that, one who did not seem afraid of anything? She had to admit she had a grudging respect for his crazy ass. But she had to hit him back and soon. Cane would never stop until he had all of Detroit. She couldn't wait to see if he could do it.

Yolanda was out on the street, dealing, trying to keep everyone cool. She was also getting information on Marly and the twins. If they could bail out the twins, they would jump bail, and then they could regroup and get Cane. Marly, though, was in on a murder charge. She was not getting out for a long time.

LoLo sat up in the bedroom of her safe house. She had been so many places lately that she was running out of them. This was where she came when she was really desperate. The little one-story house on the east side was nothing to look at, but the neighborhood was nice. The last place someone like Cane would look for her.

A man came in carrying a glass of orange juice. "Here, drink this."

"Thanks, baby," LoLo said, taking the glass. The juice was sweet and cold as it ran down her throat.

"It's bad this time, Lo," said the man. "This Cane boy is bad news."

"Don't worry, Bumper," said LoLo. "I'll take care of it."

Bumper Dixon sat next to LoLo on the bed. He was older than LoLo, almost forty. A handsome man, Bumper was tall and muscular in build. His skin was light brown, his hair was short and wavy, and his eyes were a soft hazel. His face nonetheless was etched with the hardness of his past. Deep lines of regret and pain were also within his princely visage.

Bumper had been an actor before he got hooked on coke in Los Angeles, and he had come back to Detroit in shame. He'd kicked around hustling and did time for possession. He was not a hard type but was not the kind of man you took lightly either. He'd done his share of violence over the years.

Bumper had met LoLo at a club and had become her man that same night. LoLo had never seen a man so nice-looking, and to her surprise, he was the one who came after her. Seems Bumper liked short women.

LoLo confessed her profession to him. Bumper was taken aback at first, but he genuinely liked her. They became a couple, LoLo dealing and Bumper hustling but never working for her.

They stayed together for a year before LoLo offered to take care of him so he could stop hustling. She would give him money, and all he had to do was be her refuge, comfort, and sex partner. LoLo didn't believe in love. Love made women weak. All she needed was a man, some good sex, and a safe house.

Bumper didn't like the idea of being kept by a woman, but the money would give him the freedom he wanted. He took the deal. LoLo knew he had other women, but Bumper was cautious and never threw them in her face. Once LoLo had popped over in the middle of the night, and he'd put one out of his bed. It was a great relationship.

There was a knock at the door. Bumper quickly reached under his bed and pulled out a little black Smith & Wesson .380. He went to the door and looked out. He smiled and let Yolanda in. "Hey, motormouth," Bumper said.

Yolanda walked in without a word and went to the bedroom. Bumper followed her.

"So," said LoLo, "what happened to my Girls? They okay?"

Yolanda shook her head. "Prosecutor set some big-ass bail."

"How much?" said LoLo.

"Fifty thousand each. And Marly's gone. No bail."

"Dammit!" said LoLo. "I knew Marly was gone. I ain't got that kind of cash for the twins. I need them." She started to get out of the bed.

"You got to rest first," said Bumper. He made her lie back down. He took the glass of juice from her and set it on an end table.

"We got other people," said Yolanda.

"These girls are shooters," said LoLo. "Most of the others are too weak to even lift up a damn gun. I'm gonna need hard women to get Cane. He'll be coming after me for sure. I know him. Just when you think he's not going to do anything—"

There was another knock at the door. Yolanda and LoLo grew quiet. Yolanda pulled out her gun. Bumper got up with his .380 and put his fingers to his lips. "Shh," he said.

He went to the door and looked through the peephole. He put his gun to the door and said, "What you want, girl?"

"Let me in, Bumper," said Ramona on the other side of the door. "It's me, Ramona."

"She ain't here," said Bumper. "Ain't seen her in a while."

"Let her in," said LoLo. She had gotten out of the bed and was standing in the doorway. "Go on," she said.

Bumper opened the door but kept his gun out. Ramona and Jesse walked in looking like death warmed over. Ramona went to LoLo and hugged her.

"Damn, you hard to find, girl," said Ramona.

"Yeah," said LoLo, glad to see her. "You know Bumper?"

"Yeah. Glad I remembered you," said Ramona.

"Uh-huh," said Bumper. He closed the door.

Jesse said nothing. He looked out the window and saw Nikko drive away in the car. He felt awkward standing in the living room of the house.

"I thought I'd never see you again," said LoLo. "At least not in this lifetime." She looked at Jesse and said, "So, you must be the killer."

"My name is Jesse, and I didn't kill anyone."

"Hey, I believe you," said Bumper. He laughed and put his gun away. Yolanda kept hers out.

Jesse felt ill at ease with these people. They were criminal types, all of them. Except Bumper, who looked like he fell out of a magazine.

"You don't know what I've been through," said Ramona. Pointing at LoLo's bandaged arm, she asked, "What happened?"

"Cane," Lolo said bleakly.

"You two look like shit," said Bumper. "I'll get you a drink."

"No, thanks," said Jesse. "We won't be here long." He looked at Ramona, as if to signal her. She turned to LoLo.

"LoLo, you know I'm in deep," said Ramona. "I need that black case I gave you to get me out of it."

"The case?" said LoLo. She walked away from them and sat in a chair. "Bumper, I think you'd better get them drinks."

Cane lifted the black metallic briefcase from the trunk of his Lincoln outside the house on Daniel Street. It was beautiful. Dark and cool. He could almost see his face in it.

"Where did Little Jack get this?" he asked Tico.

"LoLo was hiding it at that house I was in," said Tico. "When we left, Little Jack grabbed it. He said LoLo was always guarding it and shit. He figured it was worth something."

Cane shook the case, but nothing moved inside. "How you supposed to open this thing?" he said. "It don't have a latch on it."

"Don't ask me," said Tico. "It's junk. They probably just bought it off some crackhead."

"I'll bust it open later," said Cane. "Right now we gotta pay Jaleel a visit. If he's stealing from me, I need to relieve him of those funds. My H arrives in two days."

Tico nodded and walked to the driver's side of the Lincoln. Cane tossed the black case into the car's deep trunk and closed the lid, locking it inside.

6

Jesse Rollin'

He was sick.

Jesse felt so close to the black briefcase and freedom that he could feel it. But the case was gone, in the possession of yet another lowlife criminal.

From what he could understand, the woman named LoLo was obsessed with a drug dealer named Cane. He'd slashed LoLo badly in a fight and apparently killed one of her people. They talked about this Cane like he was the devil himself. LoLo was consumed with her hatred of the man and wanted Ramona to help, which meant she wanted Jesse too.

He didn't know what to do. He needed the black case, but joining a drug crew was certainly going over the line.

They sat and talked in back of Bumper's house. It was a converted back porch, but it was comfortable. After bringing them drinks and feeding them, Bumper had disappeared.

"So, I hear Cane is planning a big drug buy," said LoLo. "He's moving into heroin. If we can find out where, we can get him."

"LoLo, that could be too dangerous," said Ramona. "Too many people. And you're already hurt."

Jesse noticed Ramona's deep concern about her friend LoLo. That troubled him. He was thinking only about the black case. LoLo was thinking only about revenge. Jesse had no idea where Ramona's loyalties were right now.

And he definitely couldn't figure out the big woman, Yolanda. She hardly ever spoke and kept watching him suspiciously.

"If we want to stop the deal, we have to make sure he can't buy the drugs," said Jesse. "That means cutting off his money."

"Excuse us," said LoLo, turning to him with a contemptuous look. "But we talking business here, Mr. Lawyer. What do you know about rollin'?"

"Only what six-fifty drug cases have taught me," said Jesse. "Six hundred and fifty grams and you go to jail for life. If the buy is a six-fifty, and it probably is, he's got a load of cash somewhere. We get to it, and he'll have to deal."

"Okay, bad-ass," said LoLo, still scornful. "How we gonna find his cash?"

Jesse was silent. He had jumped into the conversation without thinking and had no idea where to begin. He just didn't want to leave his destiny up to a bunch of drug dealers—and women at that. "I don't know," said Jesse. "But if I can—"

"Uh-huh, just what I thought," said LoLo. "You don't know shit. Why don't you just be cool and leave business to people who know what the fuck they're doin'?"

"But if we think about it, we—" Jesse protested.

"Mona, can't you control your nigga?" asked LoLo. Yolanda uttered a short laugh.

"Jesse," said Ramona, "can you let us talk for a while here? I'll fill you in later." She seemed embarrassed, but not as much as he was.

Jesse got up and went into the kitchen. Bumper was sitting watching a small TV and drinking a beer.

"Come on in, my brother," said Bumper. His eyes seemed to shine. "You don't wanna mess with LoLo when she's talking business."

"I guess not."

Jesse reluctantly sat down. He disliked being dismissed by the women. And what was worse, he now was sitting in the kitchen with Bumper, who was obviously some kind of pretty-boy prostitute for LoLo. This must be how women felt when they were abased by know-it-all men, he thought.

"So, that your woman?" asked Bumper. His voice was smooth, almost musical.

"Ramona?" said Jesse. "Yes, she is, I guess."

"She really likes you," said Bumper.

"What makes you say that?"

"She didn't even look at me when she came in. See, I never

forgets a woman. I met her a long time ago. Back then she was checking me out, big time. But not anymore. She's all into you."

"Thanks, I think," said Jesse. Bumper was a vain, arrogant bastard. But then he had reason.

"How is she?" asked Bumper.

"In bed?" asked Jesse. "I don't feel comfortable—"

"Come on, nigga," said Bumper. "Right now them women are in there talking about how big your dick is, how you put it in, how fast you came, and everything. I know them. So come on, give it up."

Jesse had no interest in bonding with Bumper. He came off like a pimp or something, like he was trying to seduce him. Still, he didn't want to get on his host's bad side. "She's great," said Jesse. "I have no complaints."

Bumper burst into laughter. "Damn, man, you sound like a white boy! You supposed to say, 'The shit was slammin'! I was all up in the pussy! It was all that!' You know what I'm sayin'?" He laughed again.

Jesse laughed despite himself. He knew what Bumper was talking about. There was a way that black men talked about women that he'd forgotten. It was all macho posturing and bullshit, but it was an accepted means of communication. "That's what I meant," said Jesse.

"I been kickin' it with LoLo for a long time," said Bumper. "And she can fuck like a champ. I love little women. They know how to move that thang, you know?"

"But she's not your only woman, is she?" asked Jesse knowingly. He couldn't imagine this man with just one woman.

"Naw," said Bumper. "But she's my main one. I love that girl, but she loves the life more than me, you know. I keep trying to get her out, but . . ." He trailed off, and his handsome face looked a little sadder. "You know how hardheaded women can be."

"I know," said Jesse. "Believe me, I know."

"If I was you," said Bumper, "I'd take that fine little piece in there and break, just run away. This thing you in, you ain't gonna never get out of it, man."

"I have to get out of it," said Jesse. "I promised her that she'd be okay. I don't break my promises."

"You serious, ain't you?" asked Bumper.

"I'm afraid so," said Jesse.

"So whatcha gone do when you get out of this?"

That he didn't know. He thought about Connie. He still had feelings for her, but Ramona had taken his heart. He couldn't imagine his life without Ramona now. Connie was a wonderful woman, but Ramona represented a part of him that was important, a part that he shunned, a part he realized that he needed to reclaim.

"Maybe when it's over, I'll go to Disneyland," said Jesse.

Jesse and Bumper shared a laugh. Jesse took a beer and drank with Bumper. He could remember being uncomfortable with people like Bumper not too long ago. But he was also remembering what he was like before he changed. He used to love the friendship of black men, deep in culture and that almost mystical understanding that black people shared. He remembered, and it didn't seem so bad. In fact it was soothing given his situation. Solace. He hadn't felt that in a while.

Jesse was used to hiding behind his profession. That barrier let him believe that he was different, better. But now he was just another black man in trouble. If the men he had put in prison could see him now, they would— Jesse's eyes got wider. Without a word he jumped up and headed to the back room.

"Hey," said Bumper. "Where you goin', man?"

Jesse came in and found LoLo, Ramona, and Yolanda in an intense conversation.

"Ramona," said Jesse, interrupting the debate.

"Got some more big ideas, Capone?" said LoLo. She glared at Jesse, obviously disturbed at his intrusion.

"I'm sorry," said Jesse. "But I think I got it."

7

King

Cane opened the big razor as Tico and Q held the man. Little Jack sat quietly in a corner, watching. Since freeing Tico, Cane had kept the little boy close to him. He saw the boy as an investment. He didn't want him to waste away in the crew. He could raise Little Jack to be a great man, a leader, like he was. And one day he would teach him what he knew about God, fear, and all the real important things in life.

The thin man named Jaleel Jackson struggled as Tico and Q each held an arm. They'd surprised Jaleel in the process of counting his receipts. Cane and his men had descended on Jaleel and cleared the house. Now it was time to do business.

Cane was in need of money for the buy with Minnesota. The fat man seemed harmless, but all the reports Cane got told him that Minnesota and his people were not to be trifled with. If he didn't have the money, Minnesota would kill the deal and him too.

They were at a location near Grand River and Fenkell. Jaleel was one of Cane's lower-level dealers. He ran a profitable house, but he was keeping a lot of the money to himself. Not only was Jaleel disloyal, but he made Cane look bad. So he had to teach him a lesson that everyone would remember.

"Where's my money?" said Cane. "I know you've been stealing from me. So I'm only going to ask you once. After that this talks for me." He gestured with the blade.

"The money is right there," said Jaleel. In the middle of the floor on a table was a pile of money, the receipts from the day.

Cane moved closer to the man. Tico held his right arm, and Q held the left. Jaleel's torso made a big target. Cane watched the frightened man's eyes, enjoying what he saw in them.

"That's all the money I got," said Jaleel.

Cane nodded to Tico, who held out one of Jaleel's arms. Cane flattened Jaleel's palm and sliced his baby finger open. A red line appeared; then blood began to drip from it. Jaleel screamed. Cane remembered that Jaleel was a punk, a weak man who used drugs and detested violence.

"Nine left," said Cane. "When the cuts heal in a few minutes, I'll open them back up."

Cane watched him narrowly. He could tell that Jaleel was weighing the consequences of telling the truth. Tears welled in Jaleel's eyes, and his arm shook as Tico held it out. Cane slit open another finger. Jaleel yelled again, and Tico fought to keep his hand steady, not wanting to get blood on him.

"Eight," said Cane, his eyes shining.

"Okay, okay," said Jaleel. "I did it—"

"Where is my money?" Cane asked.

"The kitchen, behind the stove."

Cane nodded to Little Jack. The boy ran into the kitchen and soon returned with a small box spotted with grease. Cane took it and opened it. A small stack of bills was inside. The largest was a twenty. Cane closed the box and went back to the bleeding man.

"Where's the rest of it?" Cane asked. Jaleel's fingers were dripping blood on the floor. "What's in that box is just bitch money. So where's the rest of it?"

Jaleel's eyes widened, and Cane watched in muted amusement. Would he lie, or was he smart after all? Jaleel seemed afraid to speak and afraid not to.

"That's all of it, man. I swear!" said Jaleel.

Cane promptly turned on his heel and went into the backyard. He returned carrying a little brown chihuahua in his arms. The dog was wearing a gold collar.

"No! Not King," Jaleel pleaded. "All right, all right. It's in the kitchen. Behind the cabinets."

Cane nodded to Little Jack, who took off again. Soon he returned empty-handed.

"Where is it?" Cane asked Little Jack.

"I don't see nothing in there," said Little Jack.

Cane dropped the razor to the little dog's neck. Jaleel jerked, but Tico and Q held him fast.

"I said, *behind* the cabinets. Behind the wall!" Jaleel yelled.

This time Cane went into the little kitchen. One of the cabinet doors was open. Cane rapped a fist on the back of the cabinet. It made a hollow sound. Cane punched the back of the cabinet hard, and it broke. He pulled the pieces out, and he saw money stacked up behind the walls. Cane tested the other cabinet walls and found that they lifted easily from the back. The cabinets were filled with money, enough to make the buy with Minnesota.

The sight of so much stolen money made him enraged. He hated a thief. He walked back into the living room.

"Let him go," he said to Tico and Q.

They released Jaleel. He groaned and grabbed his hand, trying to stop the bleeding. He ran into a bathroom.

"Tico," said Cane, "you and Q get that money. We'll take it to the place later."

Jaleel came out of the bathroom with his fingers wrapped tightly in a towel. He saw Cane standing before him, still holding the little brown chihuahua.

"King," Jaleel called to the dog. "Come on, boy."

"From now on I'm gonna have a man here watching you," said Cane. "And you'll never know who it is."

"Okay, okay," said Jaleel. "Just put down King, please."

"I hear you treat this dog better than most people," said Cane. He placed his hand around the little dog's throat. He took off the gold collar and threw it to Little Jack, who put it in his pocket.

Under normal circumstances he would have taken Jaleel out, but with the heroin coming, that meant a new business, and he'd need this house and Jaleel. He was a good roller, just not too bright.

"You got your money," said Jaleel, watching with fearful eyes. "You don't need to do this, man."

"Cane," said Tico, "we got what we want. Leave the mutt alone, man."

"It's either you or King here," said Cane to Jaleel. "Make your choice."

Jaleel was silent. Cane tightened his grip on the little dog's throat, holding him out from his body. The chihuahua kicked and fought desperately, its cries muffled off by Cane's steely grasp.

Jaleel watched in horror. Tico just shook his head. Q uttered a laugh. Little Jack cringed, turning his face away. After a moment the dog stopped kicking and hung limply in Cane's grasp.

He threw the dog to Jaleel, who was now in tears. Jaleel tried to catch the dog but was too late. The carcass fell on the floor with a thud.

"I'll be watching you," said Cane. "Next time that'll be your ass on the floor."

Cane walked out of the house, followed by the others. Jaleel fell to his knees, weeping over the body of the dead animal.

8

Takedown

"I know a man who can help us," said Jesse to LoLo. He stood in the makeshift den, looking down at the women who sat together. "He's an informant, a damned good one. This man knows everything."

"Fuck that," said LoLo. "Any muthafucka who'd drop on his own kind is out."

"Wait," said Ramona. "I mean, if Jesse says that this is good, we should check it out."

"Oh, so you and your man here running my shit now?" said LoLo. "It ain't happening. I'm not concerned with you two lovebirds and your shit. I want Cane."

"All that ain't necessary, okay?" said Ramona heatedly. "It's just a suggestion."

The two women started to quarrel again. Jesse was taking a step toward them when he felt a hand on his shoulder. He turned and found Bumper looking at him very seriously.

"You don't wanna do that, my brother," said Bumper. "This is how they do things."

Jesse stood with Bumper as Ramona and LoLo cursed and yelled at each other. Yolanda just watched with an expressionless face.

"Damn, you hardheaded," said LoLo. "Okay, let's try the shit, but if it don't work, it's my way." She turned to Jesse. "So who is this man?"

"A guy named Hardaway," said Jesse. "He used to be a probation officer. He talks to a lot of ex-cons who give him info. And he sells it to the cops. I know where he lives."

"Okay," said LoLo. "We give him some money and—"

"He won't take it," said Jesse. "Hardaway is a hustler, but he won't sell anything to dealers."

"Sorry-ass bastard," said LoLo.

"That's a damned good hustle," said Bumper. There was a touch of admiration in his voice.

"How do we get to him?" asked Ramona. "Won't he try to run you in for that reward?"

"Yes," said Jesse. "That's why we're gonna kidnap him."

The room abruptly fell silent. Ramona seemed to be proud of Jesse's suggestion. LoLo looked at Yolanda. The big woman nodded ever so slightly.

"Okay," said LoLo. "When can we get to him?"

"Tonight," said Jesse. Jesse checked his watch. "Damn, I'm late. I need to use your phone."

North drove along looking for Florence's car. They'd almost gotten King and the Blake woman following her the other night. It was weird following the lady cop when the police were on her too, but they'd managed it. And unlike the cops, Florence wasn't able to shake the killers.

They'd lost her tonight, but as soon as they picked her back up, they'd stick to her.

"I say when we find her, we take her and persuade her to tell us where King is."

"Yeah, like you persuaded that woman lawyer?" said North.

There was a stony silence between the killers. The murder of Karen Bell was unplanned and unnecessary to their goal.

"I still say we should have killed that King guy too." The killer rubbed the scar on his face.

"That would have raised too many questions," said North. "Besides, this whole fugitive thing is the kind of distraction we need right now."

"So do we grab this lady cop or not?"

"Not yet. Sooner or later she'll go back to King. Then we can get that black case and clean them all."

The killers drove on, moving past a little bar in Hamtramck

where Florence's car was hidden neatly behind a big red delivery truck.

Florence sat impatiently by the pay phone in the back of the shabby little bar. It was after midnight, and Jesse was late calling her. The streets were crawling with cops and volunteer patrols for Devil's Night. She hoped that Jesse was all right. That Ramona Blake woman he was with looked like real trouble.

The phone rang. Florence picked it up on the first ring.

"Florence?" said Jesse.

"What the fuck are you doin'?" asked Florence. "I've been waiting here for a goddamned hour!"

"Calm down," said Jesse.

"I am calm," said Florence. "As calm as I can be, knowing that I'm being followed."

"The police?"

"No," said Florence. "I think it's the bad guys. And I'm sure they don't know that I've made them. I lost them right before I came here."

"Holy shit," said Jesse. "Florence, you've got to get out of there. When you left us at Packer's— They must have followed you. They came after us, but we got away."

Florence contemplated this for a moment. "Damn," she said. "I had the cops on me too that night. I'm getting to be a popular girl, huh?"

"Don't fuck with these guys. I think they may have killed Yancy, Karen Bell. I don't think they'd mind getting rid of you."

"Yeah, but what if I can get them first?"

"No!" said Jesse. He was almost yelling. "No way I'm gonna let you do that!"

"Sorry, Jess, but you ain't in no position to stop me. Look, we need a break in this thing, and if I can snag these guys—"

"They'll kill you," said Jesse.

"You know, I think if they wanted to do that, I'd be dead already."

"I'll turn myself in before I'll let anything happen to you."

"Then you'd better do it soon," said Florence. "Because I plan to take them as soon as I can set it up."

There was silence on the line. "Okay," said Jesse finally. "But get some help or something."

"Listen, I don't have any new info for you," said Florence. "But I'll be here same time tomorrow." Then she added, "I hope."

"Okay," said Jesse. "I guess I can't stop you."

"No, you can't," said Florence.

"Be careful, Flo."

"I will. And don't call me Flo, goddammit."

Jesse hung up the phone and cursed. Florence was playing Russian roulette with those men. He had to get that case soon before she was in a box with all the others.

LoLo and Bumper were in the kitchen talking. Yolanda sat in a chair watching Jesse. She made him nervous. Big and silent, she seemed like the type of person who would kill you, bury you in her backyard, then have a barbecue.

"So what did she say?" asked Ramona.

"I think the killers are on her trail," said Jesse. "They're probably trying to use her to get to us."

"What's she gonna do?" asked Ramona.

"She's going to try to take them out," said Jesse, frowning. "She didn't say what that meant. I take it she means alive. They're no use to us dead."

Jesse sat on the arm of a sofa feeling sad and frustrated. This thing was out of control now. Everyone he cared about was screwed up because of him. Moreover, he was reverting back to what he used to be. He had suggested kidnapping Hardaway the way you might decide to buy a pair of shoes. And the worst thing was, he didn't hate himself for it. Now he remembered how strong the lure of crime was. The life, as they called it, was better than nothing, and without that black briefcase that's what he had, nothing.

Ramona went over to Jesse and put an arm around him. She looked beautiful. He was in the greatest trouble of his life, but at least he'd found her. His spirits lifted at her touch. Maybe he could win this game and get his life back. She smiled at him, and he saw in her eyes what he felt in his heart. It was a strange, bittersweet emotion, and he knew in that moment that he loved her.

"No time for feeling sorry, honey," Ramona said. "We got some work to do."

Jesse stood up and kissed her, not caring that Yolanda's steely gaze was still upon him.

9

Money House

Jesse and the crew waited outside the little house on Kentucky Street. They were parked several houses from Hardaway's home. Jesse and Ramona were in the backseat of an old Monte Carlo. They all had guns, and Jesse was very nervous about that.

Bumper had stayed behind, and Jesse felt out of place with the women. It was late in the night, and the street was deserted. The patrols were probably still out for Devil's Night, but they'd be thin by now.

"Think he's got an alarm on this place?" LoLo asked no one in particular.

"I doubt it," said Ramona.

"He's got steel bars on the windows," said Jesse. "And that usually means that's all he was willing to spend. We can probably get in through the basement. But we have to move fast. This guy probably sleeps with a gun."

"You've done this before, huh?" said LoLo.

"Long time ago," said Jesse.

"Shit, being a lawyer ain't no different," said LoLo. "Just a different kind of stealin'."

Jesse heard Yolanda laugh softly.

"I'll go in," he said. "Then I'll let you all in."

"If I hear shootin'," said LoLo, "I'll wait a minute for you. If I don't see you come to the door, we outta here."

"Thanks for the vote of confidence," said Jesse. He opened the door and got out.

"See you in a minute," said Ramona.

Jesse ran to the side of the house. The street was nice, and there were occupied houses all the way down the long block. Hardaway's house was bigger than most, and he had a big two-car garage.

He moved to a window at the base of the house. The window was dirty, and it was dark inside the basement. Leaning down to test the window, he found it locked. He took out his .38, wrapped in a towel he'd brought. With a sharp tap he cracked the window. He pushed a big piece of glass inside. It fell, and Jesse heard it break on the floor. If there was a dog in the basement, or a person, he would hear the sound, but not the people sleeping upstairs. Funny how you never forgot, he thought.

There was no movement inside, so Jesse slowly pulled the remaining glass away from the window. He pulled the shards outside so that they made no sound. Soon the window was open. Jesse felt for a latch, found it, and turned it. The window opened in. He slipped through and lowered himself to the floor. It was dark inside the basement, but he didn't look for the lights.

His heart pounded a drumbeat in his ears. His lawyer's mind kept saying, Breaking and entering, kidnapping, carrying a concealed weapon—thirty years, at least. Jesse moved to the staircase. The steps were made of wood, and he was terrified as he tried them and heard a loud creak.

"Shit," he said, stopping. If he walked the stairs regularly, he might make too much noise. Jesse decided to take them two at a time. Less time, less noise. He stretched and went up. The stairs creaked, but not too badly. Jesse opened the door at the top of the stairs and went into the house.

It was dim, but the light from outside allowed him to see. The place was nice. The basement led into a little bathroom, which led into a kitchen. Jesse went to the side door in the kitchen and opened it. He went out to the front of the house and waved to the women in the car. He saw them get out and come his way. Jesse went back inside.

LoLo and Ramona soon appeared. "Where is he?" asked LoLo.

"Upstairs, I think," said Jesse.

"Go get him," said LoLo. "I'll stay down here. Any shit jumps off, I come up shootin'."

Jesse and Ramona went up the stairs to the bedrooms. The staircase was carpeted and made no sound. They went to a big door and cracked it. No one was inside. They checked the other room, but no one was there either.

"Fuck," said Jesse. "He's not here."

When they walked back downstairs, LoLo was peeking out a window. "There's a car out here," she said.

"It's gotta be him," said Ramona.

They waited until they saw him come to the side door; then they hid themselves.

The short, fat man seemed happy as he entered the little kitchen, singing a tune.

Hardaway pulled a large roll of bills from his pocket as he walked into the dining room. That was when Jesse grabbed him. Hardaway struggled, and Jesse pushed his face into a wall. Hardaway was fat but very strong. He reached for a gun in his pocket, dropping the roll of bills. Ramona stepped up, snatched Hardaway's gun, and shoved it behind his ear.

"Calm down, baby boy," she said.

LoLo walked up behind them and quickly tied a blindfold over Hardaway's eyes. Jesse tied his hands.

"Okay, okay," said Hardaway anxiously. "Take the damned money."

"We don't want money," said Jesse.

"Like hell," said LoLo. She stooped and picked up the wad of cash.

"We don't want to hurt you," said Jesse. Hardaway was silent. Jesse wondered if he recognized his voice.

"Okay," said Hardaway. "Take what you want. Just do it and get the fuck out."

Hardaway seemed scared despite his defiance, but Jesse didn't feel sorry for him. The man was almost a criminal himself. Jesse remembered how Hardaway had blackmailed Denise Wilkerson at the prosecutor's office.

"What we want is information," said Ramona. "I want to know where Gregory Cane's money house is."

"Don't know no Cane," said Hardaway.

LoLo put her gun on Hardaway's crotch. When she cocked the gun, the sound was loud in the little room. "Okay, muthafucka," said LoLo, giving the barrel a shove. "What's really important to you? This little information or the five years of fucking you got left?" She looked fierce as she said the words, and Jesse had no doubt that she would do it.

Hardaway had no doubt either. "He's got a place," he said."It's on Littlefield somewhere."

"That's a big-ass street," said LoLo. "Which block is it in?" She shoved the barrel into him again.

"Don't know the address," said Hardaway, grunting in pain. "But I know it's got a blue Samson on it."

"If you lying to me," said LoLo, "I'm coming back for that dick, old man."

"What's a blue Samson?" Jesse asked Ramona in a whisper.

"A door," said Ramona. "A big steel door."

He saw LoLo counting Hardaway's money. "Give him the money back," said Jesse.

"Get the fuck outta my face," said LoLo. She pushed Jesse out of her way and walked out of the house.

Ramona and Jesse proceeded to tie Hardaway to a chair. Jesse left enough slack in the rope so that he could get out eventually. He unplugged the phones and took the cords. That would buy them some time.

Jesse walked toward the door. He stopped and went back to Hardaway. He knelt by the bound-up man. Hardaway was unhurt and seemed more angry than anything else. "Sorry about this," he said.

"Fuck you," said Hardaway.

Jesse locked Hardaway in and got into the car with the women. Yolanda pulled off.

"Y'all want a taste of this cash?" asked LoLo. She passed some bills to Yolanda.

"No, thanks," said Jesse.

"Big surprise," said LoLo. "How 'bout you, Mona? I know you want a bite." LoLo held out some bills over her shoulder.

Ramona hesitated, and Jesse could tell that she wanted to take it. They would always need money.

"Keep it," said Ramona.

They started at Eight Mile and went south. They rolled around for an hour on Littlefield, looking for a house with a big steel door. LoLo knew the kind of door they were looking for. When a dealer wanted to keep people out of a place, he put in a steel-reinforced door. A company called Samson Security made them.

"It's that one there with the nasty picket fence," said LoLo suddenly. "A Samson like that cost a thousand dollars. And look at the car out in front."

A new Lexus coupe was sitting in front of the little run-down house. It was in contrast with the other average, basic transportation–type cars on the street.

"I see your point," said Jesse. He was moderately impressed with LoLo. She certainly knew her stuff. But she was still a lowlife. If he hadn't been with them, he was sure that Thomas Hardaway would be dead right now.

Yolanda went around the corner and parked two blocks away. It was quiet and dark on the street. Yolanda popped out of the car and got a pump-action shotgun out of the trunk.

"Wait," said Jesse. "We don't wanna go in shooting."

"I'm not arguing with you this time," said LoLo. "Some things got to be done a certain way. I don't know what you think you signed up for, but this ain't no game for punk asses."

"We can get the money without any of us being in danger," said Jesse. "If this Cane is smart as you say, I'm sure he's got a lot of heavily armed men in there. I can get them out, get us in without any gunfights."

LoLo looked at Jesse, contemplating her choice. Jesse had been right so far, and they would certainly be outnumbered. She looked at Yolanda, who nodded softly again.

"Okay," said LoLo, "but if you fuck this up, it's on your ass."

"Wouldn't have it any other way," said Jesse.

Jesse waited in the shadows as the police cruisers pulled up. Their cherry lights were on, but the sirens were silent. Jesse was in the backyard of the house next door to Cane's money house. It was dangerous, but he needed to stay close.

He had called the cops, saying that there had been gunfire at the house and had given them the address. Only something of a serious nature like that would get them out in a decent time, and he knew LoLo wasn't going to wait long.

A pair of uniformed cops got out of the cruiser. Jesse waited until they approached the house; then he pulled his gun and shot in the air twice. The cops hustled back to the cruiser, pulling their sidearms. The cops in the second cruiser did the same.

As Jesse ran away, he heard one of the officers calling for backup.

He ran through an alley back to the block where the women were. They had moved even farther down the street. Jesse got to the car and got inside.

"Now what?" asked LoLo. She seemed angry.

"Now we wait and let the cops do our job for us," said Jesse.

They sat there as more police cruisers came. The cops called to the house on a bullhorn, but no one inside said anything.

A news van pulled up, but the cops made it move back down the street, away from the confrontation.

After about a half hour someone in the house opened the big steel door and the cops poured inside. Soon six young black men in handcuffs were walked out.

"What if they find the money?" asked LoLo.

"Cane is too smart for that," said Jesse as if he knew the man. "He's probably already thought of that, and he has it in a place that you can only find if you're really looking."

The cops searched the house as they put the occupants in a police van. Jesse and his crew watched from their vantage point in the next block. A few neighborhood people came out and watched the raid.

Jesse and the women sat in the car and waited as the cops locked down the house. They came out with men, guns, and a big paper bag. "There's probably money in that bag," said Jesse. "But if I'm right, they let the cops find it to throw them off."

"You'd better be right," said LoLo. They didn't make their move on the house until the sun was up.

"Shit," said LoLo. "Where is it?" She threw a chair against a wall. The house was a mess. The police had ransacked it. And Jesse and company had broken in the back and ransacked it again, looking for the money. They'd been in the basement, the upstairs and even broken open a wall. Nothing.

"It's here," said Jesse. "I know it is."

"We got fucked!" yelled LoLo. "The cops got all the money." She kicked an old sofa.

"Maybe we're just not thinking," said Ramona. "You know how Cane is. He wouldn't hide the money anywhere obvious."

"I know one thing," said LoLo. "Cane is probably out right now hitting my people, and I'm here jacking off!"

Jesse didn't say anything. He didn't want to argue with LoLo in her present state. She was a hothead and not very smart. He guessed that only her ruthlessness had gotten her to where she was.

Ramona walked across the room. She'd been on her feet for a while and was about to sit on the old sofa. She crossed the fireplace and moved to the little sofa and sat down.

Jesse watched her, glancing down to the floor. He saw that the fireplace looked like it was never used, but there was a little soot on the hearth. He walked to it, got on his knees, and looked up the chimney. Jesse took his head out of the chimney and turned to the others, who were now looking at him curiously.

"Jackpot," he said.

10

Tune-up

Florence watched the van from her bathroom. They'd been sitting on her all night. They obviously didn't want to harm her, or they would have tried something already. Still, she hadn't slept much last night.

The blue van was parked halfway up her street on Ardmore. Florence hoped that they couldn't see her watching them. She had the curtain closed and was peeking through a crack in it.

She had to do something. She guessed that they wanted her to go back to Jesse. They would follow her and then probably kill them all. But she was not going near Jesse until these guys were on ice.

Florence was nervous, but she was also excited. She was a real cop again, and it felt good. She'd been riding a desk, doing bullshit case interviews, for too long. She suddenly realized that she hadn't had a drink in a long time. Her blood was filled with something better now.

Florence left the bathroom, put on her clothes, and drove downtown on the Lodge Freeway. She saw the van behind her every so often. She even lost them once, but they picked her back up by Grand Boulevard. They were good but not great.

Florence got off the Lodge Freeway at the Jefferson exit. She rode past downtown to the IHOP. She went inside and had a leisurely breakfast. Since Jesse was gone, her cases had been reassigned. No one came to her for work, and she was not about to ask for any. The blue van rolled by.

She couldn't play this game much longer. Sooner or later they'd figure out she was on to them, or they'd get frustrated, grab her, and beat out what they wanted. She needed to make the next move, catch them before they could think.

Florence left the restaurant and went into the parking lot. She heard one of those annoyingly loud car alarms squelch next to her car. Suddenly an idea struck her. Florence got in her car and left. She waited until she saw the van behind her, then drove to a gas station. She parked by a public phone. She didn't see where the van went, but she knew they were watching.

Florence got out of the car and went to the phone. She dialed a number.

The killers watched Florence on the pay phone with great interest. She seemed to be having an intense conversation. Her face was red, and she gestured wildly.

North gripped the steering wheel so hard his knuckles popped. She was up to something, he thought. Why else would she use a pay phone?

They watched for five more minutes as Florence ranted. She got back into her car and drove away. They waited, then followed her. Florence went to 1300 and left her car in the garage. The killers were not suspicious. A lot of cops got free car service from the city.

Florence walked from 1300 over to Frank Murphy and went inside.

They waited for her. Whatever she was up to, it seemed urgent. They had to stick to her. She might be setting up a meeting with King. If she was, they would take them out and end this troublesome case.

It would be easier now that the cops were no longer following Florence. Shows how much they knew about anything. But the killers knew. Florence was the key, and something had happened in that phone conversation.

They waited all day for Florence. Something was about to jump off. And when it did, they would be ready.

11

Girlfriend

Cane and Tico pulled up to the money house on Littlefield. The big steel door was closed, and the house looked peaceful.

"Stupid-ass niggas," said Tico. "Shootin' at a cop. When they get out, I say we smoke all of 'em."

"We got Minnesota to deal with first," said Cane. "Once we get the goods, all business will be settled."

"Well, when we do, just let me handle it," said Tico. "I hate this kind of shit."

They got out of the Lincoln and walked to the house. The street was quiet. All the cars that once lined the curb were gone, their owners at work.

Cane and Tico climbed the stairs. Tico took out a big ring of keys and picked through them. They had so many places it was getting hard to keep them straight.

Tico pulled out a big red key and opened the steel door. They walked into the wreckage of the place. Chairs were broken, furniture on its side, and glass was everywhere.

Cane surveyed the damage and thought that Tico's suggestion to kill the rollers guarding the money was not so bad after all.

Cane stepped on broken glass, and it crunched loudly beneath his shoes. He had wanted to come as soon as he heard, but he didn't want to take a chance the cops were here.

"Grab the bag," said Cane. "I'll watch the door."

He had to get his money out to a safe place. Minnesota was

coming with his future. He couldn't take care of LoLo before then, but he wouldn't tell Minnesota that. Cane's plan was to make the buy, flood the streets with his product, then deal with LoLo.

Tico walked over to the chimney and looked up. He stuck his hand up and pulled down a big garbage bag. There was a note stuck to it.

"What the fu—?" Tico said. He pulled off the note and handed it to Cane.

Cane read the little piece of paper.

Dear One-Eye,

I got your money. If you want it back, be at the pay phone at the gas station on Jefferson and Jos Campau at seven o'clock. Bring that black briefcase you stole from me and that motherfucker Little Jack.

Your Girlfriend

Cane threw down the letter and screamed. Tico picked up the letter, read it, then opened the garbage bag. Inside were old clothes, rocks, and junk.

"Cane, what are we gonna do?" asked Tico. "Minnesota's coming tomorrow."

Cane said nothing. He walked to a window and looked at the bright sun. He held up a fist. Tico started to walk toward him but stopped. When Cane got into his sun thing, it was not wise to mess with him.

Cane stood in the window, looking at God. Now it was really a war. If he didn't make the buy with Minnesota, they would surely kill him. This was a cheap shot, he whispered to the sun. Cheap and just like Him.

Cane stood there for a moment, cursing under his breath. Then he turned and walked over to Tico. Cane's head was framed by the sunlight behind it, and for a second it looked like he had no face. Tico shifted backward, frightened of his boss.

"Come on," Cane said. "We have to find Little Jack."

They were holed up in another of LoLo's hideouts, a two-family flat near the graveyard where Davison and Six Mile intersected. A woman named Carter lived in the ground floor with a brood of children. LoLo gave her money now and then, and the woman let LoLo use the upstairs.

They'd been there all day, planning how to take Cane and his men. Jesse watched in awe as the women passed a big joint, and Ramona intricately laid out the plan. She had obviously been the brains of the outfit back in her day. Jesse was strangely proud of her attention to detail and command over the others in these moments.

LoLo held a mean-looking black gun with a red seal on its stock as she took a drag on a joint, then passed it. The weapon was brought by a white gun dealer named Pierre, who called it a Stiletto. Jesse had never heard of such a weapon, but it looked like it could mow down an army.

LoLo paid for the weapon with Cane's money. She also used some of it to bail out two young black girls they called the twins. Seems they were in prison for assault with a deadly weapon. They were shocked to see Jesse and made the normal jokes about him being a wanted man. LoLo seemed happy. She had her army to do battle with Cane.

LoLo was having fun spending Cane's money. In fact Ramona, Yolanda, and the twins seemed happy about their advantage over Cane.

But Jesse was worried. LoLo was a dangerous woman. He'd seen enough criminals over the years to tell she was the real deal, a stone killer. She was mean, short-tempered and had that look, that disregard for life in her eyes that could stop your heart. She was like a demon, and she definitely didn't care about dying. Yolanda was just as bad, big, strong, and not too bright.

Jesse was also concerned that LoLo didn't care about the black case. She only wanted to kill this man named Cane. And if Cane was the man he'd heard about, he knew this and would try to kill them first. Any way Jesse sliced it, being in business with these women was a losing proposition.

"Don't hog the blunt, bitch," said one of the twins to Yolanda.

"DeSheeah," said LoLo, indicating the twin with the blond braids, "you and DeShawna take Little Jack and whoever else Cane brings." DeShawna looked just like her sister; only she had short, spiky dreadlocks. "Mr. Cane belongs to me," said LoLo. She lifted the Stiletto. "I'm gonna cut his ass down to nothing but that dead eye."

"What about the black case?" Jesse interjected. The room fell silent. He was uneasy. He felt they would slice him up and devour him at any moment. It was every man's nightmare to live in a world dominated by women. He could now tell other men that the reality was far worse than the dream.

"That's your damn problem," said LoLo. "I got other things to worry about."

"I'll keep my eye on the case," said Ramona.

"I just don't want anything to happen to it," said Jesse. "I think we need a plan."

"Mona said she got it covered," said LoLo forcefully. "Mona, your man worries too much."

"I'll give him something to worry about," said DeSheeah. She flicked her tongue out.

"I'll give him something to eat," said DeShawna. She slapped five with her sister. "Mona, let me borrow him for an hour."

"You better go break off a broom handle, bitch," said Ramona. The other women roared with laughter. Even Yolanda smiled.

Now Jesse knew how women felt when men disrespected them. It was not nice. He noticed vaguely how they called each other bitch as a term of affection, the way black men called each other nigger. He wondered if Ramona was putting on for her friends, or had she really gone all the way back to what she was? Their journey had made them both digress, but he realized she didn't have as far to go as he did, which meant she didn't have as much resolve.

Ramona got up from her seat and came to him. She was wearing a new pair of jeans that hugged her legs and ass nicely. She wore no bra, and her T-shirt left little to the imagination. Her braids cascaded over her shoulders.

"I need to talk to you in the back," she whispered to him. She looked upset. His intrusion into their conversation had obviously embarrassed her again.

Ramona walked to the little room off the kitchen. Jesse followed her. Inside there was an old TV, a bed, and little else. The moment he stepped in, she grabbed him and kissed him hard. She pushed him into the door, closing it, and began to undress him.

"Wha—?" he asked. He was cut off by another kiss.

"Get those pants off," said Ramona. She smiled at him.

"Ramona, we don't have time—"

She pulled off her T-shirt and kissed him again. Then she placed his hands on her breasts. "I need this," she said.

Jesse pulled his hands back and moved away from her. "What are you doing?" he said, upset with her.

"I'm just—I'm nervous about all this. I need you, okay?"

Jesse didn't answer. He'd always thought of himself as reasonable when it came to women. But he was not. He was like all other men. He had a place for women, and it was beneath all men. And when he met women who wouldn't stay there, he got mad. He moved closer to Ramona, who was still topless.

"I'm sorry," Jesse said. "I just feel out of place here."

"I know," she said. "It's all over your face. If it's any consolation, I think LoLo likes you, and she don't like many men."

"Thanks, I needed to know that," he said sarcastically. "I'm just worried that our mission is getting lost in all of this. All I want is that case, so we can go on with our lives."

Ramona kissed him. "I like the way you say *our lives*. Makes me want to take those pants off you." She reached for Jesse's zipper, but he stopped her.

"I have to say something first," Jesse said. He stopped, taking a moment. He was filled with emotion and didn't know where to begin. "I don't know how this will turn out, you know, but I've been—" He hugged her instead, stroking her hair and rubbing her back.

"I love you too," Ramona said softly into his ear.

He pulled her head from his shoulder and kissed her. She started humming her little song as she took his pants off. Soon they were both naked and on the little bed, twisted around each other. Jesse laughed a little as Ramona held up a condom.

He rolled on his back, and soon Ramona was on top of him, moving and humming blissfully. He looked up at her. Her eyes were closed, and she had a heavenly smile on her face. She leaned over and kissed him, her hair falling into his face. She kissed his cheek, then moved her lips to his ear.

"Tell me," she said.

He knew what she wanted. He'd walked up to his admission but was unable to speak it. He understood that saying it meant more pressure and misery for them both.

Jesse pulled her face in front of his, pushing her hair aside. He saw his own face in her dark eyes.

"I love you," he said.

12

Cathedral

St. Martin's Church looked haunted as they approached it on the shadowy street. Jesse and Ramona sat in the back of the car as LoLo drove and Yolanda rode shotgun. The twins had broken off from them in their own car earlier.

The church was on the east side just outside Hamtramck. It was an old Catholic church whose time had run out. Normally, when the archdiocese abandoned a church in the inner city, a black congregation would buy the building and move in. But in this case the city had other plans for the land. New homes would be built on this formerly sacred land.

The area was deserted. All the homes had been bought and vacated. There was not a person or a store for blocks. On a patch of land in front of the church a green and white sign read: NEW CITY PROJECT.

Jesse stared up at the dark November sky. The church's pointed rooftops and hulking gargoyles seemed to stare back. The church took up a city block. There was only one street leading to the church and so only one way to get out.

It was seven o'clock. LoLo stopped the car in front of the church. The twins' car was up the street. They were going to wait there and close Cane in when he showed. If anyone was with him, they would take them out.

LoLo and Yolanda got out of the car. LoLo pulled out a mobile phone, and dialed. She looked annoyed as she did. Jesse remembered that she didn't like to do business on the airwaves. LoLo listened on the phone a moment, then handed it to Yolanda.

"Nine o'clock, St. Martin's on our side," she said, then hung up.

LoLo took the phone back and put it away. She leaned into the car and looked at Ramona and Jesse. "Two hours and the shit is on."

Florence pulled up to the building. The construction crew was gone, and the new store was abandoned. It was almost complete, so she'd be able to move around inside. She had picked this place on Grand River because it was close to the freeway, and there were many ways to get in and out of the area.

She got out of her car and walked to the building. It was hard to see in the dark, but she assumed the van was not far away.

Florence walked into the half-finished structure. She waited, then went to an open window and looked down the street. Sure enough, two big men got out of a van and moved her way. They walked together down the dark street.

Florence surveyed the area. There was a second floor, but it was not finished. Beyond the building in the rear, machinery and supplies were piled up. That might be a safe retreat, she thought. She could hide behind the wood and bricks out there if she had to. Florence took a step and kicked something that made a loud clang. On the floor were red gas canisters. Stupid construction men, she thought. Kids could find this stuff. She carefully moved the canisters out of her way.

She looked back at the two advancing men. They were on her block now. She could almost make them out. One was black; the other white. The white one was the bigger of the pair. Seeing the black guy reach inside his coat, she checked her own gun. She'd brought extra clips just for them. All she had was the element of surprise, and she had to make the most of it. If not, no one would hear from her again.

Florence noticed that to access the rear, you had to run across an area filled with debris. There were nails and jagged metal all around. She took one last look at the killers, then cleared a path for herself with her foot. She swept as much of it away as she could.

When she returned to the window, there was only one man coming her way. The black one had disappeared.

★ ★ ★

Jesse and Ramona stood in the big doorway of the church. LoLo and Yolanda were still by the car, watching the street. Their plan was to trap Cane after he got to the church. The twins would drive up behind him, and LoLo and Yolanda would take them out. Plain and simple. No prisoners. They had not even brought the money. LoLo had no intention of ever giving it back. Jesse had argued, but this time he lost.

His job was to make sure that Cane didn't get away if they missed him. He hoped it wouldn't come to that. Suddenly he felt a hand on his arm.

"I didn't want you to come," Ramona whispered. "I think that this might be bad for everyone."

"Sorry, but I have to protect my investment," he said.

"Headlights!" LoLo called out. She turned briefly to Jesse and Ramona, holding up a fist.

The big Lincoln slowly rolled their way. Jesse's body tightened. LoLo and Yolanda seemed to stiffen too. LoLo pulled out the Stiletto and placed it under her arm. They all took cover behind the church's set of stone pillars.

The Lincoln came closer. Behind it the car with the twins inside started up and closed in.

As the Lincoln drew closer, Jesse could make out two men in the front. Then the car stopped in the middle of the deserted street, the engine idling. It was about thirty feet from Jesse and the women.

What the fuck is he up to? said LoLo to herself. "If he starts to run, shoot," she said to Yolanda.

The Lincoln stayed put as the twins' car stopped about ten feet behind it. Jesse could see the girls. They smiled, holding guns. Cane was in the passenger seat of the Lincoln. Q sat behind the wheel. In the backseat Little Jack sat nervously.

Cane looked at them for a second, then reached for the dashboard. They heard a metallic clang. The Lincoln's trunk popped open. Gunfire sounded, and the twins' car was riddled with bullets.

Where the fuck did he go? Florence whispered to herself. She was nervous as the lone man walked closer to her. The black one couldn't have gone far; she thought she'd only been away for a few seconds. He was probably doubling around behind her. That way she couldn't run out the back as she'd planned. She was getting rusty. She should have known that. If these guys killed for a living, then they were experts on keeping their prey contained.

She quickly went out of the building into the rear. She would have to use the element of surprise. She ran to a stack of lumber and crouched behind it.

A few nervous minutes passed. Then she heard someone climbing a fence. She peeked around the side of the wood and saw the black killer walking to the building. His back was to her, so she couldn't get a good look at his face.

Florence wanted him to go. Then she could get away, and her plan would be complete. She didn't want a confrontation with the men; she just needed to lure them away from that van.

She cursed silently as the black man walked her way. He was looking for a place to hide. That was it, she thought. She'd have to take him.

Florence ran up behind the black killer and shoved her gun into the back of his head.

"Don't even fucking breathe," she said. "Drop that gun right now."

The man was silent. Then he dropped his gun from his gloved hand. It had a long silencer on it.

Florence was about to hit him and run when the other man emerged from the building under a light. He was a lot bigger than he looked from a distance. He saw Florence and raised his gun.

"Hold it!" Florence said. She saw him standing under the light and got a good look at his face. She had never seen him before.

Without warning North shot his partner in the chest. His gun was muffled by the silencer. The black killer fell backward, knocking Florence to the ground. Florence shot at North wildly. Her shots thundered in the night, echoing off nearby buildings. North ran back into the building, covering himself in darkness. Florence got to her feet and moved behind a big earthmover. A volley of shots made her move away from it. She ran back farther, behind a stack of bricks. She dropped her gun, but it landed next to her.

"Fuck," she said.

She stuck her head out from behind the bricks and saw North running to his fallen partner. She shot at him but missed. He fired a succession of shots that hit the bricks, breaking some of them into pieces. Florence ducked down.

North grabbed his partner and his gun and dragged the black man by his feet into the darkness of the building.

Florence took a random shot to keep him at bay. She needed one of them alive but couldn't be timid about this.

She peeked out from behind the bricks. She saw light in the dark building. It was a spark, then a small fire.

"Oh, my God—" Florence could see the big man running by the light of the fire. The black killer was on the floor inside, consumed in a column of flame.

Tico stopped firing from the trunk of the Lincoln as Q hit the accelerator. The Lincoln roared off in reverse, swerving around the dead twins. LoLo and Yolanda fired at it. LoLo's Stiletto spit out bullets quickly, ripping a line into the Lincoln's hood.

Jesse moved from behind a stone pillar and fired three shots at the moving car. He was nervous, but he had to have that case. The Lincoln was fast, and he couldn't get a bead on it.

He looked over to Ramona, who had a gun out in front of her but had not fired. She looked distraught, and her hands shook. Jesse realized the last time she fired a gun, her sister was killed. He went to her and took the gun away.

LoLo kept firing, then took off running toward the car. "Not this time, muthafucka," she said.

"No!" said Yolanda. She tried to grab her, but LoLo was too fast. Yolanda shot at the moving car, following her boss.

"Wait!" said Ramona. Ramona tried to take off after them, but Jesse held on to her.

"It's too late," said Jesse. "We've only got one chance now."

The Lincoln stopped, smoke coming from the hood. The doors flew open, and Cane, Little Jack, and Q ran out and ducked behind the car.

Tico got out of the trunk and fired at LoLo but missed. She pulled the trigger of the Stiletto. The gun caught Tico in the leg, ripping it to pieces. He collapsed to the ground, screaming. LoLo quickly sprayed Tico with bullets. His body jumped as it was struck. Glass flew, and holes popped into the car's metal. The Stiletto emptied, and LoLo had to stop to reload. She was on fire and paid no mind to the fact that she was now out in the open.

Yolanda shot at the car to keep the men down. She was shocked when she saw Cane stand up and throw something at LoLo. He moved so fast that he was gone before she could get a bead on him.

The knife hit LoLo in the chest. With a hoarse grunt she dropped the gun and fell to one knee. She was reaching for the knife when a shot from Little Jack hit her in the arm and she fell backward.

Together Little Jack and Q popped up and fired at Yolanda. Q's shot was wide, while Little Jack's hit the big woman in the head, but not before she got off her own shot, which caught Little Jack in the stomach. The boy fell to the ground, uttering a sound like a child crying.

A few moments passed. Then Cane stepped out from behind the car. He walked quickly to LoLo. Q went to Yolanda.

"The big woman is dead," said Q. "The boy's been hit, but he's alive."

"Fuck him," said Cane flatly. "There's two more by that church. Go get them. I need one alive—the woman," he added.

Q turned, but Jesse and Ramona had vanished. "They gone," he said.

"Then they're in the damned church," said Cane. "Fuck it, just don't let them come out. Wait for me."

Q picked up LoLo's Stiletto and headed for the church. Cane turned to LoLo, who was still clutching the big knife.

"Don't suppose you know where my money is?" he asked. Blood flowed from her wound. He put his hand on the big knife and twisted it savagely. LoLo screamed. Blood ran from her mouth as it filled her chest.

"Fu' you," she managed to say.

"Have it your way." He pulled the knife from her chest and stood. LoLo gurgled something as she weakly reached up for her attacker. Cane placed his foot on her chest and shifted his weight on to her. He held her there as the life flowed from her and she died.

Cane turned to the Lincoln. Tico sat on his ass filled with bullet holes, his leg almost severed. His eyes were wide open in a surprised expression. No time for mourning, he thought. He closed Tico's eyes, then went to Little Jack and quickly felt his neck. He was gone too.

Cane turned to the big church. Q stood by the door, waiting. God was cruel, Cane thought. He'd taken friends and prosperity from him tonight, but one of those people in that church knew where his money was. And he was going to find it.

Cane went to the Lincoln and took the black briefcase from the floor of the backseat. It was covered in glass and had a few dents in it. What was this thing that a bullet couldn't penetrate it? Whatever it was, they wanted it, and he would use it to lure them out. Cane lifted the case and walked toward the church. He stopped at the women's cars. No money in either one. He cursed. He knew LoLo would never give it up easily. But that money had to be somewhere.

Cane moved closer to the church. It seemed to shoot up out of the ground into the dark sky, like a living thing. He could not remember the last time he'd been in a church. He dreaded entering the sacred place. Surely this was all part of His plan. But it was night. That made things just about even.

From the back of a small crowd Florence watched as the firefighters put out the fire in the half-finished building. They'd find the body sometime later, she thought. It was probably so badly burned that they'd never make an ID. That bastard was smart, she thought. He couldn't take the body, but he couldn't leave it either, so he'd destroyed it. He was good, all right, but not good enough.

"What the fuck happened?" asked Randall, walking up beside her. Florence moved away from the people, out of earshot, and Randall followed.

"Things got out of hand, that's all," she said.

"I heard gunshots," said Randall. "You okay, princess?" He grabbed her arm gently. Florence was still shaken, and his touch felt good.

"Yeah," said Florence. "So, did you do it?"

"Yes," he said. "I strapped it on good, like you showed me, but I don't know why you wanted to do this. Why in God's name would you put your own Lojack on someone else's car?"

"I'll tell you everything, I promise, but right now I gotta go."

Randall leaned in to kiss Florence, but she stuck out her hand and shook his and left. In her car on the seat was the Lojack car recovery equipment. She'd had a friend install it in her car at police headquarters. She knew the killers had seen her, but she figured they'd never suspect this.

Florence turned on the system. She entered her code from her own Lojack. Soon a blip registered on the monitor. The bastard was not far away.

Now it was her turn to do the following. She watched the monitor as she drove along. The killer was moving fast. He's scared, she thought. Just what she needed. She sped up, not wanting to give him a lot of time. Suddenly the van stopped on the monitor.

"Gotcha!" said Florence. She hit the accelerator. The killer was probably at home. He'd botched the job of getting her, and he'd had to kill his friend to boot. He was probably pissing acid right now.

She was going to get the killer's address, then expose him. She was navigating the sharp turns on Ponchartrain, headed toward Palmer Woods, when the killer's van started to move again.

"Fuck," she said. Florence pulled over and waited. The killer was moving toward downtown. She went that way. She drove to Livernois and got on the freeway.

Florence grew more excited as the killer started to go downtown. Maybe he was meeting whomever he worked for. He'd made a mess of things, and he needed to tell them about it.

Florence followed the killer off the freeway and down Jefferson Avenue. She followed the van into downtown, then out of it. The killer rolled toward Belle Isle, going farther east.

She was right behind him when two cars ahead of her hit each other. She lost sight of the van as traffic stopped. She had no time. She swerved around the accident, going into oncoming traffic. Horns blared, but she made it past the pileup and took up the chase, but the van was gone.

She rolled around the area where she'd lost him, cursing and pounding her dashboard. Suddenly she hit the brakes.

"Jesus, Mary, and Joseph," she said.

The van was nowhere to be found, but she was at the corner of Dwight Street. The tracking system showed that the van was nearby.

She looked down the block and saw armed guards. Florence turned her car around. She didn't dare go all the way. She drove back to Jefferson Avenue, knowing that there was only one place that van could have gone on Dwight Street. Alex Manoogian Mansion, the mayor's house.

★ ★ ★

The heavy church door opened. It creaked like the lid of a coffin in a B movie. Cane and Q stepped inside. It was dark. Debris, pews, and junk were piled everywhere.

"They probably ran," said Q. He had the Stiletto in one hand.

"No," said Cane. "We would've seen them." He motioned for Q to keep going. "We don't have a lot of time," said Cane loudly. "Cops are coming soon. All them gunshots."

Nothing. All they heard was the wind whistling outside. Cane started tapping the black case with this hand. The sound echoed off the stone walls.

"I got that thing you wanted," said Cane loudly. "I don't know what's in it, but you can have it. All you gotta do is tell me where that bitch hid my money."

"Cane, man, they're gone," said Q.

"Shut the fuck up!" said Cane.

Their eyes widened as Jesse stepped out from behind a stack of pews on the church's altar. His hands were over his head.

"Okay," said Jesse. "Let's deal."

"Where's the woman I saw?" asked Cane.

"Gone," said Jesse. "She ran."

"Bullshit," said Cane. "Women run this crew. Bring her out or I kill you right now." He pulled out his razor.

"Go ahead," said Jesse, "you'll never get that money if you do."

Cane looked at Jesse with hatred. He wanted to kill him, but he wanted that money even more.

"Okay," said Cane. "It's your world."

"First," said Jesse, "you leave that black case right here. I go with you and get the money."

"No," Cane said. "Tell me where it is, and you can have the case right now."

"Sorry," said Jesse. "This deal is not negotiable. Now, put the case down, step away from it, and let's go. Otherwise kill me now, and take your chances. I'm sure whoever you're buying heroin from has relied on you to have that money. If you don't, I guess I'll be seeing you in hell."

Cane slammed the case on the floor defiantly. Then he and Q left it behind as they walked toward Jesse. Jesse kept his hands up, where they could see them. They stopped ten feet from him.

"What's in the case?" asked Cane.

"I don't know," said Jesse.

"Damn," said Q. "This is that nigga that killed that lawyer. He busted out some girl who killed the mayor."

"Come on, muthafucka," said Cane, "let's go and get my—"

They all heard a gun being cocked. Cane turned to see Ramona holding a gun on him.

"No!" said Jesse. "Ramona, take the case, and run—now!"

"I'm not leaving you here," she said. "Now you," she said to Q. "Drop that gun, and move out of the way."

"Ramona," said Jesse, "just take it and go."

"No!" she shouted. "Now you two drop the gun and get away from him!" Her hand shook as it held the gun on the men.

Suddenly Cane dropped into a crouch and sprang toward Ramona, raising the big razor. It happened so fast that she had no time to move. Ramona fired her gun.

Jesse saw that Q was also surprised. Jesse rushed forward and jumped on Q, grabbing for the Stiletto. Q was knocked sideways, dropping the machine gun. Jesse landed on him with all his weight. In a flash Q grabbed a gun from his waistband and brought it into Jesse's face. Jesse stared sharply into the gun barrel, but Q didn't shoot.

The hesitation was what Jesse needed. He grabbed Q's gun and desperately struggled with him for it. The weapon was twisted out of Q's hand and fell to the floor. In another split second Jesse had pulled his own gun from the back of his pants and put it to Q's forehead.

"Don't make me," he said.

Jesse rose to his feet, the gun still trained on the drug dealer. Glancing over, he saw Cane, holding Ramona with one arm. In his other hand he held a razor at her throat. Ramona's gun was on the floor next to them. The black case was not far away.

"Okay," Cane said in a dead, flat voice. "Put the gun down, or I drop her ass right now."

"Shoot him!" Ramona yelled.

"Shut the fuck up!" said Cane. He pressed the razor to her neck.

Jesse didn't move. He held the gun on Q and watched Cane. Ramona's face was filled with resolve. She didn't care what happened to her now.

"Let her go, or I'll shoot him," Jesse said with determination.

"Go on, I don't give a shit about that nigga," said Cane.

"He's for real," said Q. He was silent as Jesse jabbed the gun into his head.

"Last chance," said Cane. "Drop it or I'll slice this bitch," yelled Cane.

"All right," said Jesse. He took the gun from Q's head and started lowering it to the floor.

"Just drop it!" yelled Cane. His grip loosened, and Ramona grabbed his arm, pulling it away from her throat.

Jesse immediately lifted the gun, but Ramona was too close.

Ramona slipped out of Cane's grasp and pushed herself away from him. He lashed out with the razor, cutting Ramona's hand right down the middle. She fell to the floor, blood running from the gash.

Now Cane was open, and Jesse whipped up the gun and squeezed the trigger. The gun clicked impotently. It was empty. Jesse thought vaguely that he'd spent bullets shooting at the Lincoln.

Q grabbed Jesse and punched him hard. Jesse's head snapped back. He grabbed Q by the shirt and hit him in the stomach.

Cane ran toward the two men, the razor in his hand. Jolted with fear, Jesse shoved Q into the advancing Cane, and all three men fell to the floor.

Jesse pushed away desperately, trying to get free. Yet Cane was faster, getting to his feet first, raising the big blade.

A gun fired. The bullet struck Cane in the meaty part of his thigh. At the impact, Cane stiffened and grunted loudly.

Ramona lost the gun as the recoil of her shot knocked the weapon from her hand. The gun hit the ground and bounced away from her. She scrambled to her knees, stretching for the weapon.

Jesse ran to the Stiletto, still lying nearby, and grabbed it.

"No!" yelled Q. "Don't kill him!"

Jesse pointed the weapon and fired. The gun jumped as a short burst of bullets hit Cane in the torso. He toppled backward, the razor still in his hand. His body thudded on the stone floor.

Jesse trained the Stiletto on Q, who was looking sadly at Cane's body. Without a word Jesse walked over to Q's gun and kicked it into a corner.

Q went to Cane and cursed. "Dammit, dammit . . ." he said over and over.

Jesse went to Ramona, who was bleeding badly. Her arm, hand, and one of her legs were bloody.

"You okay?" he asked.

"Hell, no," she said. "It hurts like hell."

Jesse tore his shirt and tied off her wound. He kept his eyes on Q, who hovered over Cane like a grieving widow.

"We just wanted the case," Jesse said to Q. "Good luck finding the money to buy your damned drugs."

"So, you two don't want to get in on the deal?" asked Q.

"I'm not a criminal," said Jesse. "We're innocent, and this case is going to prove it." Jesse grabbed the black case. It looked like life itself. "Can you make it?" he asked Ramona. "I need to keep this gun on our boy over there."

"I'm cool," she said.

Q stood up and turned to them. He looked angry and frustrated. "I need that money," he said.

"You must be crazy," said Jesse. "See you in jail."

Q held up a hand, then rolled up his pants leg. Alarmed, Jesse dropped the black case and put both hands on the Stiletto.

"Don't panic," said Q. "I'm just taking out my badge." He pulled out something strapped to his leg. Slowly, keeping his hand in view, he approached, holding a bright badge in hand. "Jamerson, DEA," he said. "Now that you've killed my fucking collar, I'd like to know where that damned money is."

"DEA?" asked Jesse. He was apprehensive, but he could tell the badge was the real article.

"Undercover," said Jamerson. He put the badge away. "I've been with these punks for a few months. We had a clean bust on him and a little East Coast syndicate until you stole the fucking money." His voice no longer sounded like that of a gang member. He was law enforcement all the way.

"He's lying," said Ramona. "Let's get out of here."

"I could have shot you," Jamerson said to Jesse. "Remember?"

"Yeah," said Jesse, remembering all too well. "You could have. Look, I don't want any part of this. I just need what's in this case. So I'll tell you where the money is."

Jamerson pulled out a pen and a little pad and wrote down the address of the two-family flat by the graveyard. Now Jesse knew he was legit. No drug dealer carried a notepad.

"Of course you know I have to place you under arrest," said Jamerson. He put the notepad away.

"I know," said Jesse. "But you can tell them that I pulled a gun on you." Jesse waved the Stiletto. He smiled a little, turned, and walked away with Ramona.

The two turned back when they heard a sound. Cane was on his back, coughing up blood and writhing. Jamerson ran back to Cane and placed a hand on his neck again. When Jamerson stood up, his eyes were wide, and he looked a little scared.

"Jesus, he's still alive."

13

Late Calls

Richard Steel was not feeling good. He was working too hard and not eating right. Tonight it was after eleven, and he was just leaving work. D'Estenne was to blame. The bastard was pushing for a conviction on a Dearborn corruption case to use as election fuel. Jesse's little trouble had really hurt him in the polls. Jesse. What the hell was he doing? When he had seen him at the casino, his heart had almost exploded. Just when he thought he had seen it all.

Richard walked out of Frank Murphy to his car. There were still a few cars in the lot. He couldn't believe any human being was here at this time.

Richard had reached his car when he saw a shadow rise from the opposite side of the car. He backed away, turning to run.

"Richard, it's me," said Jesse. He was standing next to Ramona holding a big black briefcase. "I need your help."

Jesse rolled the bandages tightly on Ramona's hand. The bleeding had stopped, but she was still in pain. She was tough, he thought. Never once had she complained as they were trudging through the cold November night.

They were in Richard's basement. Jesse had told him the whole story on their way over. Richard's face was expressionless as he took it in. Jesse felt that he was taking a chance, but Richard was the only person other than Florence who had seen him since he had run, and he had not turned him in.

Jamerson had called the DEA and the cops. When Jesse left,

Cane was still alive. They were going to get the money and try to set up Cane's supplier. Whoever he was, he was going to get a big surprise tomorrow night.

"She should get this stitched up," said Richard. "It looks bad."

"Can't do that right now," said Jesse. "So, can you get the U.S. attorney to listen to me?" He had to go to the feds. D'Estenne was the state prosecutor, but Jesse didn't trust him or the local police to do the right thing. If the feds thought there was government corruption of any kind, they could invent a jurisdictional reason to investigate.

"I don't know, Jesse," said Richard. "This is a farfetched story."

"Jamerson at the DEA will back me up," said Jesse.

"I told you not to trust a white man," said Ramona. Jesse smiled a little. She was her old self again. "Let's go and bust that damned thing open."

"Ramona, please," said Jesse. "Richard, look, they killed the mayor and a friend of mine. We can't let them get away with this."

Jesse had never seen Richard so torn. He was usually a decisive man, but if he made the wrong choice here, it could be terrible. If he helped Jesse, he could be aiding and abetting a criminal, and if he didn't help, he'd miss out on being a hero.

"Okay," said Richard at last. "I'm in. What do you want me to do?"

"First," said Jesse, "I want to know why you helped me in Canada."

Richard looked at Jesse curiously. "You may be an asshole, Jesse, but I know you didn't kill Karen Bell. I wasn't going to be the one who ratted you out. The whole thing smelled bad, and I—that man from the mayor's office wanting to 'help' us with the case. I was wrong about that. Then when you got in trouble . . . It was too much of a coincidence. I knew something was up. And . . ." Richard trailed off. "D'Estenne and I went to see her behind your back when she got picked up." He pointed at Ramona. "I didn't want to do it, but he made me. Kept talking about damage control. Man, he's really been losing it lately."

Jesse just nodded. "And what were D'Estenne and Ellis Holmes doing at the casino with you?"

"Well," said Richard, "D'Estenne is scared of the election. Xavier Peterson is closing in the polls, so he's pulling out all the stops. Chapel, Swiss is thinking about starting a new white-collar crime division."

"Ellis hinted that there might be a place for me there soon," said Jesse distantly.

"Actually," said Richard, "I'm being considered to head it up." He smiled ever so slightly. Same old Richard, thought Jesse.

"I told D'Estenne," Richard continued. "And he insisted that Chapel, Swiss back him for county prosecutor, or they couldn't have his influence."

"I see," said Jesse. "Well, thanks again. I need to use your phone. Florence, my old investigator, and I have a phone rendezvous. I need to get her over here. She was trying something dangerous tonight. If she doesn't pick up that phone, then I'll know—I'll know she failed."

"I'd better make some coffee," said Richard. "I'm sure the U.S. attorney will want to bring an FBI agent with him."

Jesse glanced at Ramona, who had a concerned look on her face. Her eyes darted to Richard. Jesse went to her and whispered in her ear, "Don't worry. I haven't forgotten my promise."

14

Pandora

FBI agent Mel Sanford had been working a half hour on the black case on Richard Steel's dining room table. Richard's wife was pissed at the invasion, but not so much so that she didn't go back to sleep with their kids.

Nathan Williams, the local U.S. attorney, listened intently as Jesse retold his story. Williams was about fifty, black, and very much a fed. He had a crew cut, he was clean-shaven, and he even had on a crisp new shirt. Jesse wondered if he had thought about putting on a tie.

Williams looked skeptical but seemed fascinated that somehow Yancy's death was tied to a conspiracy.

Jesse had almost kissed Florence when she walked through the door. She had failed to get the killers, but at least she was still alive. She regaled them with the story of the killers, the fire, and losing one of the assassins to the mayor's mansion. Williams suggested that Florence let the FBI use her Lojack tracker to find the man. She didn't argue.

Ramona was nowhere to be found. Jesse had suggested that she make herself scarce in case Williams didn't go for it. Jesse finished the story, and Williams leaned back in his chair.

"I want you to know, Mr. King," said Williams, "that no matter what's in that case, you stay in our custody."

"I understand," said Jesse. "But Yancy was killed for what's in that case, so I have no problem with that. If there's nothing inside, then maybe I did kill those people."

"Bullshit," said Florence. "I followed that fuckin' van to the mayor's house. That means Crawford is up to his dickhole in this shit. Jesse is telling you the real deal, and I'll back him up."

Williams and Richard cringed a little. They'd obviously never been around a woman like Florence.

"And where's the girl?" asked Williams. "She's our eyewitness in this."

No one spoke. Jesse looked at Dick Steals, who shook his head.

"I can't tell you," said Jesse.

"Can't or won't?" said Williams.

"Both," said Jesse. "She's completely innocent, and I won't put her in jeopardy again."

The phone rang. Richard answered it and brought it to Williams. The FBI agent listened on the phone just saying a lot of uh-huhs. Then he hung up.

"That was Special Agent Freeman," said Williams. "Mike Jamerson of the DEA checks out. Also we got an ID on your burned corpse. His name is John Lake, a bodyguard. Formerly with Chicago PD and, I'm sorry to say, the FBI. And Jamerson had two messages for you."

"What was that?" asked Jesse.

"He said that their action for tomorrow was still on, and the bastard you shot made it," Williams said.

"I see," said Jesse. Jamerson's message was easy to understand. They would arrest Cane's drug supplier tomorrow, and Cane had not died despite being shot seven times. God must really love him, Jesse thought.

"Okay," said Williams, "I think it's safe to bring out the young lady now."

Jesse got up and walked upstairs. He returned with Ramona. She looked like she had been asleep. She surveyed the room, then looked at Jesse curiously.

"It's okay," he said. "He knows about Jamerson." Turning to Williams, he said, "This is Ramona Blake, your eyewitness."

"Well," said Williams, standing, "I guess you've had quite a month, young lady."

"One I'd like to forget," said Ramona.

"Got it yet?" Williams asked Sanford.

"Getting there," said the other man. "Gotta be careful. Some of these things destroy their contents if they're not opened properly."

"Take your time," said Williams.

Sanford was about thirty but had a baby face. He was a computer and fraud expert. He had been pissed off at the late call until he saw the black case. He said it was a Grieger Box, a security case invented by a man named Barry Grieger from one of the State Department's many think tanks.

"Crawford could have had Yancy hit to keep casinos from coming to Detroit," said Richard. "Crawford killed the casino commission; that's real evidence."

"But it doesn't make sense," said Jesse. "Crawford has never been opposed to casinos. I think he just did it to win the election next year."

"The money," said Williams. "That's the key. We need to see what financial fallout there was from Yancy's death. Then we'll know why that van was at the mayor's mansion."

"How do we know they went to see the mayor?" asked Ramona. "I mean, a lot of people hang at the mansion. I used to. There are always a lot of people there. It could be anyone."

The men all stopped talking. Ramona's insight was keen, and they seemed shocked that she possessed it. Jesse remembered how awkward he had felt when he was the odd man out with the female dealers.

Smiling at Ramona, he said, "She's right. It could be anyone." Then he turned to Richard and said, "I hate to bring this up, but our boss might be involved."

"D'Estenne?" said Richard. "I don't think so."

"Yancy was not going to endorse him in the election. Crawford did. And maybe someone had a vested interest in keeping D'Estenne in office."

Richard rubbed his chin, thinking. "I don't know," he said. "I don't think Frank would kill to stay in office. Still, he has been under a lot of pressure lately."

"Let's not rule out anyone," said Williams. "Situations like this tend to be—"

"I got it!" yelled Sanford. "Sir, I think I can open this thing now."

Everyone crowded around Sanford as he held up the case. Jesse's heart started to beat faster. His fate was inside the black box. He hoped he would not be like Pandora, who regretted ever opening hers.

"I don't know how the mayor got hold of a GB," said Sanford.

"Yancy had friends everywhere," said Williams. "Quite a few in the Justice Department."

"See here," said Sanford, "the key is the handle. It's the only visible seam. The reason you don't see the others is that it has these shadowy lines in it. Watch."

Sanford pulled out the handle. He slipped a thin metal rod inside the base where the handle met the case.

"This would be where the key went, but since we don't have it . . ."

Sanford turned the metal rod, and everyone heard several clicks.

"Now, the other side," he said.

Sanford did the same to the other side. More clicks. Then he laid the case down flat. Jesse could see now that two square flaps of metal were sticking out from the base. Sanford turned them up, and the case opened slightly with a tiny hiss.

"The mechanism is hydraulic," said Sanford, clearly proud of himself. He grabbed a small mirror on a stick.

"Open it," said Jesse.

"Not yet," said Sanford. "If there is a destruction mechanism inside, it will be triggered if the box is opened without a key. That means it might be on now. But if memory serves me, the GB uses a laser system. If I can reflect the beam back, the box will open."

"And if you can't?" asked Jesse.

"The contents will be destroyed before we can get them out."

Jesse held his breath as Sanford put the tiny mirror into the box and moved slowly from left to right.

Suddenly the box's lid opened fully with a loud hiss.

"And that's that," said Sanford.

Inside the case were a thick envelope and a CD jewel box. They were strapped down. Jesse took the envelope and opened it.

"It looks like information on municipal bond law," said Jesse, scanning the papers. "Yancy was concerned about a bond issue that happened over a decade ago. Richard, do you have a computer?"

"I'll bring it in," said Richard.

In a few minutes Richard had the system set up. Sanford put the CD in the drive and went to the display program.

"There's a big wave file on this," said Sanford.

"What's that?" said Ramona.

"A sound file," said Sanford. "Here, let's play it." Sanford clicked the mouse a few more times.

"This damn thing working, Louis?" It was Harris Yancy's voice.

Jesse could feel the chill spread through the room. He'd heard Yancy's voice once before on the tape, but everyone else reacted to the voice from the grave.

"Just talk, you old fool," said a man in the background. He laughed.

"That has to be Louis Franklin," said Jesse. "He supposedly committed suicide." He was sure now that it was no suicide. Yancy had made a call to Louis the night he died.

"Okay," said Yancy, *"this is just a reminder to you, Louis. If we file this fiscal year, then the bond debt must be dealt with quickly. We cannot let our deadline pass, or we're fucked. That's a legal term, Louis."* Yancy laughed.

Jesse saw Ramona's eyes turn sad. He held her hand.

"Anyway," Yancy continued, *"if the city files, we'll have the power to manipulate a lot of our business partners. I'd like the authority used judiciously. While we're getting rid of liabilities we'll make our credit rating better, getting ready for the casinos that should be coming in the year 2000. What we want to do is make sure the filing goes to the right court, so that no one gets any ideas about replacing me. This is imperative. I'm losing some control over the city, but I will not be at the mercy of some asshole in a robe. That's it, Louis. All the other info is in the hard files. When you're done, send me copies. Mr. Nicks will come for them."*

There was some shuffling noises; then the file stopped.

Jesse, Richard, and Williams all looked at each other. The lawyers were all on the same page.

"Yancy was going to put the city into bankruptcy, a Chapter Nine," said Jesse.

"Bullshit," said Florence. "Cities can't go bust."

"Yes, they can," said Williams. "The government created the law just for municipal corporations."

"Orange County out in California filed one," said Richard. "They made a lot of bad investments and went belly up. It was a mess."

"So that's why Crawford was moving around money," said Florence. "Bastard didn't have any."

Jesse looked back at the papers from the envelope. "Yancy was trying to wipe out some kind of massive bond debt with a bankruptcy or the threat of it," said Jesse. "Then he was going to use the new, improved Detroit to bring casinos here. But someone knew about it and had him killed. Agent Sanford, pull up the file list."

Sanford did.

"That one right there," said Jesse. "The one Louis Franklin so comically called BIGLSRS.DOC. I think it's a list of people who stood to take the biggest losses in the bankruptcy."

Sanford brought up the list. There were a lot of names and companies listed. They were primary bondholders from the issue back in 1982.

Michael Talli's name was next to a two-million-dollar loss. COG, home of Reverend Junior and the MACs, was up for a half million. Jesse shook his head. He didn't think a church could afford to lose that kind of cash. D'Estenne's name was there. He got sacked for fifty thousand. Even Louise Yancy was down for twenty-five thousand.

That was hardly enough money to kill a mayor for. The list was long, going on for many pages, but there was not a loss big enough for murder. Talli's loss was the biggest of all.

Jesse's heart sank. He might have cleared his name with Williams, but the people who had hired the killers were still a mystery.

"Dead end," said Richard. "We'd have to investigate everyone on that list to get to the bottom of this."

"Then we'll do just that," said Williams firmly. "We have the manpower."

"Bonds," Jesse said. That was the key.

"What?" asked Richard.

"Muni bonds," Jesse repeated. "None of us really know what they're all about. But I know someone who does. We need to wake up one more person."

Ellis Holmes had almost screamed when he saw Jesse. An FBI agent had brought him over. When he saw all the federal law enforcement, he panicked. Williams calmed Ellis down and explained everything to him.

Ellis regained his composure, and soon he was looking over the BIGLSRS.DOC file.

"Holy Hannah," said Ellis. "A major Chapter Nine filing. Do you know what that would do?"

"We know," said Jesse. "What we don't know is how the bonds figure into all of this."

"It's simple," said Ellis. "There are many different types of muni bonds. The '82 bonds were tied to the treasury. The city promised to pay them back based on future tax revenues. Stupid, but everyone was stupid in the eighties."

"The city has been losing its tax base," said Jesse.

"Right," said Ellis. "So when these bonds come due, the city might be technically bankrupt. Good enough to file bankruptcy."

"Okay," said Jesse. "So Yancy knew that. Who would have wanted to prevent that?"

"Everyone who had a bond," said Ellis.

"But no one on that list was into the '82 issue for a bundle," said Jesse.

"Sure there is," said Ellis. "You see, the '82 bonds had limits on ownership. So, if you wanted to buy over two million, you had to use other companies. A number of these companies are owned by the same entity."

"Dummy companies?" asked Williams.

"No, they're legit; they're just owned by the same person," said Ellis. "But I only see a couple I recognize."

"I can do a search," said Sanford. "The computer will make a list of all companies that have the same ownership." He went to the computer and quickly typed out a few commands.

Jesse bent over the computer as it listed the name of a common owner. He stood straight up. "Steven Brownhill," he said.

The others reacted with shock. The file showed that Brownhill owned over four hundred paper companies that owned bonds. He had purchased a majority of the '82 bond issue. Jesse did a quick calculation of the numbers.

"Seventy million dollars," said Jesse. "That's what Steven Brownhill stood to lose if the Chapter Nine had gone through. That's enough money to have anyone killed."

"So Brownhill had Yancy killed to protect his money," said Williams. "He must have known that Yancy was trying to free up the city's debt in order to get casinos."

"Everyone knew Yancy wanted those casinos to save Detroit," said Jesse. "I guess none of us knew how badly."

344 / Gary Hardwick

"Brownhill could have been at the mayor's house tonight," said Florence. "The killer in the van could have been going to see him."

"Or Crawford's in it with Brownhill," said Williams. "How do we prove it?"

"There's only one way," said Jesse. "We need the killer."

"Our men have located him," said Williams. "They're waiting on me to take him."

"Good," said Jesse. "Let's do it." Jesse looked troubled as Williams picked up the phone and dialed.

"Hey, look at this," said Sanford as he sat at the computer. "Mr. King, I think you should see this."

Jesse moved to the computer screen. He watched as Sanford scrolled through screen after screen of a document. Jesse's face contorted into a scowl. He turned to Ramona.

"Son of a bitch," he said.

15

Odd Jobs

Jeffrey North lay wide awake in his bed. He was worried that his boss would have him killed for screwing up the case. But then again, he didn't know yet. He had lied to him and said that King and the girl were dead and the black case was destroyed. That would buy him enough time to get out of town.

Jeffrey North was a former career army intelligence officer who'd been drummed out of the service for selling drugs to enlisted men. He'd managed a conditional discharge and become a police officer, then later a security expert. He'd fallen into his current profession when a Texas employer needed a mistress to disappear. He soon became known for this talent and opened a new business.

He and John Lake had really blown this one, North thought. The job on the mayor had been neat, until the girl got away. Her escape made the frame on Louise Yancy fall apart. Then they'd screwed up and killed that lawyer. He should have gotten out then, but he kept thinking he could fix it.

Then John Lake had to go and get himself shot. North was not about to negotiate with the lady cop named Florence. John got sloppy, so he was expendable.

North was in his home in Palmer Woods, planning to leave the country in a few more hours. Detroit was too hot for him. Brownhill had a lot of money and influence. But if he was lucky, he'd get away, get to his money, and disappear.

Suddenly his bedroom door was kicked open. FBI officers flooded into the room. North reached for his gun, but an FBI officer had a laser sight right in his face. North stopped and put his hands up.

Williams walked through the crowd. "Jeffrey North," he said, "you're under arrest for the murder of a public official, the late Harris Yancy. You're also under arrest for the murders of Louis Franklin, Karen Bell, and John Lake. You're also under arrest for possible violations of the RICO Act as well as—"

FBI officers pulled North from the bed as Williams continued his list of violations. Then the FBI officers read North his rights. They were rough as they handcuffed him. They seemed to enjoy pushing the big man around.

Jesse and Ramona walked in. Ramona didn't say anything. She just glared at North.

North said nothing. He stood there in his bare feet, staring at them. Even handcuffed, he looked menacing.

Jesse glared at North with hatred. The man had killed Yancy. He wanted to beat him, hurt him. Ramona stood close to him, looking at North with rage in her eyes. She had reason, he thought.

Florence pushed her way through the crowd. "That's him," she said to Williams. To North, Florence said, "I was at your little barbecue, you fuck. See you in jail."

Williams smiled and turned to North, who stared at Florence as though she were the devil himself.

"We know you work for Steven Brownhill. Do yourself a favor, and help us get him." North was silent. He kept looking at Florence, the only person who had seen him commit a crime. "Fine," said Williams. "Get him out of here, fellas."

An officer put shoes on North; then they led him away. Halfway to the door North stopped short and turned to Williams.

"Okay," said North. "I can deal."

16

New City

The room was packed with media. All the TV stations and newspapers were represented. It looked like the president himself would make an appearance. D'Estenne, Reverend Junior, and Michael Talli all sat on the dais of the fund-raiser. Behind them in big green letters was a banner that read NEW CITY PROJECT.

Lester Crawford spoke passionately to the audience. He was talking about the future of the city and the uniting of the races. The dais was filled with the who's who of Detroit. Everyone knew what this event was about: Detroit was coming back.

Steven Brownhill was spearheading a renewal of Detroit's ravaged east side. He'd put together the coalition to get the financing for the project. Crawford was interrupted every so often by applause as the audience grew more and more excited.

Steven Brownhill was in good spirits. The little problem with Harris Yancy was over, and now he could breathe easier. He had to admit that Jesse King had helped him quite a bit. With his silly escape after the second murder, King had drawn all the attention away to himself.

Brownhill watched as Crawford drew closer to announcing him. This would be his finest moment. The purchase of the 1982 bonds had been a complete fiasco. Who knew then that the country would forget about the inner cities and focus on the goddamned military? It was a colossal blunder, and it had almost cost him his family's fortune.

Brownhill had taken over the family trust in the late seventies.

His father had never thought that he was capable, but then his older brother was crippled in a plane crash. Young Steven was given the call.

But he'd blown it. Those bonds were potentially worthless, and the bankruptcy would have ruined him. He'd lost money all through the 1980s. He'd taken a beating in the junk bond craze and missed out on the S&L scams.

When Brownhill found out Yancy was about to put the city into a bankruptcy, he panicked. He called Yancy, trying to convince him not to take the risky action, but Yancy would not back off. He assured Brownhill that the Chapter Nine would not stop him from getting his money. He would just get it later—much later. But Brownhill had already borrowed on the bonds, securing the debt with everything he owned. The bankruptcy would drag on, the lawyers would get rich, and the money would never come back in time.

Yancy was just a glorified dogcatcher, a civil servant. He didn't understand how America worked. Money ruled everything: politics, love, and even death. So he had to eliminate Yancy and his dreams of casino gambling. It was the most cost-effective way to get what he wanted.

Brownhill was still pissed at North and Lake, his two assassins. They couldn't even kill an old man and a whore. He didn't like using them, but North had a good reputation, his partner in this crime had insisted.

Brownhill clapped as the audience started to applaud for Crawford again. Brownhill disliked being so close to the murders. Normally he would have had a subordinate do the dirt for him, but again his partner would have it no other way. Since they had planned the murder together, his partner wanted to make sure that Brownhill had a lot to lose.

As the body count grew, Brownhill thought seriously of having both assassins executed. He was relieved when North told him the case had been closed. Now he would lay low for a while, get on with business, and one day North and Lake would disappear. Then the case would really be closed.

Crawford was finishing up his speech. This would be a start of a new life for him, Brownhill thought. After this project was completed, the city would be so grateful that it would find a way to pay those bonds.

Brownhill smiled a little. He'd done it. It was scary for a while, but he'd weathered the storm. And after this was all over, he'd get into politics and eventually Washington. Maybe in time even God would forgive him.

". . . and so I give you the founder of the New City Project," said Crawford, "Steven J. Brownhill."

The audience stood and applauded. The TV cameras all turned to Brownhill. The cameras flashed, and his wife kissed him. He smiled for them all and walked over to the podium, taking out his speech.

Brownhill shook hands and posed with Crawford. Then Brownhill took the podium and tried to quiet the audience. Soon they all sat down. Brownhill thanked them and flattened the pages of his speech.

Suddenly a flood of armed men entered the room. There was already security, but these men wore FBI jackets. Brownhill's heart exploded as the men drew closer to the stage. In the advancing crowd Brownhill saw two ghosts: Jesse King and Ramona Blake.

As the FBI agents advanced, the dais was shocked, and the audience gasped and murmured loudly.

The lead agent went to the podium and handcuffed Brownhill. He didn't fight at all.

Jesse, who still looked like hell, walked up to the microphone and turned to the crowd. "Ladies and gentlemen, I am Jesse King, and I am here with the FBI and U.S. Attorney Nathan Williams to arrest Steven Brownhill for the murder of the late Harris Yancy."

The crowd exploded. The TV and newspaper people rushed the stage. Williams had his men hold off the reporters and the bodyguards, as Brownhill was read his rights.

Jesse looked at Williams, who nodded. Jesse moved over to the dais with two FBI men behind him. He was going to arrest Brownhill's coconspirator in the assassination.

Jesse walked toward D'Estenne, who was looking at him with wild disbelief. Jesse moved by him. He moved to Reverend Junior but didn't even look at the minister as he went by.

Michael Talli went pale as Jesse stopped in front of him. Jesse cleared his throat, gave Talli a mean look, then moved on. Talli breathed a sigh of relief and took a drink of wine.

Jesse stopped again, this time in front of Mayor Crawford.

"Hello, Mr. Mayor," said Jesse. "I need you to step away from Mrs. Yancy, sir."

The FBI agents went to Louise Yancy and arrested her. Seth Carson, a tall, good-looking man of fifty, was seated next to her. His mouth hung open as Louise was read her rights. An agent grabbed him.

"Just the lady," said Jesse.

The agent let Carson go as he and the other members of the dais were cordoned off by the federal agents. Jesse walked over to Louise. His face was angry and just a little sad.

"You pulled the security assignment that night," said Jesse. "I checked the log, and you were there that day, right after Walter Nicks. Samuel, the house director, keeps a list of people who come in along with the times."

Louise Yancy was silent. Her eyes were filled with tears. Seth Carson yelled something to her as the FBI agent moved him away from her.

"I checked the contents of a disk your dead husband made," said Jesse. "It had all of Brownhill's dummy companies on it, including BoldCom, which is headed by Seth Carson. It also had an outline for a proposed property settlement for the divorce Mayor Yancy was going to file against you. Implicating yourself was brilliant. You knew you had an airtight alibi in Carson. Sooner or later the case against you would fall apart, and you and Brownhill would be in the clear. And later Seth Carson would run for mayor like he's been threatening to for so long and you'd be first lady again."

Louise Yancy started to say something but instead doubled over, crying. The FBI men tried to straighten her as she collapsed to the floor. They had to pick her up and carry her off the platform.

Williams and the FBI cleared a path in the chaos and started taking Brownhill and Louise Yancy to the door. Reporters descended on them, flashing pictures and yelling questions. Outside there was a federal van waiting. The Detroit police officers were now working with their federal counterparts to maintain order.

Jesse was escorted through the crowd to the entrance. He'd left Ramona in the hallway and couldn't wait to see her. He found her standing next to an FBI agent, smiling at him. She waved at him with her bandaged hand.

Jesse headed her way, but halfway there he was cut off by a

woman in an elegant evening dress. She filled his field of vision, cutting off the sight of Ramona's smiling face.

Jesse was speechless as Connie, his fiancée, grabbed him and pressed her tear-filled face into his, smothering him with kisses.

17

Light of Ages

It was mercifully dark as Cane opened his eyes in the hospital room. He felt the presence of others, but he could only see darkness.

He vaguely remembered being shot and the paramedics putting him on the ambulance. Then he'd blacked out and gone where He could never go, the darkness of his soul.

Cane moved slightly. He felt the numbness of the drug he'd been given in the operation. Tubes ran from his body into a machine and IV bags.

He was alive.

He had won again. Through all of this God had tried to foil him, belittle him, and in the end He tried to execute him. He remembered the dark pit in juvenile detention and the strength he'd gotten from it. Now he was even stronger than he'd ever imagined. He had defied death again.

His good eye began to focus, and soon he saw shadows in the room. He tried to move his arm and couldn't. He was restrained. And then he remembered: He was going to jail. No matter, he thought. He would grow strong there, and one day he would get out and continue his work against God.

"When he's lucid, we can read him his rights," said a voice.

Cane saw a shadow approach. A light flashed across his vision.

"Doctor, his eye's responding."

Cane watched as another shadow walked over to what looked to be a wall and reached up. The window opened, and sunlight filled the room.

Cane yelled with anger.

He tried to free himself from the bed, but he was too weak, and the restraints held him fast.

People rushed to him in the hospital bed and began to grab at him, yelling medical terms.

Cane continued to scream as someone shoved a needle into his arm. Soon he felt a numbing wave pass over him, then another stronger than the first. The waves continued as his strength waned. He stopped his struggle, turning his head slowly to the side, away from the terrible sun.

18

Promises to Keep

Jesse sat on his sofa like a condemned man as he waited for Connie. He'd been spared the task of facing Connie last night. Williams and the FBI had needed him, and he had managed to stretch the meetings and news interviews out all day. But now he had to face her. He had to tell her that he could not marry her.

Jamerson and the DEA had taken their drug courier, a man they called Minnesota, on the river. The coast guard and the DEA had trapped the yacht containing enough heroin to get the whole city high. They had made arrests all around.

The arrests of Louise Yancy and Brownhill were all over the newspapers. Brownhill maintained his innocence for a while. He might have made it a hard-fought trial, but when Jeffrey North, his hired assassin, turned state's evidence, Brownhill cut a deal, confessed everything including bugging Karen Bell's phone and Louise Yancy's involvement. Jesse's phone had not been tapped by Brownhill or anyone. He had just been paranoid, he guessed.

Ira Hoffman had called Jesse and apologized for his remarks in the press. Jesse forgave him. Ira just hadn't known him well enough to believe he was innocent.

Mayor Crawford tried desperately to distance himself from Brownhill. He had just given a speech calling Brownhill a visionary, and now Brownhill was in prison for murder. Brownhill's partners Margaret Blue and Willie Gibbs were not implicated with Brownhill. They promised that the New City Project would go on. Crawford promised that the 1982 bonds would be honored.

The procasino forces were winning a vote on a state initiative in the elections. Despite the best efforts of Mayor Crawford and the MACs, legalized gambling was coming to Detroit.

D'Estenne was still in the race for county prosecutor. The polls showed that he was winning by a good margin. The Yancy case had embarrassed him, but with Crawford's endorsement, he was projected to be the winner.

Jesse had voted against him.

Richard Steel announced his retirement from the prosecutor's office. He would be joining Chapel, Swiss to start a white-collar crime practice. He offered Jesse a job and floored him with the starting salary. Jesse didn't know what to do. He still had his job at the prosecutor's office. He was also reinstated to the bar since all charges against him and Ramona were dropped. But he didn't give Richard an answer. He was mulling it over.

He'd taken a moment to visit his sister. Bernice's house was beset with reporters, but he had to talk with her. She was still in rehab and doing fine. She even looked like she'd gained a few pounds.

Jesse talked with Bernice for a while, telling her not to give any reporter a story unless she was paid for it. She would need all the money she could get. Jesse left, but not before he gave Bernice some money. Bernice cried. She knew what it meant. He believed in her again.

Ramona visited her sister, Cheryl, and celebrated her freedom. Ramona told Jesse that she hadn't talked to her mother, and didn't plan to. She had given up on that relationship ever working.

Ramona didn't question him about Connie. She understood that Connie had no way of knowing what had happened to Jesse on his adventure. But Ramona didn't offer to make love to him, and he didn't ask. She was waiting for him to end it. He respected her for that.

There was a knock at the door. Jesse answered it, and Connie stood in the doorway, looking radiant in a fur coat. She hugged Jesse and kissed him passionately. Jesse pulled her away, a little too soon.

"Something wrong?" Connie said.

"Sit down, Connie," Jesse said.

Connie took off her coat and sat next to Jesse on the sofa. Jesse looked at her and didn't know where to begin. No matter what he felt in his heart, Connie would see it as a betrayal, and he guessed that she would be right. Ramona was special to him, but he had made a promise to Connie, one that was sacred even if people didn't treat it that way anymore.

Connie took his hands in hers and smiled. "I've got so many things to say to you, Jesse."

"I know, Connie, but let me talk first—"

"I never stopped believing in you. I knew you didn't kill anyone. I lost a lot of friends over that, but I don't care. No one knows you better than I do—"

"Connie, hold it for a minute," said Jesse. He squeezed her hand firmly. "Let me talk. I don't want you to misunderstand me here."

"I'm sorry," said Connie. She put her hand on his face. "It's just that—I'm very excited and all."

"I can't marry you," said Jesse.

Connie looked dumbstruck. She regarded Jesse as if seeing him for the first time. Her hand trembled on his cheek. She pulled it away, as if embarrassed.

"I don't want to lead you on," he said.

"It's her, isn't it, that woman? Like the newspapers said. You love her. I didn't want to believe it."

"It happened after I ran away—Connie, it doesn't matter when it happened, but it did."

"And what about me, Jesse?" asked Connie. "I love you too."

"I know. Connie, listen. You and me have always been an odd match. Our backgrounds are worlds apart. This woman—Ramona—is just like me. We both walked out of a bad world and into a better one; only she never forgot where she started like I did. She gave me back something, Connie. She gave me back myself."

Connie started to cry, and Jesse's heart crumbled. He knew it would be painful, but tears always got to him.

"Are you going to marry her?" Connie sniffled.

"It hasn't come up yet. I know it sounds old-fashioned, but I need you to release me from my promise to you."

Connie was silent as she wiped a tear from her eyes. "I'm leaving, Jesse," said Connie. She stood up. "I should be mad at you, but I'm not. I don't want to be with a man who doesn't want me. I'm just disappointed in you."

He didn't know what to say. There was no good way to break someone's heart. He thought of several comforting things to say, but they all sounded insulting at this moment.

Connie grabbed her coat and went to the door. She opened the door and stopped. With her back to Jesse, she said, "I release you." Then she left.

Jesse buried his face in his hands. The last thing he ever wanted to do was hurt Connie. But he had to follow his heart, be true to himself. It seemed that was all he had left. He'd watched families crumble all his life. He couldn't start one with Connie based on a lie.

Jesse felt a hand on his shoulder, and he looked up into Ramona's face.

"I know you asked me to stay in the back, but I couldn't," she said. "I heard it all." Ramona wiped a tear from her eye.

"Why are you crying?" asked Jesse.

"Because I feel bad for her—and because I'm happy."

Jesse stood and embraced her. He kissed her passionately and felt some of his guilt slip away.

"I'm going to be a wreck for at least a month," said Ramona.

"Come on," said Jesse. "I know what can cheer us both up." He pulled some coats from his closet and led her out of the apartment.

They went to the top floor. Jesse led Ramona to a door that read ROOF. They opened the door and took the stairs to the roof of Jesse's building.

The sun was setting. It swept over the city skyline in a glorious wave of light.

"I come here when I need to remember what's really important," said Jesse.

"It's beautiful," said Ramona.

She moved closer to him as the cold November air chilled her face. Jesse embraced her as they watched the sun's rays bounce off the river, reflecting its light into their eyes.

·A NOTE ON THE TYPE·

The typeface used in this book is a version of Plantin, designed in 1913 by Frank Hinman Pierpoint (1860–1937). Although he was an American, Pierpoint spent most of his life working in England for the Monotype company, which he helped found. The font was named after Christophe Plantin (1514?–1589), a French bookbinder who turned to printing and by midcentury had established himself in Antwerp as the founder of a publishing dynasty—like Pierpoint, one who "made good" away from home. Plantin was not, however, a designer of type, nor was the modern font strictly speaking a revival (Pierpoint was unenthusiastic about Stanley Morison's revivals at Monotype in the 1920s). Plantin was based on what is now known to be Robert Granjon's Gros Cicero font, created for but never used by Plantin, which Pierpoint found in the Plantin-Moretus Museum. Later, its full-bodied but compact quality attracted Morison to Plantin as the model for Times Roman.